THE RISE OF THE
AUTOMATED
ARISTOCRATS

A BURTON & SWINBURNE ADVENTURE

MARK HODDER

THE RISE OF THE AUTOMATED ARISTOCRATS

an imprint of Prometheus Books
Amherst, NY

Published 2015 by Pyr®, an imprint of Prometheus Books

Cover image © Jon Sullivan

Cover design by Jacqueline Nasso Cooke

Inquiries should be addressed to

Pyr
59 John Glenn Drive
Amherst, New York 14228
VOICE: 716–691–0133
FAX: 716–691–0137
WWW.PYRSF.COM

19 18 17 16 15   5 4 3 2 1

Library of Congress Cataloging-in-Publication Data

Hodder, Mark, 1962-
    The rise of the automated aristocrats : a Burton & Swinburne adventure / by Mark Hodder.
        pages ; cm
    ISBN 978-1-63388-052-8 (pbk.) — ISBN 978-1-63388-053-5 (e-book)
    1. Burton, Richard Francis, Sir, 1821-1890—Fiction. 2. Swinburne, Algernon Charles, 1837-1909—Fiction. 3. Time travel—Fiction. 4. London (England)—Social conditions—19th century—Fiction. 5. Steampunk fiction. I. Title.

PR6108.O28R57 2015
823'.92—dc23
                                                                    2015004951

Printed in the United States of America

This one is for my brother

MIKE SHANNON

AUTHOR'S NOTE AND ACKNOWLEDGMENTS

As has been the case with the previous Burton and Swinburne novels, this is a tale of an alternate reality in which famous historical characters are featured. Though their names are recognisable and their biographies have been consulted for information about their personalities, beliefs, and politics, they are not portrayed in a manner that should be regarded as reflective of the real people. The members of my cast are approximations whose motives and actions relate only to the events of the fictional world I have created. Moreover, there are occurrences in this novel that are heavily exaggerated accounts of real happenings. As always, I have sought redemption for my audacious hijacking of history and its personages by including an appendix in which information concerning the real people and events can be found. Hopefully, this will encourage my readers to explore the remarkable truths that have inspired my tall tales.

My thanks, as ever, to my partner, Yolanda, who has once again endured me being shackled to a keyboard for weeks on end—a show of patience made all the more remarkable considering that this novel was begun at the same time our twins, Iris and Luca, were born.

Thanks, too, to Rene Sears of Pyr and Michael Rowley of Del Rey (UK), who put up with my excuses ("The babies were sick on the manuscript. I'll retype it and send it next week. No, *really*! Yes, I *do* use a typewriter! What's so weird about that?")

7

THE FIRST PART

A NEW PAST

You cannot fight against the future. Time is on our side.
—William E. Gladstone

CHAPTER 1

THE EXCEEDINGLY STRANGE DEMISE OF SIR RICHARD FRANCIS BURTON

> Personally I ignore the existence of soul and spirit,
> feeling no want of a self within a self, an I within an I.
> —Sir Richard Francis Burton

Death was everywhere. Burton felt it burrowing through the marrow of his bones, saw it in the evening light that oozed across the forested peaks overlooking Trieste, heard it in the autumn leaves crunching beneath his feet, and discovered it busily at work in the water barrel at the side of the house. He looked over his shoulder and called to Doctor Grenfell Baker. "Help me, will you, old fellow? There's a robin in here."

Baker, who was examining the thinning rose bushes, turned and strode over. "Drowned?"

"It will be if we're not quick. I can't lean in far enough. My back is stiff as a board."

The doctor looked into the barrel, stretched down his long arms, and scooped out the little bird. He gave a snort of amusement. "You and your feathered friends! Are you adding ornithology to your already bloated list of interests? Here." He placed the struggling creature into Burton's waiting hands. "What was it yesterday? A swallow?"

"Yes, tapping at a window." Burton cradled the twitching robin in his palms. "That's a bad omen."

"Nonsense. It's because you put breadcrumbs on the sill every morning."

"Ah, it was not that window, but another."

Burton gently blew onto the robin's wet feathers and, when the bird was sufficiently dried, slipped it into the inner pocket of his fur coat. "I'll warm it a while then put it into a cage until it's regained sufficient strength." He took up his cane, which he'd leaned against the barrel, and gestured with it. "Walk with me around to the veranda, will you? I'll join Isabel to watch the sun set."

They set off, moving slowly, Baker adjusting his stride to Burton's hobbling gait.

The aged explorer sighed and frowned. "Funny, that swallow."

"Why so?"

"All its fellows have departed for the winter."

"There are always stragglers."

"You know the alchemists held that birds symbolise the migration of the soul?"

"Yes, I did know that. Are you having morbid thoughts again?"

"I'm almost seventy years old. What else is left to me?"

"Plenty. You have your holiday in Constantinople to look forward to. Your move back to England. The end of your governmental duties. No doubt, you'll have the reaction to your translation to cope with, too, though I wish you could be spared that. How much of it remains to be written?"

Of my existence? Precious little I fear, Doctor.

"Nothing at all. I completed it this morning. By God, I've put my life's blood into *The Scented Garden*. It is the crown of my life. Whatever the outcry, I'll not regret writing it."

"It will ruin your reputation."

Burton gave a throaty chuckle. He slipped his hand through the crook of Baker's elbow. "I had no reputation at all when I discovered the original Persian manuscript. That was in Sindh, in India. I was a stripling of twenty years, but I immediately recognised that its translation would 'make' me. It documented every transgression a man could imagine, and in doing so demonstrated that the morals under which we labour are nothing but a human contrivance. When it was destroyed in the Grind-lays Warehouse fire of 'sixty-one, I felt I'd lost a part of myself. I've spent my life searching for another copy to no avail. What I have written is a reconstruction based upon what I can remember of it, and perhaps that makes it even more the truth of me. Aye, you are right. In the short term, my reputation will likely be wrecked, but it matters not, for I shall be dead. And farther into the future, when minds are less hidebound by convention and religious constraints, then the significance of my trans-lation will be acknowledged. Future generations will know me through its pages, and that, I rather suppose, is the closest thing to immortality I can hope for."

He jerked to a halt and gazed bemusedly at a flowerbed. Amid the withered blooms and ossifying stalks, there had grown a single bright-red poppy, entirely out of season. The sight of it made him feel inexpli-cably empty and sad.

"What outré music," he murmured.

"Music, Sir Richard?"

"It's stopped now. Did you not hear it? I suppose it drifted up from the town. Maybe a choir practicing. Rather a haunting sound, I should say."

"I heard nothing."

Burton gave a little grunt, tore his eyes away from the poppy, and resumed his walk.

They rounded a corner of the house and the Gulf of Trieste came into view. The Mediterranean was a deep, glittering turquoise beneath the sinking sun.

Baker shook his head despairingly. "The truth of you, you say? No, sir, I don't believe so. I take your good lady wife's view that, no matter your intention, you'll be remembered as a pornographer if the book sees the light of day. It will eclipse all your other achievements. The pil-grimage to Mecca. The hunt for the source of the Nile. The translating of the *Arabian Nights*."

"What you two regard as pornography," Burton responded, "I intend as anthropology. The customs of our race, including those associated with the act of procreation, must be studied and recorded if we are to understand the motives at the heart of us. We are creatures of the natural world and are thus subject to its laws, such as those so eloquently described by Mr. Darwin. Yet we overlay our existence with stratum upon stratum of ritual and storytelling until little authenticity remains. Why? That question has ever been my subject."

"I'm not sure society is ready to accept such an unequivocal analysis of its complexion."

"Not now, maybe, but Time makes everything possible."

A tremor ran through Burton's body. He halted, suddenly breathless, immobilised by a curious conception of history as multiplying ribbons of light that split and intertwined in a convoluted dance, their movement following the labyrinthine melodies of a throbbing, exotic refrain.

Pulling his right hand from Baker's elbow, he examined it, utterly baffled by the notion that it should be a mechanical thing of engraved brass and tiny cogwheels and pistons. Of course, it wasn't. He saw only knobbled joints, bluish fingernails, nearly transparent liver-spotted skin, and raised veins and sinews. The hand of an old, old man.

The moment passed.

Burton swayed and leaned heavily on his stick.

Baker gripped him. "Steady! Is it your heart?"

"No. No. Just a—a—just my mind playing tricks. I heard that music again."

"There was nothing. Do you need to stop for a moment?"

"I'm all right. Go inside and fetch a cage for the bird, will you, old fellow? I can walk the rest of the way unassisted."

"I really don't think—"

"I'm perfectly fine."

The doctor hesitated for a moment, then nodded and hurried into the house, entering through a side door.

Burton looked again at his hand and shook his head in bewilderment. He gazed around at the garden, at the orchard beyond it, at the low, dark mountains and the coruscating sea. A nightingale started to sing, and its strain drew out again the deep sadness that had touched him a few moments ago. Everything felt achingly beautiful yet oddly illusory. A warm breeze—it was extremely mild for the time of year—brushed his face, and he was shocked to feel a tear trickling down his cheek. Impatiently, he swiped the droplet away with his coat cuff. "Sentimental fool!"

He stood silently for a couple of minutes then resumed his walk, rounded to the front of the house, and saw his wife, Isabel, sitting at a table on the veranda. She greeted him as he stepped up and sat beside her. "Hallo! Where's Grenfell?"

"He's gone inside to fetch a birdcage. We rescued a robin from drowning. It's in my pocket."

"Oh! The poor little mite! Was it much distressed?"

"It's young. I think it'll recover."

"Thank goodness. Do you want coffee?"

"Please."

Isabel took up a steaming pot and poured while Burton lit a Manila cheroot and started to smoke. He stared at the handle of his cane. "Nearly time to go."

"Yes. We should sort through our luggage. Do you think your old Saratoga trunk can withstand another voyage?"

"I expect so." He gave a small smile. She'd misunderstood his meaning.

"By the by," he said. "Have you seen my favourite cane? I can't remember where I left it."

"Isn't that it? You've been using it for long enough. Which is the other?"

"The sword stick. The one with the silver handle shaped to resemble a panther's head."

Isabel pushed a cup and saucer in front of him and looked puzzled. "I don't recall ever seeing such. Not in all the years I've known you."

Doctor Baker stepped out, placed a cage on the table, and quipped, "For your patient, Doctor Burton."

"Thank you," Burton replied. "Do you happen to remember a silver-topped walking cane? Handle like a panther's head?"

"Not at all. Is it lost?"

"Apparently."

"Perhaps it'll turn up when you pack for England. I'm going up to read. I'll see you at dinner." He went back inside.

Burton sipped his coffee then retrieved the robin from his pocket and put it into the cage. Isabel cooed over it. He watched her and remembered when she'd been tall and slim and beautiful. How time ravaged the body. How merciless. How cruel and implacable.

To be young again. To have another chance. To correct the mistakes I made. To turn right when I wrongly turned left. To better value those people I never recognised as the finest I would ever know.

He grinned at an unbidden recollection of his now seldom-seen friend, the poet Algernon Swinburne, falling dead-drunk out of a hansom cab into the gutter before reeling to his feet and engaging in a furious argument with the driver who'd dared to charge him half a crown when Swinburne knew—*knew!*—that all cab rides, no matter the distance, cost a shilling.

How long ago was that? Thirty years?

"What are you chuckling about?" Isabel asked.

"Algy."

"Was the cane a gift from him?"

"No. He just popped into my head. I've no idea why."

They sat and watched the sun setting, their conversation sporadic and their silences comfortable.

At a quarter past eight, they went inside and up to their chambers to prepare for dinner. Burton found himself dawdling. Their meal would be served at nine as usual—they had long ago adopted the Mediterranean habit of dining late—but he delayed changing his clothes and instead pottered about his rooms, needlessly shifting things from one place to another, putting some away and lingering over others—such as his collection of swords, mounted in brackets on a wall—to brood on the memories they generated.

"This is a *khopesh*," he told Isabel, pointing at an oddly shaped blade, one of a pair. "I brought it back from Mecca."

"You've told me before."

"Egyptian, thought to have evolved from battle axes. Often, they are ceremonial and not even sharpened, but given an edge and swung with force, one of these could cut through bone like a hot knife through butter."

"Charming. Is the lecture finished? We should go down."

"You go. I'll come in a few minutes."

"No, darling. I'll wait for you."

Fifteen minutes late, they joined Grenfell Baker at the table. While they ate, they chatted about their future life in London and other matters. All appeared normal, but Burton detected a peculiar light in his wife's eyes and realised she suspected the truth and was scared.

There was nothing he could do about it.

Time will have its way.

At eleven, they went back upstairs, and Isabel and Baker helped him to prepare for bed. As usual, he endured their assistance with bad grace, grumbling at his immobility, feeling humiliated that he'd become such a burden, such a confounded invalid.

Baker bid them good-night. Burton got into bed. Isabel, with difficultly, lowered herself to her knees and said her prayers, repeatedly mentioning her husband in her long litany of requested blessings. For her sake, he tolerated it without comment.

You appeal to nothingness, my wife. You plea into a void for mercy and for forgiveness for actions and thoughts that no one judges but you. There is no God. There is no succour. There is no afterlife. There is only Time.

Outside, a dog howled.

Isabel rose. "What a horrible noise."

"The poor thing knows the unseasonal heat doesn't long survive after the sun goes down," Burton said. "It's predicting a chilly night."

"I'll fetch an extra blanket."

"No, don't. I hate to feel swaddled."

She joined him in bed. "Shall we read?"

He nodded. She passed him his Robert Buchanan. He opened it at random, but his eyes immediately drifted away from it to the window. He gazed out at the splattering of stars. For three hours, his mind wandered. He remembered, from his childhood, stories about Spring Heeled Jack, a supernatural creature that assaulted women before leaping away; he thought about Mrs. Angell, his housekeeper in the old days; he kicked himself for not including his friend Richard Monckton Milnes among the many people to whom he'd written these few days past; he mourned over the death of his colleague, friend, and spiteful enemy, John Hanning Speke, though the man's demise had occurred more than a quarter of a century ago.

At half past two, he said to Isabel, "When we are back in England, I have it in mind to purchase a clockwork servant. They are expensive to buy but cost nothing to run, so money is saved eventually."

"A what?"

"A clockwork servant. One of Babbage's creations."

She put down her book and placed her fingers over his. "The mathematician fellow? I've not heard of them. Clockwork? Are you sure?"

"Edward has one. He named it Grumbles. Very efficient."

"Edward who?"

"My brother."

Her hand went to her mouth. Her eyes widened. "Dick, your brother is in an asylum. He has been since 'fifty-nine. You remember the head injury he received in India? He was never the same after that."

He knew she was right. He knew she was wrong. He felt confused.

Burton tried to draw a breath, but it wouldn't come. He croaked, "Open a window. There's no air in the room." Suddenly, pains were shooting through his limbs. He thrashed helplessly. A moan was torn out of him.

Isabel held him and cried out, "What ails you so, Dick?"

With tremendous willpower, he forced himself to lie still, dropping his resistance and allowing the throbs and stabs to flow through him unchecked. "It's all right. It's all right. I'm recovered now." He was unable to keep the hoarseness from his voice. "It's just a gouty pain in my left foot. The usual thing but it took me by surprise. When did I have my last attack?"

"Three months ago. Shall I call the doctor?"

"No, don't disturb him. He'll be asleep. Besides, he can't do anything for it."

She hastened from the bed to a chest of drawers and returned with a horseshoe magnet in her hand. Pulling back the sheets, she held it to his foot. "Does it help?"

"A bit," he lied.

Unfamiliar names ran through his mind. Trounce. Honesty. Lawless. Raghavendra. Krishnamurthy. Bhatti. Who were they? And Mrs. Angell? He'd never had a housekeeper!

"Do you remember Stoker?" he asked.

"The theatre man? Irving's manager? Yes, of course I do. We've dined with him on a number of occasions."

"I have the unaccountable belief that I knew him as a child."

"He never mentioned it. Surely he would have. And you've never spoken of it before. I think your mind is playing tricks."

"Perhaps it is. I imagine I knew Wilde, too."

"Oscar? Great heavens above! I sincerely hope not!"

"What is wrong with me, Isabel? I feel oddly divided, as though there's more than one of me."

"I fear you're having one of your old fevers. They always had that symptom. Remember when you returned from Africa stricken with malaria? For weeks you were convinced that you were two people in one body, forever at war with yourself. You used to—"

Her voice faded away. Oblivion enveloped him. From it, a vision emerged. He was in a featureless desert, squatting beside a tent, fascinated by a scarab beetle pushing a ball of camel dung alongside the fringe of the canvas. "The sun across the heavens," he murmured. "Day and night. Light and dark. Presence and absence. Life and death. One and zero."

When he was next aware, it was half past three and Isabel was distraught.

"I couldn't rouse you. You were gasping for breath."

He told another falsehood in order to comfort her. "Just a deep sleep. I was dreaming. I saw the little flat we'll buy in London, and it had quite a nice large room in it."

"Then we'll make that your study," she replied. "You can hang your swords on its wall and put your—"

She vanished into blazing whiteness as his chest tightened viciously. A thousand tortures. Agony beyond comprehension. He couldn't even scream.

There eventually came further cognisance of time passed. Grenfell

Baker's voice sounded from afar. "Try to keep your respiration steady, Sir Richard. Here, drink this. It will offer some relief."

Swallow. Bad taste. Pain.

"Your wife has gone for the priest."

Priest? Priest? Bismillah! Am I dying? Help me! Save me!

He squeezed his eyes shut and when he opened them again she was there, weeping. Knives twisted between his ribs. It was unendurable. He reached for her, weakly clawing at her arm. "Chloroform! Ether! Or I'm a dead man!"

"The doctor says it will kill you!" she wailed. "He's doing all he knows!"

Life. Death.

One. Zero.

Music. An intricate rhythm. Curious melodies. Peculiar harmonies. The sound gripped him and dragged him through a whiteness that was everything and nothing. He fragmented. Every decision he'd ever made unravelled. All his successes and failures frayed away. He lost cohesion until nothing of him remained.

Zero. Zero. Zero.

Gathering weight.

The pressure of her arms beneath him.

No, not her arms. The ground.

Burton opened his eyes and saw a flickering orange light. Flames reflected on a canvas roof. He was in a tent.

He sat up.

El Balyuz, the chief abban, burst in. "They are attacking!" He handed Burton a revolver. "Your gun, Effendi!"

What is this? What is happening?

Pushing back his bed sheets, moving like an automaton, with no control over himself, Burton stood, put the pistol on the map table, and pulled on his trousers. Astonishingly, his body was that of a young man. He took up the gun again, looked over to Lieutenant George Herne, and grinned. Words spilled unbidden from his mouth. "More bloody posturing! It's all for show, but we shouldn't let them get too cocky. Go out the back of the tent, away from the campfire, and ascertain their strength. Let off a few rounds over their heads if necessary. They'll soon bugger off."

Recognition.

This is Berbera! My God! 1855! My first African expedition. We were attacked. I received a spear through my face. Why am I here again?

"Right you are," Herne said. The lieutenant moved to the rear of the tent and ducked under the canvas.

Burton, occupying his own flesh like a passenger, able to observe but not influence, checked his gun. "For Pete's sake, Balyuz, why have you handed me an unloaded pistol? Get me my sabre."

He shoved the Colt into the waistband of his trousers and snatched his sword from the Arab.

"Speke!" he bellowed. "Stroyan!"

Almost immediately, the tent flap was pushed aside and John Hanning Speke stumbled in. His eyes were wild. "They knocked my tent down around my ears. I almost took a beating. Is there shooting to be done?

"I rather suppose there is," Burton responded. "Be sharp, and arm to defend the camp."

He felt the urge to rush forward and grip his old comrade.

I forgive you! I forgive you! Let us forget it all and start anew. It is good to see you again. So good! I never meant any of it, John. I don't know how such enmity came between us.

He was unable to do it. His body wouldn't accept his commands. Helplessly, he waited with the others. They checked their gear and listened to the rush of men outside.

Herne returned from his recce. "There's a lot of the blighters, and our confounded guards have taken to their heels. I took a couple of pot-shots at the mob but then got tangled in the tent ropes. A big Somali swiped at me with a bloody great club. I put a bullet into the bastard. Stroyan's either out cold or done for. I couldn't get near him."

Something thumped against the side of the tent. Suddenly a barrage of blows pounded the canvas while war cries were raised all around. The attackers were swarming like hornets. Javelins were thrust through the opening. Daggers ripped at the material.

"Bismillah!" Burton cursed. "We're going to have to fight our way to the supplies and get ourselves more guns. Herne, there are spears tied to the tent pole at the back. Get 'em."

"Yes, sir." Herne went off but almost immediately ran back. "They're breaking through!"

Burton swore vociferously. "If this blasted thing comes down on us we'll be caught up good and proper. Get out! Come on! Now!"

He plunged out into the night. Somali natives were milling about, brandishing their weapons. Jostled and thumped, Burton looked over his shoulder to check the others had followed. He saw Speke emerging from the tent, saw him struck on the knee by a thrown stone, saw him flinch and stumble back.

Don't say it! Don't utter those damnable words!

They came anyway. Burton yelled, "Don't step back! They'll think that we're retiring!"

Two short sentences—uttered without thought—that Speke would fixate upon and twist into an accusation of cowardice, inciting in him a fierce resentment, leading to betrayal and ultimately, to his death.

Despairingly, Burton turned to defend himself. He was shoved this way and that, hacking with his blade, caught up in a crush of bodies. Amid the chaos, the campfire, swollen out of all proportion, caught his eye and held it.

Suddenly, everything else dwindled from awareness and, as a javelin slid into his cheek, knocked out two molars, sliced across his tongue, and transfixed his face, he lost all physical sensation.

Flames. Only flames. There was nothing else.

Grindlays Warehouse.

In 1861, when the depth of Speke's perfidy had become apparent, and Burton was at his lowest ebb, Grindlays burned to the ground, taking with it all the documents, costumes, artefacts, and mementoes Burton had stored there after returning from his many years of travel and exploration, depriving him of every material thing he'd ever valued. At this juncture of his life, he'd married Isabel Arundell, the only remaining constant.

He saw her now, a blazing bonfire illuminating her face, reflecting in the tears on her cheeks, making them look like rivulets of blood.

Snapping out of his trance, he walked toward her. It was a winter evening. He was back in his garden in Trieste.

"What a ghastly time I've had of it!" he exclaimed as he approached. "I'm sorry to have caused such a fuss. By God, I thought I was done for. Was it another heart attack? I feel perfectly healthy now. Even my rheumatism has let up."

She didn't respond.

"I dreamed I was back in Berbera with John Speke. A nightmare. It was extraordinarily vivid. Isabel?"

Sparks and glowing scraps of paper spiralled up through the smoke. The bonfire crackled and snapped. He watched as she reached into a carpetbag at her side, pulled a handful of letters from it, and threw them into the conflagration.

"What are you doing?"

Still no answer.

"Isabel?"

Something felt wrong.

She took a thick sheaf of paper from the bag.

His translation of *The Scented Garden*.

"Wait!" he cried out. "No! Don't do that!"

Lady Isabel Burton consigned her husband's *magnum opus* to the flames.

Burton shrieked as he felt it—and himself—consumed.

It was Grindlays all over again, reducing him to nothing.

White. White. White.

Zero.

Hands took form, easing out of the featureless glare, shapes congealing around them. He didn't immediately recognise them as his own, for rather than being gnarled, liver-spotted, and transparent, they were tough and healthy and young.

A note was pushed into one of them. Raising his eyes, he saw Arthur Findlay of the Royal Geographical Society, an expression of utmost sympathy upon his face. Burton read the note, already aware of the news it bore, and reacted to it without any volition of his own.

"By God! He's killed himself!"

John Hanning Speke—who, two years after the Berbera incident, had accompanied him into central Africa in search of the source of the

Nile and who subsequently claimed to have discovered it without Burton's help—was dead.

The Bath Assembly Rooms. 1864. This is where I was supposed to confront Speke and condemn him, humiliate him. Where I'd make him pay the price for his disloyalty. Instead, just prior to the conference, he shot himself while out hunting. An accident, perhaps. Or suicide.

Burton put the note onto the table and rose from his chair.

This is the day I was forever broken.

He heard himself say all the things he'd said on that occasion: to Findlay; to Sir Roderick Murchison, president of the RGS; and to the other members of the committee. Then he stumbled out of the room and into Isabel's waiting arms.

She was young again. Beautiful.

Contorting emotions that made no sense at all mauled at him. How could he love and, at the same time, fear her?

"What ails you so, Dick?"

Don't be concerned. It's just a gouty pain in my left foot. The usual thing. When did I have my last attack?

He said, "John has shot himself."

She fussed but he couldn't bear to be near her. Burton needed to flee; he required space in which to think. He tore himself away, spoke to Sir Roderick, told him he'd address the waiting audience, and watched from within himself as the familiar events unfolded, as the same sentences were uttered and the turning point of his life was played out once again.

Is this my reckoning? Am I being judged?

The outer Burton escaped to a quiet room and there wept for Speke. The inner Burton wept too, the memories and replaying emotions overwhelming him. When both regained control of themselves, the one sat and wrote out a makeshift presentation concerning the valley of the Indus while the other watched through his host's eyes and waited for the astonishing dream to end.

It kept going.

Thirty minutes later, Burton was standing at a podium in front of an audience. He saw eager faces, hungry for sensation and scandal. He began his presentation. Words spilled from his mouth and trailed away until, in the faintest of whispers, he said, "I'm sorry. I can't continue."

Burton fled from the stage, grabbed his coat, hat, and cane, exited the Assembly Rooms, and stumbled down the steps to the street. There, he paused, breathed deeply, and suddenly had full control of himself. Utterly amazed, he looked down at his strong 43-year-old body and whispered, "I'm alive." He put a hand to his chest. His heart was racing but not failing. He laughed, moaned, stifled a sob, clapped a palm over his mouth, and clenched his teeth to prevent himself from hollering like a maniac. Pedestrians, dressed in the styles of three decades past, walked by and glanced curiously at him. A horse-drawn hansom clattered over the cobbles.

He looked up. Dark clouds were drifting across a blue sky, threatening to obscure it. He guessed, from the sun's position, that it was half one in the afternoon or thereabouts.

His senses felt amplified. Everything he observed, he saw in exaggerated detail. Every sound possessed startling clarity. Odours filled his nostrils and touched the back of his tongue—burning coal, cooking food, animal waste, vegetation. Each scent brought with it a scintillating memory of days long since passed.

"It can't be real. It can't be!"

Leaning with both hands on his cane, he fought to quell the fit of shaking that suddenly gripped him. Then it occurred to him that the building at his back was filled with newspaper journalists, all clamouring for further news of Speke's death, all eager to question him, all bound to follow when they realised he'd exited the premises.

He hurried away.

Isabel. What about Isabel?

"We were staying at the Royal Hotel," he mumbled. "I'll meet her there later."

Shock. She'd burned *The Scented Garden*.

How many betrayals can a man endure?

No, he wouldn't consider that now.

Besides, if this is 1864, then I haven't even written the bloody thing yet.

He passed a street singer who was warbling about a "four pence ha'penny cap," turned left at a junction, and hastened along with no idea of his destination. It was enough just to walk. His muscles, joints, and bones were entirely free of arthritis, rheumatism, gout, and the myriad of other ailments that had accompanied him for so long. He felt clean and powerful. Temperament, he realised, was as much a function of the body as it was of the mind. This younger physique made him feel like a sharp blade, in contrast to the blunted edge of old age.

He gave a bark of exuberance. Passers-by stepped out of his path.

Oh! The brutal countenance of Sir—no, *Captain!*—Richard Francis Burton in his prime. The blazing eyes! The savage jaw! The swarthy skin and pronounced cheekbones! The scar and long Oriental moustache!

"Hah!" he bellowed at a studs-and-laces vendor.

The man threw up his hands and staggered back.

Bismillah! Control yourself!

"My dear fellow," Burton said. "I'm so sorry. Forgive me. I'm a little overexcited."

"Holy Moses! Excited is it? Blimmin' well barmy, more like!" the vendor exclaimed. "Shoutin' at them what's a-mindin' their own blimmin' business. There ain't no call for it."

"Barmy? Yes, perhaps so, perhaps so. My sincere apologies. Is this 1864?"

"Is it 1864, he asks now! Of course it blimmin' well is! What are you, escaped from the loony bin or summick?"

"In a manner of speaking, my man, that might well be the case. Good day to you."

Burton moved on. His eyes flicked back and forth, eating up every inch of the environment. Worn paving. An overgrown hollyhock. A cracked windowpane. A fat pigeon. A blind beggar. A discarded beer bottle. The flaking paint on the side of a passing carriage.

The world felt astonishingly lucid and profoundly tangible, more so than Trieste had ever done.

An urge to run gripped him, to escape, to plunge out into the world and lose himself before Death realised its oversight and reclaimed him. He removed his top hat and held it by its brim, flung up his stick and caught it by its middle, and set off. Pedestrians scattered. Men protested, "I say! Steady on!" Women gave little squeals of alarm. His legs pumped. The air streamed across his face. His lungs embraced the exercise without complaint.

Down the road, around a corner into a less populated one, past houses and stores and workshops.

"Free!" he yelled. "Free! Free!"

Finally, he stopped, bent with his shoulder against a wall, roared with laughter, whimpered in shock, and panted until his respiration settled. When he straightened, he saw a policeman glaring at him. Burton replaced his hat and gave a sheepish smile. He nodded an apology, knuckled his brim, and moved on.

A few minutes later, as he was passing a carpenter's yard, a weight dropped onto his right shoulder. He yelped, jerked up his hands, and swatted at it. There was a flash of bright colour and an indignant squawk. Burton stumbled to one side and instinctively fell into a fencing pose, stretching out his cane like an épée.

Its end was pointed at a parakeet.

The bird had jumped from his shoulder onto the railing in front of the yard. It peered at him side-on, head cocked, and gave a click of its beak and a little cackle.

Burton lowered his stick. "Just an escaped pet."

"Bollocks and filthy gut stench," the bird responded.

"Good Lord! A fugitive from a foul-mouthed owner, it appears."

"Message for Sir Richard Francis fornicating flop-bellied Burton."

He gawped. He'd encountered taking birds of course—as a matter of fact, Isabel kept a rather-too-vocal mynah—but he'd never heard of one that could do more than mimic. And *Sir*? He'd not been knighted until 1886. If this was really 'sixty-four, how did it know to call him Sir?

"You are invited to meet the reborn," the parakeet continued, "at the stinking Slug and Lettuce. Message bloody well ends, and up your claggy tubes, toilet breath."

The feathered herald poked its tongue out of its beak, blew a raspberry, and took wing. Burton watched as it fluttered away over the rooftops. He opened his mouth as if to speak, closed it, checked again that his hat was straight, turned, took two steps, stopped, and muttered, "Ah. Now I have it. It's the only explanation."

Plainly, he was still on his deathbed in Trieste. His heart was on the outs, and his brain, starved of oxygen, was, in its distress, generating this deeply compelling hallucination.

He sighed, disappointed, and looked around. "It feels so completely real. What an incredible organ the human brain is. How marvellous that it should ease my passing with this simulacrum of youth."

Burton walked on and frowned. "But why reconstruct this day of all days? Surely a happier one would have been more appropriate. Unless—"

Might it be that a man is defined by the incidents in his life that he can't let go of, the ones that haunt him into his dotage? Are they experienced again at the moment of death in order to be cleansed from the soul, so each individual is purified before passing through the gates of paradise?

Was he here that he might forgive himself?

Except, of course, he didn't believe in sin or the soul or the afterlife. *Did I get it all wrong? Was my atheism a mistake?*

Rounding another corner, he found himself back on the busy thoroughfare, though farther along it. Market stalls lined either side of the street and a flock of sheep was being driven between them, causing much chaos. From amid the shouted objections, good-natured insults, and shrill bleating, the voice of a newsboy hollered, "Read the latest! War in America! Come buy, come buy, come buy a paper! Latest from America!"

Burton picked out the source of the declamation, a tiny ragamuffin, and walked toward him.

"And the parrot," he said to himself. "Why would I fantasise such a capricious ingredient as that? 'Meet the reborn,' it said. The reborn."

Pushing past an old gypsy woman who shoved a sprig of heather into his face and advised him to "be lucky, me deario," he approached the newsboy.

"Paper, sir?"

"No thank you. Can you direct me to the Stinking Slug and Lettuce, lad? A public house, is it?"

The boy grinned, exposing a mouthful of green and gappy teeth. "Ha ha! It is, sir, but 'tain't so bad as all that."

"I beg your pardon?"

"It's the Cat an' Fiddle what's the stinkiest drinkin' 'stablishment in the city, far as I know. The Slug 'n' Lettuce is perfickly 'spectible. Yus, I can tell you 'ow to find it." The boy paused and rubbed the grubby fingers of his right hand together.

Taking the hint, Burton fished in his trouser pocket, found a few coins, and dropped them into the waiting palm.

"Crikey!" the urchin exclaimed, and quickly pocketed the payment before the amount could be reconsidered. He pointed along the road. "Thataway 'n' turn left into Quiet Street. You'll see it. 'Tain't far to walk."

"Much obliged."

Burton moved forward, navigating the crowd while experiencing an oddly disjointed mix of familiarity and alienation. He felt engulfed by distant memories come alive. After the relative silence of his secluded home in Trieste, the cacophony of this English thoroughfare battered his already overloaded senses. He suddenly found it impossible to string any thoughts together. His eyes were too full, his ears too encumbered, and his olfactory faculties—more chained to memory than any other sense— were working overtime.

He felt his guilt at abandoning Isabel during this moment of crisis jumbling with a multitude of other irreconcilable emotions concerning her. It was as if he'd known her hundreds of times over, each relationship founded on a slightly different basis. He loved her. He hated her. He depended on her. He resented her. He wanted her. He feared her. She was his other half, his wife, his friend, his acquaintance, his supporter, a stranger, his opponent, his enemy, his nemesis.

He shook his head, trying to clear it, then shoved through the crowd, causing indignant oaths to be uttered, and stumbled to the junction with Quiet Street. Mercifully, the road lived up to its name, and he emerged from the throng and entered it, gulping at the air like a drowning man.

He stopped and steadied himself, one hand on his cane, the other on a garden fence.

This is it. My old heart has stopped. I'm about to expire.

His breathing gradually settled. He didn't die. The illusion held.

He saw the Slug and Lettuce just ahead, a small ivy-clad building with walls that bulged outward as if on the point of collapse.

"Brandy. That's what I need. Heaven or hell, if they exist, whichever

I enter, I'll arrive there drunk." He gave a bark of laughter. "Yes, by God, that's the Burton of old!"

A warrior on a mission, he strode toward the drinking den, pushing all other considerations aside and dwelling only on the euphoria of his restored physique.

As he neared the public house, he heard the patrons within talking, shouting, singing, and laughing. When he opened the door, it was to reveal a crowd of lunchtime drinkers, mostly of the working class, all breathing an atmosphere thick with blue tobacco smoke. Entering, he shouldered through to the bar and, being identified as a gentleman by his attire and bearing, was immediately served. The men to his right and left, who'd been waiting before him, made no complaint. They knew their place.

Burton turned and surveyed the mob while his drink was being poured. He smelled sour beer and body odour, bad breath and unwashed clothes, stale urine and rancid lard. He saw good-humoured labourers, clerks, stallholders, and dolly-mops. He heard gossip and jokes and ribaldry. He didn't spot anyone who appeared to be "reborn."

He swallowed his brandy in a single gulp and marvelled at the taste, which he now realised had been terribly dulled by old age. After requesting and receiving a refill, he slid payment across the bar, turned, and pushed his way through to the ill-lit back of the room. There, he stopped, staring awestruck at a small man seated at a table.

The little fellow looked up, his eyes widening, and gave a piercing shriek of recognition.

A face from the distant past.

An old friend restored to youth.

Algernon Charles Swinburne.

CHAPTER 2

A GATHERING OF THE INEXPLICABLY RESURRECTED

If the misery of the poor be caused not by the laws of nature,
but by our institutions, great is our sin.
—Charles Darwin

"**W**hat?" Swinburne shrieked. "What? What?"

Burton stammered, "You're—you're young."

Of course he's young, you dolt! It's 1864! But what's he doing here?

Swinburne leaped to his feet, his chair falling backward. "You know? You know that I—that I—but look at you! You're alive!" The poet slapped a hand to his forehead. "My hat! Why didn't I realise it? I knew there was something about this date. It's the day Speke shot himself, isn't it? I should have remembered you'd be in Bath."

Burton put his glass on the table, dropped his topper and cane, and pounced on his friend. They gripped each other by the elbows and laughed hysterically, heedless of the people around them. Tears streamed down their cheeks.

"I don't—I can't—it isn't—how can it—?" Words tumbled from Burton's mouth. He was again stricken by an ungovernable trembling and had no idea what he was saying. Yet, even as he struggled to control himself, he was aware that Swinburne's reaction to his arrival, which was equally unrestrained, had greater emotion behind it than was warranted from a man who, in 1864, had seen him fairly frequently.

"It makes no—are we—gah!" the master poet cried out. "Surely it's—gah!—but—gah! Eek!"

Burton stood panting, his thoughts disarranged. The last time he'd met with Swinburne, his friend had been a little old man, bald, grey-bearded, bent-backed, and subdued—the excessive energies of his youth long faded. Now, here he was in all his diminutive slope-shouldered glory. His thick, wavy, red hair was sticking out almost horizontally from his over-large head, his bright green eyes were wide, and his surplus of electric vitality had been restored causing him to twitch, hop, and dance just as it had done so many years ago in the early days of their friendship.

It was miraculous.

"Algy, stop. Calm down. We're making a scene. Let us sit and talk quietly."

"Poo-poo to all that! This is beyond the bounds!"

"Yes, I know. But let's do it anyway."

Burton pulled out the poet's chair and pushed his friend down into it. He ordered beers and more brandies from a potboy and settled at the table.

They stared in wonder at each other, and a curious silence descended upon them. The hustle and bustle of the Slug and Lettuce continued unabated, but it was as if an invisible screen had suddenly separated the two men from it. Burton contemplated the possibility that he might be slipping into some form of shock and remembered how he'd been enveloped by a similar quietude after the spear had been thrust through his face at Berbera.

Snap out of it. Don't allow the world to become dreamlike. You might wake up.

He opened his mouth to speak but hesitated. As Swinburne did the same, Burton stopped him with a raised hand and slight shake of his head.

"Wait a moment."

Think it through. Why is—Ah. Yes. This day.

He jabbed a finger toward the other. "You, my friend, should not be here."

Swinburne threw out his hands as if Burton had stated the perfectly obvious. "You're telling me! I should be dead! You'll think me mad, and I very well might be, but the Swinburne who sits before you is not the one you know. That is to say, he's—I'm—I was—I should be forty-five years older. I've been restored to youth and sent back to—" He made an all-encompassing gesture, "to here, from the future, from my deathbed. It's perfectly incredible. Perfectly ridiculous. Perfectly true!"

In his mind's eye, Burton saw again a scarab beetle pushing a ball of dung.

Not just the sun but the whole of existence, created and manipulated by Life itself. Sentience. The source of All.

His mind was wandering. With an effort, he reined it in.

"I believe you, for less than an hour ago, I was also breathing my last. I was in Trieste. It was 1890."

"Nineteen years ago," Swinburne whispered incredulously. "I remember."

"Nineteen years?"

"I mean to say, you died nineteen years before me."

It took Burton a moment to absorb that information.

"So you've come from—?"

"1909. The last of it I remember, it was evening, and I was suffering from pneumonia. Everything turned white, and suddenly I found myself clinging to Culver Cliff. Do you recall me once telling you about how I climbed it in my youth to prove to myself that I possessed courage?"

"Yes, I remember."

"Well, there I was, inexplicably back at the scene, with seagulls screaming at me and the wind ruffling my hair. Of course, I considered it a dream. But nevertheless, rather than falling, I climbed, though I hardly knew what I was doing. I made it to the top, collapsed onto the sward at the edge of the precipice, and there fancied I heard somebody address me. Before I could turn my head to see whom it might be, I fainted. When I regained my senses, I was aboard a train. Now I had time to think, and when I realised that I'd somehow become young again—and that this was something more than the idle imaginings of a slumbering mind—I have to confess, I became somewhat hysterical."

"Understandably," Burton murmured. He felt distracted by the increasingly thick veil that appeared to surround them both. The babble of voices and sharp clink of glasses had reduced to an indistinct hum. He could only focus on his companion. Everything else was obscured and blurred. Desperately, he clung to Swinburne's words, praying they'd keep him tethered and prevent him from slipping away, back to Trieste, back to pain and decrepitude, back into Death's embrace.

Swinburne continued, "The guards objected to my behaviour and threw me off at the next stop, which proved to be Salisbury. There, I saw a newspaper, noted the date and—after checking my ticket and the labels on my luggage—came to the conclusion that I'd been travelling to Cornwall for a holiday. I vaguely recalled the occasion. Now, though, I hadn't a clue what to do. I was all set to catch a train back to London when—" He stopped, giggled, and waggled his right forefinger around his temple to suggest insanity. "Out of the blue, a parakeet landed on my shoulder, insulted me, and told me to immediately board the express to Bath and come here to the Slug and Lettuce to meet the 'reborn.' I suppose, now, that it was referring to you."

"I received a similar directive, also from a bird." Burton said. "What is it, thirty, forty miles or so between here and Salisbury? Not far for a bird to fly. I daresay it could have been the same one."

Their drinks arrived. When the potboy set down the tray, the clatter possessed greater volume than it should, and in an instant the crisis passed. The world snapped back into focus. Burton's senses were assaulted, and he accepted the battering with immense relief. Everything was real. Sight, sound, smell, taste, and touch; vivid, solid, and marvellously present. He was alive. Algy was here. None of it could be doubted.

They raised their glasses and took a deep draught. Then they regarded each other, recognised a shared appreciation of their reinvigorated senses, and burst into such uproarious laughter that tears again spilled down their cheeks.

Burton felt the hinges of his jaw aching and revelled in the mild discomfort. He heard a nearby patron say to another, "They've started early, ain't they? They'll be in the gutter afore too long," and it made him laugh all the more.

They regained control of themselves, swallowed their beers, shifted attention to their brandies, and sat quietly for a few moments.

Burton patted his pockets until, with an exclamation of pleasure, he located a Manila cheroot, which he immediately lit and drew on, grunting with the sheer luxury of it.

Everything felt like new.

"To see you again!" Swinburne exclaimed. "It's marvellous. How I mourned your passing. I wrote you an elegy." Tipping back his head and closing his eyes, he declaimed:

> *"Night or light is it now, wherein*
> *Sleeps, shut out from the wild world's din,*
> *Wakes, alive with a life more clear,*
> *One who found not on earth his kin?*
> *Sleep were sweet for a while—"*

His right elbow suddenly spasmed upward. He squeaked and used his left hand to slap down the wayward limb. "Oof! My twitches have returned with a vengeance. I was far more sedate in my dotage. I don't know whether to resent them or be delighted." He grinned. "Actually, that's a lie. I'm cock-a-hoop!"

"It interrupted your recital, at least," Burton said. "I'll have no more of that, if you please." He shivered. "Death! By God, these past few years I've felt it at my shoulder every minute of every bloody day. I saw it in the mirror—my own skull pushing through the skin of my face. I watched my wife being slowly consumed—" He noticed a shadow pass across his companion's features at the mention of Isabel, "and now, by some mysterious means, I've shaken it loose. Life, Algy! Life!"

Swinburne gave a jerky half shrug, half twitch. "Yes, you're right. Life. No more of the other stuff. No more debilitation and decay."

They drank a toast to that.

"So," Burton said. "Isabel. Tell me."

Swinburne grimaced and shook his head.

"Come on, old friend. I couldn't miss the expression on your face. Out with it."

"Ugh! And pah!"

"I beg your pardon?"

"Pah! I say!"

"By which you mean?"

"Pah to Isabel, Richard. Pah to her, and pah to her again! And that's all I have to say on the matter."

"I see. And such unpoetic sentiment is prompted by—?"

Swinburne crossed his arms, uncrossed them, crossed them again, then frowned and compressed his lips.

Burton rapped his knuckles on the table top. "Come on! Come on! I'm filled to the brim with conundrums. I lack capacity for another."

The poet loosed an inarticulate cry. "Confound it! She burned *The Scented Garden*! Burned it! That and all of your diaries and notes!"

"I know."

"I never spoke to her again. I couldn't stand the thought that—Hallo? What? Pardon? How can you possibly know? You were dead."

"Before I found myself here, when my heart was failing, there were hallucinations. At least, that's what I thought they were. Like your Culver Cliff episode." Burton touched the long scar on his face. "I experienced again the disaster at Berbera. You recall, when my camp was attacked? And I saw her at a bonfire, throwing my work into its flames."

A confusion of emotions welled up in Burton—rage, sadness, loss, love, despair, resignation—then were gone, leaving nothing but a strange and aching absence, as if he'd had a tooth removed. Isabel was nearby, restored to her prime, lovely and alluring, yet he suddenly knew he'd never see her again. The notion didn't disturb him as much as it should have.

Abandon her? You can't. Not even you are that ruthless.

Swinburne shook his head sadly. "A terrible and stupid thing to do. It utterly ruined her reputation. She was roundly condemned by the press and lost most of her friends just when she needed them the most. Is—is she here, in Bath?"

"Yes."

"What are you going to do?"

"I can't think about it right now. I can hardly think about anything."

"I know exactly what you mean. My head is crammed with visions that make no sense. I'm remembering things that never even happened."

Burton raised an inquisitive eyebrow. Swinburne shrugged. "Fantasies. *Alice in Wonderland* nonsense." He paused. "Hmm. A case in point. I feel that I've met Charles Dodgson—you know, Lewis Carroll, the author of that book—yet I'm equally convinced that I haven't."

"Yes," Burton responded. "Yes. Was I with you? There was—a storm? You were swimming in the sea. Then—" He squeezed his eyes shut and clutched at fleeting impressions. "A carriage ride. Dodgson saying something about literature and travel."

"Steam transportation making the world smaller," Swinburne muttered. "The booklets sold at stations—the little thrilling romances where the murder comes at page fifteen and the wedding, at page forty—surely they are due to steam."

"Yes. He said that, I remember. But when? When were we with him? I can think of no such occasion."

"Nor I. And the carriage—not a horse-drawn affair but a queer sort of contraption more akin to a locomotive. I can picture all sorts of such machines. I see myself in a flying chair and on a penny-farthing that has a little engine. I recall big spidery contrivances. Animal monstrosities, too. Giant swans and colossal horses. I even imagine myself to be a vermillion-coloured jungle. If I allow my mind to roam freely, I instantly slip into an opium-like reverie."

"I've been pushing it aside but—if I let it—the same happens to me. Much of what I think and feel is blatantly nonsensical. But—" Burton drew his brows together. "Another mutual illusion. This jungle of yours. I've seen plenty, but never a vermillion-coloured one. Except, somehow, I feel I have, and I am possessed of the notion that I've been in it, too."

"I didn't say I imagined myself *in* it. I said I *was* it, which is utterly ridiculous." Swinburne looked at Burton with uncertainty. "It's as if—I have the idea—I feel almost as if I've lived many lives over and am recalling them all at once. Are my eyes bulging? Am I foaming at the mouth?"

"No," Burton answered. "And I share the identical sensation."

He glanced around at the dingy interior of the Slug and Lettuce, at its low-beamed ceiling and stained walls, at the hustle and bustle within them, at the dirty, pockmarked, and expressive faces of its customers. Many a glance was being cast in his and Swinburne's direction. Their demeanour and behaviour had attracted considerable curiosity. One man in particular was standing alone, tankard in his right hand, bowler hat in his left, staring at them intently. He possessed a thickset, burly physique, frosty blue eyes, and a wide brown moustache. Upon seeing he was observed, he gave a slight start and shifted awkwardly from foot to foot. He then appeared to reach a decision and moved through the crowd toward them.

Without taking his eyes from him, Burton said, "That man, as with Dodgson, I think I've met before but am also aware that I most certainly I haven't."

Swinburne followed his gaze. "Oh, it's just my brother." He emitted a squeak of surprise. "What in blue blazes am I talking about? No it isn't! I've never laid eyes on the fellow!"

The man arrived at their table, put down his glass, and self-consciously touched his right forefinger to his eyebrow in greeting. "I'm—um—forgive the intrusion, gentlemen, but—er—my name is William Trounce—Police Sergeant William Trounce—and I was wondering—that is to say—oh dash it!—does the word 'reborn' happen to mean anything to you?"

"It certainly does," Burton said. "You'd better sit down, Detective Inspector."

"Sergeant," Trounce corrected. He put his hat on the table, pulled out a chair, and joined them, fidgeting awkwardly, plainly nervous. "I'm sorry to—the thing of it is, you see—" He put his hands over his face and groaned. "By Jove! What in the name of God is happening?"

Swinburne said, "Might it be that you died and now find yourself in your own past?"

"Yes!" Trounce exclaimed. "Yes, I swear to it. But it's not—how did you—how—?"

"It has happened to us, as well," Burton put in. "We were just discussing the fact that we're also experiencing memories that aren't our own. For instance, I feel an instantaneous familiarity with you, Mr. Trounce, almost as if we've spent considerable time together, which most assuredly is not the case."

"I share that sentiment," Swinburne added. "You feel like family, Pouncer. Sorry. Pouncer? I mean Will—er—Sergeant Trounce."

"William, please," Trounce said huskily. He looked from one to the other then grabbed his tankard and emptied it. Burton, who'd finished his own drinks without even noticing, snapped his fingers to attract the potboy's attention and ordered another round. If the alcohol he'd so far consumed was having any effect, he was too agitated to notice it.

"It's been a very long time since I got sloshed," Swinburne commented. "I'm strongly inclined to address that grievous negligence. William, my name is Algernon Swinburne—'Algy' will do—and this is Sir Richard Burton, the famous explorer."

"And the king's agent," Trounce said.

"The what?" Burton asked.

Trounce moved his lips wordlessly, obviously grappling with a notion that wouldn't come. His face bore an expression of complete helplessness. "I don't know why I said that."

"There hasn't been a king since William the Fourth," Swinburne noted. "And no monarchy at all since Victoria's assassination."

Trounce winced. "I should know that better than anybody. I was there when she was killed. It ruined my life. Even me being here—" He made a gesture that suggested not just the tavern around them but the world—and time—beyond it, "might be traced back to her death, after a fashion."

"How so?" Burton asked.

"You'll have me committed if I tell you."

"The madhouse might be the best place for all three of us."

"Humph! I can't argue with that." Trounce smoothed his moustache with his fingertips and gave a small and decisive nod. "I'm a London City policeman. Have been all my life. I joined the Force when I was barely out of short pants but—well—you mistakenly called me 'Detective Inspector,' sir, and I bloody well should be by now, but it all went bad for me right from the start." He paused and they waited, allowing him to gather his thoughts. "Do either of you recall the old stories about Spring Heeled Jack?"

A chill skittered up Burton's spine. His mouth went dry. His hands curled into fists, and his knuckles turned white.

"Never explained," Trounce went on. "A phantom that assaulted young women before taking mighty leaps to evade pursuers. Spotted again and again in the late 'thirties."

Swinburne said, "I remember the tales."

"On the tenth of June, 1840, I was pounding my usual beat, which took me along the Mall, onto Constitution Hill and through Green Park. I always timed it so I'd be in the park when the queen and Prince Albert emerged from the palace for their daily ride. Crowds tended to gather for the occasion, and there were often protestors. Poor little Victoria wasn't as popular before her death as she was after it. However, on this particular day I was late, having been distracted by a notorious pickpocket known as Dennis the Dip. I was nineteen years old and eager to make my first arrest. Stupid! It was just a five-minute delay, but it cost me my reputation. By the time I was entering the park, the assassin, Edward Oxford—"

Again, Burton shuddered, as a wave of inexplicable fear and sadness ran through him.

"—had drawn his flintlock. I heard the first shot and broke into a run. Then—"

Trounce stopped. His face paled. The potboy approached, and even before he'd set down the tray, the policeman had grabbed a tankard from it and taken a long draught.

Swinburne said to the lad, "Keep 'em coming."

Trounce waited until the boy had departed then continued in a hoarse voice. "A freakish apparition raced past and stopped in front of me. A man, on short stilts, in a tight white costume and a black helmet, with blue fire playing all around him. Spring Heeled Jack! I swear by all that's holy. Spring Heeled Jack! The creature yelled, 'Stop, Edward!' then the second shot was fired and Victoria was killed. The phantom leaped right over my head, and when I turned to look for it, it had vanished into thin air. I managed to gather my wits enough to continue on to the scene of the murder. By the time I got there, a man had tackled the assassin and accidentally killed him. He then ran off."

"The 'mystery hero,' as he became known," Swinburne put in.

"Yes. I chased after him, followed him into a thicket of trees, and found there nothing but a top hat lying on the ground. The man, like Spring Heeled Jack, had vanished as if by magic."

Pulling a red-and-white polka-dot handkerchief from his pocket, Trounce blew his nose. "No one believed my report," he went on after a pause. "I became the laughing stock of Scotland Yard. So, while my fellows got their promotions, I didn't. I stayed a constable until close to retirement when they finally—out of sympathy, I suspect—made me a sergeant." He heaved a forlorn sigh and took a rather more modest swig of his beer than the previous. "I didn't help myself by spending time, against the commissioner's express instructions, investigating the old Spring Heeled Jack sightings. I even carried on after my retirement, which brings me to today—that is to say—to Tuesday the twenty-second of January, 1901—" He cleared his throat and looked at Swinburne. "Which isn't today at all, is it? This is 'sixty-four?"

"It is, and I find that as difficult to swallow as you do."

"Humph! Well, this morning—that morning—I was on my way to Stratford to meet another witness to the assassination, a former road sweeper known as Old Carter, when I ran into a petty criminal I'd put away in my younger days. Vincent Sneed, his name was. A nasty, vicious piece of work with the biggest nose you could possibly imagine. He recognised me, I recognised him. He had a grudge and a repeater in his pocket, I was unarmed and none too fast on my eighty-year-old feet, and—bang!—next thing I knew I was flat on my back on the pavement and everything turned white. I dreamed. Imagined myself to be flying through a city of towers in some sort of aerial ship. When I woke from it—"

"Aerial ship?" Burton interrupted. "Like Renard and Krebs's *La France?*" He corrected himself. "No. Much larger and considerably more sophisticated." He gave a grunt of surprise. "How the devil do I know that?"

"*Orpheus,*" Swinburne murmured.

"Yes!" Burton and Trounce chorused.

The three men looked at each other in astonishment.

"The word came to me from nowhere," Swinburne said.

Flustered, Trounce resorted to his beer again. Burton and Swinburne followed suit.

They sat in silence for a minute before Burton quietly said, "Continue, please. I feel that your account is drawing us closer to some manner of explanation for our current predicament. If 'predicament' is the appropriate word."

"It isn't," Swinburne interjected. "And I'll risk my reputation as a poet by stating that no suitable word exists."

Trounce wiped froth from his moustache. "As an old man, I'd always expected to die in my bed. Instead, I'd been shot dead. I was certain of it. I considered every thought my last. Memories—some my own, some obvious fantasies in disguise—came and went until one predominated. It was as clear as day, this recollection, of an occasion near enough forty years before when I'd gone to Bristol to interview a woman named Clayton, formerly Hurd. I'd found an old newspaper article in which it was reported that, the same year as the assassination, Spring Heeled Jack had assaulted her. Apparently he'd pounced on her, sliced hair from the back of her head, and made his escape. Except, it gradually dawned on me that this wasn't a memory at all. I really was in Bristol. It really was 1864. I was in the past, and I was—" he tapped the middle of his chest, "like this. Young!"

"Your wits returned to you today," Swinburne said. "I mean *today* today, not the other today."

"Er. Yes. I think."

"You'd awoken in your own past," Burton clarified.

"I had, and at a particularly inauspicious moment."

"Why inauspicious?"

"Because, on this particular day, I was only free to travel to Bristol on account of having sent a messenger to inform Chief Commissioner Mayne that I was sick and bedridden. It was a falsehood, and not only did the whole endeavour prove fruitless—from the woman's description it was obvious to me that her attacker was nothing more than a prankster—but my deception was discovered." Trounce picked up his bowler hat and lightly tapped his fist against it as if considering whether it would withstand a hefty punch. "I'd been seen and recognised at the railway station. My chief tore into me. I was disciplined and marked down as unreliable. From that moment, I knew I'd never amount to anything. I'd succumbed

to an unhealthy obsession, and it had ruined my prospects. This day—"
He waved his hat around his head. "Friday, the sixteenth of September,
'sixty-four, is the exact day that my life took a turn for the worse, the day
I finally realised that I would never make the grade at Scotland Yard."

"And your presence here in the Slug and Lettuce?" Burton asked.

Trounce blinked rapidly and, as if unable to give any credence to the
words that came from his own mouth, said, "I was standing outside Mrs.
Clayton's house, wondering what in the name of heaven was happening,
when a parrot landed on the gatepost and told me to catch a train to Bath
and come here to this place. It called me a—what was it?—a skunk-
scented, slack-tongued nitwit."

Swinburne gave a snort of merriment.

The policeman gritted his teeth, and the threatened punch was delivered to his bowler, leaving a dent in its crown. "I don't like birds, I don't
like being insulted, and I don't like mysteries, even when they restore me
to my prime."

"Nor I," Burton agreed, "and if our particular mystery has a solution, the current date may be a clue toward its discovery, for in common
with you, William, I've always regarded this day as the occasion of my
ruination."

"In what—if you don't mind—I mean—humph!—how so?"

"A colleague of mine shot himself dead today. It was the culmination
of a sequence of events that shook my confidence in myself and damaged
both my good name and my self-regard. Though in the case of the former,
it wasn't so good, and in the case of the latter, I'll confess that a little
more humility was probably required anyway. I say that with the benefit
of hindsight, of course."

Burton looked at Swinburne. "I don't recall this being a time of any
great significance for you, though, Algy, so perhaps I'm barking up the
wrong tree."

"Are you joking?" Swinburne objected. "Bark away! Perhaps not this
specific date but certainly this period. 'Sixty-four is when my reputation
as a poet was secured and when my little indulgences grew into such
grandiose passions that my ability to write was all but destroyed by them.
Eventually I had to be taken in hand by Theo—" He turned to Trounce.

"Theodore Watts-Dunton. A friend of mine who, in 1879, when my excesses had caused my health to fail, virtually kidnapped me, kept me in seclusion, and weaned me off the bottle. Were it not for him, I'd have died a great many years earlier than I did. I survived but, according to the critics, the same could not be said of my talent."

Trounce glanced at the empty glasses that were fast accumulating on the table. Swinburne, noting the look, grinned. "We are restored. We deserve a little debauchery after suffering our prolonged twilight years, do you not think? Nudging my toe onto the road to ruin is not the same as taking a headlong plunge along it. I shan't be doing that again, I can assure you. Presuming, that is, that we are here to stay."

Trounce gave a slight smile. "You make a good case, lad. By Jove, a few hours ago, these fingers of mine were near enough paralysed by arthritis. To clap 'em around a tankard again, well—" He raised his glass. "I have to drink to that!"

They imbibed and regarded each other thoughtfully.

"A second chance," Burton said. "For me to throw off the chains of disappointment; for you, William, to free yourself from a destructive obsession; and for you, Algy, to not let your zeal get the better of you. Are all who make mistakes offered this manner of reprieve? Do they all, at death, return to a key moment in their past? Is that how existence functions?"

A female voice came from beside him. "No, Sir Richard. It is not."

A REMARKABLE CONTRAPTION
OVER RED BLOSSOMS

DO YOU HAVE A CLOCKWORK SERVANT?
THE WONDER OF THE AGE!

Powered by a spring mechanism that requires
winding just once every twenty-four hours!
Stronger than a man!
Self-maintaining!
Obeys every command!
Fitted with a babbage calculator that can:
Predict your requests! Evaluate every option! Make astute choices!
Possessed of such a sophisticated synthetic intelligence,
you'll swear it's alive!

EVERY HOUSEHOLD NEEDS ONE!

A woman, almost entirely concealed by a voluminous dark green cloak and hood, had stepped out of the crowd and now stood beside the table. Politely, the three men got to their feet. She had a walking cane in her right hand. With her left, she reached up, slipped back the cowl, and revealed a beautiful face. Her eyes were black and almond-shaped; her lips full with squarish corners; her skin dusky; and her hair, deepest jet, wound about her head and held with pins. She was, Burton guessed, in her mid-twenties. His nostrils detected the scent of jasmine.

"Good day to you, gentlemen. I am Sadhvi Raghavendra. No doubt you all recognise me but can't think where from. An explanation for that and for everything else you are currently experiencing awaits. I have a landau outside. Will you join me? Our destination lies a little over five miles to the east of here. There, a certain individual will provide you with all the answers you need." She smiled. "Or shall I leave you here to get pickled?"

"My hat!" Swinburne responded. "You present quite the dilemma, dear lady."

She held the cane out to Burton. "I expect you've missed this, Sir Richard."

Accepting her familiarity without question, the explorer took the stick and found that it had a silver handle fashioned to resemble a panther's head—the same cane he thought he'd mislaid during his final evening in Trieste. He pulled the handle up to expose a few inches of concealed blade. Sliding it back, he murmured, "Captain. It is 1864. I was—will be—knighted in 1886. Where did you get this?"

"You gave it to me. And the date your knighthood was, or will be, conferred varies considerably."

"Varies? How can it vary?"

"I shall tell you a little *en route*. Will you accompany me?"

"Are you the owner of an impolite parrot?"

She smiled. "No. You are. Parakeet. His name is Pox. He was recently recruited to the group to which I belong."

Burton hefted the cane, holding its handle in front of his eyes. Without averting his gaze from it, he said, "I think I shall forgo further drinks. Algy? William?"

"I'm with you," Trounce said. "I don't mind confessing that I have little inclination to deal with this tomfoolery alone. It's too much for me. I'm just a policeman."

"Blast it!" Swinburne muttered. "My ability to taste is restored and already I must deny it its pleasures. Have you nothing at our destination with which we can wet our whistles, Miss—forgive me, what was it? Revenger?"

"Raghavendra. And I daresay we can rustle up a brandy or two." She smiled at him with an amused twinkle in her eyes.

"Then I bow to the majority. Let's be off."

They drained what remained of their beer, and Burton called over the potboy to settled the bill. He handed his old cane to Trounce and kept hold of the new one. The three men followed the young woman through the crowd and exited the Slug and Lettuce. As promised, a landau was waiting for them, its two horses standing patiently.

"Proceed, please," Raghavendra called up to the driver.

The man, whose face was badly disfigured by a harelip, pulled a clay pipe from his mouth and clicked his tongue. "Cottles Wood, ma'am? Middle o' nowhere? You're certain?"

"If you please."

"Rightio, ma'am."

They boarded the carriage, which rocked and creaked beneath them, and, once they'd settled onto its wooden benches, it moved off. Almost immediately, Burton exclaimed, "Wait! I should leave a message for Isabel. She'll wonder where I am."

Swinburne uttered a little sound of disdain.

Raghavendra said, "It will serve her better if you don't."

"What do you mean by that?"

"As I said, everything will be explained, your wife's destiny included."

Burton sighed. "Destiny? By Allah's beard, this was a very odd sort of day the first time around. Now it's considerably odder. Very well. Isabel will have to fret awhile."

"She must be used to it by now," Swinburne put in. *"Pay, pack, and follow.* Do you remember that, Richard?"

"The message I left for her when I was recalled from Damascus."

"You departed without her. Without even telling her you were going."

"That was in 1871. We'd been married for ten years by then. She was accustomed to my ways. Here, now, 1864, our marriage is but three years old."

Raghavendra smiled. "She's a strong woman. She'll be all right. Take my word for it. I happen to know a great deal more about her than even you do."

"I'm inclined to believe you, though that sentiment is baffling since you are a stranger to me."

"A stranger you feel you know, same as Detective Inspector Trounce, here." She nodded toward the policeman.

"Sergeant," Trounce said. "By Jove! Why the devil do you all insist on promoting me?"

"Because it's your proper title, sir, the one you more usually bear. You are one of Scotland Yard's finest."

"Piffle!" Trounce growled. He pushed out his chest a little and smoothed his moustache. "Balderdash, I say!"

"No doubt you think otherwise because your career was blighted by your preoccupation with Spring Heeled Jack. Am I correct?"

The policeman uttered a cry of amazement. "What in blue thunder do you know about that?"

"I know your interest was justified. He is the reason you are all here. Spring Heeled Jack was not a supernatural creature, William, but a man. His name was Edward Oxford."

"No, that was the name of Victoria's assassin."

"And also of the assassin's great-great—I don't know how many greats—grandchild."

"My dear young lady, that is arrant nonsense and you know it. Oxford was killed at the scene. He had no descendants, and, even were I wrong about that, there is no way you could possibly know about them, particularly if they were great-great-whatevers. Really, you cannot pull the wool over my eyes. I've spent a lifetime investigating the events of that day, as well as all the individuals involved. I know the history of the assassination back to front and inside out."

"I don't doubt it, but the history you refer to is not the one I'm speaking of."

"Eh?"

"We should return to the pub," Swinburne suggested. "We're too sober for this."

Raghavendra winked at the little poet. "You probably are, and I'm afraid the story only gets more fantastic. Oxford's descendent—whom, for the sake of clarity, I shall henceforth refer to only by his nickname of Spring Heeled Jack—was a man from the distant future, from the year 2202. He created the means to journey backward through time to 1840, where he intended to watch his ancestor attempt to shoot Queen Victoria. The assassination, you see, should have failed. The history that Jack travelled back through was one in which it *had* failed, one in which Victoria had reigned for nearly sixty-four years before dying of old age on the twenty-second of January, 1901."

"Tripe!" Trounce barked. "Absolute bilge water! And that is *today's* date. I mean, not today, but the day I've come from. It's the day I was—I was—"

"Shot dead. I know. Time employs coincidence as a means to emphasise significant moments and events. Occasionally it does so with a rather cruel irony." She paused for a moment, and Burton saw sadness touch her eyes. "Anyway, as I say, Spring Heeled Jack travelled from the future and interfered with the past. He altered events. He caused the assassination to succeed and accidentally killed his own ancestor. You saw him do it, William."

Trounce's eyes widened. "He killed—? You mean he was the 'mystery hero'?" He shook his head and made a gesture of dismissal. "You are jabbering! How could he be the stilted creature *and* the mystery hero? They were present at exactly the same moment."

"When one possesses the ability to move through time, such paradoxes become almost commonplace."

The Scotland Yard man was silent for a moment. He emitted a groan. He eyed his bowler, which was on his lap, as if contemplating whether to fling it out of the carriage's window. "Forgive me, but it would be obvious to even a gullible idiot that you are indulging in fantasy, Miss Raghavendra. Why is it then, that despite myself, I'm half convinced?"

"Perhaps because the bizarre claim that a man can project himself through time, while easily dismissed by most, undoubtedly feels a little more credible to a man who is currently sitting in his own past."

"Humph!"

Trounce looked at Burton for support. The explorer shifted in his seat and ran his fingers over his chin. He opened his mouth to speak, stopped, thought a moment, then said, "Why the stilts and costume?"

"The suit was actually a very sophisticated machine. It was the means by which Edward Oxford—Jack—literally jumped through time."

"I see. And you expect us to believe that everything which occurred subsequent to the assassination—every circumstance from the tenth of June, 1840, all the way to the future year of 2202—was obliterated and overwritten by new events as a result of his actions?"

"Overwritten, yes, precisely, Sir Richard, and not just once but many times, in the manner of a palimpsest. You see, Spring Heeled Jack had broken the natural mechanism of time, and actions taken subsequent to his meddling caused the new version of history, which he'd created, to split again and again, so that now there are many iterations of the world all existing contemporaneously. What we refer to as the Original History, from the future of which he had come, may still be among them, not obliterated but obscured by a proliferation of alternates. My companions and I have been searching for it. This, your world, is the closest to it we've found. Your life—and yours, Algernon, and yours, William—have, as far as we can ascertain, been more or less identical to the ones you lived in Original History. In fact, the assassination and the political ramifications thereof—the empire becoming a republic, for example—are the only aspects of this world that indicate it to be a variation."

Burton examined the silver handle of his cane. "Let us suppose I give credence to your claim—and I'm hardly in a position to refute it—why is it that the three of us have fallen from our respective deathbeds straight into our own past?"

Raghavendra folded her hands on her lap and looked out at the houses that were slipping past outside. The landau was passing through a residential district on the outskirts of Bath. Without averting her gaze, she answered, "I and the other members of the expedition to which I belong are from a different history than this one. In our history, we departed from the year 1860 and journeyed to 2202, there to confront and kill Spring Heeled Jack, thus preventing him from doing any further mischief. His experiences, you see, had made him insane and very dangerous. During our return journey, our leader has been repairing the processes of time. How, I cannot explain. He will tell you himself. Suffice to say that all the variants are being isolated in such a manner that they will no longer be able to taint or in any way influence the history my fellows and I call our own. And with regard to that, you are invited to join us there, to live again, to have a second chance. We retrieved Pox from one of the alternate time streams, as we call them, and now we have retrieved you."

"Splendid!" Swinburne announced. "Absolutely smashing! Why?"

"That will become clear within the hour."

The poet gave a spasmodic kick and glowered at the young woman. She laughed at his expression, leaned forward, and patted his knee. "If you refuse the offer, I will miss you terribly, Algy. I really will."

"What? What? What?"

She laughed again and sat back, saying no more.

Burton looked out of the window and watched as the houses thinned in number and gave way to countryside.

This is happening.

His final night of life felt increasingly distant and phantasmagorical. He tried to recall its details and found them to be unfocused. There had been a bird drowning in a water barrel. He'd called Doctor Steinhaueser over to—

No. John Steinhaueser died in 'sixty. It was—it was—Bismillah! What is the name of my doctor? Baker! Yes!

He'd called Baker over to help him rescue it. A starling? A sparrow?

He couldn't remember, despite that the event had occurred, from a subjective point of view, just a few hours ago.

Minutes passed without a word spoken.

Glancing at Swinburne, Burton saw that his old friend had slipped into a daydream. Trounce, too. Again, he wondered whether shock was affecting the three of them.

Raghavendra met his eyes, and, though she said nothing and made no gesture, he sensed that she understood the peculiarly disjointed quality of his current situation. She radiated sympathy, compassion, and reassurance in a manner that struck him as almost supernatural, as if she could somehow feel the imbalance in him and was offering clairvoyant support as he struggled with it.

She is a Sister of Noble Benevolence. They possess that ability.

He averted his eyes.

How do I know that?

The landau passed through a small village signposted Monkton Far-leigh, crested the brow of a hill, and proceeded down a long slope into a wide, shallow valley. A patchwork of green fields and woods stretched to the horizon. Burton's attention was attracted to a broad meadow bisected by a low wall beside which a group of people were standing, two police constables among them. He suddenly felt uneasy.

"I'm sorry, Sir Richard," Raghavendra murmured. "The significance of where we landed our ship didn't immediately occur to us. As I said, Time has a tendency toward unfortunate coincidences such as this."

With a shudder, Burton realised the meaning of the little gathering by the wall. Huskily, he said, "That is where John Speke shot himself yesterday afternoon."

"Yes, it is."

He swallowed. His mouth felt dry.

"Ship?" Swinburne asked in a dreamy tone. He cleared his throat and blinked, forcing his attention back outward. "A ship, did you say? I see no water."

"A rotorship. A flying machine. The *Orpheus*. She is landed in a clearing in Cottles Wood. We are nearly there."

"*Orpheus*. We remembered the name. But how do we know it?"

"Because you each had a counterpart in the history I come from. My expedition's presence here is causing a resonance through which you are vaguely recollecting aspects of those other lives."

"Had," Swinburne responded. "Past tense."

"Yes."

"The other Burton, Trounce, and Swinburne—our *doppelgängers*—are dead?"

"No."

"Then what?"

"Have patience, sir."

Swinburne rolled his eyes and sighed.

A couple of minutes later, Raghavendra called up to the driver. "Stop here, please."

The carriage slowed to a halt and its passengers climbed out, finding themselves in a country lane at the edge of a wood.

"Here?" the driver asked. "It's a fair walk to the next house, ma'am. Ain't nought hereabouts 'ceptin' rabbits an' trees. No reason fer anyone to be here, 'less they're poachin', which you plainly ain't."

"We're having a picnic," Raghavendra said, passing the fare up to him. He took the coins.

"Aye, well, the clouds are gatherin' and I reckons it's going to rain soon, ma'am, and even if it weren't, a picnic ain't no cop without a spot o' grub to go with it, if you'll forgive the observation."

"No need for concern," she answered. "It's all arranged. Thank you. Good day."

He shrugged, saluted her, gave a flick of the reins and a click of his tongue, and steered the landau around and back the way they'd come. They stood and watched it go. It rounded a bend and drove out of sight. The clip-clop of horses' hooves faded. But for the faint rustle of leaves in the slight breeze, silence surrounded them.

"Follow me, please." Raghavendra lifted her cloak and skirt a little and stepped off the road onto a dirt path that led into the trees. The light became dappled as they trailed after her and the verdure closed overhead.

Soft soil squelched beneath their feet. Occasionally they pressed themselves against bushes as they skirted the path's edges to avoid puddles. Though the weather was rapidly deteriorating, they all felt uncomfortably warm.

After they'd traversed a quarter of a mile, Swinburne observed, "There's rather a preponderance of red flowers, don't you think?"

Burton, who'd been searching his memory and had found it to be brimming with anomalous oddities, realised that the poet was quite right. The farther into the woods they walked, the more they found themselves surrounded by vermillion blossoms, which grew in patches beneath the trees and, in many instances, on vines that climbed the trunks.

"Out of season," he said.

"Not at all," Trounce countered. "September, isn't it?"

"No, not these. I was thinking about a poppy in the garden of my home in Trieste. It caught my eye this evening. I mean, last night. Um.

That is to say, in 1890. It was the same bright shade as these blooms and shouldn't have been growing at that time of year."

"*Tempus flores,*" Raghavendra said. "Time flowers. They tend to follow wherever we go."

"Extraordinary!" Swinburne exclaimed.

"More so than you think. It was you who named them, Algernon, and they have a greater connection to you than you could possibly imagine."

"Miss Revenger, you underestimate me. As a matter of fact, just a little while ago I was gripped by the fancy that I had somehow been transmogrified into vegetation almost identical to this. Can you explain that peculiar coincidence or shall you spout more of your 'time has tendencies' hoo-ha?"

"Yes."

"Yes what?"

"Yes, more hoo-ha. And it's Raghavendra, as you well know."

Swinburne stamped his foot in exasperation, inadvertently splashing mud over Trounce's trouser leg. "Now look here," he began, then stopped in his tracks and gaped.

They had emerged into a clearing. The ground was a thick carpet of heaped scarlet flowers, but their colour was dulled by dark shadow, for floating twelve feet above them there was a massive contraption with lines so unfamiliar and exotic—its design so utterly alien—that Burton, Swinburne, and Trounce could barely take it in. They saw a dirigible with pointed ends, baroquely moulded struts and panels, a multiplicity of graceful pylons with spinning wings at their tops, ornately framed portholes and curving glass at the front and rear, spindled projections the function of which couldn't be guessed at, and gleaming pipes from which wisps of white steam emerged.

Spelled out upon the side of the craft—it was indisputably a vessel of some sort—in lettering that reminded Burton of the elaborate design values currently fashionable in France—fashionable in 1890 not '64, he had to remind himself—was the word ORPHEUS.

"My hat!" Swinburne whispered. "The size of it! How does it stay up?"

Trounce cleared his throat. "You surely don't expect us to—to—to board that—um—"

"She's perfectly safe, Detective Inspector, I assure you. Ah, there's Daniel."

A man had stepped out of a door in the side of the machine and was descending a ramp. He reached the ground and Raghavendra led them toward him, her cloak billowing and flapping in the downdraught caused by the craft's wings. The fellow was a little shorter than average height, slightly plump, hatless, with sandy hair and a kindly face. His chest was crisscrossed by a leather harness that secured two mechanical arms against his sides, supplementing his own. Their motion was smooth and quite natural. Indeed, it was an artificial hand that the man extended to Burton as he drew near.

"Sir Richard! How marvellous to see you back in the flesh, so to speak."

Burton, rather awkwardly shaking what felt like a metal gauntlet, vaguely recognised the individual and, before an introduction could be made, said, "It's, um, Goode, isn't it?"

"Gooch. Daniel Gooch. Yes, of course, I forgot you wouldn't know me from Adam."

"What do you mean by 'back in the flesh,' Mr. Gooch?"

"Algernon, William," Raghavendra interrupted, "Daniel is our ship's engineer."

"Engineer!" Trounce exclaimed. "Ah! Yes! I thought I recognised the name. I think I once read about you in a newspaper. You're the—er—whatsit—the cable-across-the-Atlantic thing. That man, aren't you?"

Gooch scratched his head with metal fingers. "Am I? Yes, probably. I wouldn't be at all surprised. It sounds like the sort of project I'd undertake."

"You aren't sure?"

"Multiple histories. Numerous Gooches. Gets confusing. Shall we go aboard? The others will be delighted to have you back."

They followed him onto the ramp.

Swinburne said, "According to Miss Revenger, you have a supply of brandy."

"Good old Algy!" Gooch chuckled. "Oops! Pardon me if I seem a little overfamiliar. You see, we've been a long time away, and it's been a slow voyage back, and it hasn't been quite the same without you. I must confess, I always found the other one a little less—I don't know—he didn't have your—"

"Daniel," Raghavendra interjected. "Our guests aren't yet aware of the full story."

"Of course. Of course. My apologies."

"Let's say hello to the captain first," Raghavendra said. "Then we'll go to the lounge."

They entered the ship, turned to the left, and passed through a door into a semi-circular chamber. Large windows dominated its curved walls. There were control consoles and panels of switches, levers rising from the floor, wheels and flashing lights. A tall, uniformed man of military bearing, with a finely clipped beard of snowy white and cold, grey eyes, gave an almost imperceptible start of surprise as he saw Burton.

"Oh," he said. "Remarkable! Sir Richard, Algernon, William, welcome aboard."

Gooch introduced him. "This is Nathaniel Lawless."

Burton shook the man's proffered hand. "The expedition commander?"

"No, Sir Richard, just captain of the *Orpheus*. Our leader is on the observation deck."

A deep, disembodied voice said, "Are you playing some sort of game, peculiar creatures?"

It was as if the room itself had spoken.

Lawless grimaced and pointed a finger upward.

The three reborn looked up and saw a brass sphere fitted into the middle of a concave ceiling.

"The ship's Mark Three babbage," Gooch said. "Its synthetic brain."

"And the only clear-thinking one present," the metal globe added. "Our voyage appears to have befuddled you all. Why are you acting like strangers? Why did you order us sideways when we should have gone back? I have no objection to flying this ship for you, but I do wish you'd have the common decency to keep me informed as to what we're doing and why we're doing it."

"And a thorn in my side," Lawless added. "It was originally designed to replace a full crew and to make the calculations necessary for the various stages of our voyage through time. When we were in the twenty-third century, the engineers of that age tampered with it. They said they were—to use their terminology—'upgrading' it, making it better and more efficient. All they appear to have done is installed into it a thoroughly irritating interest in human affairs and a propensity to refer to us as 'peculiar creatures.'"

"An accurate description, don't you think?" the Mark III said. "You're such whimsical little things."

"Little?" Lawless responded. "You are smaller than any of us."

"I was referring to your intellect. I have severe reservations concerning it. I have no option but to obey your orders, but I consider it perfectly reasonable to ask for them to be adequately explained. If I knew what you were up to, I'd be better able to assess your capacity for rational thought."

"Assessing us is not a part of your duties," Lawless said.

"I'm not permitted a hobby?"

"Is it alive?" Swinburne asked.

"Oh, how I wish it was. Then I could kill it. No, the intelligence is artificial."

The sphere said, "There! A perfect demonstration of muddled thinking. How can intelligence be artificial? Would it not be more accurate to say that mine is generated by a constructed mechanism rather than by a little bundle of sticks and juice, and it is there that the artifice, as you judge it, is located?"

Lawless clapped a hand to his forehead. "Now we peculiar creatures are bundles of sticks and juice! It gets worse by the blessed minute." He sighed forlornly. "I can't wait to get home and have the damned thing *adjusted*." He supplemented this statement by dragging a meaningful finger across his throat.

"Ungrateful wretch!" the babbage complained. "After all I've done for you."

Raghavendra, with a twinkle in her eye, said, "I think we should leave you two alone, Captain. You apparently require more time to work out your differences."

"Oh, Lord help me!" Lawless groaned.

"You see?" the Mark III commented. "He calls upon a deity. Superstitious! Lacking logic! Ridiculous! Can we please get this voyage over and done with? I require a little peace and quiet that I might work out how to best cure you of your mad illusions."

Chuckling, the young woman led Gooch and the three newcomers off the ship's bridge and along a corridor.

"A talking machine?" Trounce asked. "Trickery, surely?"

"No, just very advanced science, William," Raghavendra answered.

"But it has an attitude."

"It surely does. But the things it says are generated only by a very complex sequence of algorithms."

"And what are they?"

"From the Latin, *Algoritmi*," Burton put in. "The name given to Muḥammad ibn Mūsā al-Khwārizmī, a Persian mathematician."

Trounce frowned. "An Arabian was speaking to us through a ball in the ceiling?"

"He's been dead for centuries."

"But," Raghavendra said, "the mathematical principles he created are at the heart of the device, as is something called the Oxford Equation, which allows it to guide us through time. Here we are."

She opened a door and they passed through into a well-appointed room that, portholes aside, looked as if it more properly belonged in a country house than in a flying machine. A handsome young Indian greeted them. "Hello there, good fellows! If you don't remember, I'm Maneesh Krishnamurthy."

Handshakes were exchanged.

A parakeet on a perch screeched, "Sheep fumblers! Giggling bum-slap swappers!"

"And you've already met Pox," Raghavendra observed. "Eugenically bred, in a different history, to carry messages. If he knows you, he can find you, unless you're shut indoors or out of his flight range. Very useful."

Krishnamurthy added, "And very rude. A flaw in the eugenic design." He moved over to a cabinet and got to work with glasses and a decanter. "Our illustrious leader has been in a deep self-induced trance for a considerable period but should be conscious enough by now to communicate with you. Have a thimbleful first, to steady your nerves."

"Good chap!" Swinburne enthused.

Trounce slumped into a seat and fanned himself with his hat. "It's too much. I was shot dead. Shot dead in the street. And now all this. I think, if you don't mind, I shall go to sleep. Don't bother rousing me. For all I know, I'd awaken to find myself attending my own funeral, by Jove!"

Krishnamurthy handed him a glass, well filled with spirit. "Here you are. Get that into you. It will make you feel much better." He offered another to Swinburne.

"Hurrah!" the poet cheered. "I shall soon climb aboard the sobriety wagon, and so must savour this while I may."

Burton noticed that Raghavendra, Gooch, and Krishnamurthy were all watching Swinburne and Trounce with expressions of unmistakable fondness. He, too, had received glances that suggested he was well known to them and well regarded.

It amazed him to discover that he returned the affection. Where the emotion had come from, how or why it had arisen, these questions he couldn't answer, but he knew for certain that these people were his colleagues and his friends. Trounce, whom he'd met just this afternoon, he trusted implicitly and liked tremendously. For Gooch and Krishnamurthy—Lawless, too—he had complete respect and admiration. As for Raghavendra, she appeared to generate an additional degree of fondness, a depth of friendship that had comforted him considerably after the death of his fiancée—

Fiancée? What the hell am I thinking? I'm married! And Isabel is alive!

He tried to conjure into his mind an image of his wife's face. Instead, he saw her heat-blurred figure standing by a bonfire. Despondency descended upon him. He didn't understand it at all, and the heavy emotion didn't lighten when Raghavendra stepped over and placed a hand on his arm, again as if she knew exactly his inner turmoil.

"There is a certain degree of disorientation that accompanies a journey through time," she said softly, "which is not made any easier by our dealing with many disparate histories. Be aware that, as with the foreign memories, much of what you feel belongs not to you but to other Burtons, who have had different experiences to your own."

"My wife is waiting for me, Sadhvi," he said—the informality came to him with such ease that he didn't even notice it—"yet I feel as if she is no longer there, as if she is dead. Did my counterpart from your history suffer her loss? Is that where my feelings spring from?"

She responded with a slight nod of the head. "It is. We have observed the many different iterations of Isabel as we've travelled back from 2202. In some histories, such as my own, she is killed. In others, like this one, she marries you, lives vicariously through you, and, after your death, ruins her own reputation in a misguided attempt to preserve yours. In others still, you abandon her and she goes on to achieve great things. I have seen her, in Arabia and Africa, become a legendary warrior woman named Al-Manat. I've witnessed her as a secret agent for the crown, as a tireless campaigner for women's suffrage, as a successful author, and as an explorer whose achievements surpassed even your own. Undoubtedly, by leaving her you cause great pain, but the distress provides her with the impetus to break free from the constraints of society and become, in her own right, an extremely accomplished and celebrated individual."

"Nevertheless," Burton murmured after a moment of contemplation. "How could I live with myself, with the guilt, if I don't today return to her?"

"You have already grown old with her, dedicated your life to her."

"And at its end, she betrayed me," he whispered.

"And herself. She paid a terrible price. Now, you have the opportunity to spare her that unhappy ending. But you don't need to decide yet. Wait until you know the full truth of what we're doing."

She turned and called to Swinburne and Trounce. "It's time. Will you accompany me, please, gentlemen?"

The poet glanced at Burton, who offered a shrug and a nod. Trounce got to his feet with a sigh almost of despair. "As if I'm not giddy enough with it already, now there's more to come."

Raghavendra ushered them toward a door.

Daniel Gooch said, "See you later."

Krishnamurthy added, "Don't worry. Our leader is a bit strange, but he knows what's what better than the rest of us all rolled into one."

"Skudge puddles!" Pox squawked.

They followed the young woman into a passageway. It had no portholes but was warmly illuminated by bracket-mounted oil lamps. They walked past doors to either side. Though all were closed, Burton somehow knew they opened onto passenger cabins, and, as he passed a particular one, he was stricken by the sensation that his old colleague William Stroyan, who'd been killed in Africa forty-five years ago—

No. Now it is just nine years ago.

—was inside. He stumbled to a halt, dazedly raised a hand, knocked on the portal, and called, "Bill? I say! Stroyan?"

Raghavendra turned back, reached out, and gripped him by the wrist. "Don't. He's not in there. It's merely an echo."

Burton blinked and pulled his hand away. He put it to his head and winced. "What?"

"You're responding to a circumstance that a different Sir Richard experienced."

"Not a good one, by the feel of it."

"No, not a good one. Bill Stroyan was murdered on this ship. He was my friend, too, and I miss him terribly."

They moved on, and as they passed the various cabins, Burton thought about another man who'd gone to Africa with him—John Hanning Speke—and wondered whether he'd shot himself dead at this juncture in all the other histories, too.

They came to double doors. Raghavendra turned. "Gentlemen, I shan't enter the observation deck with you, but may I remind you that, not very long ago, you were each experiencing the end of your life. Thanks to the individual beyond these doors, you are restored to health and youth. That you might understand why, I urge you to do whatever you are instructed, without hesitation or reservation."

She twisted a doorknob, pushed the portal open, and stepped back from it. Burton saw through the opening a large chamber with walls and ceiling made of glass and, sitting cross-legged on the floor in the middle of it, a figure entirely enshrouded by a cloak and hood.

Burton, Swinburne, and Trounce entered the chamber.

Behind them, Raghavendra pulled the doors shut.

The scene, Burton thought, should have been rather more mystical. Candles, shadows, and the coiling smoke of incense would have been appropriate to it. Maybe a pentagram chalked onto the floor and some unfathomable hieroglyphs scrawled across the glass. But no. Broad daylight shone through the transparent ceiling, illuminating the figure that was remarkable only because it was hidden within the copious robes.

There were three small bottles on the floor. The seated form raised a sleeve-swathed arm and indicated them one after the other. A deep but whispery voice emerged from the hood. "Will you sit, please, gentlemen?"

Glancing at one another, they did so. Trounce emitted a groan as he crossed his legs then mumbled, "Sorry. Unnecessary. It slipped my mind that I'm capable."

A rustling chuckle. "It feels good to be at your best again, yes, William?"

"Physically, I can't deny it. A darn sight worse for the brain, though. Who are you?"

Burton peered at the figure, trying to pierce the shadow cast by the hood, but could see nothing.

"I shall explain everything," came the response. "But first, you will oblige me by drinking from the bottles. The concoction will aid your comprehension."

"Is it alcoholic?" Swinburne asked.

"No."

"I'll not be poisoned!" Trounce objected.

Burton looked down at the bottle in front of him. Its label bore the words, *Saltzmann's Tincture.*

The name sounded familiar.

The cloaked man whispered, "William, if I wanted you dead, I'd have left you on the pavement with Sneed's bullet in your chest."

"Humph! I suppose."

Swinburne uncorked his bottle and upended its contents into his mouth. He smacked his lips. "Hmm. Rather like honey or mead."

Trounce clicked his tongue then drank.

Burton followed suit. He felt the liquid ooze down his throat.

"I asked who you are," Trounce said. "Shall you answer?"

"It's rather complicated," came the reply.

The tincture was having an almost instantaneous effect on Burton.

He felt warmth seeping through his capillaries. He sensed countless possibilities stretching away from him into innumerable futures.

"I have my given names," the figure said.

Sunlight coursed through the explorer, shone out through his pores.

"And I have the names that I've adopted for one reason or another."

Colours were detected as flavours. Sounds were heard as textures. Touch was received as scent.

"And I have the names imposed upon me by others at various times in my life."

Though he sat motionless, Burton felt himself toppling forward and backward and sideways. Time became a permeable concept. He soaked into it and found no boundaries, no channels, nothing that flowed. He was everywhere in it. He was everything of it.

"At the moment, perhaps it would be best to go by one I've recently given myself; one appropriate to the circumstances I find myself in, for I am tasked with the manipulation of time, and therefore of reality as we perceive it."

As Burton slipped away and eased slowly into another iteration of himself, he saw arms reach up to a hood, saw strong but very pale fingers grasp the material, saw it yanked backward, and saw a face he felt he would recognise if only he could properly focus his eyes upon it. They, however, refused to cooperate, and he was possessed by the curious conviction that the man seated before him had more than one head. For an instant—or perhaps for an eternity—it appeared that three heads occupied the same space. Then five. Then one. Then three again.

"I," the individual said, "am perfectly impossible. I am self-created. I am paradox personified. I call myself the Beetle."

A SOJOURN IN THE FUTURE OF A DIFFERENT HISTORY

Love and praise, and a length of days whose shadow cast
    upon time is light,
Days whose sound was a spell shed round from wheeling
    wings as of doves in flight,
Meet in one, that the mounting sun to-day may triumph, and
    cast out night.
        —Algernon Swinburne, "Birthday Ode"

The cloaked man and the observation deck flexed and shifted out of perception. Once again, Sir Richard Francis Burton occupied his own mind as if he were a passenger in it. He was subjected to thoughts, memories, and impulses that weren't his own, though they felt as if they were, and he found himself to be a separated fragment of consciousness that witnessed but could not motivate.

He was walking. It was all wrong. He was too tall. Physical sensation had about it a peculiar second-handedness, as if his body were operating some distance away and somehow relaying what it experienced back to him. His self-awareness was all askew. At the back of his mind, he could detect a ceaseless muttering as a part of him calculated how to move each leg, where to place each foot, how to maintain balance, what to do with his hands, where to direct his eyes. All the silent, instinctive, and automatic functions of the brain that usually went unnoticed were now akin to the background thrum of an engine, such as could be detected aboard a transatlantic steam ship.

It was so disconcerting that the environment didn't immediately register.

Then it did, and all thoughts of himself were immediately vanquished by it. He was overcome. He could look, but he couldn't process what he saw. It was simply too incredible to comprehend.

A moment of mental immobility then the disorientation passed. Piece by piece, he started to make sense of the visual and aural stimuli.

Initially, he thought he was back in Africa, striding through a jungle beneath a purpling evening sky. On closer inspection, he realised this was not the case, for the tangled vines, knobbled trunks, and twisting limbs of the flora surrounding him followed the contours of buildings, which ranged in dimension from low blocky structures to slender towers of such unbelievable height that their upper reaches were made faint by the atmosphere. Here and there could be glimpsed patches of brickwork, the angles of doorways and windows, panes of cracked glass, a sharp corner, the outline of a colonnade, a sloped roof, a cornice, and a myriad of other architectural elements, making it apparent that he was in what had once been a vast city, the substance and form of which was being consumed by vegetation. No! Not merely consumed—but mimicked and replaced! Where had once stood a tenement building there was now a cluster of huge nut-like growths, their inner flesh melted away, the remaining shells melded together like adjoined rooms, with oval doorways and window openings apparently having grown without human intercession; where once had soared a breathtaking tower, now there stood a colossal trunk, its wood riddled with hollows and passages, its branches blending into those of neighbouring columns to make bridges; what had once been a macadam-surfaced thoroughfare lit by gas lamps was now a wide moss-covered trail illuminated by glowing fruits, berries, and gourds.

All of it was every shade imaginable of red. There were Tyrian purples, deep maroons, bright crimsons, dusty violets, dazzling scarlets, soft hues of rose, earthy rusts, diaphanous magentas, glimmering tints of ruby, shadowy carmines, and luscious blushes of raspberry.

It should, perhaps, have struck him as hellish but, instead, he envisioned the entire world as a single living entity with this city as one of its pulsating organs. The vibrancy of its life was all around him. Sap throbbed like blood through translucent vines. Sac-like growths palpitated as if breathing. Pods shivered and rattled, seemingly engaged in some esoteric discussion.

There was a pervasive intelligence about it.

And life supported life.

Amid the riotous tangle, colourful butterflies danced through the air, and heavily laden bees droned industriously. Pollen swirled like a light mist, except that drifting tendrils of it sometimes made a sharp change of course that in no way related to any movement of the atmosphere.

There was a plethora of marvellous perfumes. Burton knew this, but he couldn't experience them. He didn't know why, but he had no sense of smell.

Birds chattered and sang and whistled.

Squirrels gambolled along branches.

Spiders weaved their webs.

And there were people.

They were moving through the rapidly deepening twilight, gossiping and laughing and conversing and singing and gesticulating and offering him friendly salutations as they passed. They called him "guv'nor."

Most of them walked the trails. Some clambered from bough to bough. Others flew.

The majority were perfectly human in appearance. Many were not.

A woman, wearing a broad-brimmed hat, a tight-fitting jacket, and knee-length knickerbockers, scuttled across his path and plunged into the undergrowth. She had six crab-like legs.

A man, in a one-piece chequered costume, crawled by on all fours. His torso was preternaturally long, like that of a Dachshund.

There was a boy with suckered tentacles playing with a spinning top. There was an elderly gentleman with eight eyes leaning against a thick stem, softly singing, "I didn't know I loved you 'til I saw the sky—" There was a girl with gossamer wings, a portly fellow with a single horn curving upward from his forehead, a faun, a centaur, a manticore, a cyclops, a sphinx.

Folklore and legend had come alive, as if liberated from the depths of human consciousness.

Where am I?

As soon as the question was asked, the astonishing answer was provided. To his left, in a gap between corrugated leaves, on a patch of wall partially obscured by a bunch of grapes, a rusty metal sign proclaimed *Gloucester Place*.

Knowledge welled into him.

It was March the 19th, and the year was 2203. London. The *Orpheus* had come here from 1860 and had thus far remained for a little over thirteen months. During that short space of time, the phenomenal jungle had grown, dismantling the layered structure of the city.

The vaulted roof that, for generations, had enclosed the old ground-level metropolis was gone, and the working masses who, like troglodytes, had toiled beneath it, were free. Green Park, Regent's Park, Hyde Park, and St. James's Park, previously raised up to the exclusive heights, were now back where they belonged. The towers, once the province of the elite, were open to all.

The Burton of Trieste knew—because the Burton he currently occupied knew—that the aristocratic few who'd once held sway over the majority had, for the most part, fled the city, convinced they'd find some remote enclave, an island perhaps, untouched by the jungle, in which to reassert their dominance. They wouldn't succeed. The verdure was spreading at a prodigious rate. Wherever they went, it would catch up with them eventually.

The world was changing and changing fast, and today was the tipping point. Something was going to happen this very evening, and everyone was aware of the fact, though no one could predict the nature of the event.

From up ahead, he heard a booming voice cry out, "Hear the word! Hear the word! The rapture is nigh! The rapture is nigh! Hear the word!"

He also became aware that someone was addressing him. He looked down to his right and was rather startled when the motion caused his neck to emit a soft whir.

Algernon Swinburne was at his side, hatless and dressed in an absurd one-piece red-velvet suit with an Elizabethan-style ruffled collar.

Trounce was on the other side of the poet, sans moustache, his hair down to his shoulders, his waist much slimmer, his clothes plain, white, and functional.

Swinburne was saying, "—that Ireland is habitable for the first time in three hundred and sixty years or so. I wonder whether the whole business of the potato blight and the carnivorous plants that drove away the population had its origin in one of the alternate histories, and if the vegetation was somehow a different and much less benevolent iteration of this, our own jungle."

"Well you, of all people, should know." It took Burton a moment to realise that he'd articulated the sentence—and, indeed, that it *was* a sentence, for it had sounded like an orchestra of handbells and bagpipes. Not his own voice at all. Not even a human one.

What am I?

"It was a version of you, after all," he continued to wheeze and chime, "that received a dose of a venom designed by Prussian eugenicists, and who transformed into this jungle as a result of it."

The poet looked up at him, and Burton thought he detected in his friend's eyes that he was also riding inside himself, with no power to influence what this variation of Swinburne did or said.

"True, but it also caused that particular Algernon to develop a wholly different order of sentience than the human. I have no better idea of what he—or, rather, *it*—is up to than you do."

"It appears to me that, since we arrived in this future, human sentience has itself altered considerably. Might the pollen carry the venom? Is everyone slowly mutating into vegetation?"

"There's been no evidence to suggest it. And let us not forget that the air is thick with nanotechnology, too, which previously functioned to keep the population subdued. That microscopic machinery has now blended with the pollen, so we all have neither one thing nor the other in our bloodstreams, but rather an amalgam of both. All except you, of course."

Why not me?

"But to return to my point," Swinburne continued, "has it not occurred to you that if the disaster in Ireland had never happened there wouldn't have been the great Irish exodus to America and the history of the Anglo-Saxon Empire might have been very different. The politicians who forged that continent's alliance with the old British Empire were, after all, Irish-Americans."

"Were they?"

"Haven't you been reading *The History of the Future?* The Kennedy family? The nineteen sixties, seventies, and eighties?"

"I've been preoccupied."

"I noticed. What with?"

"Need you ask?" Burton extended his arms and was shocked to see that there were six of them, all fashioned from polished brass and made flexible by cog-wheeled joints, rods, and miniature pistons. One of them ended in a stump. Another had a large gun affixed to it. All were fitted with extendible tools of various sorts.

This is why I'm an exception. I'm a machine.

From amid the mental noise of his motion, more memories surfaced, and Burton was suddenly aware that the life of the *doppelgänger* he occupied made his own story—judged as extraordinary by his contemporaries—appear dull by comparison. Indeed, so outré was it that his counterpart now inhabited this mechanical body, which had originally served to keep the great engineer Isambard Kingdom Brunel alive before it was hijacked by the insane mind of Spring Heeled Jack, the time traveller.

Swinburne went on. "My proposition is that we must extricate the notion of cause and effect from the restrictive shackles of sequence. Once we accept that an effect can come—from the perspective of our regimented perception of time—before its cause, then we might understand that coincidences, far from being nothing but chance, are meaningful elements of a bigger process."

The poet reached out and tapped his forefinger against one of Burton's brass arms.

"The Irish famine is one such example. You are another."

"Me?"

"The transference of your consciousness into the black diamonds inside that body's mechanical brain can be easily explained. You had me shoot you dead so your brain's terminal emanation would overwrite the presence of Spring Heeled Jack, which existed within them. Thus you wiped him out of existence while also ensuring that your mind survived the fatal injuries he'd inflicted upon you. As fantastical as that might be, it at least makes sequential sense. What's more difficult to comprehend is the fact that you've ended up in that body at this particular juncture in history."

A woman with wide bat-like wings swooped over them and landed on a branch, wrapping her prehensile fingers, toes, and tail around it. Her face was illuminated by a dangling pear-like fruit, which exuded a soft yellow light. She smiled at Burton, blinked her big, round black eyes, reached for the fruit and plucked it, then turned and launched herself back into the air, flapping away.

"This particular juncture?" Burton watched her go. He noted that stars were beginning to prick the sky.

William Trounce spoke for the first time. "Algy has a point. You might be the only person in the entire empire who doesn't feel the imminence of the rapture."

"I wish you wouldn't call it that."

"Humph!"

Trounce gestured ahead to where, hidden from view by clumped leaves, the voice continued to proclaim with foghorn volume, "Hear the word! The rapture is nigh! The rapture is nigh!"

"It's what the people have named it."

Swinburne said, "I understand and share your dislike of the word, Richard. In your native time period, it had specific connotations. However, I feel certain that, whatever happens tonight, it will bear no resemblance to the Rapture of defunct Christianity. It'll be quite different. An evolutionary leap, perhaps. A deeper integration with existence engendered by the assimilation of botanical and technological elements into the human body."

"As predictions go, that's rather a specific one," Burton observed.

The poet shrugged. "Call it intuition."

It occurred to Burton that this was not the Algernon Swinburne he'd known during his lifetime, who'd been plucked from his deathbed in 1909 and restored to 1864, there to imbibe in the Slug and Lettuce with the equally revitalised Burton and Trounce. Nor was he the one familiar to the version of Burton inhabiting this mechanical body, with whom the poet had shared adventures so extraordinary that the recollection of them was almost impossible for the inner Burton to comprehend. No, this Swinburne possessed a gravitas neither versions of the explorer would have attributed to him.

Again, unbidden, knowledge blossomed. During the voyage to this future, the "authentic" Algernon Swinburne—and William Trounce, too—had been killed. The men walking beside Burton were copies. Clones. And brothers! Carried by the same woman!

Burton, who possessed no familiarity with the concept of cloning, suddenly did, and the wonder of it was that it failed to astonish him, this because his mind was already overloaded. He received but could not process. Such information might perhaps make sense eventually— as it obviously did to his host—but for now all he could manage to do was watch and listen, allowing the bizarre experiences and memories to overlay his own in the manner—just as Sadhvi Raghavendra had said—of a palimpsest.

He recalled that he was, in reality, sitting with his companions before a cloaked man aboard the *Orpheus* and began to will himself to return to that place. Then he stopped, afraid that he'd peel away illusion upon illusion until he was back in his bedroom in Trieste, in the throes of a heart attack.

"Hear the word! Hear the word! The rapture is coming! Any time now! Be prepared! The rapture is nigh!"

Just ahead, the source of the loud pronouncements came into view: a distorted figure squatting on the corner of a junction between two trails, with a wagon loaded with fruit, nuts, and vegetables in front of it. Short and bulbous—dressed in baggy garments and with a flat cap upon its broad head—the creature was little more than a blob with seemingly boneless arms protruding from it and a head that grew straight from the torso without mediation from anything resembling a neck. The froggish face, jutting forward, was split by a mouth so wide that its corners touched the tiny vestigial ears.

The man—if the street vendor could be so classified—suddenly expanded his throat and cheeks, puffing them out tremendously, like a balloon, so that he even more resembled a bullfrog, and opened the phenomenal mouth to blast, "Hear the word! Hear the word! Land for all! Homes for all! Food for all! Sky for all! The rapture is just minutes away!"

"Ouch!" Swinburne muttered, putting his fingers into his ears. "What ho, Mr. Grub! What ho! Put a sock in it, will you, old fellow!"

"Hallo, Mr. Swinburne," the living trumpet responded. "Hallo, Mr. Trounce. Hallo, guv'nor." His head split into so broad a smile that Burton marvelled the top half of it didn't fall off.

"You've not joined the exodus, then?" Trounce asked.

"Me, sir? No, sir! This is me patch. There's been a Grub a-standin' 'ere since time immum—immim—imm—umm—"

"Immemorial," Swinburne offered.

"Aye, that's the word. Since time immaterial. I'll not abandon it fer nuthink, even if it means I'll be the last bloke livin' in London."

"I doubt it'll come to that," Trounce said. "There's plenty content to stay."

"True enough, sir, true enough. It'll be a different sort a London, though, won't it?"

"It already is."

"Aye, but I ain't referrin' to the jungle. What I mean to say is, it'll not be a city no more. Soon, there'll be no such thing anywheres."

Burton chimed, "You can confirm it? Cities are decentralising?"

Grub bent an arm upward and scratched the side of his jaw. "If'n I take yer meanin' correctly, guv'nor, yes, that's the word. People is leavin' all the old cities an' spreadin' outward into smaller communities." He gestured around at the vegetation. "Homes for all. Food for all. Anywhere. Least there will be once the jungle covers the globe."

"And governance?"

"Takes care o' itself, don't it?"

"Smaller settlements," Swinburne mused. "Microcommunities. Easily maintained by their population. With no competition for resources, there's little motive for crime or warfare. The jungle is bringing peace to the world."

"And 'appiness," Grub said. "I ain't never imagined it could be like this, sir." He turned his face upward. The red foliage reflected in the outer edges of his little protuberant eyes and stars were mirrored in the pupils.

"One more piece left to place in the jigsaw, if'n I might put it like that, an' it's a-comin' this very evenin'." To Burton, he said, "All o' this is 'cos of you, guv'nor. Folks hold you as their champion."

Burton shook his head, his neck ratcheting. "No, I mustn't be idolised. The people were, for too long, dominated by those who held themselves as better than the rest, and they, in turn, were presided over by the mind of a single man—and he a lunatic. You are free now. The world is yours. As for me—" He held out his six arms. "I have no place here. I'm not even human."

"You're the most 'uman of us all," Grub protested. "You sacrificed your life for us. Sort of. If'n yer know what I mean."

"Whether that's true or not, I don't belong here. I have to take my leave of you. I've come to say good-bye, Mr. Grub. Tonight, I shall witness the rapture, whatever it may be, and afterward, my friends and I will board the *Orpheus* and return to our own time."

Grub scratched his head. "I've asked you before an' I'll ask you again, 'cos I can't get me noggin' around such wonders—you're really from the past?"

"We are, and it's high time we went back to it."

"I'll spread the word, then. The people will want to see you off."

"I'd prefer it otherwise. I can't bear partings and I have a distaste for ceremony. Will you delay any pronouncement until the morning?"

"If that's what you ask, that's what I'll do, of course."

"Thank you. And thank you, too, for the part you played in the revolution. It was you who mobilised the people and you who prevented them from running wild after we defeated those who ruled over you."

Grub bobbed his flat head and gave a loose salute. "The workers ain't inclined to riot, sir. They are too busy gettin' on with gettin' on. Always 'ave been." He turned to Swinburne and Trounce. "But you two gents— surely you'll stay?"

"We shall," Swinburne answered. "Though we possess the memories of the men from whom we were cloned—that is to say, the Swinburne and Trounce from 1860—we are native to this time and will, we're certain, be subject to the rapture."

"You feel it in you? The expectation? It's powerful, hey? I feel an imm—immin—"

"Yes, we do, and 'imminence' is the word you're looking for. In fact, we should get back to our friends, before it's too late. We'll seek you out again tomorrow, old chap."

"Right you are, sir." The vendor again addressed Burton. "Good-bye. Thank you. From every single one of us."

After handshakes were exchanged, Burton, Swinburne, and Trounce turned and retraced their steps, following Gloucester Place down to a barely recognisable Portman Square—it being little more than a clearing in the jungle, though one of unnaturally angular dimensions. In its centre, the *Orpheus* was floating a little above the rust-coloured and mushroom-dotted lichen that covered the ground.

They boarded it and joined Captain Lawless on the bridge.

Swinburne said to him, "The others will be at the Monument Flower by now. Let's go straight there."

Lawless looked up at the ceiling. "You heard the man, *Orpheus*."

"I'm busy," the Mark III said. "Why don't you walk? It's hardly any distance."

"Busy doing what?"

"Contemplating."

Lawless looked at Burton with an expression of exasperation. "I'm sure the bloody thing is getting worse every day. Babbage created it as a calculating machine. This era's scientists have made of it a thinking machine. And a thoroughly irritating one, at that."

"What are you contemplating, *Orpheus*?" Swinburne asked.

"My own existence."

"Oof!" Lawless exclaimed. "That is easily explained. You were built. Built to operate this ship. At my command. And I command you to fly it to Green Park. Do you understand?"

"Perfectly. Though none of that explains *your* existence."

"How about leaving me to worry about that?"

"Hurry," Trounce put in. "The rapture is almost here. I feel fit to burst."

Swinburne put a hand to his brother's elbow. "Don't worry, Pouncer. Nothing will happen without us."

"How can you possibly know that?"

"I just do."

The *Orpheus* eased smoothly into the air. Burton looked out through the window and watched the jungle sinking past. It thinned, dropped out of sight, and he was suddenly looking at a half-moon, visible through a forest of black columns that rose from a twinkling blanket, the speckled lights of which appeared as a counterpoint to the stars above. The glowing jungle swathed the land for as far as the eye could see, from horizon to horizon.

The rotorship steered a course southeastward then circled a colossal obelisk—a knotted trunk half a mile in circumference and so inconceivably tall that its upper reaches were lost from view.

New Buckingham Palace.

Orpheus sank down just to the north of it, coming to rest on the eastern slope of Green Park.

The small expanse of land, uncluttered by jungle, consisted of a lawn dotted only by a few isolated bushes, the berries of which offered a paltry illumination, and thickets of trees around its fringe, which also offered some measure of light. As Burton, Swinburne, Trounce, and Lawless disembarked and started down the shallow slope, the explorer was able to make out Queen Victoria's monument silhouetted ahead of them. It had been erected, he recalled, in 1842 on the spot where, two years before, a bullet had killed the monarch. Designed by a little-known artist named Henry Corbould, and, according to its creator, based on a vivid dream, it took the form of a huge flower of no identifiable species, though it somewhat resembled a cross between a rose and a tulip.

Controversial when erected, the memorial had weathered the storm of criticism and, by the time of Burton's death in 1890, was an accepted and celebrated element of London's landscape. The monument was twenty feet in height but appeared considerably larger to the explorer as he now approached it. Were he able to frown in puzzlement, he would have done so, for a trick of the light made it look as if the monument was slowly swaying, its spiny petals gently curling and uncurling.

He gasped—a sound that resembled the susurration of a brushed cymbal.

The movement was no illusion.

A new set of facts bubbled to the front of his mind. In this version of history, Spring Heeled Jack had caused the memorial to be demolished, perhaps in an attempt to forget the crime that had contributed to his madness. Thirteen months ago, Swinburne, moved by a whim, had buried the ashes of Burton—the Burton whose consciousness now occupied this brass body—on the same spot. From those ashes, the plant had grown and flowered, its bloom remarkably similar in form to the old monument.

The four men joined a group of people standing at its base. One of them stepped forward to greet them.

"The blossom is getting more active by the second. I was starting to worry you might not arrive back in time. You said your farewells to Mr. Grub?"

"We did, Tom," Burton said. The Burton of Trieste was amazed to see, in the other's features, echoes of his old friend Thomas Bendyshe. The Burton of brass knew him to be a cloned descendent of that man.

Looking past him, the explorer spotted the rest of the crew of the *Orpheus*: Daniel Gooch, Sadhvi Raghavendra, and Maneesh Krishnamurthy.

Trounce looked up at the massive flower. "We haven't missed anything, then?"

Bendyshe replied. "A lot of leaf curling and some odd pops and whistles. We all feel certain it'll be the source of the rapture."

Burton said, "You base that assumption on what?"

"The excitement we're experiencing. The expectation. It's definitely emanating from this thing."

Krishnamurthy moved closer to them and added, "Those of us from the *Orpheus* feel it, but it's affecting those native to this time with much greater intensity."

Burton extended his arms slightly. "I sense nothing, but I trust your and the others' instincts. So a vegetable is going to change humanity?"

"It wouldn't be the first time."

"Maneesh?"

"The humble potato. It could be argued that its arrival in Europe sparked the agricultural revolution, which in turn lead to the industrial revolution and the rise of empires."

"Hmm. I little while ago, Algy proposed that the Irish potato blight altered the course of history."

Krishnamurthy grinned. "Well, there you are. As hard as it may be to swallow—I refer to the fact, not to the spud—it's from such innocuous items that the human world takes its form. We can't discount the possible influence of—" He stopped and gaped as heavy bunches of berries hanging from the plant suddenly erupted with light.

"Hello!" Bendyshe exclaimed. "Your arrival appears to have added to its agitation, Sir Richard!"

Swinburne whispered, "It's been waiting for us. Now the show can begin."

Above their heads, a rattle sounded, and with a creaking of its woody stalk, the flower turned and bent, giving the impression that it was looking down at them. Bladder-like organs at the back of its outermost petals expanded like balloons, then contracted, and as they did so, air was blown through the central bud, the petals of which moved like lips. A dreamy whistle emerged and was shaped into words.

> *"One, who is not, we see; but one, whom we see not, is;*
> *Surely this is not that; but that is assuredly this."*

> *"What, and wherefore, and whence? for under is over and under;*
> *If thunder could be without lightning, lightning could be without thunder."*

"Bloody hell!" Daniel Gooch cried out, throwing up his supplementary arms. "Will wonders never cease? Now we have to deal with a talking flower!"

Standing at his side, Nathaniel Lawless said, "All aboard the *Orpheus*. This is beyond the bounds. Too much for us. Let's go home."

"Not too much for me," Swinburne murmured.

"Or me," Trounce said.

"Or me," Bendyshe agreed.

Sadhvi Raghavendra turned to Lawless. "I understand your reluctance to stay, Captain. I have the distinct impression that this world won't allow those of us from the past to remain in it for very much longer.

However, I also sense that we are, for the moment, perfectly safe. We can witness, but we must then depart as planned."

The captain jerked his chin in acknowledgement and gazed with an air of bemused disapproval at the flower.

"Doubt is faith in the main: but faith, on the whole, is doubt:
We cannot believe by proof: but could we believe without?"

Burton wished he could control his host's body. He wanted to say, *You wrote those words, Algy. It was a poem entitled "A Higher Pantheism in a Nutshell"—your mockery of Tennyson's "The Higher Pantheism." When was it? 1870 or thereabouts? Is the plant really a eugenically created version of you? What lunacy am I witnessing?*

He couldn't give voice to the thought. Instead, he looked down as Gooch stepped to his side.

"Why now, I wonder?" the engineer muttered.

"Why now?" Burton clanged.

"If there's one thing we've learned during our recent adventures, it's that the timing of events is meaningful. So this rapture thing—why this evening? What's the date?"

"The nineteenth of March," Burton responded. "It has no significance I can think of, unless you count the fact that it's my birthday."

"It is? Do you know your hour of birth?"

"Half past nine in the evening."

"Interesting. It's close on that now."

"I hardly think it has any bearing on the matter." Burton paused before adding, "I just turned forty. Yet, taking the current year into consideration, I'm also three hundred and eighty-two years old."

He watched as the flower's bladders again inflated and contracted.

"Why, and whither, and how? for barley and rye are not clover:
Neither are straight lines curves: yet over is under and over."

With a squeal of bending wood, the flower suddenly dropped down until its petals were just inches from Burton's face.

"Happy birthday, Sir Richards," it wheezed. "Birth and birth."

"Gad!" Gooch blurted, stumbling backward in surprise.

"Sir Richards?" Burton echoed.

"Thee and thee."

It knows I'm in here!

The blossom chanted:

"Two and two may be four: but four and four are not eight:
Fate and God may be twain: but God is the same thing as fate."

"You can converse?" Burton asked. "You understand me?"

"Better than you know."

"Gad!" Gooch cried out again.

"Incredible!" Krishnamurthy muttered.

"Then answer me this," Burton said. "Are you Algernon Swinburne?"

To his right, the human Swinburne had become uncharacteristically silent and motionless.

"Was. Was. Was." The flower emitted a sound that resembled a chuckle. "What! What! What!" It leaned closer to Burton until its petals were almost touching the side of his brass face. "Many happy returns. You do *want* to return, I presume?"

Return to life? Return to the past? Return to corporeal form?

"Yes."

"Then accept my gift."

With much rustling and a slight screech, the plant straightened until its blossom was again directed at the sky. Burton heard it quietly recite,

"More is the whole than a part: but half is more than the whole:
Clearly, the soul is the body: but is not the body the soul?

"One and two are not one: but one and nothing is two:
Truth can hardly be false, if falsehood cannot be true."

It fell silent.

Burton looked at Swinburne, Trounce, and Bendyshe. They were standing glassy-eyed, as if in a trance.

Sadhvi Raghavendra gestured. "There!"

"What is it?" Krishnamurthy asked, his tone subdued and hoarse.

A part of the base of the central stalk—as wide and knurled as the trunk of an ancient oak—had started to distend. It squeaked, groaned, and grew paler, the bark stretching thin, a large swelling bulging outward. There came a sharp crack and a split appeared, bisecting the protrusion vertically. It widened and, with a soft squelch, a sap-covered sac was extruded from it. The membrane flopped heavily onto the plant's exposed upper roots and rolled to the ground where, veined and translucent, it undulated as something shifted inside it.

"Is that—?" Lawless croaked.

Uttering a small cry, Raghavendra hurried forward and crouched over the quivering membrane. "Maneesh! Help me!"

Krishnamurthy hesitated, then joined her, squatting down. "It's not possible."

"Help me get him out," she said.

Burton chimed, "Him?"

He watched as his friends tore at the skin and heard it rip like linen.

Krishnamurthy gasped and toppled backward, sitting heavily on the ground. Mucilaginous white liquid spilled from the sac and splashed around him, soaking his trousers.

"Breathing!" Raghavendra announced.

She turned her face to Burton. Gazing past her, he saw, naked and hairless, an old man lying on his side, his legs curled up, knees against his chest, his arms folded to either side of them. His skin appeared to be a peculiar wormy-blue colour, though in the glow of the plant's fruits and berries, it was difficult to be certain.

"Who?"

Raghavendra reached down and, placing a hand to either side of the newborn's face, gently turned his head so that his features were visible to Burton. "He looks like you."

She was right. The thrusting jaw, hard mouth, sharp cheekbones, and deep-set eyes were unmistakably those of Sir Richard Francis Burton, though very aged. About seventy, Burton automatically estimated.

What the hell? That's the face I see in the mirror! That's the man I was in Trieste, when I died!

With a hiss of pistons, he took a step backward. He tried to speak, but the words wouldn't come, his voice generator producing nothing but a discordant tone, almost a whine. Through mechanical eyes, the passenger, the old man reborn, watched incredulously as Raghavendra eased her arms beneath his unconscious double and lifted it until the naked figure was sitting up. The hairless head rolled forward and white fluid spilled from its mouth. There were no signs of consciousness.

"Look," she said, indicating, with a jerk of her chin, the liver-spotted cranium.

Burton saw eleven small bumps circling the scalp like a crown.

"What are they?" he managed to clang.

"I have no idea. But——" She fell silent.

"But what?"

"This fellow looks like an older you, but it goes no further than that. He's empty. I feel no presence."

Daniel Gooch peered at the unconscious man's face. "But not dead? Then who is he?"

"Nobody."

"Nobody, Sadhvi? He must be somebody."

"There's nothing. A complete absence of—of mind."

"How can you know that?"

Krishnamurthy said, "She's a Sister of Noble Benevolence, Daniel. You know what that means."

"I've never really understood it."

Over their heads, the flower purred:

"Parallels all things are: yet many of these are askew:
You are certainly I: but certainly I am not you."

Raghavendra said, "Oh!" as, one after the other, the bumps on the old man's head split, their edges puckering open to reveal deep cavities.

In unison, Swinburne, Trounce, and Bendyshe said, "Half past nine. Happy birthday. A gift of diamonds."

Burton looked at them. "Are you still with us?"

They didn't respond.

"Diamonds? Where? What of them?"

No answer.

Gooch moved closer to the sagging form and, bending over Raghav-endra's shoulder, peered into the eleven holes. He pulled a box of lucifers from his waistcoat pocket, lit one, and held its flame close to the man's head, illuminating the openings. "They have irregularly faceted sides," he said. "Something occurs to me. You'll consider me loopy."

Nathaniel Lawless gave a wry laugh. "Daniel, we're three and a half centuries in the future, standing beside a giant talking flower that just gave birth to a fully formed old man. Nothing you say can possibly compete with that for lunacy."

Burton asked, "What are you thinking, Daniel?"

"A gift of diamonds."

"You understand the significance?"

Gooch straightened, folded his mechanical arms across his chest, and ran the fingers of his natural right hand through his sandy blonde hair. "We're up to our eyes in bloody diamonds—black ones that, at a certain time and in a certain place, were considered extremely rare. Thanks to Edward Oxford's various exploits, those same stones now exist in the here and now many times over, having arrived in the Nimtz generators attached to the multiple iterations of his time travelling suit. Personally, I'd like to chuck all the bloody things into a pressure furnace. They give me a headache."

"They give everyone a headache," Raghavendra said. "Pressure furnace? What would that achieve?"

"It would reduce them to carbon dioxide. However, since we'll never make it home without our ship's Nimtz and the Mark Three babbage, both of which contain such diamonds, I'm loath to reduce our supply until we're back where we belong. It's a maxim of engineering that machines only ever require spare parts when there are none available."

"Your point?" Burton asked.

"My point is that the gems in the machinery aren't the only ones. There are also eleven in your head, Sir Richard. They used to hold Brunel's consciousness. It was overwritten by Spring Heeled Jack's which, in turn, was erased by yours." With his left hand, Gooch indicated the unconscious man's head. "Eleven diamonds and eleven faceted openings in this chap's skull. What's the betting they're a perfect fit?"

"Are you suggesting that—that—" Burton began. His mechanical voice petered out.

"That we remove the stones from your body's probability calculator and fit them into the cranium of this new Sir Richard? Yes, that's exactly what I'm suggesting." Gooch rubbed his chin. "I think the jungle just gave you the opportunity to be human again."

"Human? Born from a plant?"

"Near enough human, anyway. More so than the contraption you currently occupy, that's for certain."

"But he's old."

"He's flesh. You'll regain your lost senses. Taste. Smell."

The plant whispered, "Birth day."

Gooch continued, "Providing we keep the diamonds in close proximity to each other while moving them, you'll not be in any danger, and if there's no result, we can easily return them."

Raghavendra, still supporting the limp body, looked up at Burton. He was surprised to see that her eyes were brimming with tears. "Richard, we have to try!"

Burton turned his eyes from Raghavendra to Lawless, from Lawless to Krishnamurthy, from Krishnamurthy to Gooch, from Gooch to Swinburne, Trounce, and Bendyshe—these three standing together, frozen, poised as if waiting, their thought processes somehow suspended.

"How," he asked, "does any of this relate to the rapture?"

"I don't know," Gooch responded. "But somehow it must. The contemporaneity of events is too extraordinary to ignore."

"There's something else to consider," Raghavendra put in. "Without a mind, this body will die. And soon. Already, his breathing is becoming irregular."

Burton took two paces forward and crouched, his body buzzing and whirring. He reached out and touched the man's face with a brass forefinger. "You're sure?"

"I can feel the imbalance growing within him."

After a minute of consideration, Burton clanged, "I'm heartily sick of being entombed in this machine. It has made me immortal, but I feel like I'm buried alive. I can't bear the torture of it any more. We'll try. Even if it gives me only a year or two of life, I'd rather die old with my senses restored than live forever without them. Daniel, what do you need?"

Gooch unfolded his metal arms and extended a set of tools—screwdrivers, spanners, and pliers—from his wrists. "Nothing more than these. We can do it right away."

"What will I feel?"

"Physically, nothing. Mentally, your capacity to think will diminish as I remove each stone from the probability calculator. Ultimately, you'll black out, like being chloroformed but without the unpleasantness. Providing this fellow's brain has the ability to process the electromagnetic fields stored within them, as I place each diamond into his skull, your consciousness will gradually be restored. If it doesn't work, we'll put you back where you are, and you'll wake up none the worse for the experience."

"Very well. Let's get on with it. I beg of you, be careful, my friend. I'm quite literally placing my life in your hands."

"You can count on me."

Gooch moved around Raghavendra to Burton's side and applied his tools to the brass man's head.

Inside Burton's mind, and undetected by him, the second Burton wanted to scream. Everything he'd thus far witnessed was so far out of the ordinary that he thought it could only have been induced by the Saltzmann's Tincture, which was obviously a hallucinogenic drug of particular potency. Yet it all felt horrifically real—and oddly familiar, too. Now he was about to endure some manner of brain surgery, and there was nothing whatever he could do to prevent it.

Wait! I'm in here, too! Don't put me back in that body! You don't understand! It's old! It aches! It's going to die! Not again! Better this machine than that!

At the periphery of his vision, he saw Gooch's hand place something that resembled a brass skullcap onto the grass. There came a slight grinding sound followed by a click.

What are you doing? Stop! Stop!

"I'm going to extract the first stone. Are you ready?" Gooch asked.

"Yes. Proceed," Burton said.

No!

Half a minute, then, "It's out. How do you feel?"

"Fine."

"Good show. Now for the second."

Suddenly, the sensation of floating.

"And now, Sir Richard?"

"I don't think I can move."

"As expected. Let's do the next."

Click. Click.

"Done."

Stop! I don't like it! I'm afraid!

"I just—clang!—zzzzzz!—went blind."

"You've apparently lost some control over your vocal apparatus, too. In a minute, we won't be able to communicate. I'll keep talking, but you may not comprehend my words. Don't be concerned."

Perhaps I'll survive this. I'm not this Burton. I'm a visitor. What happens to him doesn't necessarily happen to medicinal. Medicinal? Why shell me that behind?

"Are you still able to think?"

"Basking yellow in my—zzzzzz!—fretwork," Burton clanked.

Sadhvi Raghavendra's voice: "What did he say?"

"Nothing intelligible. I've removed his ability to express himself through language."

"Can he understand us?"

"If he can, it won't be for much longer."

Wooden highest of table momentum!

"Fifth one out," Gooch said. "The babbage is processing just half of the electromagnetic field that comprises his mind now. Let's do the next."

Burton tried to summon an image of Isabel but couldn't work out how her vision locations related to her head-shape space. His experience, he knew, needed to be otherwise.

Tonic. All of you chicken cold.

Colours suddenly slantwise wrong.

"Light master." Gooch noise. "Earlier garnish is that much off."

Intonation: "Friendly beneath in stacked embarrassments. Slowly?"
"Barleycorn."
Level level level.
Shake. Hardly the Trounce.
Hello.
A desert. He stepped out of his tent.
The horizon.

CONCERNING IMPROBABILITIES AND IMPOSSIBILITIES

Monarchy degenerates into tyranny, aristocracy into oligarchy, and democracy into savage violence and chaos.
—Polybius

Burton opened his eyes and saw the Beetle and the glass walls of the *Orpheus*'s observation deck.

To his right, William Trounce groaned and muttered, "Drugged!"

To his left, Algernon Swinburne was moving his lips as if attempting to give form to words that wouldn't come.

The Beetle's eyes were dark and penetrating, with dilated black irises surrounded by a thin and glittering silver border. Burton felt as if they could perceive his every thought.

There were eleven lumps circling the hairless head.

Or heads.

One. Three. Five. One.

Strain as he might, Burton couldn't properly distinguish the features. Only the eyes appeared fixed; every other element of the man's countenance was multiplying, unifying, and sliding in and out of perception, as if both there and elsewhere. Unquestionably, though, this was the same person whose abnormal birth he'd just witnessed, except—

Very quietly, he said, "You are considerably younger."

"Yes," the Beetle responded. "My course through time is the reverse of normal and is very rapid."

"You are me?"

"I can't deny it. Though it's not wholly accurate. The concept of a *you* and a *me* no longer properly applies. I might just as easily claim to be a Swinburne or sentient vegetation or an intelligent machine. I am—" He paused, then recited:

"All Faith is false, all Faith is true:
Truth is the shattered mirror strown
In myriad bits; while each believes
his little bit the whole to own."

Burton said, "From my *Kasîdah of Hâjî Abdû El-Yezdî*. I wrote it in 1880."

"And in 1859," the Beetle rejoined, "after meeting Abdu El Yezdi in person."

"There is no such person. I invented him."

"You did, indeed. I might claim that you invented me, too."

"Then you are confirming my suspicion that this is all an hallucination? That I am still in the throes of a heart attack in Trieste?"

"No, Sir Richard, this is real. At least, as much so as anything else in a universe whose very fabric is woven out of imagination, projection, interpretation, and belief; a universe that is nothing but a reflection of the sentience that discerns it."

Trounce let loose a deep breath, leaned forward, and rapped his knuckles against the floor. "Enough of this gibberish! And will you please keep your confounded head still, man!"

"I'm sorry, William, I can't alter your sensory limitations."

"What the blazes do you mean by that? Are you insulting me?"

"I'm not. It is merely that the human mind is conditioned to apprehend only one possible path at once—one fragment, if you will. In me, all of them are made apparent. That is why I quoted Sir Richard's poem. I am the mirror reconstructed."

"Humph! Paths. Fragments. Mirrors. Mumbo jumbo. Is there a

single occupant of this flying contraption who can resist the temptation to speak in riddles?"

The Beetle gave vent to a rustling laugh, his head—or heads—blurring as he tipped it—or them—back. "Hah! Good old Trounce! I apologise if my answers feel to you like obfuscation."

"They don't feel like anything at all, least of all answers."

"Then I shall attempt to clarify. Let's start with a question. Can you agree, William, that at its heart, the universe turns on a single question, it being that either things exist or they don't?"

"I suppose."

"If the answer is that things don't exist, then we need go no further. Indeed, we cannot, for we aren't here. Since we patently are, then the answer is that things *do* exist. From that circumstance, further questions unfold. Is a thing this or is it that? Is it likely to do this or likely to do that? I put it to you that the answers to those questions are wholly dependent upon there being a conscious observer, that if no one is present to witness a thing be or a thing happen, it cannot be or happen at all, but must remain suspended between possibilities."

"Rhubarb!" Trounce put in impatiently. "The notion is preposterous."

"Is it? Then you suggest that when a tree falls in a forest, it makes a noise even if there's no one within hearing range?"

"Of course it bloody well does."

"Yet sound is merely a certain range of vibrations in the air—among many other vibrations—that impact against the ear and are then interpreted by the brain. If no ear is within range, there can be no interpretation, thus there are vibrations but no sound."

"Phonographic recording. A device left in the forest."

"Merely a bridge—a surrogate ear designed to document and reproduce the disturbance in the air, and one that, ultimately, still requires a real ear attached to a conscious mind."

Trounce scowled and squinted at the Beetle, as if, by sheer willpower, he could overcome the elusive quality of the man's head. "What will you claim next? That the tree cannot be seen if there's no one there to look at it? That it cannot be touched?"

"Quite so. All our senses operate within an extremely constrained sphere. What you see is a narrow range amid a vast sea of light, and if you were able to perceive the tiniest components of a substance, you would find no difference between what is solid and what is not, between what is considered an object and what is considered space." A slight shrug. Five heads. Three heads. One head. "It takes us back to the root question. Do things exist independently of us or do they not? Yes, they do, but only in the form of probability, neither this nor that until we decide."

Trounce gave a snort of derision. He cocked a thumb at Burton. "So the source of the Nile wasn't there until Sir Richard found it?"

Burton murmured, "I didn't find it. Speke did."

"It was believed to be there because we subjected the Nile to the most common of the narratives we habitually employ, it being that everything has its origin, its period of life, and its end; in the case of a river, its source, its course, and its mouth. The question was whether any European could reach the source, which for centuries was considered an impossibility. However, when something becomes more plausible to the observing mind than the opposite, then it is made actual. By the same token, we do not travel to the moon because such an achievement is inconceivable. One day, we'll think otherwise, and merely by thinking it, we'll sow the seeds that will ultimately make it not just possible but inevitable."

Trounce lowered his face into his hands. "By Jove!" came his muffled voice. "Now we're off to the blessed moon!"

Swinburne, who'd been sitting quietly with his brows drawn together, said, "Habitual narratives? You touch upon a matter I've oft considered. It strikes me that the human organism has a tendency to shoehorn all that's perceived into a limited number of preconstructed sequences, the most common of them being—as you suggest—that of a beginning, a middle, and an end. These are then endowed with an unwarranted veracity, as if the framework holds greater truth than the elements that are hung upon it."

"Bravo, Algy!" the Beetle replied. "You have pierced the heart of the matter, for sequences—narratives—when applied to a probability, either extinguish it or cause it to blossom into being. The notion of sequence is the notion of Time. Time is the factory of consciousness and reality is its product."

Burton opened his mouth to speak but, before he could utter a sound, Swinburne interrupted him.

"As a poet, I seek to write that which is timeless. I do so by employing structures based not upon sequence but on meter, juxtaposition, and rhyme."

"And that is how the mirror is repaired," the Beetle responded. "Not by forcing its fragments into a linear sequence but by piecing together corresponding edges and angles. Practically speaking—"

Trounce dropped his hands from his face and arched a sceptical eyebrow.

"—one must seek the truth through coincidences, patterns, themes, symbolic harmonies, and nonlinear correlations. In these, a unity can be apprehended, and in that can be seen a reflection of the self."

Burton said, "And your identity? The mirror reconstructed?"

He detected a slight smile amid the confusion of the Beetle's features, and for the briefest of instances, recognised his own face looking back at him.

"In all the many histories, Sir Richard, different versions of you have struggled with the consequences of Spring Heeled Jack's meddling. Across those time streams, your unified mind—shared between all your iterations and operating at an unconscious level where the only language is that of symbolism—has assembled and understood the meaning of events. In the mirror thus made manifest—in me—the totality of you is reflected. Swinburne is part of you. Trounce is part of you. Everything is part of you." The Beetle gave a dry chuckle. "If you divide the elements of that truth into sequence, you will render me an impossibility, for I obviously defy narratives—how can I be the consequence of an expedition that I myself instigated and which I'm now travelling back to instigate all over again?" He placed a hand over his heart. "I am a closed loop, an utter paradox that consumes itself until it is gone. In the normal manner of thinking, I am inconceivable. However, the intellects of many Burtons have been forced along strange routes to unusual conclusions, and thus was I made."

Burton regarded the Beetle. The whispery quality of the man's voice suddenly felt to him a little less human, as if air was being forced not through vocal cords but through internal petals.

He asked, "And now?"

"Now I must undertake various tasks in various periods of various histories in order to make my own existence possible. In one, I'll found an organisation called the League of Chimney Sweeps and will ensure that the Swinburne of that history is one day made an honorary member of it. I'll also stow away aboard another *Orpheus* that I might warn its crew that a saboteur is aboard. I'll see to it that a gentleman named Herbert Spencer is rescued from a gang of particularly dangerous fellows known as the Rakes. I'll arrange for a rogue occultist named Eliphas Levi to be shown the error of his ways. And in the time stream that is this ship's destination, I'll travel back a few months prior to its departure and will cultivate a red jungle in an abandoned factory." He smiled. "I must do what has already been done, and then I shall do it all again and again and again, and with each reiteration, the circle will tighten until it eventually makes itself extinct and the damage to time will be repaired, and there will be but one history and one Burton and one Swinburne and one Trounce and an infinity of unrealised probabilities."

There followed a short silence before Trounce mumbled, "As clear as mud."

Burton said, "It makes very little sense, yet I somehow understand it."

One, three, five heads nodded. "Uncountable Burtons, each contributing a unique insight to the subconscious intellect that links you all, each vaguely aware of the possible sum of its parts."

"Very well. I accept all that you have told us. You have not explained, though, why you have yanked these two fellows and me from our deathbeds."

"Pavement," Trounce corrected.

"I intend no ingratitude," Burton continued, "but I would like to know why I am here."

He felt a sudden sadness emanating from the strange figure before him. The Beetle flickered as if his presence had briefly folded to some other place, then he was back.

"*My* Swinburne and Trounce, if I might so call them, have remained in the year 2203, while I—well, let us say that the Burton who's returning to 1861 is not the Burton who departed."

"Not by a considerable degree," the explorer concurred somewhat dryly. "And I say that with confidence despite never having met the chap."

"So I intend to recruit you three as replacements."

Swinburne clapped his palms together and rubbed his hands. "Splendid!"

"Wait, Algy. Hear me out. It's a little more involved than that. You three men finished your lives with certain issues unresolved and—if you'll excuse the observation—with some measure of disappointment. I can offer you the opportunity to live again and to make different choices, but not here in the past of your own history, where you'd encounter only the same options. You'd also know what is to come, which means you could shape events to your own advantage—an irresistible prospect, which I cannot allow. However, if you travel sideways with us into *our* history, you'll arrive in an 1861 that is rather dissimilar to the one you remember. There, you'll be plunged into entirely new circumstances. You should know that the tightening of the circle, of which I've spoken, will cause events to develop with unnatural rapidity, and you'll be required to fight the instability that will undoubtedly result, including the consequences of the *Orpheus*'s return from the future. You'll become entangled in matters of considerable magnitude. They will change you. The second half of your new lives will be markedly different from the second half of your old lives, and they'll not be easy. Through them, you'll become a new Burton, a new Swinburne, and a new Trounce."

Again, a period of silence.

Burton murmured, "What if we decline?"

"I shall have no recourse but to return you to whence you came."

"Thunder and lightning!" Trounce cried out. "You'd condemn us to our deaths?"

"Condemn? Let me tell you, William, there is a beauty in the tranquillity and transcendence of death that you would yearn for if only you could know it in life. It is not the end you perceive it to be. It is simply a liberation from the constriction of narratives."

"How could you possibly know that?"

"I have died many times."

"Humph!"

"I accept," Swinburne said.

Burton sighed and remembered the pervasively cold ache of rheumatism and the stiffness of his old bones. He stared at the Beetle, seeing clearly only the dark pupils with their strangely metallic outer rims. He swallowed and spoke, his voice quiet and steady. "When I was a young man, I was convinced I'd one day be immortalised as the translator of *The Scented Garden*. Then the original manuscript, which I'd purchased from the library of the Emir of Sindh, went up in flames. As an old man, I pieced the damned thing together from memory, still believing it would secure my name for posterity. Then, I have learned, it was burned again, this time by—by—bismillah!—this time by Isabel, of all people! I was, it appears, on the wrong road from the start." He shrugged and clicked his tongue. "I accept."

The Beetle said, "William?"

Trounce, still sitting cross-legged, slapped a palm onto the deck. "Confound it! You've drugged me! Mesmerised me! Befuddled me with gobbledegook!"

"I've spoken the truth, and you know it."

"The deuce I do! And what of this other world of yours? This 1861? How in blue blazes are we to fit in? We'll not know up from down! Am I supposed to pretend to be this other Trounce? Masquerade as a Detective Inspector? Go home to my—to my—" His eyes suddenly welled up with tears. Angrily, he dragged his sleeve across his face and said, huskily, "to my wife?"

"A justified concern, my friend, but already the mere proximity of this ship and its crew has given rise to unaccountable memories, is that not so?"

The policeman offered a reluctant grunt of confirmation.

"When you are fully immersed in the other history, such recollections will prevail. It will feel somewhat akin to slipping your foot into a comfortable old shoe."

"And what of our current memories?" Swinburne asked.

"They'll rapidly fade into the background. With an effort, you'll be able to raise them, should you feel inclined to do so."

Trounce again clapped his hands over his eyes. "Oh, God help me! To blazes with the whole thing! I accept! I accept!"

The Beetle took a hold of his hood and pulled it up. From within its shadow, he said, "In my former incarnation, I—which is to say, *you*, Sir Richard—wrote a report outlining the events of this expedition. Certain matters were excluded from it, primarily those circumstances that led to my birth. It is vitally important that my existence remain a secret, for I am the embodiment of the Oxford equation and am thus the seed of humanity's future. I must be allowed to enter the collective consciousness in the correct manner. Edward Oxford's time spanning exploits caused growth to occur out of season and you have seen the consequences. Now I am eliminating the weeds and preparing the ground. No more false starts. No more mistakes. So, sealed lips, please, gentlemen. The Beetle must never be mentioned. Agreed?"

They each made a sound of acquiescence.

"As for you three, no one but you, me, Sadhvi Raghavendra, Krishnamurthy, Gooch, and Lawless will ever know that you are not exactly who you purport to be, and after a short while such a distinction will cease to matter, anyway. Sergeant Trounce, you are hereby promoted to Detective Inspector. I wish you well. Sir Richard, Algernon, I will remain aboard this vessel when you leave it and shall depart in my own manner and without ceremony. Do what needs to be done and rely on your instincts, for they will guide you correctly. Now, if you'll excuse me, I have a great deal of work to do." He made a slight gesture of dismissal with the fingers of his right hand.

Burton knew he'd get nothing more from his mystifying counterpart. He stood and offered a helping hand to Trounce, who took it and heaved himself to his feet. Swinburne hopped up, too, and they backed away from the motionless Beetle then turned, opened the door, and stepped out into the corridor.

Sadhvi Raghavendra was waiting.

Burton regarded her and felt disorientated. He knew he'd last seen her in this same place but also thought he'd last seen her standing beside the Monument Flower in 2203.

"I expect he gave you a lot to think about," she said to them.

"He gave me nothing but a bloody headache," Trounce complained. "'Scuse my language, ma'am."

"As always, it's bloody excused. The headache is no surprise. The black diamonds in the Beetle's skull are not the only ones we have aboard. In fact, we are carrying a lot of them. The resonance they emit powerfully affects the psychic parts of the human mind. In the average person, proximity causes headaches, though those aboard this ship have become somewhat immune. In people with well-developed clairvoyant abilities, the gems, even from considerable distance, can cause death."

"Humph! As far as I'm aware, my mind has no clairvoyant parts at all."

"But nevertheless suffers due to the emanations. Either that or your session in the Slug and Lettuce is wearing off. Come through to the lounge. Let's get some coffee into you."

As they followed her along the passage, Burton asked, "Sadhvi, what happened? What was the rapture?"

"How much did the Beetle show you?"

"My—or should I say *his*?—final moments in the brass machine. His birth, or arrival from death, or whatever it was."

"Ah. Or should you say *yours*. Baffling, isn't it?"

"Good Lord," Trounce groaned. "Will you people never let up?"

They entered into the comfortable chamber, which was now occupied only by Pox, who greeted them with, "Ghastly sponge heads!"

"Make yourselves comfortable. We'll be under way in few minutes. Captain Lawless is on the bridge as usual, Daniel is in the engine room, and Maneesh is attending to the Nimtz generator. A tiny crew, but most of the ship is automated."

"Nimtz generator," Swinburne said. "As was spoken of in our shared vision. Exactly what is it?"

"Exactly, I couldn't say, such matters not being my area of expertise, but basically it is a machine created by Edward Oxford and reproduced, albeit in a much larger and clumsier form, by Charles Babbage. It manipulates something called chronostatic energy, thus making movement through time possible."

"I see. It sounds like uncommon nonsense."

Burton smiled at the poet's paraphrasing of *Alice in Wonderland*. *Uncommon nonsense, indeed!*

The three men settled into armchairs positioned around a low table onto which Raghavendra placed an already steaming coffee pot, four cups, a jug of milk, and a bowl of sugar. She sat, leaned forward, and attended to their beverages, obviously familiar with their preferences. No milk but four heaped teaspoons of sugar for Burton, milk and two for Trounce, milk and one for Swinburne. For herself, just a splash of milk.

Old friends, some of whom had never met before, reunited.

She sipped, put her cup down, and leaned back.

"March the nineteenth, 2203. Daniel took the black diamonds from the brass man's babbage and slotted them into the holes in the old man's head. As each diamond went in, the skin closed over it. For about twenty minutes, nothing notable happened, though I sensed a presence gradually building within the prone form. At precisely half past nine, he opened his eyes and smiled."

Raghavendra blinked rapidly and pursed her lips. She shook her head slightly.

"It's very difficult to find the words for what then occurred. A very powerful wave of what I can only describe as clairvoyant energy was transmitted from him. It was utterly overwhelming. Those of us from 1860 were knocked senseless by it. We recovered some few minutes later to find that Algy—I mean the other Swinburne—and William and Tom Bendyshe were—" She stopped and frowned. "Different."

"In what manner?" Burton asked.

Raghavendra lifted a hand and felt her hair, caught her bottom lip between her teeth, and appeared to look inward, as if putting her thoughts into order. "They and the man we now call the Beetle had become very difficult to look at. It was as if they each had multiple heads occupying the same space, there and yet, at the very same time, elsewhere. But there was something else. It was like—um—" She stopped, considered, then went on, "There is a certain component of the human system, generally unrecognised by anatomists, that is called by clairvoyants the astral body. As far as I understand, it is a subtle electromagnetic field that follows the contours of the flesh but which also, in an exceedingly rarefied form, extends some distance outward from it."

"The *farr*, according to Persian tradition," Burton said. "It translates as *glory*."

"Nincompoop breeders!" Pox shrieked.

Raghavendra ignored the bird. "Ah. Then I shall employ that word, for it is a perfect fit. What I sensed was that my friends were now each in possession of a vastly more powerful and very greatly extended astral body. In fact, their *farrs* were so expanded that they commingled not only with each other but also with the equally amplified astral bodies of every individual on the globe. In short, humanity had become one single organism of which every man and woman was but an element. Furthermore, the red jungle had become an integral component of that organism, and the grand total, the immense and unified *Being*, radiated a sheer joy that I could barely grasp, so intense was it. That, Sir Richard, was your *glory*. Nathaniel, Maneesh, Daniel, and I were virtually incapacitated by it. For sure, we all had in our bloodstreams the pollen and nanotechnology that was now a constituent of this new humanity, but in us it was functioning to resist the rapture rather than to incorporate us into it. Plainly, with our origin lying in the year 1860, we were not sufficiently progressed to withstand such a wonder. Indeed, we all felt horribly uncomfortable, as if we were suddenly a mote in evolution's eye. The Beetle, Algy, William, and Tom assisted us to the *Orpheus*. There, they bid us farewell. I regret to say that our parting was not as I should have liked it. Their presence was too much for us to withstand. I felt as if I were staring wide-eyed into the sun. We stumbled aboard, somehow managed to close the doors behind us, and instructed the ship to take us home. We then collapsed and lost consciousness. When we awoke it was to find to our astonishment that the Beetle had accompanied us aboard. He'd also taken command of the ship, slowing its passage backward through time, that he might, as he put it, 'start stitching the wounds in history,' though how he means to achieve that end, I cannot tell you. He also proposed that we should voyage sideways into alternate histories, first to fetch Pox then to pluck you gentlemen from the end of your lives."

"And here we are," Burton said. He picked up his cup and drank from it. His hand was shaking.

Too much to take in. It's real. I know it's real. But how can it be?

A deep thrumming sounded, the floor vibrated, and, through a porthole, he saw the trees drop out of sight.

Raghavendra said, "Off we go. Home to our own world and our own time, where you three will establish yourselves and live again."

"Cretinously!" Pox contributed. "Twonk rubbers!"

"My first task shall be to compose a poem," Swinburne announced, "comprised entirely of that feathered fiend's insults. It'll be a masterpiece."

Burton stood, crossed to the glass, and looked out. He saw the patchwork fields sinking beneath the ship and spotted again the wall and the small group of people standing by it. He could see their faces were turned toward the *Orpheus*, though they were too distant for their expressions to be clear. He guessed they reflected absolute astonishment.

"Our destination, Sadhvi. Events have unfolded differently there. Does Lieutenant Speke still live?"

"No. He died a hero at Berbera in 'fifty-four."

"A better death than he suffered here."

"Most assuredly."

"And my wi—and Isabel. How did she die?"

"Not well, I'm afraid, Sir Richard. She was murdered by one of your enemies."

The ship plunged into the clouds. There was nothing to see outside but grey. Burton's face was reflected in the window. He watched the ghostly other and the ghostly other watched him.

"My counterpart has enemies?"

"He is, or was—and now you are—the king's agent, commissioned by the prime minister on behalf of His Majesty to protect the empire from threats too peculiar in nature for the police. It has involved antagonists. Some of them have been very powerful."

Burton raised his eyebrows. He counted backward from Gladstone, the prime minister of 1890.

The Marquess of Salisbury. Gladstone again. The Marquess. Gladstone. Disraeli. Gladstone. Disraeli—Gad! Those two went at it like duellists!—the Earl of Derby, John Russell, and—ah!

"Your Palmerston apparently possessed considerably more faith in Richard Burton than my own did."

"My Palmerston was hanged as a traitor in 1842."

Burton turned. "Good God!"

"Our prime minister is Disraeli. Our king is George the Fifth, the son of Ernest Augustus of Hanover."

Trounce uttered a sound of surprise. "Not as barmy as his father, I should hope! And what of Albert? What has become of him?"

"The prince works in a diplomatic capacity, and with consummate skill. He brokered a peace accord between our empire and the German Confederation."

Swinburne said, "My hat! Then your history is certainly far different to this. We are a republic, and in my final years, a war with the *Deutsches Reich* was all but assured."

Raghavendra nodded. "That war will come in this and in every other history but my own. It will devastate two generations of men, lay Europe flat, and extend across the entire globe. The consequences of it will reach so far forward in time that the very evolution of the human race, the rapture, will be badly delayed. However, where we are now going, you three gentlemen—together with a faithful band of followers among whom this crew is counted—have created conditions through which the great disaster will be averted."

Swinburne's left leg twitched with such vigour that he kicked the table and slopped the coffee. "Us? But I'm a mere poet! Richard is an explorer and writer! Mr. Trounce is a policeman!"

"And I, a nurse." Raghavendra turned her palms upward. "History is shaped by individuals. No matter a person's circumstances, all have a part to play. Not one single man or woman can be counted as insignificant."

Orpheus's voice suddenly reverberated through the ship. "Prepare yourselves, peculiar creatures. We are about to traverse time. Sideways and backward. Destination: midnight of the nineteenth of March, 1861. A primitive era due to your ridiculously inadequate ability to organise yourselves."

Pox blew a raspberry.

Raghavendra said, "I warn you, this will feel a little strange. It used to be a lot worse, but since the ship's brain was improved, our jumps through time have been considerably easier on our stomachs."

"Perhaps that compensates a little for the brain's personality," Swinburne suggested.

"I doubt the captain would agree. He considers the babbage an absolute pain in the—"

Raghavendra, her words, and the ship blinked into whiteness.

"—neck."

In an instant, everything was back, but the lounge was suddenly darker, there now being no daylight streaming through the portholes, and when Burton looked out, he saw neither cloud nor the Somerset countryside but rather the twinkling lights of nighttime London.

"We're descending," Raghavendra said. "Finish your coffee and take up your hats and canes, gentlemen. I'll escort you to the exit. We'll be staying overnight in Battersea Power Station before meeting with the minister in the morning."

A curious presentiment caused Burton to clear his throat. Something lurked at the periphery of his mind and refused to come into focus. Before it could be clarified, the ship's voice sounded again.

"Jump successful. We'll be on the ground in two minutes. Welcome home, peculiar creatures."

The three men followed Raghavendra out of the lounge and along to the door through which they'd entered the ship. Trounce glanced at Burton, and the explorer recognised that this man, whom he'd met a just little while ago but who already felt like an old friend, was feeling nervous. He offered him a slight nod of encouragement. The policeman rubbed a thumb over his moustache and said, "Then it's done. We've left everything behind. I know you'll think me a silly beggar, but I can't get it out of my head that I'll never wear my blue striped pyjamas again. Of all the blessed things to miss! A pair of bloomin' pyjamas!"

"My pipe," Swinburne said. He tapped his chest. "At this age, I hadn't taken up the habit, but in my dotage I enjoyed nothing better than a contemplative puff in the garden." He took a deep breath and exhaled with satisfaction. "Young lungs! I shall start smoking earlier and reap the benefits all the more!"

"That's the spirit," Raghavendra said as they arrived at the boarding hatch. "Look forward, not back."

There came a gentle bump and the ship was immediately filled with a deepening whine as its motors slowed.

"1861," Krishnamurthy announced. "I wonder what we've missed? Shall we see?" He took hold of a handle on the left side of the door and nodded toward its opposite. "Would you, Sir Richard?"

Acting without thinking, Burton took hold of the other handle and, in concert with Krishnamurthy, lifted, pulled, and slid the door aside. A ramp emerged from the bottom lip of the portal and smoothly slid down to the ground. It was only then that it registered with Burton he'd somehow known how to do something he'd never done before.

Chilly night air rushed in carrying with it droplets of moisture and a multitude of disagreeable odours. Filled with curiosity, the explorer peered out and was dazzled by the blazing lights of the power station beside which the *Orpheus* had landed. The structure, which didn't exist in his own world, was blocky and massive, with four tall chimneys rising from its corners, each of them, by the looks of it, fashioned from copper.

Daniel Gooch exited the lower deck, joined them, and placed a metal hand on Burton's shoulder. "I expect you chaps could do with something to eat. It's a bit late in the day, but we can't expect our inner clocks to immediately readjust, can we? Come on."

However, before they could step out of the ship, they were interrupted by Lawless, who emerged from the door to the bridge. "Mr. Gooch? I think we might have a problem."

Gooch turned. "Eh? But we're landed."

"We are. And the moment we touched the ground, the Mark Three announced that it had received a transmission."

"A what? Here? There's no radio in 1861, Captain. What manner of transmission? Who from?"

"That's the problem. When I asked, the babbage didn't respond, and is remaining silent."

"It can't choose not to answer."

"I know, yet I can't get a single word out of it."

"That's both strange and uncharacteristic. Mind you, if the blessed contraption has developed a fault, we must thank our lucky stars that it's happened now, rather than during our voyage. I'll examine it in the morning. Our stomachs must take priority."

Lawless made a sound of assent. "I'll join you for supper after I've given the ship the once-over."

Returning his attention to Burton and the others, Gooch led them down the ramp.

The explorer pulled his coat tighter. Trieste had been warm. So, too, had Bath. Here, the air was wintery.

They crossed hard, well-worn ground to a huge gate in the station wall. A normal-sized door was inset into it and upon this the engineer rapped his knuckles. "Hey there! Open up!"

Immediately, the lock clicked and the portal swung inward. A figure stepped into view.

Burton, Swinburne, and Trounce all took a pace backward. A manlike machine had responded to Gooch's hail. Constructed from polished brass, it was slender and about five feet five inches tall, with a canister-shaped head. Its "face," across which the lights of the *Orpheus* reflected, was featureless but for three raised circular fittings set vertically in the front. The topmost of them resembled a tiny porthole, and through it could be seen a great many spinning gears, as small, complex, and finely crafted as the workings of a pocket watch. The middle circle enclosed a mesh grille, and the bottom one was simply a hole out of which three very fine five-inch-long wires projected. The neck consisted of thin shafts and cables, swivel joints and hinges. A slim cylinder formed the mechanical man's trunk. Panels were cut out of it, revealing cogwheels and springs, delicate little crankshafts, gyroscopes, flywheels, and a pendulum. The thin arms ended in three-fingered hands. The legs were sturdy and tubular; the feet, oval-shaped and slightly domed.

It did not at all resemble, Burton thought, the hulking mechanism his other self had occupied in the future, being far smaller and more delicate in appearance.

"Good evening," it said in a pleasantly mellifluous and lilting voice. "My name is Fiddlesticks. I presume, by the arrival of the *Orpheus*, that you are Mr. Gooch? Please, come in. My masters will be delighted to see you."

"Hallo, hallo!" Gooch exclaimed. "Have there been developments? New voice boxes? You sound superb!"

The engineer passed through the door into a courtyard and stepped aside to allow entry to Burton, Swinburne, Trounce, Raghavendra, and Krishnamurthy.

Fiddlesticks said, "Mr. Babbage made many improvements to his devices before his disappearance, sir. Our voices being but one of them. This way, please."

They followed the contraption toward another set of big double doors.

"Disappearance?" Gooch asked.

"Mr. Babbage hasn't been seen for the past four months or so. No one knows where he's gone."

"Good Lord!"

The clockwork man attended to a lock then opened one of the inner doors sufficiently for them to pass through it into the station.

Burton shielded his eyes. Big glass globes were hanging from the high ceiling of the cathedral-sized interior. Captive lightning crackled and popped inside them, casting incandescence into every corner of the great hall. As his vision adjusted to it, he saw a vast floor crowded with bewildering contrivances of metal and glass. There were things that pumped and sparked and buzzed; things that showered sparks and sent lines of electrical energy between themselves, snaking through the air, so that the station was filled with the sharp tang of ozone; things that assaulted the senses and muddled the mind.

Nearby, an elderly, white-haired man was bent over a knot of pipes examining a row of gauges, the indicators of which were swinging wildly back and forth. Another mechanical man was standing beside him, and Burton now realised that there were a great many of the clockwork devices attending to various tasks. Machines operating machines.

"Mr. Faraday!" Gooch called.

The man at the pipes straightened, turned, and cried out, "Daniel! You're back, by gosh!"

"We are," Gooch countered.

Faraday walked over, a little unsteadily—Burton guessed him to be nigh on seventy years old—and shook the engineer's hand, then Burton's, then each of the rest in turn. His eyes were rheumy and his manner rather vague. "How wonderful to—to—um—to see you again. We'd practically

104

given up on you. Splendid! Er. My goodness! Was the—the thing—the mission—was it a success?"

Gooch nodded. "It was."

"And the—er—the future? What was it like? Marvellous? What scientific advances? In what state the people? Do we achieve the whatchamacallit—Utopia, I mean? Have you brought machineries of the future back with you? By gosh! Can I examine them?"

"Steady, man!" Gooch protested. "Don't overexcite yourself. We thought it best not to infect our own time with too much. The Mark Three babbage calculator aboard the *Orpheus* has been enhanced with future techniques, but aside from that, we are empty handed."

Faraday gave a disappointed sigh. "I suppose you've acted correctly. As Mr. Whatsisname—er, Darwin—would no doubt say, um—"

"Evolution must develop at its own pace," Raghavendra offered.

"Yes. Exactly. But—" Again, a despondent sigh. "But you say the Mark Three has been augmented? May I ask how?"

"A full explanation later," Gooch said.

"But will you not give me at least a hint? Something to think about?"

Gooch smiled at the other's impatience. "In a nutshell, Mr. Faraday, easily manufactured crystalline silicates will be at the heart of calculating machines in the future. The substance offers near infinite capacity for information storage and processing. The Mark Three has been supplemented with such, and now operates with greater rapidity and efficiency."

"I say! How fascinating. Crystalline silicates, hey? I look forward to seeing them demonstrated."

"Hmm. That might be easier said than done. Apparently the Mark Three has just lost its voice. A fault of some sort."

Krishnamurthy said, "Mr. Faraday, what's this about Charles Babbage making off?"

"Oof!" the scientist responded, ushering them across the floor. "He hasn't been seen since—um—since—since—when was it now? Yes, November, I believe. November. He removed all his work over the course of a week. No one realised what he was doing until it was too late."

"What on earth could have prompted that?" Gooch asked. "Was he acting abnormally in any way?"

"No more so than usual. His is a great loss, Mr. Gooch. He took all his prototypes with him, all his—you know—his—er—blueprints and notes. Made off with the things, too."

"Things?" Gooch asked.

"The—er—the black diamonds. All of 'em."

"I'll be damned!" Gooch shot a loaded glance at Burton, as if to ask, *Do you realise the diamonds' significance?*

The explorer did, though he wasn't sure how.

"He had absolutely no right to take the stones," Gooch protested.

"Indeed not," Faraday agreed.

With Fiddlesticks at his side, the old man led them between coils, towers, banks of dials, and panels of switches until they came to a central area of workbenches and control consoles. Here, Krishnamurthy and Raghavendra uttered inarticulate shouts of surprise, and Gooch, stumbling to a halt, threw out his four hands and shouted, "Idiot! I'm a confounded idiot! My God! I should have realised!"

Their eyes were fixed on a giant, six-armed figure of brass, standing as motionless as a statue beside one of the benches.

Burton, too, couldn't avert his gaze. He felt as if he were somehow looking at himself, and a terrible sense of claustrophobia gripped him.

"Sir?" Faraday said to Gooch.

"Brunel. He's here."

Faraday shrugged. "Ah. Yes. Well. Er. I'm afraid that's debatable. We've been unable to revive him. The old chap hasn't shown the slightest sign of life. He's not budged an inch."

Gooch shook his head and took Faraday by the elbow. "No, you don't understand. My reference was to the body not to the mind. I'm sorry to have to tell you that Mr. Brunel is dead. We learned that in the future. His presence in the machine's diamonds has been overwritten by a fragment of Spring Heeled Jack's mind." He jabbed a metal finger toward the motionless figure. "That is our enemy. He'll remain in this state for many years. They'll put him in the British Museum, and there he'll bide his time until, eventually, he'll revive and establish a foul autocracy. Spring Heeled Jack will rule the world until we defeat him."

"Gosh! Really?"

Krishnamurthy stepped forward and peered up into the likeness of Brunel's face that adorned the front of the brass man's head. "Um, Daniel, couldn't we now prevent any of that from ever happening? What if we melted him down and found a means to drive the presence out of the diamonds?"

"That wouldn't be difficult," Gooch responded. "A strong electrical current passed through the stones would be sufficient."

"Phew!" Krishnamurthy said. "We could prevent everything we experienced in the future from ever happening."

Gooch put his hands to his head. "What a paradox! It would mean we couldn't do what we've already done. Nevertheless—" He ran metal fingers along the line of his jaw.

For half a minute, no one spoke. The lightning sizzled overhead. Burton watched its light playing across Brunel's polished brass form.

Brunel's? Oxford's? Mine?

He shuddered.

"It appears, gentlemen," Sadhvi Raghavendra said, "that our mission requires further action in order be completed. However, this is perhaps the first occasion where we can claim that time is on our side, so before we commit what remains of Spring Heeled Jack to oblivion, may I suggest we see to our own needs first? My hollow stomach requires urgent attention."

Gooch nodded. "Quite right, Sadhvi." He addressed Fiddlesticks. "Would you see to it that some food is brought to Mr. Brunel's office? A cold platter will do. Have rooms prepared for us, too. We'll eat, sleep, and deal with conundrums on the morrow."

"Right away, sir."

The next ninety minutes were, for Burton—and he could see for Swinburne and Trounce, too—exhausting. He was, he had to remind himself, an old man. Not physically any more but still mentally, for sure. It had been a long, long time since he'd had to process so much that was new and strange, and for now, at least, his capacity to do so had reached its limit. He ate without tasting and listened to Gooch, Faraday, Krishnamurthy, Raghavendra, and—a little later—Nathaniel Lawless converse without full cognisance of what they were saying. He vaguely gathered that the Mark III had altogether ceased to function, and the Beetle had somehow vanished from the *Orpheus* without so much as a good-bye. When talk turned to world affairs, he learned that Britain had established a frail peace with China, the latter caving in after Lord Elgin had bombed the Old Summer Palace; in America, Lincoln had been elected, but the states were dropping out of the union like toppling dominoes; Italy had unified; Bazalgette's London sewer system was now fully operational; the East End, which had burned to the ground almost two years ago, was now being rebuilt, its northern parts being turned into residential districts while its riverside area would—like the Tooley Street district on the opposite side of the Thames—consist mainly of wharfs and warehouses; Disraeli and Gladstone's notorious battle of wits, which in his world had commenced toward the end of the 'sixties was, in this one, already well established; and, since the signing of the trade alliance with the German Confederation, there were some who were already—and accurately—predicting that the British Empire would one day be called the Anglo-Saxon Empire.

Too much to take in.

His eyelids drooped.

He saw Isabel.

He saw flames.

He saw his young self, gazing, with haunted eyes, out from a mirror. Behind his reflection, there was a medium-sized chamber containing a bed. Barely recalling the end of the meal and not sure how he'd ended up in the room—and not caring—Burton turned, stumbled across the floor, collapsed fully clothed onto the blankets, and immediately dropped into the deepest of sleeps.

He dreamed that his reflection remained in the mirror and stared at him as he slumbered and that the room behind the watcher was as real as the one it reflected.

THE MINISTER AND A
MECHANICAL IRREGULARITY

The difference between a misfortune and a calamity is this: If
Gladstone fell into the Thames, it would be a misfortune. But
if someone dragged him out again, that would be a calamity.
—Benjamin Disraeli

*Allāhu Allāhu Allāhu Haqq. Allāhu Allāhu Allāhu Haqq. Allāhu
Allāhu Allāhu Haqq. Allāhu Allāhu Allāhu Haqq.*

"By my Aunt Blodwyn's bulging bustle!"

Swinburne's exclamation broke into Burton's internal chant. The
explorer opened his eyes and sighed. The world would not be ignored.
There was no escaping it.

Trounce was sitting beside him in a landau, Swinburne and Gooch
opposite.

They'd departed Battersea Power Station half an hour ago—at
around nine o'clock—and were being followed by a second carriage carrying Raghavendra, Krishnamurthy, and Lawless.

The explorer moved his tongue around his mouth, feeling the gaps
where the spear had, in Berbera, knocked out a couple of his molars.
None of the remaining teeth were rotten or worn.

He was still young.

It's not going away.

"What is it now, Algy?" he murmured.

109

"A two-legged vehicle," Swinburne answered. "Walking!"

"A stamper," Gooch said. "Put into commission far more quickly than I anticipated. I thought they'd take at least another couple of years to develop." He clicked his tongue forlornly. "With Brunel dead and Babbage gone astray, it might be the DOGS' last innovation for some considerable time. By golly, I've never known the station to be so badly attended. There are more clockwork people in it than fleshy ones. It's as if the heart's gone out of the place."

"Dogs?" Swinburne asked, and answered himself. "Ah, yes, the Department of Guided Science."

Looking out of the window, Burton wondered whether a cessation of Battersea Power Station's operations might not be a good thing for London. He'd always considered the capital too overcrowded and noisy, but the metropolis he remembered paled in comparison to what he saw now. The drizzle, the chill, and the buildings were all familiar, but the streets were another story entirely. Their fringes were seething with people: lords and ladies, vagabonds and thieves, vendors and entertainers, clerks and businessmen, urchins and prostitutes; while throbbing and rumbling through the middle of the city's swollen arteries there was such a heterogeneous jumble of vehicles that the explorer was hard put to separate them from one another. Horse-drawn carts, cabs, and carriages were present in profusion, but clanking and grinding and rattling among them were contraptions of outlandish and in some cases ludicrous design, all powered by steam, and all pumping a billowing veil of vapour across the scene, so that they waxed and waned in and out of sight, as if uncertain of their own essence. The stamper was there—a brass-bound and studded box of polished oak with windows and doors, carrying passengers inside, the whole of it raised up on mighty legs of metal with backward-pointing knees. The thing pounded along, honking and hissing like an enraged goose, sending cursing people and whinnying horses scattering from its path. Too, there were many mechanical carriages like the one in which Burton rode, identical in form to the usual landaus, hansoms, growlers, and phaetons, but each was pulled, rather than by a horse, by a small tall-chimneyed locomotive similar in design to Stephenson's famous *Rocket*, though less than half the size. Of "penny farthing" bicycles, there were countless, but instead of relying on their riders' leg muscles for momentum, they were powered by miniature engines. There were also metal spheres, their motive force being a vertical band that rotated vertically from the back to the front around their circumference. They were rolling in and out of the traffic like giant marbles.

Those were the means of transportation that Burton managed to at least half comprehend, but there were others which he did not: contrivances that banged and groaned, jiggled and bounced; that jerked or lurched or rolled or hopped along in a manner that couldn't possibly offer anything resembling comfort to their drivers and passengers. He wondered why anyone had bothered to create such impractical machines. The answer came to him in the form of a maxim commonly quoted in this world: *The DOGS bark, "Because we can!"*

The madness wasn't confined to the ground; the sky was teeming with it, too. There were leather armchairs with spinning wings somehow keeping them aloft, titanic rotorships like the *Orpheus*, and unsteady-looking constructions that flapped metal wings and dipped and bobbed through the air. Of the latter, Gooch noted, "Ornithopters! My colleagues must have solved the problems. The damned things were always impossible to control."

"How are collisions avoided?" Burton asked.

"There's a lot of sky. Unlike ground travel, one has altitude to play with. Nevertheless, flight remains hazardous. There's an average of three smashes per day. Probably more now. It appears considerably busier up there than it was a year ago."

Their landau steered into Trafalgar Square and entered the Strand. Burton looked with interest at Parliament's clock tower, the home of the famous Big Ben bell. Partially concealed by a web of scaffolding, it was almost twice as tall as he remembered, and its architecture was considerably altered. Upon making an enquiry about it to Gooch, he was told, "The old one was destroyed by a bomb." Immediately, the explorer recalled the event as if he'd been there.

He sighed and glanced at Swinburne and Trounce. The poet appeared to be enjoying himself immensely, craning his neck as he leaned out of the window, peering this way and that, taking it all in, careless of the steam and coal smoke that curled around him. Trounce, by contrast, was sitting pale faced and nervous, holding his bowler by its brim and sliding it around and around through his fingers.

The three of them had, over breakfast at the station, shared the fact that they'd each awoken with their heads full of new information. Burton, for example, now knew that he lived not in Trieste but at 14 Montagu Place, a house he recalled having rented a room in at some point in his other life—though, peculiarly, as much as he tried, he couldn't pinpoint exactly when. Similarly, Swinburne was currently resident at 16 Cheyne Walk, which he shared with the artist Dante Gabriel Rossetti, it being a house he'd moved into in 1862 in his former existence but which, here, he'd apparently occupied considerably earlier.

Burton found himself clinging to mundane information such as this, for it gave to him a sense that he'd been reborn into a proper corporeal world rather than into an unfathomable and unanticipated heaven or hell. Unfortunately, there were other recollections, which—as much as he tried to suppress them—insistently arose to suggest that hell might be a much more viable possibility.

Isabel had been killed by a *nosferatu*. A vampire.

An older Burton from yet another history had inadvertently created this one.

There had been confrontations with crazed scientists, with clairvoyant dictators, with the rampaging forces of the Prussian Empire, with werewolves and monsters.

It was all confused, entangled, and illogical, as if cause was refusing to always precede effect, as if an event in one history could have consequences in another.

Time streams, Raghavendra called them, a term coined by Bertie Wells.

He wondered who Bertie Wells was, then pictured in his mind's eye a small man dying two nasty deaths.

He shuddered.

Allāhu Allāhu Allāhu Haqq.

He couldn't reenter the meditation, couldn't avoid the man he was tumbling into.

Sir Richard Francis Burton: king's agent.

The landau rocked to a halt, and the driver banged on the roof and called down, "Venetia Hotel, gents."

They exited the cabin, jumping down to the pavement. Trounce inadvertently bumped into an individual who was strapped into a machine that carried him along on four mechanical legs.

"Watch where you're stepping, man!" the pedestrian protested.

The Scotland Yard man managed an uncertain "humph!" and watched incredulously as the quadruped scuttled away.

"Three and six," the driver told them.

"I'll think you'll find it's a shilling," Swinburne countered.

The corners of Burton's mouth twitched up. Different world, same old friend. There was comfort in that, at least.

Gooch paid the driver the proper fare, despite the poet's further objections, and they waited while the second carriage stopped and its passengers disembarked.

"How do you like our London?" Raghavendra asked Burton as she approached.

"It's an insane asylum."

Trounce muttered, "Seconded."

Captain Lawless, at her side, smiled and gave a grunt of agreement. "That's why I used to prefer to stay in the *Orpheus*."

"Used to?" Burton asked.

"That bloody mechanical brain has taken the pleasure out of it."

The group—Burton, Swinburne, Trounce, Gooch, Raghavendra, Krishnamurthy, and Lawless—mounted the steps of the Royal Venetia Hotel and were greeted at its door by a clockwork man upon whose chest plate the initials R. V. H. were engraved. "Shall I have the bellboy fetch your luggage from the vehicles, sirs?"

"We have none," Burton responded. "We're merely visiting a guest."

The machine opened the portal to them. "Right you are, sir. Mr. Bromley, the reception clerk, is at his desk to your left as you enter. Good day to you."

As they walked into the lobby, the clerk looked up, recognised Burton and acknowledged him with raised brows and a polite nod, and called out, "He's expecting you, Sir Richard. Nice to see you again."

Gooch murmured an explanation. "I sent Pox last night to announce our arrival."

"I hope the insults were pithy."

Burton straight away wondered why he'd expressed such a sentiment.

They climbed the ornate staircase to the fifth floor and passed along a corridor to suite 5. Automatically, Burton took the lead, and when he arrived at the door, he eyed it for a moment before, with a mystifying reluctance, raising his panther-headed cane and rapping on it. Half a minute later, the door swung open to reveal another clockwork man.

"Hello, Grumbles," Burton said.

Grumbles. My brother's servant. Wait! My brother? My brother is—the minister?

"Good morning, gentlemen, ma'am. Will you come in, please? The minister is in his reading room. May I take your hats, coats and canes?"

"Nice new voice, Grumbles," Gooch said.

"Thank you, sir. It suits very well."

After handing over their outdoor garb, the group—the word *chrononauts* persistently occurred to Burton—was led by the gently whirring and ticking mechanism through a parlour and into a large library. The chamber was all books. They lined every wall from floor to ceiling, teetered in tall stacks on the deep red carpet, and were strewn haphazardly over the various tables, chairs, and sideboards. In the midst of them, by the window, a giant of a man, wrapped in a threadbare red dressing gown, occupied an enormous wing-backed armchair of scuffed and cracked leather. His hair was brown and untidy, and from it, a deep scar ran jaggedly down the broad forehead to bisect the left eyebrow. His eyes, which fixed on Burton as he entered, were intensely black. The nose, obviously once broken, had been reset crookedly, and the mouth—the upper lip cleft by another scar—was permanently twisted into a superior sneer. It was a face every bit as brutal in appearance as Burton's own, but the heavy jaw was buried beneath bulging jowls, and the neck was lost in rolls of fat which undulated down into a vast belly sagging over thick legs. The fellow was so obese that, despite the two walking sticks propped against one of the tables, it was impossible to imagine him in motion.

"So you're back, at last," the minister said. He narrowed his eyes at Burton. "You look different."

You can bloody well talk!

While it was true that Burton was astonished at his sibling's corpulence, the thought hadn't been just a sarcastic reaction. The Edward Burton of his own history, after being severely beaten by Singhalese villagers in 1856, had become so pathologically withdrawn that, by 1858, he wasn't speaking at all and, the following year, was committed to Surrey County Lunatic Asylum. He'd still been there in 1890.

"We were—we were away for over a year," the explorer stammered.

"I'm well aware of that. Why did I have to wait? However long you spent there, you could have been back a minute after your departure. For crying out loud, if you have the ability to transcend time, why not bloody well use it? All of you, find somewhere to sit. Grumbles, serve tea, coffee, or whatever."

Gooch, clearing books from a chair, said, "We felt it wise to remain true to subjective time."

"You didn't consider that it would be in the interests of the empire for the prime minister to know the outcome of your expedition sooner rather than later?"

Gooch sat and, out of habit, looked at Burton for support.

Burton spoke without thinking. "As its leader, I judged otherwise. And please bear in mind, brother, that those of us who travelled aboard the *Orpheus* have witnessed three and a half centuries of the empire's future. It might be argued that we can comprehend what is best for it better than anyone else, and that includes you."

That'll hit where it hurts!

With a slight shock, he realised that he'd slipped into his counterpart's role as if it were second nature. He knew, as if he'd always known, that Edward, in addition to being the minister of chronological affairs, was also Disraeli's most trusted advisor. Indeed, the information at his fat fingertips was so deep and so broad ranging in nature that, on occasion, it might be justifiably suspected that Edward was the empire's primary mover and shaker in the great games currently being played between Britain, Prussia, Russia, and China. To suggest to Edward that anyone knew more than he concerning such matters was to strike a blow where it counted.

The minister responded with a taut silence, steepled his fingers in front of his chin, and locked eyes with Burton, who, while matching the implacable stare, realised that somewhere along the way the competitive relationship of their youth had got very, very out of hand.

He felt that he was in over his head. He wanted to shout, *Stop! I'm not who you think I am!*

Edward said, "Do you have a written report?"

"I do." Burton turned to Krishnamurthy. "Please, Maneesh?"

Krishnamurthy, who had a leather satchel hanging from his shoulder, took a thick file from it and handed it to Burton who, in turn, passed it to the minister. The explorer recognised his own characteristically small handwriting upon its cover. He—the *other* he—had written it during his sojourn in the twenty-third century.

Edward gave a snort of disdain. "I see you still hold the government in contempt."

"Pardon?"

"The title you've inflicted upon the document. *The Return of the Discontinued Man*. Must you insist on such childishness?"

Amusement spiked through the explorer. Suddenly, he rather liked his *doppelgänger*. Glancing across at Swinburne, he saw a gleeful twinkle in the poet's eye. Trounce, too, appeared more at ease. Already the three resurrected men were settling into their new circumstances, which, just as the Beetle had predicted, felt as familiar as favoured old footwear.

"Strange affairs and curious cases require melodramatic titles," Burton said. "They offer a forewarning of the contents."

"Then the future was—?"

Swinburne offered the confirmation. "Strange and curious, Minister."

"Indeed. See to yourselves while I read it. Grumbles will attend you."

Without further word, the minister opened the file and ignored them completely.

After a few minutes, Burton gestured for Swinburne, Trounce, and Gooch to join him in the parlour.

There, he drew his friends closer with a waggle of his fingers and whispered, "Remember, there's nothing in the report to suggest we're anything other than the men he knows."

Swinburne grinned. "Should we continue the charade?"

"It's becoming less of one by the minute, don't you think?"

Trounce rubbed the side of his jaw. "The odd thing is, I feel like me, and I feel at home. Yesterday, I'd never have suggested that we could get away with it, but today I'd say we can."

"Agreed," Swinburne said. "I find myself wondering whether I dreamt my old age."

Burton made a sound of agreement. "If it becomes apposite to reveal the truth, we shall, but I suspect that Edward might regard us with suspicion if he knew the full story."

"He most certainly would," Gooch put in. "He doesn't like the inexplicable. That's why Disraeli gave him the role. It's the job of the minister of chronological affairs to identify the abstruse and get rid of it."

"I wouldn't like him to regard me as such," Burton said.

"You can count on me and the rest of the crew to keep our lips sealed," Gooch said.

Grumbles entered. "Can I get you anything, gentlemen?"

They each made a sound or gesture to indicate the negative. The clockwork servant bobbed his head in response, moved to a corner, and stood motionless.

"What of the accounts of future history given to us by the Cannibal Club?" Gooch asked.

For an instant, Burton didn't know what the engineer was referring to, then, in a flash, he remembered. The Cannibal Club, currently—in 1861—little more than a band of his hard-drinking bachelor friends, would soon found a secret dynasty, making allies available to the chrononauts as they travelled into the future. The *Orpheus* had visited the years 1914, 1968, and 2022 en route to 2202. In each, the descendants of the original Cannibals had handed over a record of events, so that by the time the travellers had reached their destination, they possessed a full chronicle of centuries to come.

But how to use such information?

The "time stream" they'd navigated would continue to exist whatever their current actions. However, any deviation from its events would cause a new stream to branch off from it, and this world would follow that path rather than the original. Had that already happened? Contorted logic suggested so, for the exact moment of the *Orpheus*'s departure in 1860 contained within it only two possibilities—either the ship would return or it wouldn't—and all the history the expedition had chronicled from that moment forward must have therefore been suspended between those two prospects, neither of which could be realised until the homeward voyage had—or hadn't—been completed. That meant, simply by coming back, the expedition had changed the future from one fashioned by two possibilities into one created from a single fact.

The *Orpheus* was home. *The History of the Future* could not be regarded as a reliable record.

If Burton was correct, that also meant the Cannibals had no further need to plan ahead.

"Maneesh has it in his satchel," Burton said. "I haven't yet decided whether to hand it over to my brother or not."

"Why the hesitation?" Gooch asked.

"If it goes to Edward, it goes to the prime minister." Burton paused. He thought about the history he'd come from and the controversial wars in South Africa and Afghanistan that "his" Disraeli had plunged the country into during the late 1870s. What would the man do now if he knew how history was likely to develop?

"Can I allow such knowledge to fall into the hands of a man with such power?" he mused. His mouth twitched in amusement. "The absurdity is that my brother wrote—or rather, will write—the first part of the document himself."

Lawless entered the parlour from the library and approached them. "He hasn't said a word. Are we expected to kick up our heels here all day while he reads? There's only so much tea a fellow can drink."

"He reads as fast as I do," Burton said. "It won't take him long."

"I suppose I'll settle with a newspaper, then. Might as well catch up on events."

"I'm with you," Gooch said. "I say, Grumbles, is there any danger of toast and marmalade? I skipped breakfast."

"I'll see to it right away, sir."

The two men returned to the library to rejoin Krishnamurthy and Raghavendra. The clockwork man departed for the hotel kitchen. Burton, Swinburne, and Trounce were left to themselves. They looked at each other.

"My hat!" Swinburne said. "This is all immensely strange. Is it my imagination or has life picked up a considerable turn of speed? I feel like I left myself behind in Bath. Shall we hop on a train and go back?"

Trounce rubbed his chin. He'd forgotten to shave and his jaw was stubbled. "Tempting, young fellow, very tempting, but—do you know what?—I'm actually looking forward to seeing my office at Scotland Yard. Never had one before but—by Jove!—somehow I know exactly what the room looks like."

Burton said, "Just as we were told, it's evident that we'll feel at home in no time at all, but let us make a pact. If any one of us suffers in any respect from these unexpected circumstances, then let the other two offer unqualified support. William, you may feel somewhat disadvantaged in that Algy and I were friends in our previous lives whereas you were unknown to us. Let me be frank, the man I've become obviously holds you in very high regard. That opinion is now my opinion. I shall stick by you, you can be certain."

"Count me in on that," Swinburne said. "Already, I regard you as family."

Trounce reddened. "Humph! Well, I wouldn't go that far—that is to say—humph!—I suppose—likewise, likewise." He paused, frowned, and put his fists to his hips. "Um. While we're on the subject of—er—shared impressions, I—I find myself anxious about a matter that was brought to our attention last night. I wonder whether you feel the same way."

"Babbage?" Swinburne asked.

"Yes."

Burton considered this, following a train of thought that, if acted upon, would plunge him even deeper into this strange new world. "There are words that want to spill out of me. Part of me—the old man from Trieste—has no clue what they mean." He put a hand over his heart. "This new me comprehends their significance. I'm positive you will understand them, too. They are these: Charles Babbage is old, eccentric, and, in my opinion, increasingly mad. Nevertheless, he understands the Oxford equation, upon which the principles of time travel operate. He designed a version of the Nimtz generator that has propelled the *Orpheus* through the centuries, and he is in possession of black diamonds, which make the vanquishing of time's strictures possible. In short, I consider him a loose cannon possessed of extraordinarily powerful knowledge and with dangerous resources at his disposal. The fact of his disappearance, as you say, William, is a matter of great concern. Apparently, I'm the king's agent. I intend to embrace the role. I think I shall take it upon myself to trace his whereabouts. Will you two help me?"

"Absolutely, I will," Trounce responded.

"Try and stop me," Swinburne agreed. His left knee spasmodically jerked up.

"Then we have a mission. Perhaps in pursuing it we shall find a release from the disappointments and frustrations of our former lives and, too, our previous existence might help us to weather the damage done to the men whose identities we've occupied. I, for one, already feel a lessening of the crippling pain caused by Isabel's murder. I know I've lived a full life with her. I'm also aware that, at its end, she acted on impulse and destroyed everything I had laboured for years to achieve. Those things combined mean that I have loved her and lost her, but am now free of her. That particular story has ended."

Trounce gave a curt nod. "And I was correct about Spring Heeled Jack. My instincts have been proven reliable, though they ran counter to the opinion of the whole of Scotland Yard."

"And I," Swinburne added, "was transformed into foliage."

They looked at him. He laughed and hopped up and down waving his arms. "Inspiration! A completely different cognisance of life! My hat! I shall write as never before!"

"It's settled," Burton said. "Let us throw ourselves into this new world and, as Sadhvi recommended, not look back."

Hell, if I can deal with the manipulative mountain my brother has become, I can deal with anything.

For the next two hours, they perused the minister's library, read the newspapers, drank tea, then coffee, then brandy, and quietly conversed among themselves.

Grumbles saw to their every need until, at midday, Edward Burton dropped *The Return of the Discontinued Man* onto the floor beside his chair and, raising his voice, demanded that everyone attend him.

They gathered, moved books, and sat down.

The minister glared at his brother. "My department now has five reports concerning Edward Oxford and the consequences of his meddling. Every one of them has been given an absurd title. They are ill written and replete with illogical nonsense and loose ends, and not a single one of them presents anything resembling a proper conclusion. You killed the man. Good. Well done. But how did you do it? Why leave that out? This is not a serial in a penny dreadful, brother. I don't want melodrama and suspense. I want answers."

"The account tells you everything you need to know," Burton said.

And you don't need to know that your brother has become the Beetle and I'm an imposter.

"I shall bloody well decide what I bloody well need to know!" The minister lifted a book from the table beside his chair and flung it at his servant. "Grumbles! Will you find the source of that infernal tapping and put an end to it!"

Burton realised that a persistent clicking had started a few moments ago. He said, "Answers close a narrative, Edward. You should be aware by now that we are not dealing with a narrative but, rather, with the elements of a pattern."

"Tosh! Don't you dare try to pull the wool over my eyes with such blather! How did you drive the Oxford intelligence out of Brunel's body? I demand to know! Grumbles! For pity's sake, I didn't ask you to open the blasted window!"

The clockwork man said, "There is a bird on the sill, sir. It was tapping on the pane."

"Well shoo the bloody pest away!"

With a flash of colour and a squawked "Slack-lipped peanut heads!" Pox swooped in and settled on Burton's shoulder. "Message from knock-kneed Michael Faraday. Battersea Power Station is being attacked. Help us, you cross-eyed bottom nuzzlers!"

"What the—?" Gooch cried out. "Who by?"

Pox whistled.

"He can relay messages, not answer questions," Sadhvi Raghavendra pointed out.

"A messenger parrot?" Edward Burton asked. "Here? How? I've never—attacked? The station?"

"We fetched the bird from a parallel history," Burton snapped.

The minister glared at him for a second then turned to Grumbles. "Take my brother, Swinburne, and Krishnamurthy down to the mews. Gentlemen, you will undoubtedly find rotorchairs there. They belong to guests of this hotel. Commandeer them. I'll settle the matter. Go! Hurry!"

Trounce gripped Krishnamurthy's arm. "No, I'll go."

"You will not!" the minister yelled.

Burton recalled that Krishnamurthy and his cousin, a man named Shyamji Bhatti, had originally served his brother. It was they who'd rescued him from the beating that, in other histories, had so incapacitated him. Edward trusted Krishnamurthy more than he trusted Trounce.

"It's all right, William," the explorer said. "Wait here."

Reluctantly, Trounce stepped back.

Burton addressed Pox, "Message to Michael Faraday. We're on our way. Message ends."

The parakeet launched itself from his shoulder and out of the window.

"Follow me, please," Grumbles instructed. He paced across the floor, opened the door, passed through the parlour, and exited the suite into the hallway. Burton snatched his hat, coat, and swordstick from the stand as he passed it. Following the fast-moving clockwork man, he, Swinburne, and Krishnamurthy careened along the corridor, down the stairs, and through a hall that took them past the kitchens and out into the hotel's backyard. They raced across the open space to a long and low wooden structure, the doors of which Grumbles yanked open to reveal a selection of vehicles parked within.

The mechanism stood back as Krishnamurthy plunged past and into the shed. Grabbing the rearmost rail of a rotorchair, the Indian looked back at Burton and shouted, "Help me to drag it out!"

Burton ran forward, and, together, they pulled the vehicle into the open. Swinburne, meanwhile, took a grip on a second chair and said to Grumbles, "Give me a hand, will you?"

The clockwork man didn't move.

"I can't manage it by myself," the poet protested.

"Here," Krishnamurthy said, turning from the first chair. "Let me." He took two steps back toward the shed but was brought up short when Grumbles' left hand shot out and grabbed him by the shoulder. He yelled in pain as metal fingers dug in.

"My sincere apologies, sir," Grumbles said. "This is perfectly dreadful—not at all in my nature."

The brass figure whipped up its right hand and delivered a devastating blow to Krishnamurthy's chin. The young man's head snapped back, and he crumpled to the ground.

"What the devil are you playing at?" Burton demanded.

"I really couldn't say, sir," Grumbles responded.

"Get out of the way! Go back inside!"

"Yes, sir. Certainly, sir. Right away, sir."

He didn't budge.

Swinburne emerged from the shed and bent over Krishnamurthy. "He's out cold. Have you developed a defect, Grumbles?"

"Not at all, Mr. Swinburne. I'm perfectly fine. I'm dreadfully sorry if I've caused any inconvenience. Here, allow me to assist."

One brass hand closed around the back of the poet's collar, and the other clutched the seat of his pants. Screeching and hollering, Swinburne was hoisted into the air, held above Grumbles' head, and thrown with great force up onto the shed's roof. He hit it with a crash, rolled down its slope, and plummeted back into the yard, landing with a thud in an oily puddle where he lay stunned and winded.

Burton drew the rapier from his cane.

In a pleasant tone, Grumbles said, "I hope you don't mean to assault me with that, sir. I wouldn't want you to break your blade."

"I'll shove it into your gears."

"Oh dear. I don't like the sound of that at all, and I fear the minister would object most strenuously were you to damage his property."

Eyeing the gaps in the plating of the machine's torso, Burton slowly waved the tip of his sword from side to side. He measured distances and considered which might be his most effective line of attack.

Swinburne rolled over and groaned. "I say! I'm soaked through. My clothes are ruined."

Grumbles rotated his head until the openings in it were levelled at the poet. "I shall attend to your laundry immediately. Remain where you are, please."

"I'm in a puddle."

"Indeed so, sir."

"I hope your pendulum corrodes."

Burton lunged. Grumbles reacted with a blur of movement, knocked the blade aside, pounced forward, and buried his fist in the explorer's stomach. Bending double and dropping to his knees, Burton retched and struggled for breath.

"Gracious me! I didn't mean to do that at all," Grumbles said. "This day has taken a very peculiar turn, don't you think?"

Swinburne, dripping, staggered to his feet. "You absolute rotter!"

"I know! I'm as dismayed as you are. Would you like another brandy, sir? The master had a rather splendid bottle of Cognac delivered last week. I don't think he'd mind if—"

"Yes, please."

The clockwork man stood motionless.

"Well?" Swinburne said. "Jump to it. I'm thirsty!"

"Of course, sir. Right away, sir."

"You don't appear to be moving. Fetch me a tipple. At once!"

"Yes, sir. No, sir. Yes, sir."

Burton heaved himself to his feet and was immediately grabbed by the neck. Grumbles pulled him close and, with their heads almost touching, said, "Could I trouble you to unclip the key from my back and wind me up, sir? I have to knock you unconscious, but I fear my spring has become so slack that the blow will prove insufficiently powerful."

"Go to hell!" Burton croaked.

"Yes, sir. Immediately, sir."

The pressure on Burton's throat suddenly eased. He pulled himself away and sucked at the air.

Grumbles remained frozen with one arm raised.

"Where's my libation?" Swinburne asked.

No reply.

"Hey! Bucket head!"

Nothing.

"He's wound down," Burton observed.

"Thank goodness. What on earth was that about?"

Burton rapped his knuckles against the clockwork man's head. "Good question."

CHAPTER 7

A FURTHER INCIDENT IN WHICH CLOCKWORK MEN RUN AMOK

The world is governed by very different personages from
what is imagined by those who are not behind the scenes.
—Benjamin Disraeli

Having left the still-senseless Krishnamurthy with hotel staff, and after sending a message up to suite 5 to warn the minister that Grumbles had developed a fault and should not under any circumstances be rewound, Burton and Swinburne took to the air. They'd covered half the distance to Battersea before it occurred to them that neither knew how to fly a rotorchair. At almost exactly the same moment, they lost both confidence and control, and the two flying machines dipped nose first toward the ground.

Swinburne screeched.

Burton cursed.

Aptitude that wasn't their own took over, and, as they grappled with the control levers and sent the rotorchairs skimming low over rooftops, both men praised whatever it was that had bestowed upon them the knowledge and skills of the men they'd replaced.

Ahead, the four chimneys of Battersea Power Station emerged from the city's smoke and drizzle. The duo flew over the Thames and circled the edifice but could see no signs of conflict. They set down in front of the gate—where the *Orpheus* had previously landed—and were clambering out of their machines when Michael Faraday came stumbling from the building waving his arms and shouting incoherently. His white hair was sticking out in every direction.

"Aargh!" he told them. "Yaaah! Impossible! Good gosh! No!"

"Take it easy, man," Burton said. "Speak slowly."

"They took it! They went crazy and took the blessed thing!"

"Who took what?"

"The clockwork men! They attacked us! Overpowered us! Aargh!"

"We've just had a run-in with one of the brass men ourselves. What's got into them?"

"I haven't a clue! The whole lot of 'em have flown off!"

"Off the handle?" Swinburne asked.

"Off in the whatsit."

"The whatsit? What's that?"

"The thing. Ship. The *Orpheus*."

"They stole the—?" Burton looked back at the rotorchairs. He'd assumed the DOGS had moved the ship.

"How long ago?"

"Oof! What? Er. Maybe half an hour."

"In which direction?"

Faraday gave a vague wave of his arm. "Over the thingamajig. Water. The river."

"If you're in no further danger, Mr. Faraday, Algy and I will scout around. Maybe we'll spot it."

"Yes! Go, please! Yaaah!"

Burton addressed Swinburne. "We'll circle the city in opposite directions and meet back here."

Swinburne, with his teeth chattering as a result of his wet clothing, belted himself back into his rotorchair's seat and slid down over his eyes the flying goggles he'd found in its storage box.

The two rotorchairs shot upward and separated. Burton steered his northwestward, while Swinburne took a northeasterly course. There was an unbroken, flat, grey blanket of cloud overhead, but it occupied a much higher altitude than any ship could fly, so offered no opportunity for concealment to the missing vessel. The atmosphere was dirty and wet, and visibility was bad, but not to the point where a ship the size of the *Orpheus* would be hidden by it.

As he soared across the river, Burton muttered to himself, "Yesterday, Doctor Steinhaueser and I rescued a sparrow from the garden pond. Today, I'm in a flying armchair hunting for mechanical thieves."

Something felt terribly amiss with the first part of that statement, but, recalling the pact he'd made with his fellow reborn, he refused to dwell on it.

Below, Knightsbridge slipped past, then Belgravia, Portman Square, and Oxford Street. There were other rotorchairs and ornithopters all around him and, ahead, a much bigger machine. He initially thought it might be the *Orpheus* but was disappointed when he drew alongside it and saw the name *Darling Lucy May*.

Regent's Park, Camden Town, eastward over Holloway and Islington, and southward back toward the river, passing Finsbury and the hive of activity that was the half-rebuilt East End.

Burton flew westward along the course of the Thames until he arrived back at Battersea. He landed, ran into the station, and hailed a young woman who was monitoring flashing lights on an apparatus of spinning wheels, clacking valves, and wheezing bellows. "Ma'am! Mr. Faraday?"

She pointed.

Striding in the indicated direction, he saw Faraday at a workbench, applying a pair of pliers to an arrangement of wires and unfathomable parts. The man looked up at his approach, squinted, and with far greater self-control than he'd previously displayed, said, "Aargh!"

"No sign of it," Burton announced.

"I simply cannot understand what happened," Faraday said. "Every clockwork man in the—in the place—the station! Gosh! We've had them for years. They've never gone wrong before."

"The timing appears significant, don't you think?"

"Very! Very significant indeed! Why so?"

"The ship returns after a thirteen-month absence and they suddenly go wild and make off with it?"

"Ah. I see what you mean. Yes. Significant is the word. And Fiddlesticks."

"Fiddlesticks? What about him?"

"He took the diamonds out of Brunel's head."

Burton's knees almost gave way. He grabbed at a workbench to steady himself. The future he'd visited must have already changed. If the Edward Oxford consciousness was no longer in the Brunel body, would it find another route through which to infiltrate the empire as the decades passed? Had his counterpart's self-sacrifice been in vain?

"By God!" he croaked. "Then Spring Heeled Jack is out of our hands!"

Pushing himself upright, he stood with the back of his right wrist pressed against his mouth and his eyes flicking from right to left, fighting the impression that everything around him was illusory and impossible.

"Are you quite all right?" Faraday asked.

"I should report back to the minister."

"Yes, I suppose so." Faraday held up the thing of wires and parts. "There! Mended! Now then, what was it for? Do you recall?"

"I never knew in the first place."

"Oh."

"When Swinburne arrives, tell him to meet me at the hotel, will you?"

"Swinburne? The poet fellow? Very well."

Burton's instruction proved needless. As he returned to his rotor-chair, Swinburne's landed with a thud beside it.

"Nothing!" the poet announced. "Either it made off at top speed or it's landed somewhere in the city."

"In which case it would have been seen," Burton countered. "But by whom, and how do we find that witness?"

"Through Trounce and Scotland Yard, perhaps?"

"Good idea. Let's see what he can do. You're shivering."

"I'm damp."

"We'll return these chairs and get you into something dry."

"And get something wet into me. Grumbles promised me a Cognac."

They flew back to the Royal Venetia Hotel, landed beside its vehicle shed, and were immediately set upon by two very irate men.

"What the very deuce do you think you're playing at?" one demanded.

"I say! How dare you! Those are our rotorchairs!" the other complained.

Daniel Gooch, who was also present—he'd unscrewed the top of Grumbles' canister-like head and was using tools to poke about inside it—said, "This is Lord Chumleigh and the Right Honourable Percival Braithwaite. Those machines you borrowed belong to them."

"Gentlemen, I apologise," Burton said. "I am Sir Richard Burton, His Majesty's agent. As you can see, your machines are returned safely. My companion and I were forced to commandeer them. It was a matter of national security. If you visit my brother, the minister, in suite five, he'll arrange for you to be compensated."

"But the club!" Chumleigh objected.

"Club?"

The aristocrat flapped a hand toward the shed, indicating the spot where a third rotorchair had stood. "Our friend had to leave without us. We'll be dreadfully late."

"For what, sir?" Burton asked.

"Cocktails, you blithering idiot! Cocktails! What else do you think I might mean?"

"At this hour?"

"Great heavens! Do you now dictate to me when it's appropriate to partake?"

Swinburne nodded sagely. "An outrage, that's for sure. You should know better, Richard. One must never come between a gentleman and his cocktail. It could cause the collapse of civilisation."

Braithwaite brushed his hand at the poet as if to sweep him aside. "We'll take this up with the minister chappy in due course, of that you can be certain, and I'll see to it that he has your confounded hides. Now shift out of the bally way. Let us get to our vehicles."

Burton and Swinburne stood aside as the two aristocrats pushed past.

Chumleigh gasped when he saw the seat of his machine. "What the devil? It's covered in—in—"

"Machine oil," Swinburne said. "My apologies. As you can see, I'm dripping with the blessed stuff."

"Why?"

"It keeps me supple."

"Damned fool!"

The aristocrat pulled a handkerchief from his pocket and used it to wipe down the leather seat. Moments later, with a blast of air and steam, the rotorchairs rose and disappeared over the rooftops.

Burton turned to Daniel Gooch and indicated Grumbles' dismantled head. "Have you discovered anything?"

"There's no mechanical failure that I can see. Mind you, I can only probe so far. You know these things are booby-trapped? Tinker with them too much and they first burst into flames, then the heat sets off an explosive. Very unpleasant. Babbage is extremely secretive about certain aspects of his work. What happened, exactly?"

"Grumbles put Maneesh out for the count and tried to stop us from taking the rotorchairs. It appears he was working in concert with the clockwork men at the station. They overpowered your people and have made away with the *Orpheus*."

Gooch uttered a gasp of amazement. "How in the name of God is that possible?"

"You tell me."

"I'll have to take this thing to the station for proper examination. I can see already that someone—almost certainly Babbage, I should say—has made changes to its probability calculator. There's a component here I don't understand. Maybe I can make sense of it given the proper equipment and a little time."

"Then cart it off and get to work. I'll inform Edward. How's Maneesh?"

"Conscious, but his jaw is badly broken. He'll be out of action for a fair while. Sadhvi has just set off with him for the Penfold hospital."

Burton retrieved his cane from the ground and signalled Swinburne to follow him. They reentered the hotel and ascended to the fifth floor. Trounce answered their knock. "By Jove! I'm glad you're back. The minister is livid. What in blue thunder is happening?"

Burton gestured for him to follow and led the way into the parlour. Trounce glanced at Swinburne, who whispered, "We're not about to make the minister any happier. You might want to stand by the drinks cabinet, brother. Sedatives will be required."

"Don't call me brother. It makes me feel odd. Why are your clothes glistening?"

"I dropped off a roof into an oily puddle."

"Humph! I should have guessed it would be something like that." The trio passed into the library.

Lawless greeted them with obvious relief. It lasted but an instant.

"Your ship's been taken," Burton told him.

"What?" Lawless and Edward Burton cried out in unison.

The king's agent—Burton realised with a slight shock that he was already subsumed into that role—told them what had happened. Lawless's face turned white and his eyes flashed angrily. Edward twisted his mouth into an ugly snarl, then jabbed a finger at Trounce. "You! Stop standing about. Get to Scotland Yard. There are clockwork men all over London. I want to know whether any others have misbehaved."

Trounce swallowed, blinked, sought Burton's eye, cleared his throat, nodded, put his bowler hat on his head, and moved toward the door.

"William," Burton called after him. "We need to know whether the *Orpheus* has landed anywhere in the city, too. Get some constables onto it. Make enquiries."

Trounce looked doubtful for an instant then nodded decisively. "Where do you—ah, yes, Montagu Place. Very well. I'll—I'll see what I can do and will report to you there." He left the room.

Edward Burton addressed Swinburne. "The *Venetia* has a number of brass men among its staff. Go down and see what they're up to."

"Rightio."

"Richard, fetch me a bottle of ale."

Burton's eyes fixed upon the other man's. "I beg your pardon?"

"I need a drink, damn it! Hell's bells, what am I to do without Grumbles?"

"I can tell you right now that you'll not replace him with me."

"Shut up. I blame you for these untoward events."

"Why so?"

"You come back and the very next day, all this. Am I supposed to consider it a coincidence?"

"I made a similar observation to Mr. Faraday." Burton stepped over to the drinks cabinet. "It *is* rather suggestive, that much can't be denied." He passed a bottle and glass to his brother. "Here's your beer. Maybe it will keep your mouth occupied with something other than petulant and ill-thought-out accusations."

The minister scowled at him, took the bottle, and turned to address Lawless. "What made your ship worth taking?"

"It's the best in the fleet."

"Oh, humbug! Don't be so absurd. There are plenty of rotorships in the empire, but yours is the only one that's just returned from the future. So, Captain, what is aboard it? What did you bring back with you aside from a talkative parrot? Obviously, whatever it is, that's what they're after."

Lawless looked questioningly at Burton. The explorer said, "The Mark Three babbage calculator that automates the ship's functions and manipulates the Oxford equation to allow it to jump through time—"

He stopped, suddenly taken aback by his own words.

I talk as if I know these things. I don't! This madness has nothing to do with me. I'm a retired geographer. A writer. An old man who can't even get dressed without help.

Edward poured his beer, set the bottle aside, and took a gulp from the glass. He held it up and examined the way the light glimmered through the dark liquid. Slowly, as if engrossed, he said, "What about it?"

Burton's lips moved soundlessly as he struggled with the words that wanted to come out.

He gave up and let them.

"We had engineers—descendants of the Cannibal Club—tinker with it. They replaced some of its parts. The new components have expanded the synthetic intelligence by means of calculating techniques evolved from the work of a man named Turing. They supersede those developed by Babbage by some considerable degree."

The minister took another swig then set the glass on the table at his side. His eyes met his sibling's and held them. "What else?"

"There are a great many more of the black diamonds. Multiple iterations of the same stones."

"More? By God, don't we have enough of the infernal things? No wonder I've had a headache all day. What of the various devices you wrote of in your report? What of the identity bracelets and the intelligent pistols?"

"I judged it best to leave them where they belong, which is assuredly not in the year 1861."

Without averting his gaze, Edward addressed Lawless. "Is that correct, Captain?"

"Um. Yes. That is to say, we didn't bring anything apart from the diamonds and reworked Mark Three, and I might add that whoever has taken the ship is in for a disappointment, since its brain stopped working the moment we arrived. More likely they were after the gemstones, anyway."

Edward's face darkened, highlighting his scars and the brutality of his appearance.

"Do you both take me for a bloody fool? You think this was some manner of heist? Ridiculous! No, no, no. There's more to this. You're keeping something from me. The final chapter of your report is nothing but damned obfuscation. Something else happened, and I demand to know what. Furthermore, the notion that you returned virtually empty handed is beyond credibility. You are attempting to deceive me. I won't have it! What else was aboard your ship, Captain? Or perhaps I should be asking who?"

Lawless paled and mumbled, "No one. Nothing."

"Liar! Traitor! I should have you clapped in irons and thrown into a dungeon!"

"I forgot something," Burton muttered.

"What?"

The document. The History of the Future. It's still in Krishnamurthy's satchel.

"I forgot how objectionable you can be."

His brother bared his teeth in a nasty snarl.

"And to contribute to your ill temper a little more," Burton said, "the diamonds containing the remnants of Spring Heeled Jack were taken from the station, too."

"Dolt! Incompetent fool! I should—I should—"

"What I can't quite understand," Burton went on, "is why they were left there in the first place. Babbage took all the others last November. Why didn't he take the ones in Brunel's head, too? Perhaps because he thought Brunel still occupied them? If so, it suggests he learned otherwise the moment we returned from the future. How?"

Swinburne returned and, in his high-pitched voice, declared, "I just encountered the manager on the stairs. He's in a right old flap. Apparently, Sprocket, the doorman, has done a bunk."

"And the others?" Burton asked.

"There are seven other clockwork servants in the building. They're all behaving normally."

"About face," the explorer ordered. "We're leaving." He pushed the poet back toward the door and gestured for Lawless to follow.

"Come back here at once!" the minister shouted. "I'll have the truth out of you, confound it!"

He was ignored.

"Find the bloody ship! Keep me informed. And have the manager send up someone to assist me."

As they descended the stairs, Lawless hurried ahead and said over his shoulder, "I'm going home to get my rotorchair. I'll fly over every inch of this city until I find the *Orpheus*. I'll catch up with you later."

He reached the bottom of the staircase, raced across the lobby, and exited the hotel.

Burton strode to the reception desk with Swinburne at his heels.

"Sir?" the clerk asked. He cast a disapproving glance at the poet's filthy attire.

"I hear your doorman has absconded, Mr. Bromley. Did you see him go?"

"Yes sir. Sprocket. I don't know what came over him. He's never misbehaved before. He followed your two colleagues, the injured man and the young lady, when they departed and hasn't returned."

"Ah, did he now? Thank you." As he strode away, Burton thought of something and turned back. "Incidentally, the minister asks not to be disturbed until further notice."

"Very well, Sir Richard. Duly noted."

"You're very mean to your sibling," Swinburne observed as they placed their hats upon their heads and stepped out onto the Strand.

"Apparently so. I can't help myself. But it won't hurt Edward to get off his considerable behind. He needs the exercise."

"And what of us?" the poet asked. "What shall we do now?"

Burton moved to the edge of the pavement, raised his swordstick, and gave a loud whistle to summon a ride from the seething mass of eccentric vehicles.

"We have to get to the Penfold Sanatorium," he said. "Maneesh still has the historical records, and I fear Sprocket might be intent on getting them."

A steam-horse-drawn growler drew to a halt at the kerb. Its engine emitted a gargling sigh and a cloud of white vapour.

The king's agent directed the driver to the hospital and added, "Make haste, please. It's an emergency."

"I'll do me best," the man replied, "but the traffic ain't going to part for us like the bloomin' Red Seas, if yer don't mind me a-sayin' so."

"There's a generous tip in it for you if you get us there in good measure," Burton stated as he climbed aboard.

"Back streets, then. Better hang on. It'll be a bumpy ride."

As Swinburne settled beside Burton and the carriage jolted into motion, the poet asked, "How could the doorman know Krishnamurthy has the documents?"

"Grumbles was aware of the fact," Burton answered. "He was in the room when we spoke about them. I thought he was trying to prevent us from getting to the station when he set upon us in the yard. It might be that he was actually after the satchel. However, he didn't have the opportunity to speak with Sprocket, so your question stands, and I don't know the answer to it."

They grabbed at the leather hand straps hanging over the windows, steadying themselves as, without warning, the vehicle careened to the right. The light dimmed as walls closed in on either side of it. The driver had evidently steered into an alleyway. Burton caught a glimpse of a vagabond pressed against brickwork, his eyes wide with surprise as the wheels missed his toes by mere inches.

Rounding a corner, thundering through a small, litter-strewn square and into another tight passage—this bordered by slouching tenement buildings—the growler bumped over uneven ground and scattered detritus, rocking from side to side and giving its passengers a thorough shaking.

"This is Soho, isn't it?" Swinburne said, hanging on for all he was worth. "Strange how such a squalid rookery can exist right beside the glamour of the Strand."

"The British Empire has always been one of contrasts," Burton replied. He added "Oof!" as the vehicle bounced over a pothole. "And in London, they are condensed and brought into sharp focus."

From a maze of alleyways, the growler emerged into Oxford Circus where it was immediately hemmed in by a cacophonous profusion of wheeled and multilegged machines. Drivers yelled expletives at each other. Horses reared and whinnied in distress. Spokes tangled with metal knees. Steam and smoke billowed in every direction.

"Get your bleedin' heap out o' my way!" their man bellowed. "Coming through! Coming through! And the same to you, matey! Oy! Mind out! Are you blind or what? Yeah? Well why don't you shove it where the sun don't shine!"

With a lot of bumping, scraping, and very bad language, they nudged their way across the bustling junction before, like a cork popping out of a bottle, suddenly accelerating into a narrow side street.

Once again, the opulent facade of the city gave way to the inner rot, as they clattered into the grimy backwaters of Marylebone, moving through roads inhabited mainly, it appeared, by beggars, drunkards, ne'er-do-wells, and women of ill repute.

"If Sadhvi and Maneesh stuck to the main roads, which they surely did, we might reach the sanatorium before them," Swinburne observed.

"So might Sprocket," Burton countered.

The growler scraped through a very narrow passage, navigated a tight corner, and emerged into a long, straight, and slightly wider alley bordered on either side by the featureless redbrick walls of tall warehouses.

Burton leaned out of the window and looked ahead. The far end of the alley opened onto what appeared to be a main thoroughfare—Weymouth Street, he guessed—and he could see the front of a butcher's shop.

Momentarily made light-headed by déjà vu, he collapsed back into his seat and grappled with disparate memories, but before he could get a firm grasp on any of them, the vehicle reached the junction and turned with such speed that its left side rose up and Swinburne was knocked into him.

"My hat!" the poet squealed. "The teeth will be shaken from my head at this rate!"

Burton regarded the patch of oil that had been transferred from his companion's clothes to his own sleeve. "Our cabbie must be in debt. He's certainly keen on earning that tip."

Moments later, they swung out onto Marylebone Road and were rattling toward the crossing with Edgware when the driver gave a cry of alarm and jerked the carriage to a halt with such abruptness that both passengers were propelled forward, banging their heads against the opposite wall of the cabin.

Shouts and screams reached them from outside.

"What now?" Swinburne muttered.

Throwing open the door, Burton jumped to the ground and saw, ahead at the junction, that an ornithopter had just landed in the middle of the thoroughfare. It had evidently done so precipitously, for a wagon lay crushed to matchwood beneath it, and vehicles, in seeking to avoid a collision with the wide, still-flapping metal wings, were veering to either side, bumping up onto the pavements and, in one case, as Burton watched, smashing through the front window of a bakery.

Swinburne stepped down to his side and cried out, "Look! Surely that's Sprocket!" He pointed at a landau that was skidding to a halt in front of the flying machine. A clockwork man was clinging to its back, hitching a ride like a street urchin.

"Sadhvi and Maneesh!" Burton exclaimed and started forward.

He saw the brass doorman drop to the road and stride to the side of the carriage. At the same moment, the ornithopter's hatch swung open and six mechanical figures emerged and ran the short distance to join Sprocket, who gripped the landau's door, ripped it off, and flung it aside. A cry of fright came from within.

Burton yelled, "Stop!" as he saw Raghavendra and Krishnamurthy hauled from the cabin.

"Unhand them at once!" Swinburne demanded.

The clockwork men started back toward their flying machine, dragging their captives with them. Raghavendra saw Burton and extended an arm toward him.

"Help, Richard!"

"Sadhvi!"

Two of the mechanicals turned as Burton and Swinburne caught up with the group.

"May I assist you, gentlemen?" one asked. "Perhaps you require a serious injury or a rapid demise?"

"Release them!" Burton commanded. "Where are you taking them? On whose orders?"

"At your service, sir. We aim to please. Have a nice day. Good morning. Good afternoon. Good-bye. Hello. Good-bye."

"Stop babbling and stand aside!" Swinburne shrieked. He attempted to push past the contraption, but it immediately snatched him by the back of the collar and lifted him from the ground.

"I say!" The poet pedalled his legs frantically. "Put me down!"

"As you wish, sir."

"No! Don't!"

Swinburne's sudden realisation of what would happen came too late. Once again, he was thrown high into the air.

As his somersaulting friend soared over a nearby omnibus, Burton paced forward but was immediately brought up short by the mechanism, which suddenly lunged at him. The king's agent saw a flash of polished brass as the heel of a metal hand impacted against the side of his head.

Everything went black. There was a sensation of falling. Then there was nothing.

When consciousness reignited, there came the immediate cognisance that only a few minutes had passed. Burton opened his eyes. An enormous goose was peering down at him. Black smoke billowed behind the bird. People were shouting. A horse was whinnying in distress.

The goose sneezed and expelled feathers. They floated down around its head. "Are you all right?" it asked, blinking its bright green eyes.

"I'm—" Burton pushed himself up onto his elbows. "Ouch!"

"You were knocked senseless."

"Algy? Is that you?"

"Yes. I crashed through the roof of a cargo van. It was transporting feathers for mattresses. They've stuck to my oily clothes. In terms of fashion, I doubt the look will catch on. What do you think?"

Ignoring the question, the explorer scrambled to his feet and looked around at a scene of utter mayhem. Through coiling fumes, he saw flickering flames and heaped wreckage. A rotorchair was embedded in the front of a building. Carriages and wagons were scattered around the crossroads, many of them on their sides. A wounded horse was on the ground, kicking wildly, with three men hanging onto its reins, jumping out of the way of its lashing hoofs, while a policeman tried to press a revolver to its head.

Swinburne sneezed again. "Apparently the bucket heads took off in great haste and knocked a couple of rotorchairs out of the sky as they went. One exploded when it hit the ground. There have been fatalities."

"What of Sadhvi and Maneesh?"

"Abducted."

Police constables were arriving and attempting to bring some sort of order to the scene. Burton saw one nearby, talking to a woman. He paced over, with his friend following, and interrupted.

"Constable, I'm Burton."

The uniformed man turned from the woman and saluted. "Yes, sir. The agent. Recognise you. I was at the Leicester Square incident last year. I'm Khapoor. I—that is to say—er—" He gazed in bemusement at Swinburne.

"His Majesty's special fowl," the poet snapped authoritatively. "Dispatched to investigate incidents of unlawful flying."

The policeman removed his helmet and scratched his head. "Um. What?"

"Joking."

"Ignore my colleague, Khapoor," Burton advised. "He has a peculiar kink in his brain. It causes him to quip and jape inappropriately during times of duress. He's playing the fool because he's deeply concerned. In which direction did the ornithopter depart?"

"I was just asking Mrs. Baker here that very question, sir."

Burton turned his attention to the woman. She was middle-aged, overweight, and possessed the ruddy, thread-veined complexion of a dedicated gin drinker.

"Mrs. Baker owns the bakery," Khapoor added. "It was badly damaged."

Swinburne grinned. "Mrs. Baker the baker? That's a fortuitous combination."

The woman eyed him haughtily. "There's nothing forty-tooty about a broken window, young man. An' the surname came with marriage. Me maiden name were Potter."

"Then it's a good thing you got hitched, ma'am, else you might be kneading clay rather than dough."

Burton winced. Taking the poet by the shoulders, he turned him and pushed him away. "Algy, go and pluck yourself."

He waited until Swinburne had moved off before once again addressing Khapoor. "Proceed, please, Constable."

"Yes, sir. So, Mrs. Baker, you witnessed the entire affair, is that right?"

The woman rubbed her chin with leathery fingertips. "I blimmin' well did. Nearly got clobbered by that there growler, too. I'd just stepped out o' the shop to take a few sucks on me pipe, you see, when the horny-chopper fell straight down out o' the sky an' landed with a thump on top of a coal cart. Smashed it right to pieces, it did, an' killed the poor driver dead. Traffic went this way an' that, an' I had to jump for me blimmin' life when the growler came at me shop. Right through the glass it went! That'll cost a pretty penny to replace, so it will, an' it won't be out o' my pocket, oh no. When you catch 'em what's responsible, you'll hand 'em the bill for repairs, hey?"

"We will, ma'am," Khapoor said. "You saw the machine take to the air again?"

"I were lyin' in the gutter. In the gutter! At my age! Saw the metal men bundle a lady an' gent into the flyin' machine an' hoff it went. Bang! Crash! More blimmin' hurly-burly!"

Burton asked, "Which way did it go?"

She pointed westward. "Thataway, sir."

Khapoor shook his head and said to Burton, "As soon as it vanished over the rooftops it could have turned in any direction. Those contraptions are fast, too. I doubt we'll find it."

"Hmm. Will you speak to Detective Inspector Trounce? Ask him to get word to all the city's police stations. Someone, somewhere, must have seen it land."

"I will, sir, but there's a lot of ornithopters. Even more than rotorships, and I just got orders to look out for one of them, too."

"Yes, the *Orpheus*. My goodness, Trounce spread the word quickly."

"I crossed paths with him a little earlier, sir. He was on his way to the Yard. We—"

They all jumped as a shot rang out. Burton looked around and saw that the wounded horse had stopped kicking.

Mrs. Baker clicked her tongue. "What about me blimmin' window?"

"One moment, please, ma'am," Khapoor said. "Will there be anything else, Captain Burton?"

"Not for now. Thank you, Constable. Mrs. Baker."

He left them and rejoined Swinburne, who was standing watching policemen and others attempting to right vehicles and clear the road. The poet's face was still half concealed by feathers. He turned it toward Burton and said, "You know, there's only one explanation."

"For what, Algy?"

"For the bucket heads working in concert like that. They must be able to communicate over a distance, perhaps using something like the radio devices we saw in 1914. Whatever the means, Grumbles used it to inform Sprocket that Krishnamurthy had the document. Sprocket then followed our friends, hitched a ride on the back of their cab, and called down the ornithopter."

Swinburne put on his hat, then took it off and scratched his hair, causing a cloud of feathers to swirl into the air. He put the hat back on and puffed out his cheeks. "Which makes me think about that transmission the *Orpheus*'s Mark Three received upon our arrival."

"Ah," Burton said. "Yes. We need to locate the source of it."

"But how, Richard? We're thoroughly thwarted. I don't doubt that Babbage is behind all this, but how the devil do we find him?"

"I have no idea, Algy. As you say, we're stumped." Burton squeezed his eyes shut and ground the heels of his hands into them. "My head is aching. No wonder, I suppose, after taking a blow from a metal fist. And I feel so suddenly fatigued that I can't even string my thoughts together."

"I must confess, I feel the same way, though I can't fathom why. I slept well enough."

"As did I. Perhaps it's just the effects of our journey back from the future."

Burton frowned, suspecting that he was overlooking something, but whatever it was, it refused to come to him. "Right now, there's nothing we can do except hope the police discover our missing flying machines. I suggest we withdraw to our respective homes and rest up while they get on with it."

"And while Gooch investigates Grumbles' misbehaviour."

"Indeed."

Burton hesitated and pulled at his coat cuff distractedly.

Retire from the fray? Hide at home while others do the work? I'm Burton! Why am I acting like—like an old man?

Swinburne cocked a thumb over his shoulder. "I'll stroll with you a-ways."

They returned to their landau and paid the driver, who'd been waiting patiently for them, then moved away from the crossroads and proceeded back along Marylebone Road, passing jammed traffic, swearing drivers, and cursing passengers, pushing through a thickening crowd of the curious until they finally broke free of the crush and turned right into the relatively peaceful Gloucester Place.

Ragamuffins—and a number of adults—directed laughter and clucking noises at Swinburne. He ignored them.

"It occurs to me," he said, "that Babbage was liable to go off the rails whether we completed our mission in the future or not. You'll recall what we were told about him in 1914?"

"That he lost his mind," Burton responded. "That, on the twenty-eighth of September, 1861, he destroyed all his prototypes, all the devices he had in his possession, and incinerated his every plan, blueprint, and diary, leaving no trace of his work at all other than the Mark Two probability calculators that occupied the heads of his clockwork men."

"And which will explode if anyone examines them too closely. If the history we travelled through was one suspended between two probabilities, then the fact we were told that means it is certain to happen either way."

They passed the mouths of Salisbury Place, Bickenhall Street, York Street, and Crawford Street without further conversation, each entwined in his own thoughts, each battling the exhaustion that had descended so suddenly upon them.

As they approached Montagu Place, they heard someone bellowing, "Hot baked 'tators! Hot baked 'tators! Hot baked 'tators for 'em what wants 'em! Keeps yer warm an' keeps yer full! Hot baked 'tators!"

"My hat!" Swinburne exclaimed. "It's our old friend Grub!"

Drawing to a halt, they stood and watched the street vendor. The man bore no resemblance at all to the froggish individual of the far future, but they knew this man was the forebear of that other Mr. Grub.

Centuries from now, this very spot would be a tangle of vermillion jungle. They would stand in its midst. Swinburne would feel the rapture coming. Burton would feel nothing.

Approaching the flat-capped, baggy-clothed man, the explorer exclaimed, "Hallo there, Mr. Grub. You look well."

"Lord 'elp us, if it ain't the Cap'n 'imself!" the man cried out, knuckling his forehead. "I thought you'd bloomin' well moved away, so I did! Been on anuvver of yer hexpiditions 'ave yer? Brought back an African bird, I see. An ostrich, is it?"

Burton chuckled. "This is Algernon. He fell into a feather-delivery van."

Swinburne raised his hat in greeting. "What ho! What ho! What ho!"

Grub eyed the poet. "Celebratin', was you, sir?"

"If by that you mean to ask whether I was one over the eight, I was not. I was perfectly sober. How's the world been treating you, Mr. Grub?"

"Better than it's been treatin' you, by the looks of it, if yer don't mind me a-sayin' so."

"I'm glad to hear it."

Burton said, "It's good to see you, old fellow. Home wouldn't be home without you on the corner. What's the word on the street?"

Grub scratched his chin and looked bemused. "Cap'n?"

"How do people feel about the empire, about the political situation and so forth?"

"Blimey, I don't mix with the type what thinks about things like that, sir. Cor, no! Politics is what the 'igh an' mighty uses to look after 'emselves, while folks like me just muddle along without 'em, if you'll pardon me for a-sayin' so. No offence meant."

"None taken. It was impudent to ask such a question. My apologies."

"Do you want a spud, Cap'n? Mr. Swinburne? Hot an' tasty."

"Another time, thank you," Swinburne replied.

"My landlady will have my hide if I eat before she's fed me," Burton said. "I'd better get home. Good day to you."

"Nice to 'ave you back, sir."

After they'd moved on a few steps, Swinburne said, "Wave down a hansom for me, will you, Richard? I suspect I'll be ignored if I flap a wing."

This was done, and as the vehicle drew abreast of them, the poet asked, "Shall I call on you in the morning?"

"Please do. We'll pay a visit to Gooch at Battersea Power Station."

"I wonder how Pouncer is getting on?"

"We'll call on him, too.

They parted ways and, unaccountably, Burton instantly felt alone. *What is wrong with me? Why do I feel so displaced?*

He strolled toward his house and crossed the road, narrowly avoiding a collision with a velocipede, whose driver swerved his vehicle and shouted, "Oy! Silly ass!"

Stopping in front of number 14, the explorer regarded the front door with a sense of unfamiliarity that made no sense to him. He slipped his finger and thumb into his waistcoat pocket, only to find that he'd somehow misplaced his key. Before he could step to the door and knock on it, it opened. A boy, about fifteen years old, emerged, saw Burton, stopped, and gaped.

"Ye've come home, so ye have!"

Bram Stoker.

A child! Of course. Why would he be otherwise?

"Yes, I've come home, Bram. You look different."

The boy straightened and squared his shoulders. "I've grown six inches! It's Mrs. Angell's dinners!"

"Good lad. Are you on your way out?"

"To buy Sangappa polish. Mrs. A wants to give the leather chairs in the dining room a going over, so she does."

Burton retrieved a few coins from his pocket and handed them over. "Here. Treat yourself to the latest issue of that penny dreadful you like so much."

"*The Baker Street Detective*! Crikey! Thank you, guv'nor! By the way, did Mr. Fogg come back with you?"

It took a moment for Burton to remember that Fogg—Macallister Fogg—was the fictional detective featured in *The Baker Street Detective* and that Bram persistently confused him with William Trounce.

"Yes, he did. Safe and sound."

Something else came to mind. The boy belonged to an organisation called the Whispering Web, formed by young waifs and strays, through which messages could be sent and information received at the cost of just a coin or two. From orphan to urchin, passing from mouth to ear the length and breadth of the empire, what communiqués lost in accuracy—the phenomenon known as "Chinese whispers" was an inevitable problem—was made up for by the astonishing speed at which they travelled. It was a fine, though not widely known, alternative to the Post Office.

"I say, Bram, may I add an errand to that which you already have? It'll earn you some toffees to suck on while you're immersed in Mr. Fogg's latest."

"Ask and I'll obey!" the boy answered with a wide grin.

"Put word out on the web. A rotorship named *Orpheus* has been stolen. I'd like to know where it was taken. Also, Miss Raghavendra and Mr. Krishnamurthy—you remember them?—were forced aboard an ornithopter crewed by Babbage mechanisms. Perhaps it was seen landing."

"Cripes! A new adventure, sir?"

"I sincerely hope not. How are things here?"

"All quiet, 'cept—" Bram stepped out onto the pavement and pointed up to a window. "That's been a-tapping at your study window for the past hour or so."

Burton looked up and saw Pox on the sill. He drew the last of his coins from his pocket.

"Then we'd better let it in and give it somewhere to sit. Task number three: visit a pet shop and buy a perch of the tall, free-standing variety."

"Do ye intend to keep the thing?"

"I do. The bird and I are already acquainted."

Bram took the money, saluted, and scampered off, whistling merrily as he went.

Burton entered the house and closed the front door. He placed his cane in an elephant-foot holder, put his topper on the rack, and hung up his overcoat. He lifted a small handbell from the hall table and jiggled it. At the end of the hallway, a grandfather clock countered the tinkling with a chime to mark the half hour.

He examined the pictures on the wall. One was a daguerreotype of a young man in an early police uniform. Mrs. Angell's late husband. Another, a tiny oil painting, portrayed Edward Burton at the age of about twenty-five, unrecognisably handsome and slim.

A voice rose from the stairs that led down to the basement. "Who's that what rung the bell? Is that you Elsie Carpenter? That there bell ain't for the likes of you. I'm the mistress o' this house, so there'll be no summoning by bell 'less it's me what does the summoning!"

Elsie Carpenter. The maid. Comes in three times a week.

"It's only me, Mother Angell," Burton called.

There came a loud screech. "Lord have mercy! The master's come home!"

From the door to the left of the grandfather clock, an elderly, white-haired, and wide-hipped woman appeared, saw Burton, threw her apron up over her face, and shrieked, "Home and healthy! Mercy me! Goodness gracious! Home and healthy! Not skinny as a skellington and yellow as a Chinaman like last time!" She lowered her apron and peered at him. "P'raps you avoided the jungle, like what I advised?"

"It was rather a different sort of jungle, Mrs. A."

She rushed forward and embraced him, then stood back and scrutinised his face. "Have you been eating properly?"

"Yes, but I haven't had any lunch. I'm famished."

"There's freshly made bread, cold pork pie, cheese, and pickles. I don't 'spose you've learned how to eat at a dining table like a civilised human. Bring it up to the study, shall I, like always?"

"Yes, please."

"Too much time in the company of savages, that's your problem."

"You've met my brother?"

"Tish tosh, that's no way to talk about family. Up the stairs with you. The fire's already lit."

"It is? Why?"

"I lights it every day. Don't want the damp to infect your books, do you?"

"Most assuredly not. Thank you. It's good to be home. Very good."

"Get away with you. Stop blocking my hallway." She flapped her apron at him. There was a tear in her eye. "I'll bring Fidget up."

Burton climbed the stairs and, upon reaching the landing, opened a door to his right and entered the study, peering around it with such curiosity that he almost felt like an intruder in someone else's home.

"I was away for longer during the Nile expedition," he muttered, "and didn't feel like this upon my return. What on earth has got into me?"

He saw three desks piled high with books and papers. Swords and daggers were affixed to the wall over the fireplace, with spears and guns displayed in the alcoves to either side of the chimney breast. His worn and cracked university boxing gloves hung by their laces from the corner of the mantelpiece. A bureau was positioned between the two tall sash widows, while bookcases—warped beneath the weight of books—were flush against the walls. An old saddlebag armchair stood by the fireplace, with other chairs and occasional tables scattered here and there about the chamber.

It was all as it should be and all terribly and unaccountably strange.

Crossing to the window, he slid up the sash. With a squawked "Flubber jockey!" the little bird flew in, perched on the back of a chair, and got to work preening its bright feathers.

Burton went to one of the desks.

"*Vikram and the Vampire*," he said, reading the title of a manuscript to which annotations were apparently being added. "I've already written that, surely?"

Without warning, a further wave of mental exhaustion washed over him. He removed his jacket and waistcoat and threw them onto a chair, unclipped and cast aside his collar, undid the topmost buttons of his shirt, then sat, unlaced and kicked off his boots. He saw his *jubbah*—the gown he'd worn during his pilgrimage to Mecca—slung over the back of the saddlebag armchair. He took it up, shrugged into it, and settled at one of the desks, taking a sheet of blank paper from a drawer and pulling a pen from its holder. He dipped the nib into an inkpot and began to write.

Thirty minutes later, he completed the report, an account of all that had occurred since he'd departed the Venetia, including the confession that he'd withheld *The History of the Future* from his brother. Edward would, of course, be beside himself with fury.

He folded the paper and sealed it in an envelope upon which he wrote *Burton, Suite 5*.

Stretching, the explorer rose, returned to the armchair by the fire, and dropped into it, giving a grunt of satisfaction as his hand habitually fell to a box of Manila cheroots on the hearth.

An hour later, he was smoking his third cigar, a plate containing nothing but breadcrumbs and a smear of pickle juice was on a table beside him, and next to that, there stood a bottle of port.

Fidget, his basset hound, was stretched out on the rug at his feet.

Pox, with his head folded under a wing, mumbled, "Muck snipe. Dribblewits. Twerp."

Mrs. Angell had not been impressed with the parakeet.

The explorer raised his glass to his lips and sipped. He was unable to gather his thoughts into anything resembling coherence. His mental processes had seized up.

The afternoon eased into evening.

Mrs. Angell took the plate and delivered a pot of coffee.

The room darkened.

Burton drifted in and out of a light doze. He was half aware of the red firelight reflecting on the ceiling—twice, he'd dreamed it to be the canvas roof of a tent in Berbera—and of Mr. Grub's sing-song appeals for customers, which penetrated the windowpanes, though only faintly, being mostly drowned out by the clatter and clank of the traffic.

"Hot baked 'tators! Hot baked 'tators for 'em what wants 'em! Hear the word! Hot baked 'tators! The rapture is nigh! The rapture is nigh!"

Red ceiling. Red canvas. Red leaves. Red flowers. Red sky as the sun set over the Gulf of Trieste.

Steinhaueser. It wasn't Steinhaueser. Why do I keep thinking it was Steinhaueser? Our live-in doctor was Baker. Geoffrey—no, Grenfell—Baker. And not a pond but a water barrel.

The thought flickered briefly then died, its significance instantly lost.

A tap on the door roused him. Fidget looked up and gave a little whine.

"Come," Burton called drowsily. He stifled a yawn.

Bram poked his head into the room. "Perch."

The explorer waved at a corner. "Thank you, lad. Over there will do."

The boy entered, positioned Pox's perch as indicated, then said to Burton, "Priory Park, Crouch End."

"Hmm? What about it?"

"The *Orpheus* was found abandoned there. Spotted from the air by its own captain, so it was."

Burton sat up. "By Lawless? Ah! Good! No doubt he'll fly her back to the power station."

"Aye, sir, already has. No sign of Miss Raghavendra and Mr. Krishnamurthy, I'm afraid. Can I be a-doin' anything else for ye?"

"There's an envelope on the desk. Will you see that it's delivered to the Venetia Hotel?"

"Rightio."

"Good lad. Nothing else. I'm going to turn in."

"It's fair early, so it is."

"I know, but I can hardly keep my eyes open. I think I must be having a reaction."

"A reaction, is it? To coming home?"

Burton heaved himself to his feet. "To the end of a very long journey, Bram."

"Sleep well, then, Cap'n. Goodnight to ye!"

The boy took the envelope from the desk, and withdrew.

Burton stood, crossed to Pox, prodded him with a forefinger, then continued on to the window and opened it.

"Ack!" the bird yelped. "Bollocks!"

"Message for Detective Inspector Trounce. This is Burton. Clock-work men have abducted Sadhvi and Maneesh. *The History of the Future* was also taken. I'll drop by Scotland Yard tomorrow. Message ends."

The parakeet dived out of the window. Burton left it open enough to allow for the messenger's return then stepped out of his study and climbed the stairs to his bedroom.

"Why didn't I send that message earlier?" he mumbled. "Careless of me. I must be getting forgetful in my old age."

Upon entering the chamber, he stood by the bed with his eyes half closed and waited for someone to come to his assistance. Thirty seconds passed before he realised what he was doing and wondered why in the name of Allah he was doing it.

He undressed, got into bed, and was asleep almost immediately.

His slumber was turbulent. He groaned and thrashed and called out Isabel's name, but he didn't wake until eight in the morning and did so feeling refreshed and with no recollection of his dreams.

Sitting up, he wiped beads of sweat from his forehead, took a glass of water from his bedside table, gulped it down, then lay back and rested for a further half hour.

He knew he'd come from a different time where he'd possessed a different body, but he identified the time as 2203 and the previous body as a brass machine.

Old age and Trieste did not occur to him.

CHAPTER 8

MR. DISRAELI THROWS A SPANNER IN THE WORKS

DANGER! NO ENTRY!
Construction Work in Progress
The New East End!
Fully plumbed houses and tenements. Efficient sewer system.
Well-lighted streets.
Small parks and recreational areas.
Shops, offices, work yards and other business premises.
AN END TO POVERTY.
THE EMPIRE TAKES CARE OF ITS OWN.

In the mews at the back of 14 Montagu Place, there were two velocipedes, two rotorchairs, and one steam sphere. When Swinburne—defeathered and well rested—arrived at ten o'clock, he and Burton took the rotorchairs and flew to Battersea Power Station.

Neither man made any mention of his previous life.

Gooch and Faraday, who were standing at a bench and examining Grumbles' dismantled head, looked up and greeted them. Faraday's hair was still sticking out, not having been brushed since yesterday.

"*Orpheus?*" Burton asked.

"In the quadrangle," Gooch responded, referring to a large area behind the main workshop that was open to the air and surrounded on all four sides by the building. "Nathaniel is aboard, standing guard, though

I've assured him that the vessel is perfectly secure there. They got what they wanted from it."

"Which was?"

"The Mark Three babbage, the Nimtz generator, and the black diamonds. All removed. It also means they've got their hands on the Turing modules that were added to the ship's brain."

"Looking on the bright side," Swinburne said, "they're now exposed to the Mark Three's personality. That'll teach 'em."

"Only if it's broken its silence," Gooch noted.

Burton clicked his teeth together and rapped the end of his cane on the floor. "Bloody Babbage! It has to be!"

"My thought exactly," Gooch agreed. He leaned forward over the bench, supporting himself with his mechanical arms while gesturing, with his natural hands, at the components spread across its top. "I checked the station records. It is normal procedure for clockwork men to be recalled on an annual basis for checks and fine-tuning. During the period between our departure for the future and Babbage's disappearance, he personally serviced a hundred and twenty-one machines. Your brother's device was one of them, as were all of those that worked here at the station. The remaining seventy-three are owned, presumably, by various organisations, politicians, and aristocrats—that is to say, by the people and places that can afford them—but the ownership certificates have been removed, so I can't tell you exactly who or where."

"And the tampering?"

Gooch tapped Grumbles' head. "As I said before, I can't dig too deeply into it for fear of setting off the booby trap, but I was, at least, able to retrieve this." He took a small metal fitting between finger and thumb and raised it. "Not so much a tampering, as an extending. I don't know exactly what it does, but at its heart, there's a granule of black diamond dust."

Swinburne drummed his fingers on the bench top. "And what do we know about such gems? They can distort time. They can accentuate clairvoyant abilities. They can hold a human consciousness."

The engineer shook his head. "No, a single grain of this size hasn't the capacity for any of that."

Burton asked, "Might it employ the resonance that exists between all the diamonds and their fragments as a means for communication?"

Gooch looked astonished. "I say! Yes, it's very possible! Very possible indeed! What on earth made you think of that?"

Briefly, Burton told the engineer about the kidnapping of Raghavendra and Krishnamurthy.

"Phew!" Gooch exclaimed. "You're right. There must be intercommunication. It only makes sense if Grumbles, Sprocket, and the crew of the ornithopter were able to alert one another." He straightened and stroked his chin with artificial fingers. "Hmm. The transmission the *Orpheus* received. I wonder—"

"Algy came to the same conclusion. A message from Babbage, perhaps? But how could he have known of our arrival? We hadn't announced ourselves. Even the clockwork men here in the station didn't know we'd returned until we were greeted by Fiddlesticks."

"The sound of the ship landing?" Swinburne suggested.

Gooch made a gesture of negation. "Ships set down here day and night." His brow creased. "I suppose Babbage could have been using the stones he took from the station to broadcast, via their resonance, a permanent signal, which the *Orpheus* responded to immediately upon reception of it. That way, he'd have known we were back before anyone else. He might have then ordered the ship to remain silent and to take off as soon as the station's clockwork men, following his directive, boarded it."

After a moment of consideration, Burton addressed Faraday. "How was Babbage behaving in the days before he vanished?"

Faraday shrugged. "He was his usual self—you know, idiosyncratic. Obsessive. Short-tempered. Impatient. Er, things like that."

"Nothing unusual? Unusual for him, I mean."

"Not that I noticed."

"Any new obsessions?"

Faraday patted his pockets, didn't find what he was looking for, peered at Burton, and said, "Pardon?"

The explorer repeated the question.

Faraday scratched his head. "Those doo-dahs. Round. What are they called? Circles. Children. You know."

"Eh?"

"Er. Spinning tops. No, that's not right. Hoops. Yes, hoops. The ones the nippers play with, rolling them along the streets—the roads—the—er—streets. Babbage took umbrage to them, called them a public nuisance."

"He's always hated the entertainments enjoyed by the common folk," Gooch put in. "In fact, he'd be delighted if that whole class of people—*the mob*, as he refers to them—were removed from the face of the earth."

"Oh, quite so, quite so," Faraday agreed. "That's why he developed his clockwork men in the first place. He was furious when what's-his-name refused to allow their deployment in the—er—watchamacallits."

"The who in the what?" Swinburne asked.

The scientist stared into space.

"Mr. Faraday?" Burton prompted.

"Hum? The who in the—? Ah, yes. The prime minister. Who is it? Disraeli! Old Babbage met with Disraeli last year and offered to replace all the—um—the labourers with his—you know—in the factories and workhouses."

"Substitute them with his clockwork men?" Burton asked.

"That's right. Efficiency. No wages required. Of course, Disraeli put the mockers on the idea. Supplanting the working classes wouldn't make them disappear. Quite the opposite. If they weren't occupied, they'd be free to make whatsit all over the place."

"Babies," Swinburne said.

"Mischief."

"I would have thought that objection rather obvious," Gooch observed.

"Patently," Faraday agreed. "But Babbage hadn't thought it through. He's always been funny like that." He tapped a finger to the side of his head. "Lacking a few thingamabobs in the old—er—noggin."

"Exactly when did he see Disraeli?" Burton asked.

"Um. October. No. August. Wait. Let me think. Ah, it was late in October. Yes, that's right. Without a doubt. October."

"Shortly before he absconded, then?"

"Oh! Why, yes, I suppose it was."

Gooch pursed his lips. "How might that relate to our spring-driven bandits?"

"I'm searching for the rationale behind yesterday's events," Burton responded. "If Babbage is responsible, could he be independently pursuing the idea rejected by Disraeli, or some variant thereof?"

"I can perceive no logical connection between the thefts of yesterday and the desire to disenfranchise the lower classes," the engineer said.

"Neither can I," Burton agreed, "but I'd like to know what passed between Babbage and the prime minister at that meeting." He indicated the metal part still in Gooch's hand. "If we're correct in thinking that Babbage is broadcasting orders to his devices, is there any way to trace the source of the signals?"

"Babbage is the only man I know of who might be able to create a method. It's a shame the Beetle has slipped away. He has—"

Burton and Swinburne both interrupted him with cries of surprise.

"Bismillah!" Burton said, slapping a hand to his head. "The Beetle! I forgot him. I forgot I'm an old man. Isabel. Trieste. 1890."

"What? What? What?" Swinburne shrilled. "How could we—how am I—My hat! This isn't even our world!"

Faraday blinked in puzzlement. "Beetle? Not your—er—? How is it not?"

Gooch hastily explained to his colleague, "Disorientation caused by the transcendence of time. We encountered it frequently during our voyage. Would you mind leaving us, old fellow? I have to discuss matters that are classified as confidential by the government. You understand, of course?"

"Yes. Yes. Of course. I'll give you chaps your privacy."

With a slightly awkward bow, Faraday backed away and shuffled off.

Gooch waited until the man was out of hearing range then said to Burton and Swinburne, "It's all right. Your new memories are obscuring the old. It's no surprise and nothing to worry about. I'd advise you not to resist it."

"But—but—are we becoming different people?" Swinburne asked.

"No. Just different renditions of the same men—variations more suited to this particular time stream. Still the poet. Still the explorer."

"It's happening so fast!"

"You've rather been thrown into the deep end, so to speak," Gooch said. "None of us expected this turn. We thought you'd be eased, not plunged, into your new roles." He lifted Grumbles' head. "This business has accelerated the process."

"The closing of the circle," Burton murmured. "The Beetle said events would occur with great rapidity."

He drew a cheroot from his waistcoat pocket, lit and drew on it, then breathed out a plume of smoke, cleared it with an impatient wave, and dismissed at the same time the subject of identity. Somehow, it just didn't feel important.

"Let us focus on the matter at hand. The Beetle? What about him?"

"Ah, yes. I must retract my earlier comment. Babbage doesn't have all the black diamonds. There are eleven still implanted in the Beetle's head."

"But aren't they the same ones that were taken from the Brunel machine?" Swinburne asked.

"They are. Each of them currently exists twice over in the same period of time. A very anomalous circumstance, though one that applies to a great many of the other diamonds as well, thanks to certain actions undertaken by your predecessors. If, as you suggest, Babbage is using the stones as a means of communication, I'm wondering whether our multi-headed friend might have heard his messages."

"Do you know where the Beetle is?"

"He's in the past, perhaps. Or maybe he's gone sideways into a different iteration of the present."

Burton opened his mouth to ask whether the Beetle was able to traverse time by willpower alone, but, before he could utter a sound, an inner affirmation rendered the question unnecessary.

Gooch went on, "He has to undertake a number of actions that, from a certain perspective, have already been done. It's very confusing. I'm under the impression we'll not see him for a while."

The explorer grunted his agreement. "He said as much. I suppose we'll have to do without him. Let's start with Babbage's residence. We should search it."

"You'll not find anything, I'm afraid. Prior to his disappearance, he lived here at the station. His old rooms are completely empty and scrubbed clean."

Burton closed his eyes and pressed a hand to his forehead. "If the man I'm replacing possessed any talent for investigation then I wish I could acquire it from him a little more rapidly. I don't know where to look or what to do. Daniel, I must rely on your inventiveness. Please, find a means to trace the source of that transmission."

Gooch waved his supplementary arms. "If, indeed, there was one. We may be on a hiding to nothing. I'll do what I can. Perhaps I could create something like the Field Amplifier that Babbage built last year. He took it with him, but I remember the principles of the device. It was designed to record the electrical patterns present in the diamonds. If this granule from Grumbles contains some vestige of the signal that we could analyse, it might tell us what we need to know."

Burton picked up his cane. "We'll leave you to press on with it." He drew again on his cigar and cast his eyes across the huge chamber, searching for a sense of unfamiliarity and not finding it. "As for Algy and me, I see but one path to follow, and it leads straight from here to number ten Downing Street."

"The prime minister? I doubt he'll receive you unannounced."

"I shall announce us myself. Let's see whether my position as king's agent can open the most important door in the empire."

Picking up their hats, Burton and Swinburne bid their friend farewell, departed the station, and mounted their rotorchairs.

"Richard," Swinburne said, as he placed goggles over his eyes, "I'm positive I should be stricken with the notion that I'm losing myself, but I feel the absolute opposite."

Burton flicked the stub of his cheroot away, pushed his hat into the storage box beneath his seat, and slipped his cane into a holder. "Likewise, and thank goodness, else I think we'd both be lunatics by now."

The poet grinned, gave a thumbs up, and squeezed the lever that started his machine's engine.

As they soared up and followed the course of the Thames northeastward, Burton noted that the chill air was filled with that variety of meteorological prescience that frequently portends a storm or heavy snowfall. The drizzle had petered out during the night, but the high, flat, featureless layer of cloud still obscured the sky. Pillars of smoke were rising vertically into it from thousands of chimneys, reminding him of the gigantic towers of 2203. It was as if the altitude of the capital was being established first in a gaseous form. Ghosts of things to come.

They descended toward Whitehall. Burton resisted the urge to squeeze his eyes shut and hope for the best. Rotorchairs, rotorships, and ornithopters were swarming in profusion above the rooftops and a collision felt inevitable. Indeed, another flier came so close that the explorer heard, above the paradiddle of his own machine, the other vehicle's driver yelling at him.

With a teeth-jarring thud, he landed on the cobbles of Downing Street. His rotorchair screeched along on its runners, showering sparks, and almost overturned before it came to rest.

Pedestrians, who'd dived out of its path, shook their fists and expressed their indignation in no uncertain terms.

"Bloody hell!" he muttered, breathing heavily.

Swinburne's flying chair set down more gently nearby, causing a horse to utter a panicked whinny. The driver of the wood wagon to which the beast was harnessed bawled an incomprehensible oath as he steered around the machine.

The two men dragged their vehicles to the kerb, removed their goggles, and strode along to the prime minister's residence. A constable was standing sentry duty at its door. Swinburne offered him a grin and a ragged salute. "What ho! What ho!"

"Move along, please, sir," the policeman said. "And next time you take it upon yourselves to land in the street, perhaps you'd do so with a little more care and attention."

"I'm the king's agent," Burton told him.

"Really, sir? That's funny, 'cos I'm the king of Siam. It don't make no odds as far as the landing of rotorchairs goes, though, does it? Good day to you."

Burton proffered his credentials. The policeman gave a careworn sigh, took them, read them twice, and scratched his chin. "Hello! This is a new one on me."

"You've not heard of me?"

"At the Yard, yes, sir, but I didn't know you were real."

"I can assure you that I am."

Swinburne said, "Might I suggest you make an enquiry inside, Your Majesty?"

"I don't know about that. Even if this here bit o' paper is *bona fide*, as the saying has it, that don't much matter unless you have an appointment. Do you?"

"No," Burton said. "But it's a matter of considerable urgency. Is the prime minister at home?"

"I'm not permitted to tell you that, sir. For all I know, you're a couple of anarchists and this here permit of yours is a forgery. He might be. But he might not be. And if he is, this is highly irregular. I think I'd better consult with his staff. On the other hand, if I bother them over nothing—"

"Decisiveness," Swinburne observed. "A desirable quality in a monarch."

The constable considered the poet for a moment. He cleared his throat, turned, and gave four quick knocks on the door followed by a pause then three more. The portal opened wide enough for him to squeeze through into the house. It closed after him.

"Shall I climb to the roof and slip down the chimney?" Swinburne asked.

Before Burton could respond, the door opened again and the constable stepped out.

"In you go, gentlemen. The prime minister will see you immediately."

"Ah! So he *is* at home!" Swinburne exclaimed.

"I can't confirm that, sir."

The poet gave a curtsey and followed Burton in.

They were greeted by—to the explorer's discomfort—a clockwork man.

"I am Mr. Pinion," it said. "The prime minister's secretary. You are Sir Richard? And Mr. Swinburne?"

"Yes," Burton confirmed.

"Your arrival is most felicitous. Mr. Disraeli was about to send for you. This way, please."

Crossing the black-and-white tiled floor of the lobby, the two men were led through a door to their left, passed into a small corridor, then were ushered into a medium-sized square chamber. It was decorated with draped silks, statuettes, paintings, and ornaments, all of Japanese origin.

Mr. Pinion moved to a corner and stood motionless, poised to act upon any request.

Benjamin Disraeli was seated behind a large desk. There were two empty chairs in front of it. He was writing and, without looking up, said, "Sit."

Another man was present, by a small table against the wall to the premier's right. He didn't rise to greet them as propriety required but instead sat glaring disdainfully at Burton.

The explorer felt his heart hammering. He couldn't give credence to what he was seeing.

The prime minister's other guest was Colonel Christopher Palmer Rigby.

Rigby! Bismillah! Rigby! What the hell is he doing here?

The man could only be regarded as an implacable foe. He detested Burton with a passion. The sentiment was returned in full measure. Their mutual antipathy had its roots in India, twenty years ago, when the explorer—then an ensign in the British East India Company Army—had repeatedly beaten the other out of his accustomed first place position in language examinations. Rigby had since applied himself assiduously to the spreading of false rumours about his competitor.

Three years ago, when Burton had arrived in Zanzibar to begin his expedition to the source of the River Nile, he'd found Rigby there, ensconced as British consul. His old enemy had made every effort to interfere with the expedition, so far overstepping the mark that, after Burton had lodged a complaint against him, the British government had been left with no option but to dismiss the man, replacing him with Burton's friend, George Herne.

And now, here he was again, his eyes smouldering with hatred.

Rigby, in his early forties, was slightly taller than Burton and just as

161

solidly built: his shoulders wide, his chest deep, and his biceps straining the sleeves of his long jacket. His hair was shaved extremely short, being little more than bristle, though it lengthened in front of his ears and grew down into an unkempt beard. This, together with his high-bridged and narrow nose, sneering thin-lipped mouth, and closely set eyes, bestowed upon him a horribly brutal mien.

Still without looking up from his papers and in an abstracted tone, Disraeli drawled, "You are acquainted with Colonel Rigby?"

You know damn well I am!

"Unfortunately so," Burton replied as he took his seat.

The prime minister ignored the prickly response and pushed his document aside. Leaning back, he regarded Burton, his heavy lids hooding his eyes. An effete longhaired dandy, his manner was, as always, languid and detached, his expression sleepy. The explorer knew this to be a meticulously cultivated pose which lulled opponents into such overconfidence that when the premier struck—which he did with all the speed and venom of a cobra—it always came as an unpleasant and, more often than not, politically fatal shock.

A dangerous man.

"Your arrival is well-timed. I was about to summon you."

"So I've been told."

"I haven't had much sleep, Sir Richard. I spent a considerable portion of the night in conference with your brother. He informed me that your mission has failed. We are not secure. The possibility exists that we might suffer further interference from the future. I understand, too, that items you brought back with you have been stolen from beneath your nose. Are you so careless?"

Burton glanced at Rigby. "Are we to discuss such matters in front of the colonel, Prime Minister?"

"Colonel Rigby has been made aware of the relevant facts."

"Really? May I ask why?"

"You may not. Please confirm, have you really been so remiss?"

Burton's hands, resting on his thighs, curled into fists. He struggled to keep his voice steady. "I'll answer that in a moment. First, would you please order Mr. Pinion out of the room?"

"For what reason?"

"If you'll indulge me, I'll explain once he's gone."

"I see. Mr. Pinion, you are dismissed."

"Yes, sir," the clockwork man intoned pleasantly. He departed.

Disraeli waited for a few moments after the door had closed then said, "Well?"

Burton looked the premier in the eyes. "My mission to the future succeeded but may have been undone by the events of yesterday. The diamonds containing a fragment of Spring Heeled Jack's consciousness have been removed from Brunel. Their whereabouts is unknown. If we do not recover them, we'll not be able to drive his presence out of them, which means he might still find a means to infiltrate our future history."

"But you will, nevertheless, defeat him there, surely? You have already done so."

"I defeated a Spring Heeled Jack that had been resident in the Brunel body for centuries. Now he is elsewhere, meaning he will be elsewhere in the future, too. Thus all I did there has been rendered null and void. The only advantage gained from the expedition is that we now know the nature of the threat and, providing we regain the diamonds, can neutralise it by passing a strong electrical current through them."

"What has this to do with Mr. Pinion?"

"I have reason to suspect that Charles Babbage ordered the theft of the gemstones. He might also be using his clockwork men to spy."

Disraeli brushed lint from his sleeve. "On me?"

"On the Department of Guided Science, on the Minister of Chronological Affairs, and—yes—perhaps on you, as well."

There came a taut silence, broken only by the muffled thud-thud-thud of Swinburne's right foot, which he was restlessly tapping on the carpet.

The prime minister took a document from a pile to his left and ran his eyes over it. He picked up a pen, put his signature to the paper, and slid it to his right. "To what end?"

Burton gave a slight shake of his head. "That is something I have yet to establish."

"We're currently at odds with only one foreign power, Sir Richard—

I refer, of course, to China—and its leaders are certainly far too wily to recruit such an unreliable man as Babbage to spy for them. In fact, his reputation is such that, if you are correct, he must surely be acting independently. Such being the case, do you not consider it likely that he is moved by scientific avariciousness and nothing else, for what more has ever motivated him? In that light, his spying on the DOGS and the minister might make some sort of sense, but I doubt very much indeed that he has any interest in my affairs."

"He appears to have a measure of interest in your social and economic policies."

"He does?"

"Did you not meet with him last October?"

"Ah. I did. He presented to me a scheme by which the working classes would be ousted from their jobs by his clockwork men. Less a social or economic proposal than an utter absurdity. I dismissed the notion at once."

"And immediately afterward he absconded."

"In a fit of pique, you mean? If so, it was misjudged. He was already perfectly placed to receive any of the machineries and information you brought back with you from the future. Indeed, they would have been put into his hands before any others. I rather suppose he now regrets his temper. Having isolated himself, he was left with no recourse but to steal the items in question. A genius he may be, but he also has a history of impulsive actions and outbursts. Ever has he teetered on the brink of madness."

Burton slapped a hand onto his thigh. "Yes! Exactly! A madman, now in possession of items that must be considered a threat to the welfare of the empire! You appear remarkably unconcerned, sir! People have already died. Spring Heeled Jack is alive and who knows where! Babbage has the means and the ability to directly influence the course of time and reintroduce into it a foul intelligence that I have already destroyed at—at—"

At great personal cost to myself.

The prime minister made a placating gesture. "Quite so. Quite so. Rest assured, it is my intention that Babbage is found and restrained. It is for exactly such work that the empire has a king's agent to whom every resource will be made available that the job can be completed as quickly as possible."

Burton's response was halted by a raised finger, which the prime minister then tapped against his own lips. For half a minute he said nothing, then, "The course of time, you say? As recorded in the document that was snatched from your associates?"

"After a fashion, yes."

"After a fashion? What do you mean by that?"

"It chronicles the international affairs that will shape a future which exists regardless of the outcome of my expedition. Since that outcome is now known to us, the events charted therein are, for us, liable to develop differently."

"Then it has no value?"

"The document serves as a warning."

"Concerning what? Summarise the contents, please. I'm interested to know what Babbage has his hands on."

Burton glanced at the silent Colonel Rigby.

"It is quite all right," Disraeli said. "Speak freely. I want the colonel to understand every aspect and implication of the mission you undertook."

The explorer clenched his teeth, the muscles at the hinges of his jaw visibly swelling. He fumbled for a cigar, looked at the prime minister for permission, received it via an almost imperceptible nod, then struck a lucifer and started to smoke. In a tightly controlled tone, his voice cold, he said, "Why?"

"I shall explain to you when I am ready. Your account, if you please. I express it as a request, but you must regard it as an order. Speak."

Burton shifted uneasily in his seat. Something felt wrong. He tried to read the prime minister's expression but, as always, the man's thoughts were expertly concealed behind a lackadaisical indifference. Rigby's attitude, by contrast, could not have been plainer. He was contemptuous and, more worryingly, triumphant.

Play for time. Give yourself a few minutes to get a grip on this, to think it through and work out what's happening.

"If you have no objection," he said, "I'll ask Algernon to outline the contents. His descriptive abilities outshine my own to a considerable degree. He'll do a far better job of it than I."

"Very well. Mr. Swinburne?"

The poet scratched his head. He leaned back in his chair and crossed his arms, then uncrossed them, twitched, and jerked his left elbow up. He cleared his throat and entwined his fingers, leaned forward, unlaced his fingers, reached for his pocket, changed his mind, rubbed his left eye, then peered first at Rigby then at Disraeli.

"My hat!" he said. "The jolly old future, what! Let us see. Shall we call it a saga of waxing and waning empires, of alliances and betrayals, of belligerence and appeasement, of the impact of individuals and the tidal forces of the masses? Yes, it is all those things; a saga, a tragedy, and a romance."

He steepled his fingers beneath his chin, closed his eyes, and began his narration. From the outset, he made a choice that Burton wouldn't have thought of: he spoke in the past tense, as if from the perspective of 2203. In doing so, he endowed his recitation with a significance it might not have otherwise possessed. Too, his choice of words, the variation of his tone, the well-chosen points of emphasis, the rhythm and the colour of his language, these all demonstrated what a splendid orator he was. And though Burton was somewhat familiar with the material—he'd been too preoccupied with his predicament to read *The History of the Future* but was, nevertheless, aware of its contents—he was enthralled. Despite his hostility, Rigby, too, was obviously mesmerised.

Disraeli, though, turned his attention to his papers and read them and made notes in their margins and scribbled his signature as if paying no attention to the poet at all.

It thoroughly irritated Burton.

For almost an hour, Swinburne described the course of future history. When he had finished, it was clear to every man present that the greatest danger to the British—and later, the Anglo-Saxon—Empire came not from foreign powers but from generation after generation of increasingly weak leaders, for it was they who had allowed the insane presence of Spring Heeled Jack to infiltrate their thinking machines. It was they, too, who'd meekly come under his sway, allowing him to create a foul oligarchy wherein the poor working masses were consigned to an underground world while the idle elite occupied soaring towers.

When the poet finished, no one said anything for almost two minutes. Disraeli's pen scratched on paper.

Finally, the prime minister looked up and broke the silence. "Thank you, Mr. Swinburne. So, Sir Richard, the document details people, places, and events. Does it also offer specifics where the machineries of the future are concerned? Blueprints? Plans? Diagrams?"

Burton shook his head. "No, sir, it doesn't."

"Then Mr. Babbage must be sorely disappointed, for doubtlessly that's what he hoped to find. And what of our contemporaries? Are their future actions recorded? Are mine?"

"No."

"But you can add to it the necessary detail, surely? You were in the future for thirteen months. You made enquiries pertaining to our current period? You asked the denizens of 1914, for instance, what mistakes were made during the latter half of this century?"

"I did not."

"Really? That's rather a serious oversight, don't you think?"

"We were looking forward not back. Also, you must understand that, during our voyage, the years immediately subsequent to the present were the most precariously balanced between one probability and another, the most impacted by the return or nonreturn of the *Orpheus*, and by the decisions taken thereafter in relation to that event. Because the issue was not resolved, no one was able to describe anything that stemmed from it. Even in 1914, little more than fifty years hence, they simply couldn't remember."

Swinburne added, "Our own past has in it an example of such an amnesia. The period between 'thirty-seven and 'forty has always been regarded as strangely muddled. It wasn't until a couple of years ago that we discovered why. A great many events of that period had been retrospectively rendered impossible due to a contextual shift in time."

Frowning, Disraeli pulled a black, lace-edged handkerchief from his pocked and brushed it across his nose. "How, then, did you occupy yourselves in the future once Spring Heeled Jack was defeated?"

Burton, by now on his second cigar, drew on it.

My mind was trapped inside a machine. My senses were curtailed. I felt I was buried alive and suffered an anguish you could not even imagine.

"The people of London required our help. They needed to adapt to their new circumstances. We gave assistance in the formation of a new social and political order. We aided in the overthrow of the inept ruling class."

"You became revolutionaries?"

"If you want to couch it in such terms, yes, we did."

"And you really expect me to believe that in all those months you gave no attention to the years that you yourself could expect to live through upon your return?"

Burton leaned forward and ground out his cigar in an ashtray on the prime minister's desk. Unable to keep the impatience from his tone, he said, "Even the academicians of the twenty-third century were forced to work around enormous gaps in knowledge and a peculiar absence of records. History was as riddled with holes as a Swiss cheese. Even had I been inclined to explore my own fate, I would have found it—um—I would have—"

Dizziness.

Trieste. Isabel. Death. How can I keep forgetting who I am?

Jumbled memories fell into place, some his own, but most belonging to other Burtons. He recalled stilt-walkers and giant mechanised spiders, underground rivers and sewer tunnels, African mountains and armies of beast-men, conflict and fire and pain, pain, pain.

By God, what madness have I been caught up in? What tortures and losses have I endured?

With an effort, he hauled his thoughts out of the mire. He couldn't allow himself to be drowned by the remnants of other lives. He was not those other Burtons. He was different. He, of all of them, had been blessed, for he was reborn.

He had a second chance.

He was young and fit.

He felt good.

This time, he would get it right.

"You're an incompetent fool."

Burton blinked at the premier. "I beg your pardon?"

"I said: you are an incompetent fool."

From the corner of his eye, Burton saw Rigby grinning savagely.

"I say!" Swinburne protested.

"Mr. Swinburne," Disraeli said. "Be quiet. Not another bloody word from you, if you please."

The prime minister rose to his feet and leaned forward over the desk, supporting himself on fisted hands. His demeanour had altered in an instant. Burton hadn't even suspected that a change was coming.

The cobra was striking.

"I hold you accountable, Sir Richard. I hold you accountable for an abject failure. You have returned from the future virtually empty-handed, and what little you brought back with you, you have lost. The day after your return! The *Orpheus*'s brain, stolen! The Nimtz generator, stolen! The diamonds, stolen! The manuscript, stolen! Our enemy, lost from view! And what have you done about it?" He banged his knuckles on the desktop. "Not a bloody thing!"

"You're being—"

"Shut your mouth! You kicked up your heels in the future and there neglected to ask pertinent questions and get detailed answers, and thus uninformed, you have laid the blame for the sad state of this empire's future at the feet of its leaders, who you accuse of weakness, when anyone with even an ounce of sense can see that the rot begins not with them but with an increasingly demanding *petite bourgeoisie*!"

Swinburne threw up his hands and shrieked, "What? What? What?"

Shocked, Burton could only stammer, "I—you—have—have you lost your mind? What the devil are you talking about?"

Disraeli straightened and slammed a palm down. "The middle class! That's how they'll be referred to, is it not? This money-grubbing horde? This self-serving swarm? Swinburne may have glossed over the truth in his recital, but I see it clearly! I see it! You can't pull the wool over my eyes! For all your criticism of the upper classes, it is they who give us our stability. It is they who've granted the workers greater rights than are enjoyed anywhere else in the world. Look at Great Britain, sir! We are the sole country in Europe that has not suffered the chaos of socialism. Thrones have toppled in France, in Germany, in Italy, but here, no! We have a steadfastness that you yourself have seen endure far into the future. If the 'elite,' as you call them, make one mistake, it is that they'll kowtow to the demands of this emerging rabble of uppity *parvenus* whose unfettered ambition and unquenchable discontent will eat away at our social structures. There lies the danger! The *nouveau riche* must be nipped in the bud! The aristocracy must be strengthened while our working classes are given every acknowledgment that, under the guidance of their superiors, they are the driving force of our empire's success and expansion!"

Swinburne leaped to his feet. "Acknowledgment, Prime Minister? Acknowledgment? What value has that? What of *betterment*? What of improving their lot in life?"

"They do not need to be made better. They are perfectly happy as they are. Can you not realise that they are formed by a different breeding, are fed by different food, are ordered by different manners, and are not governed by the same laws as the likes of us? We must maintain their way of life as we maintain our own. It is a misguided notion that these two separate nations within a nation can be merged into one by means of a new class that bridges the gap."

"Us?" Swinburne shrieked. "Confound your snobbery! I'll have no part of it!"

Burton stared in astonishment at the prime minister. Hoarsely, he said, "What has got into you? Have you never walked the streets of this city? Are you blinkered to the pestilence, disease, and starvation that inflict the greater part of it? Have you no sympathy, no empathy, no pity?"

Disraeli folded his arms and coldly returned Burton's gaze. "I'm a politician. My work allows no room for such emotions. I operate at a level that necessitates consideration of broader issues than those of any given individual. This office is where decisions affecting the whole of society are made."

Burton stood and pulled Swinburne away from the desk. He faced the prime minister, his expression ferocious. "You've read the reports held by the Ministry of Chronological Affairs? *The Strange Affair of Spring Heeled Jack? The Curious Case of the Clockwork Man? Expedition to the Mountains of the Moon? The Secret of Abdu El Yezdi?*"

"Utterly imbecilic titles, but yes, I have, of course. What of it?"

"Then you must surely have realised that history consists only of amassed details not of some chimerical broad stroke upon its imagined canvas. You cannot stand above it. You are not an artist at his easel."

"On the contrary, I am perfectly placed to stand above it," Disraeli countered. "The account so ably given by Mr. Swinburne has provided a frame of reference that no other person on this planet possesses. I have the big picture. It is not a pleasant one, so it falls to me to change it. It is my obligation as prime minister to do so."

"Change it by ridding the empire of the *nouveau riche?*" Burton said. "The idea is monstrous. Preposterous."

"Through the lens of sentiment, perhaps, but a politician must be cold and scientific about such matters. Do not superior people have a duty to dominate and guide their inferiors while purging society of those elements that threaten to unbalance the *status quo?* That is Darwinism, pure and simple."

Burton chopped his hand in negation. "No! No, it isn't! In the name of God, see the account for what it is! Algy spoke of international conflicts but could not recount the experiences of the millions of individuals who will suffer, who will die, who will be widowed, who will starve, who will be displaced, whose lives will be ripped apart and ruined. Would you base your decisions on such a broad focus that you overlook the calamitous details?"

"For the good of the empire, I have to."

"But your intentions are fashioned by inaccurate information. The path the world follows has already altered in its course simply by virtue of my expedition's safe return."

"And I intend to clear this new path of the pitfalls that so afflicted those who followed the other."

"At any cost?"

Disraeli ignored the question, sat, and raised a hand to his left temple, which he massaged with his fingertips. He murmured, "I have a pounding headache and a paucity of patience. You are dismissed, Sir Richard."

For a moment, Burton didn't respond, then, very quietly, he said, "I shall locate Babbage, retrieve the stolen material, and place *The History of the Future* into your hands. I hope you will read it carefully and recon—"

Without looking up, the prime minister cut him off. "Sir Richard. Enough. I cannot excuse your oversights. Nor can I rid myself of the suspicion—which your brother shares—that you are withholding vital information. Plainly, you can no longer be trusted. So when I say you are dismissed, I mean from your commission. Please leave your warrant with Colonel Rigby before you depart."

"My—my—?"

Rigby stood. He lifted a swagger stick from the table and jabbed it toward the explorer. In the deep but rather nasal tone that Burton remembered so well—and despised so intensely—he said, "You have failed in your duties and have been stripped of your post. Hand over your credentials. You must take no further action in the name of the king or the government. I will take care of Babbage."

"You?"

"I am the new king's agent. The prime minister is busy and this discussion is finished. Go home."

A NEW PRESENT

... full of presumption, affectation, petty tyranny and igno-
rance; and the civilised world have confirmed their verdict
with the damning epigram that it has fixed to this class
that "they are servile to those above, and tyrannical to those
beneath them."
                        —Karl Marx on the middle classes,
                    New-York Daily Tribune, 1854

YOUNG ENGLAND,
OLD FRIENDS, AND A BROTHEL

AN EXHIBITION OF MECHANICAL WINGS
Hyde Park, Saturday April 15th, 2 p.m.
In which courageous aeronauts will don the newly invented wings,
jump from the rotorship *Orpheus*, and fly like birds for your
entertainment and wonderment.

You will not believe your eyes!
MEN CAN FLY!

"It's atrocious!" Thomas Bendyshe bellowed. "An affront to human liberty! The criminalisation of public protests! By gad, that Disraeli fellow should be kicked in the seat of his pants!"

"I'd happily lend my foot to the project," Richard Monckton Milnes responded. "The name for his current campaign—*Young England*—originated with me. That it's been so perverted in purpose and application causes me considerable guilt. I only wish I could retract my involvement."

Sir Richard Francis Burton, sitting cross-legged in a leather armchair with a hookah at his side, exhaled a plume of fragrant smoke and in a drawling tone, his words a little slurred, said, "But it was something else entirely at the time, was it not?"

Monckton Milnes, a tall, enigmatic, and saturnine individual, took a decanter from the sideboard by which he was standing and refilled his wine glass. "Absolutely. The original Young England was founded back in 1840, in the days following the assassination. At that time, Palmerston was attempting to backdate the Regency Act to allow Prince Albert to accede to the throne. Countess Sabina—you remember her? The clairvoyant?"

Burton winced. "Of course I do. She died right in front of me."

In his mind's eye, he saw the countess, possessed by a *nosferatu*, her head twisting around until her neck snapped. Like so much at present, the recollection felt as if it more properly belonged to someone else. There was no depth of emotion attached to it.

Monckton Milnes continued, "She warned me that, though it might appear a desirable move where the welfare of the country was concerned, Palmerston's intentions were rather more unscrupulous. Aware of the prince's persistently frail health and the likelihood he would die relatively young and without issue, Palmerston was manoeuvring himself into what could easily become an unassailable position of power. He foresaw the empire slipping into republicanism with, in all probability, himself as its president. Countess Sabina warned that his actions would lead to a violent and disastrous revolution such as those that were then brewing throughout the whole of Europe."

"You told Disraeli?" Burton asked.

"The countess instructed me to do so. Frankly, I was puzzled. In those days, Dizzy was an insignificant politico with the reputation of being an unprincipled opportunist. He didn't strike me as a man who could oppose someone as cunning and influential as Palmerston."

Doctor James Hunt, seated opposite Burton, removed a pipe from his mouth. "He was considered a radical at the time, wasn't he? Disraeli, I mean."

"Quite so," Monckton Milnes agreed. "Though he was standing as a Tory candidate. I met him at one of Lady Londonderry's little soirées. He wasn't much liked. There was considerable prejudice against Jews at the time, and I must confess, I felt a little sorry for him."

"Hah!" Bendyshe yelled. "If only you'd known then what a loony he'd turn out to be, hey?"

"Great Scott, Tom! Why must you trumpet so?" Sir Edward Brabrooke complained. "You're giving me a blessed earache."

Burton, Bendyshe, Monckton Milnes, Hunt, and Brabrooke, along with Sir Charles Bradlaugh and Captain Henry Murray, were relaxing in the private chambers above Bartolini's Italian restaurant in Leicester Square. Together, they formed the disreputable Cannibal Club, of which Swinburne—currently absent—was also a member. An offshoot of Burton's Anthropological Society, it had originally been created as forum for dining and discussion but from the outset had proven a better vehicle for drinking and hell-raising. Indeed, its members' tendency to rowdiness—especially on the part of Swinburne and Bendyshe—frequently incited Signor Bartolini to banish them from his rooms, though he always rescinded, usually after being charmed by either Burton or Monckton Milnes.

Last year, the club had taken on a more serious purpose, its dedicated bachelors tasked with finding wives and starting families, so their descendants could assist Burton's expedition as it travelled forward through time. His safe return, which owed a great deal to their success, meant the Cannibals could now abandon the project. It was a confusingly contradictory state of affairs that none of them really understood.

"I rather like the sound of my descendants," Bendyshe had said, "and shan't deny them the opportunity to exist. I'll continue the search, and one way or another, I shall find my spouse and do the unnecessary."

Three months of fruitless wife hunting had passed since he'd made that statement.

Those same three months—it was now June 1861—had seen Burton at a loose end. Stripped of his role as the king's agent, he had no idea what to do with himself. None of his unfinished writing projects interested him—not *The Thousand Nights and a Night*, not *The Kama Sutra of Vātsyāyana*, not even *Vikram and the Vampire*, which required only a little attention before it could be considered complete. Whenever he considered them, he experienced the inexplicable sensation that the work was already done, that whatever he wrote would simply reiterate what already existed, not by virtue of being translations, but rather because—

And here he stumbled. Because what?

Why did everything—*everything*!—give rise to a haunting déjà vu, yet at one and the same time, strike him as bizarrely unfamiliar? It made no sense. And why, too, his permanent suspicion that he'd forgotten something?

He was flummoxed, restive, and irritated, and had in consequence so far called five meetings of the Cannibals in order to drink his uneasiness into submission. The previous four occasions had seen him achieve a thorough state of inebriation. On this fifth, he was dedicating himself assiduously to the same end.

He wasn't there yet. Only two hours had passed since the club convened—it was close to midnight—and the time had thus far been spent discussing the extraordinary policies the prime minister was rushing through Parliament. In a matter of weeks, Disraeli had taken the empire in a whole new direction, with Gladstone's opposition party offering a baffling lack of resistance.

"So following your advice," Burton said to Monckton Milnes, "Disraeli founded Young England?"

"He did. I funded it and suggested the name, following the pattern of Young Ireland, Young Italy, and Young Germany, all similarly nationalistic groups. Together with four aristocratic young gentlemen—George Smythe, Lord John Manners, Henry Thomas Hope, and Alexander Baillie-Cochrane—and supported by John Walter the Second, who was then the proprietor of the *Times*, as his son is now, Dizzy mounted a devastating attack on Palmerston, exposing him as a dangerous megalomaniac and ruining his political credibility while, incidentally, raising his own game to such a degree that he was elected head of the Conservative Party and, soon afterward, prime minister. As you know, Palmerston went barmy, attempted an armed insurrection, holed up in secret chambers beneath the Tower of London, and in October 1841 was flushed out, tried as a traitor, and hanged."

"Bloody hell!" Bendyshe thundered. "Dizzy owes his career to you. Perhaps I should apply my boot to *your* pants!"

"I suppose he does and maybe you should," Monckton Milnes ruminated. "Though once Palmerston was defeated, I withdrew my support."

"Why?" Burton asked.

"Simply because there was no further requirement for it."

"And what of Young England?"

"It continued for a while, its new intention being to promulgate the notion of *noblesse oblige*, the idea that the landed gentry has a duty to fulfil social responsibilities, that it must earn its privileges by working to improve the lot of the lower classes, rather than seeking ever more influence, as Palmerston had done. However, by the mid-forties, Dizzy's political jiggery-pokery made it apparent that he actually supported the unbridled power of the aristocracy, which so badly damaged Young England's credibility that the group disbanded and that was the end of that."

"Until three months ago," Brabrooke observed. "Why resurrect it?"

Monckton Milnes shrugged. "It's the same name and the same core group of people—less George Smythe, who died a few years ago—but the rationale appears to be the opposite of the original. This new Young England is pursuing a course by which peers are more greatly separated and insulated from the masses than ever before. The common people—or, to be more specific, the middling sorts—are fast becoming the subjects of a cold-hearted plutocracy, with all the legal routes of opposition to it being fast removed."

"I'll say!" Bendyshe put in. "These new laws of his are oppressive to an extreme. The right to detain individuals without charge. The militarisation of the police. Outrageous! The people are being denied their freedom. Dizzy has become little better than a dictator."

"As our friend Algernon is making very plain," Monckton Milnes noted. "He's treading a perilous path with his latest work. John Walter the Third is vilifying him in the *Times* on an almost-daily basis. The paper has dubbed him the 'Rabble-Rousing Rhymer.' I'm happy that Algy has found a purpose, but I worry that he's pushing harder than the authorities will allow. There are rumours that lawsuits are being prepared against him and that he'll be accused of sedition, libel, and obscenity. Already, his poems 'A Song in Time of Order' and 'A Song in Time of Revolution' have been suppressed and all published copies burned. You need to calm him down, Richard. Tell him to keep quiet and lie low for a while."

"I've not seen him for some weeks," Burton countered.

"Probably because he's sobered up and you've gone the other way,"

James Hunt observed. "I mean no offence—Lord knows, we all know how to down a few—but, you must admit, you've been hitting the bottle rather hard of late."

Burton sighed, put aside the hookah, picked up a glass half filled with brandy, and emptied it in a single swallow. "Frustration, James. Raghavendra and Krishnamurthy have been missing for over twelve weeks, Scotland Yard has no leads, Trounce's attempts to investigate have been blocked by Chief Commissioner Mayne, and I'm prohibited from looking any further into the matter. Even were I to ignore that ban—which I do—I have no notion how to proceed with the investigation."

Bradlaugh stepped closer to avail himself of the decanter. "Your brother still hasn't contacted you?"

"No."

Without declaring his intentions, and accompanied by Shyamji Bhatti, Edward had, the day following Burton's meeting with Disraeli, abandoned his suite at the Venetia, taking with him just a small amount of luggage. Burton didn't know where he'd gone and hadn't had the opportunity to ask him whether he'd been privy to the meeting last October between Disraeli and Babbage.

Two days after Edward's disappearance, Captain Lawless had been informed that his ship was to be used in an exhibition of mechanical wings. Taking umbrage that the pride of the fleet was to be employed for the purpose of public entertainment, he and his crew had departed Battersea Power Station in it and had not been seen since. The *Orpheus*, once again, was missing.

I am losing my allies.

"I say!" Bendyshe exclaimed. "What about that parrot of yours? Doesn't it possess an uncanny ability to locate the people it knows?"

"It does, and I've sent it more than a few times to Edward, Bhatti, Lawless, Krishnamurthy, and Raghavendra, and on every occasion it has flown back and stated, 'message undelivered.' It can only mean that our people are either beyond its flight range or locked indoors somewhere."

"And Gooch?" Bradlaugh asked. "Still no progress?"

"Very little. He's working under severe constraints in a field that isn't his area of expertise. His colleague Michael Faraday would have been of considerable assistance, but he left the country for America the moment Disraeli incorporated the Department of Guided Science into the Department for Industry."

"Gad!" Brabrooke said. "The DOGS disbanded! Dizzy has gone insane, I tell you. Completely insane."

"How many of his people does Gooch have with him?" Monckton Milnes enquired of Burton.

"Seventeen. He and they cleared out of Battersea Power Station the day before it was closed down. They took equipment with them and have been hiding out at a secret location ever since. Under such circumstances, developing a Field Amplifier is proving difficult, to say the least, but until it's completed, I'm stumped."

"And that bounder Rigby hasn't made any headway, I suppose?"

"I've seen no evidence that he's even investigating."

Monckton Milnes shook his head sadly. "How could it have come to this? I thought your expedition was supposed to open the way to a bright new future, and instead we have Disraeli declaring his every new policy 'emergency legislation' so its parliamentary passage can be expedited in days—sometimes hours—without any proper consultation, consideration, or discussion. Why the hell is Gladstone allowing it? And what is the emergency? China, we are told! The whole empire is being flooded with Celestial spies! Do any of you actually believe that?"

"Not I," Bradlaugh said.

"Nor I," Brabrooke agreed. "The Treaty of Tianjin was signed immediately after the bombing of the Old Summer Palace. Why would the Qing Dynasty immediately renege on it? The prime minister's claim that the Chinese are planning to attack the British mainland is risible balderdash. Our government is fear mongering. These are tactics of distraction."

Bendyshe jabbed a forefinger toward Burton. "I don't know what you told Dizzy about the future but, plainly, it has sent him over the edge."

Drawing on the hookah, Burton murmured, "I made it perfectly clear in my report that Spring Heeled Jack's ascendancy was made possible by successive generations of increasingly ineffectual aristocratic leaders. The equation is simple enough to comprehend: where power and privilege is inherited, then the qualities that earned the honours in the first place must surely diminish.

The prime minister appears to have ignored that observation entirely and is bent on establishing today exactly the sort of inviolable divide between the rich and poor that I witnessed in the twenty-third century."

He gulped at his brandy angrily. His mood was dark and had been since the meeting at Number 10. He felt as if the sudden and harsh new governmental policies were somehow his fault.

He needed to see Swinburne and Trounce. Only their company soothed the restlessness that was boiling inside him. Unfortunately, Algy had so thrown himself into his poetic but vitriolic criticisms of the empire, and was enjoying such a level of notoriety, that he'd become extremely difficult to pin down. Trounce, meanwhile, had been at odds with his superior at Scotland Yard, having strenuously objected to the arming of constables with pistols, to the right to incarcerate suspects without charges, and to the many other new powers recently granted to the Police Force. Having been twice reprimanded, he was now working extended shifts in an attempt to restore the chief commissioner's confidence in him and avoid any further disciplinary action.

The Cannibals were left as Burton's only recourse, but though he valued each of them as friends, there lurked within him the feeling that these drunken meetings were nothing but a means of avoidance, an arena in which to talk about the world when he should be confronting it head on.

Why this bloody paralysis?

Why, for twelve weeks, had he felt so forestalled in the matter of Raghavendra and Krishnamurthy's abduction? Why could he not identify a means to locate them—or Babbage—beyond that which Gooch had proposed?

Has turning forty made of me an old man?

It was a recurring and aggravating thought.

Too old for this. Too old.

"I think," Tom Bendyshe said, "that I shall take a leaf out of Algy's book and join the opposition to this dreadful regime. My little publishing concern has so far confined itself to ethnological work and material of, shall we say, a rather more saucy nature. I'm inclined to now turn over my presses to our little redheaded friend. As inflammatory as his poetry is, I'll wager it's not half of what he wants to say."

"Hankey and Ashbee are treading cautiously," Bradlaugh noted, referring to the two mutual friends who'd thus far published the poet's works. "I'd advise you to do the same. The authorities may have turned a blind eye to your volumes of erotica, but I doubt they'll stand for outright subversion. I already fear for Algy. Don't make me fear for you, too."

Bendyshe flapped his hand dismissively. "Pshaw! Don't worry yourself, old fellow. My presses are in Paris. I can't be arraigned for what's published there, and I'll ensure the material is brought to this country by suitably circuitous means."

He filled and raised his glass and bellowed, "By gad! I propose a toast to Algernon! May his barbs prick Dizzy where it hurts the most!"

The quaffing continued and intensified. Burton listened to conversations as they meandered drunkenly from one subject to another, dwindled, and arose again to follow a new and equally digressive path. He contributed to fewer and fewer of them, becoming ever more withdrawn, his thoughts folding in on themselves.

He tried to envision his future, wondered where he'd go or what he'd write, but his mind persistently skipped past all the possibilities and instead presented him with visions of his dotage. He imagined himself incapacitated, imprisoned in a declining body, the fancy quickly developing with such pitiless clarity that his hands started to shake, a cold ache gnawed at his joints, and gravity tugged at him as if eager to draw him into the grave.

Time is moving too fast, spiralling in on itself. Events are out of control. I am plummeting toward my death.

"I can't!" he cried out, lurching to his feet and dropping his half-filled glass. "I can't!"

"Richard?" Monckton Milnes asked, reaching for him.

Burton batted his friend's hand away. "Not again!"

Again? Again? What am I saying?

He stumbled to the door and snatched his outdoor vestments from a coat rack.

"Can't what?" Monckton Milnes called after him.

Burton turned unsteadily. The Cannibals were gaping at him, their faces expressing surprise and concern.

"I have—I have to go," he mumbled, placing his hat upon his head.

Practically falling through the door, he descended the stairs, hearing the muffled voice of Bendyshe behind him. "What the devil has got into him? I swear, the old boy's not been the same since his confounded expedition!"

Burton barged past a waiter, hurried through the restaurant, and plunged out into Leicester Square.

London was fogbound and insufferably warm. The sulphurous pall had enveloped the city two weeks ago, steadily thickening into a pea-souper, a "London particular." Visibility was so reduced that Burton felt he'd stepped into a limbo inhabited only by vague and silent ghosts.

One of the phantoms detached itself from the wall beside the restaurant door and, before the explorer had taken two paces, swooped upon him. Burton was suddenly wrapped in shadow. A vast hand clapped tightly across his mouth, and a thick limb embraced him from behind, pinning his arms to his sides.

A voice hissed in his ear. "Lord 'elp us, you've kept me a-waitin' for long enough. Shush now! Don't make a bloomin' sound, guv'nor. They're watchin' out for you."

"Mmmph," Burton replied.

"It's me. Follow. Quiet as you can."

Montague Penniforth.

Penniforth was a cab driver, a giant of a man, Burton's friend, and a member of the Ministry of Chronological Affairs.

The hand and arm fell away. Fingers clutched his sleeve. Tripping drunkenly over his own feet, Burton allowed himself to be drawn along close to the sides of the buildings and into a side street. There, he was bundled into a landau. Penniforth whispered, "Someone wants to see you. I'll take you right there. Here, drink this."

A flask was thrust into Burton's hands.

The carriage door closed, and the vehicle rocked as Penniforth heaved his considerable bulk up onto its box seat. There came a mechanical cough, growl, and splutter as the steam-horse started. The wheels began to grind over cobbles.

Bemusedly, Burton lifted the flask, opened its lid and sniffed at the contents. Coffee. He sipped it. Hot. Black. Strong. Well-sugared.

A foghorn sounded from the Thames. The fog muffled all other noises bar those made by the landau.

He drank the coffee and, when he'd finished, concluded that enough time had passed. He lifted his cane and used its end to push open the little trapdoor in the cabin's roof.

"What's the story, Monty?"

"Wait," came the abrupt reply.

Burton waited.

The carriage turned this way and that. Twice, its cabin bumped and scraped against brick walls. The vehicle was obviously navigating the narrow back streets.

After perhaps five minutes, Penniforth called down, "You've got hounds on your scent, an' I daresay we've not shaken 'em off, so when I tells you to jump, you 'op out while I keep goin' an' lead 'em on a merry chase. You'll find yerself at the end of an alley. Walk down it—no hangin' about—an' enter the establishment what you'll find 'alfway along."

"I'm followed? By whom and for what reason? And what establishment?"

"No time to explain, guv'nor. Jump! Now! Off you go!"

Burton opened the door and dropped from the moving carriage. His feet hit the ground, and he staggered and nearly fell. By the time he'd righted himself, Penniforth's cab had already vanished into the murk.

A denser shadow to his right marked the mouth of an alley. Burton quickly moved into it and, when he heard the chugging of approaching engines, pressed himself against a wall. Three velocipedes passed, rattling along the road he'd just left, obviously chasing the landau. Their riders were unidentifiable, their forms mere smudges in the cloud, but he had the fleeting impression that they were somehow oddly proportioned, and a chill prickled through him.

He didn't move until the vehicles' noise had faded to nothing and even then waited for two minutes before turning and feeling his way forward, peering cautiously ahead. His boots encountered litter and filthy puddles. Flecks of ash accumulated on his shoulders and hat. The corrosive fumes assaulted the back of his throat. He battled the impulse to cough.

An orange glow pierced the vaporous curtain a few steps away and to his left. He moved toward it and saw a gas lamp above a dark blue door. A small brass plaque was mounted on the portal. It bore the words *Verbena Lodge*.

"Ah," Burton murmured. "Algy."

His friend's physiological quirk didn't only inspire inappropriate outbursts of humour but also caused the poet to experience pain as pleasure. This had given rise to certain unusual tastes. Verbena Lodge was where Swinburne indulged them.

Burton thrice applied the handle of his cane to the wood. Half a minute passed before his knocks were acknowledged. The door, with a slight squeak, swung inward. A seven-foot-tall bald-headed and muscular African, dressed in long white robes, looked down at the visitor.

"I don't recognise you," he rumbled, his voice sounding as if it was rising from the depths of the earth.

"Burton. I think my friend Swinburne is here. He sent for me."

"Swinburne. There's no Swinburne."

"I see. Perhaps he goes by another name. He's a very short and excitable fellow with a taste for the lash and a propensity for versifying."

The doorman grinned, his teeth startlingly white. "Oh. You mean Mr. Wheldrake."

Ernest Wheldrake. A pseudonym Algy used when writing humorously negative reviews of his own poetry.

"I believe so."

"Come in, please."

Burton entered. The servant closed the door after him, stalked across the small lobby, and poked his head around an arched opening into the room beyond. "Madam, a gentleman is here to see Mr. Wheldrake. Should I—?"

A husky female voice responded, "He's expected, Malazo. Show him up to the Crimson Suite. Remind the girls that it's off-limits until further notice."

"Yes, ma'am."

Malazo turned back to Burton and led him to a staircase, up to the second floor, and along a corridor to a chamber on the right. He tapped on the door then opened it. Burton passed through and found himself surrounded by maroon draperies, plush redly upholstered furniture, and rather garish *objets d'art*.

The door closed behind him.

"Hallo! Hallo! Hallo!" Swinburne screeched, jumping up from a *chaise longue*. "About time! Are you perfectly squiffy?"

Eying the man who rose from an armchair beside the poet, Burton said, "I'm very rapidly regaining my sobriety, Algy. It's good to see you again. And how do you do, Mr. Gladstone? I shan't pretend I'm not taken aback to find you here."

"Old Gladbags is a regular customer," Swinburne declared airily. "He's perfectly fascinated by the doxies."

"My name is not Gladbags," Gladstone objected. His voice was icy and precise. He stood with his back ramrod straight and extended a hand toward Burton while giving every indication that he'd prefer it not to be taken and shaken.

Burton took it and shook it.

The leader of the opposition and—until his recent and uncharacteristic silence—Disraeli's fiercest critic, possessed a glowering and entirely unforgiving demeanour. It was so thoroughly puritanical that a brothel was perhaps the very last place on earth in which one could expect to encounter it. Yet, despite the permanently disapproving glare and the puckered lips, the haughty angle of the chin and the nostrils that flared as if permanently assaulted by a foul odour, there were persistent whispers concerning Mr. Gladstone's nocturnal habits, a certain breed of tittle-tattle that clung to him no matter how censorious his words and deportment.

"And you know full well, Mr. Swinburne," he said, "that my visits to this establishment have but one object, it being to turn the dox—the young ladies—from their sinful ways."

Burton removed his hat and put it on a sideboard. He laid aside his cane and unbuttoned his coat. "With what rate of success so far, if I might ask?"

"My labours are ongoing. The eradication of such varieties of wickedness that are found herein cannot be achieved in short order."

"He's still in the research phase of the project," Swinburne said. He gestured for Burton to occupy a vacant chair and, as the explorer settled into it, added, "And there is such a *delicious* variety of wickedness, Richard. The girls of the lodge are remarkably creative. Especially Madam Betsy, who, I am convinced, possesses the strongest right arm in the city. Why, she recently inflicted upon my buttocks a thrashing of such savagery that I am still hardly able to—"

"That's quite enough!" Gladstone barked. "We are here to discuss a different order of vice altogether. I refer to the perversion of the law and the ethical degeneracy that is currently sweeping through the government."

"Do you have the capacity for another drink?" Swinburne asked Burton.

"I've had my fill," he responded. He ran his tongue around his teeth, tasting coffee and traces of brandy, and regarded the leader of the opposition. "Mr. Disraeli's policies?"

Gladstone resumed his seat, pulled his jacket straight, and gave a curt nod. "Do you divine his intentions, Sir Richard?"

"My friends and I were discussing the matter this very evening."

Burton returned his attention to Swinburne. "You were missed, Algy. You've been making waves. We're all impressed but concerned. I hope you know what you're doing."

"I'm writing poetry," Swinburne said. "There's no danger in that. The arts are the one place where truth can be expressed with impunity. If such a circumstance ever changes, the world is finished." He lifted a glass of red wine from the floor beside the *chaise longue*, drank from it, then added casually, "Incidentally, I'm being followed."

Burton's right eyebrow arched upward. "As am I, according to Montague Penniforth."

"I suspected as much. That's why I had him whisk you here under cover of the fog."

Gladstone snapped his fingers. "I asked a question."

"You did," Burton agreed. "Disraeli's intentions. Well, sir, as far as I can tell, he's attempting to make the rich richer and the poor poorer while removing what few avenues exist that might allow the latter, in terms of their income and quality of life, to in any way approach the former. He is also stifling the right to protest, which is why I'm anxious about my outspoken friend, here."

"Pah!" Swinburne interjected dismissively.

Burton locked eyes with Gladstone and adopted a challenging tone. "In the apparent absence of any effective governmental opposition, it appears that the empire must rely on its poets and literati to voice concerns about the prime minister's unwarranted actions."

Gladstone responded coolly to the jibe. "We'll address that observation in a moment. Do you know where your brother is?"

"No. Why do you ask?"

The politician lifted a thick document from a small table beside his chair and, leaning forward, handed it to the explorer. Burton saw, upon the top page, the words *The Return of the Discontinued Man*. The penmanship was neither his own nor Edward's. He flipped through the pages.

"It's a copy of the report I gave to him, but this is not his hand. Someone else must have written it out. How did you come by it?"

"It was delivered to my door by a ragamuffin who made off before I was able to question him. The significance is plain, is it not?"

Burton narrowed his eyes. "Significance?"

"As leader of the opposition I should have been granted access to the original. I was not. Someone who *does* have access to it has defied the prime minister by sending this copy to me."

"And you think it was Edward?"

"Your brother hasn't been seen in the prime minister's company for three months—or anywhere else, for that matter. For a very large man, he's demonstrated a remarkable ability to disappear. Why has he done so? Because he opposes Young England?"

With a shrug, Burton said, "I don't know. Edward is a slippery customer at the best of times, which these most certainly are not. If he's up to something, I haven't been made privy to it. Perhaps it was he who sent you this. Perhaps it wasn't. The important thing is that you have it and are now aware of the historical context in relation to which the prime minister enforces his policies."

Gladstone uttered a sound of agreement. "I stand incredulous that he is pursuing such a misjudged course. Is the empire not being hastened along precisely the path you cautioned against?"

Burton returned the document to Gladstone. "Absolutely. If we continue upon it, I foresee a situation wherein, in years to come, generation after generation will be subjugated by an unassailable, unconscionably affluent, and utterly unprincipled minority that is completely lacking in ethics, vision, and leadership ability. There will be no representation. Only oppression."

"I am moved to suggest," Gladstone responded, "that the aristocracy's response to industrialisation steered us in that direction well before Mr. Disraeli's ascent to power. In almost every one, if not *every* one, of the greatest political controversies of the last fifty years, whether they affected the general public, whether they affected religion, whether they affected the bad and abominable institution of slavery—whatever subject they touched—these leisure classes, these educated classes, these titled classes have been in the wrong."

"Then we must accuse the premier of magnifying and hastening forward an already dangerous state of affairs. What is your point, Mr. Gladstone?"

"That Benjamin Disraeli is an unprincipled bounder but not one jot a fool. He wouldn't have ignored your warning. There must lay, amid all his unconstitutional measures, some element that we are missing, something within Young England that he intends as a solution to this problem of erosive patronage and nepotism."

Burton felt his pocket for a cheroot but found he'd smoked the last. "Some manner of meritocracy being established within the bounds of the upper classes, you mean?"

Gladstone gave a disdainful snort. "Really, are you so blind to the arrogance of these people? They would never submit to such a scheme."

"But if there was made a legal requirement for such—"

"Stuff and nonsense! It could never happen. If Mr. Disraeli were to even attempt such a move, the elite who fund his Conservative Party would withdraw their support, and he'd be ousted. Such is the financial stranglehold the gentry has on the political system."

"What, then, do you suggest? What might this seemingly invisible policy be?"

"That is what I want you to find out."

Burton recoiled, blinking in surprise. He glanced at Swinburne, who was grinning, then looked back at Gladstone. "Me? I'm no bloody politician."

"That, I am very well aware of. You rather artlessly indicated, a few minutes ago, that you consider me remiss in my duties as leader of the opposition party. Why am I not waging a campaign against Young England, you wonder? I shall tell you. Due to the prime minister's declaration of a state of emergency, normal parliamentary legislation is suspended. Laws are being enacted, amended, and repealed without the normal period of consultation. New policies are bypassing the House of Commons entirely and going straight to the House of Lords for approval. I am not even informed of them, let alone given the opportunity to voice my concerns. Thus it is that only the aristocracy is dealing with issues affecting the aristocracy. In the parlance of the street, the lords and ladies of the empire are writing their own ticket."

"But you have access to Number Ten. Have you not confronted the premier in person?"

"He no longer occupies Number Ten. He and his cohorts are now running the country from a secret location, supposedly for fear that the Chinese might attempt to assassinate him. He has made himself inaccessible."

"Has Lord Elgin's bombing of the Old Summer Palace really so incited the Qing Dynasty that an attack upon the empire is imminent?"

"Not in the slightest bit. It's utter humbug. The Opium War is won and done with. There is tension but no danger, no impending conflict, no spies, no threat at all."

Burton pushed himself to his feet and, with his thumbs hooked into his waistcoat pockets, his chin down, and his brow creased, strode back and forth across the room, his boots making no noise on the plush crimson carpet. After a minute had passed, he murmured, "And the king? He holds executive authority. Can he not put a stop to this?"

Gladstone took an empty glass from the table and extended it toward Swinburne. The poet lifted a wine bottle and poured.

"The fact that he hasn't done so suggests that he's in on the game."

The explorer grunted. "What about the newspapers? Don't they offer you a platform?"

"Who do you think owns them, sir? Even those that claim to back my Liberal Party are the property of peers. Did you read the piece I wrote for the *Daily Bugle*? It was so heavily edited that my scathing condemnation of the government was somehow transformed into nominal support."

Burton stopped pacing and faced the politician.

"What on earth do you expect of me?"

Gladstone examined his glass of wine, raised it, hesitated, and put it aside.

"You were not long ago Mr. Disraeli's swashbuckler. Now I want you to be mine. Find out what's happening to our aristocrats."

"What's happening to them? I should think it obvious. As you say, they are making their position inviolable."

"They are disappearing."

"What?"

"The House of Lords is less than two-thirds full, and its numbers dwindle with every session. Votes are being posted in. Absences are notable, too, at every event favoured by the nobility. Ballrooms are half empty. Gentlemen's clubs are all but abandoned. The horse tracks are losing money."

"Posted in, you say? So disappearing from view but still active?"

"Apparently. Will you look into the matter? I can't match the stipend you earned as the king's agent, but the Shadow Cabinet has allowed for a certain allocation of party funds to be made available for your commission."

Burton shrugged. "I wouldn't know where to start."

Gladstone withdrew a folded sheet of paper from inside his jacket. "Some of those who've not been seen for the past few weeks are listed here. Also—" He paused, reached for his wine, and this time took a sip. "Also, might I suggest that, if you and Mr. Swinburne are being followed, perhaps you should follow the followers?"

"To what end?"

"To discover who and why. I suspect that I'm also under observation, as are a number of my colleagues. If there has been established some manner of secret agency for such nefarious purposes, then it must be exposed to the public, else we are closer than ever to a totalitarian state."

Burton hissed a breath out through his teeth. He removed his thumbs from his pockets and took the proffered list. Scanning the names—many had addresses written next to them—he immediately recognised three: Lord John Manners, Henry Thomas Hope, and Alexander Baillie-Cochrane.

"The original Young Englanders," he muttered. His eyes flicked up, met, and held Gladstone's. "Very well. I'll undertake the job. Do I have a free hand?"

"Take whatever action you deem appropriate within the bounds of the law."

"The latter part of that statement may prove difficult. The law is becoming ever more restrictive. If I'm found out, I'm liable to be declared a traitor."

"Indeed so, but I haven't the authority to grant you immunity. Whatever risks you take must be on your own account."

"In that case, I shall try very hard not to shoot anybody."

Gladstone stood, looked with distaste at the glass in his hand—he'd taken but a single sip from it—and put it down. He brushed at his sleeve and moved toward the door. "If you need to speak with me again, leave a message at this establishment."

"You visit it frequently?" Burton gave Swinburne a sidelong glance.

Gladstone squared his shoulders. "I have promised to strengthen the moral character of its inhabitants and will not give up on them, sir."

Swinburne added, "Mr. Gladstone probes the rectitude of each of the girls in turn, Richard."

"Tiring work," Burton commented.

"Quite so, but I stand firm," Gladstone declared.

"I'm sure you do."

With a nod, the leader of the opposition turned and reached for the door handle. Before he could touch it, there came a commotion from the other side of the portal. He stepped back as it suddenly flew open, and a man burst in, panting and dishevelled.

"Trounce!" Burton exclaimed.

Wheezing breathlessly, the detective inspector looked wide-eyed at the leader of the opposition and gasped, "By Jove! You're Gladstone, aren't you?"

"I can explain my presence," Gladstone said. "I am attempting to—"

"Never mind about that," the Scotland Yard man snapped. "They're not after you. You'll be safer if you remain here. But you two—" He jabbed a finger at Burton and Swinburne. "Follow me at once—or you're dead men!"

CHAPTER 10

FIGHTING ON ROOFTOPS AND PLOTTING IN CATACOMBS

WHAT IS KILLING OUR CLAIRVOYANTS?
The Mysterious Toll Continues
Eleven Unexplained Fatalities in the Past Week

"**M**y hat!" Swinburne cried out. "What the devil—?"

Trounce sprang forward, grabbed the poet by the collar, and dragged him kicking and squealing out of the room. "Come on! Come on! There's not a second to spare!"

Burton gave Gladstone a quick nod and followed Trounce and Swinburne, grabbing his cane as he exited the chamber but leaving his hat and coat. Malazo was waiting in the corridor. Trounce said to the African, "Show me."

"This way, sir."

The tall man strode quickly to the end of the passage farthest from the stairs and opened a door. "This is the one."

A woman's panicked scream sounded from the floor below. Voices were raised in protest. Others, demanding and harsh, shouted incomprehensible commands. There was a crash that sounded like furniture being knocked over.

Trounce pushed Swinburne into the room. Burton followed, and Malazo closed the door behind him, shutting them in. They heard a key turn in the lock and a scrape as it was removed.

"Take this," Trounce said. He pushed a revolver into Burton's hand. "If it comes to it, shoot them in the head. You'll probably have to empty the chamber before they go down." He handed over a box of cartridges, which Burton slipped into his jacket pocket.

"Who, Trounce?"

"The SPG."

It meant nothing to Burton.

The room, like the one they'd just left, was luxurious, with velvet drapes, a plush carpet, and gilt-framed pictures hung on its floral wallpaper. Romanesque statuettes were arranged on its furniture, and a four-poster bed extended out from the wall to their right. The latter was occupied by a skinny, long-bearded fellow and an extremely curvaceous—to the point of being bulbous—young lady, both sitting up amid a tangle of silk sheets. Their mouths were hanging open in shock. Neither was suitably dressed for the reception of guests, a fact reflected in the rapidly deepening scarlet of the man's face.

"What ho, gymnasts!" Swinburne said to them, as Trounce hurried across to the window and yanked it open. "We're just passing through. Don't let us interrupt your contortions."

After leaning out and examining the exterior wall to the left, the detective inspector snapped at Burton, "Out and up. You first, Algy next, and I'll follow. Hurry."

Shouts and thumps came from the corridor. Someone yelled, "Get off me!" More screams. The slamming of doors.

Burton stepped to the window and saw metal rungs affixed to the brickwork outside. They went up but not down. He climbed onto the sill, reached out, gripped one, and swung himself out onto the ladder. As he ascended it, keeping a careful hold of his swordstick, he heard Swinburne say, "Goodnight, my lovelies. Mind you don't strain yourselves."

Fog swirled around the explorer as he climbed the short distance to the roof. This was, he surmised, the brothel's escape route, used when the police conducted one of their very occasional raids. He wondered whether one was occurring now but thought it unlikely. Trounce was too perturbed. This was something far more serious.

The roof proved to be of the gambrel type, the metal rungs of the ladder continuing past the gutter up the steep outermost slope but stopping at the edge of the inner, topmost one, which rose at a shallow enough angle that Burton was able to stand upon it, though it was slippery with a thick powdering of ash and soot. He bent and gave Swinburne a helping hand.

Trounce's voice came up from below. "Keep going. To the right."

Holding on to each other for balance, Burton and Swinburne moved carefully forward. It was exceedingly dark, the city's nighttime lights contributing only the faintest of glows to the billowing vapour.

They heard a splintering report as the door to the room below was broken open. The woman shrieked.

Trounce caught up with them. He grabbed Burton's elbow, pointed toward a tall chimneystack, dimly visible ahead, and hissed, "We'll get behind that. No choice but to shoot it out. We'll not outrun them."

Gingerly, across slick tiles, they traversed the slope.

"Stop!" a voice demanded. "In the name of the king."

"Who are they?" Swinburne whispered as they reached the chimney and crouched behind it.

"Devils," Trounce growled. "Look out! Here they come." He raised his pistol. "Remember, aim for the heads, multiple shots. It's the only way. By Jove, what I wouldn't give for a rifle!"

Burton knelt, peered around the corner of the brickwork, and aimed his gun at a moving light.

"Is there no weapon for me?" Swinburne asked.

"Can't risk it," Trounce murmured. "You're a rotten shot."

"So what should I do? Compose a damaging verse?"

A patch of greater darkness divided and coalesced into three eerily attenuated figures, thin-limbed and each with a bright blue light shining from the middle of its long face.

Clockwork men!

With deafening bangs, Trounce's gun discharged—one, two, three shots in rapid succession. The lead figure staggered, sparks erupting from its head. Three more shots sounded, one of which missed, but the target righted itself, kept coming, and announced, "You have attacked a police officer. You are under arrest. Give yourselves up. Reinforcements have been summoned."

"Police officer?" Swinburne exclaimed. "Your people, Trounce?"

"Hardly."

As they came closer, Burton was better able to make them out. He saw that—though the clockwork men followed the general design of such mechanisms—there were differences, the most notable being that they were taller, their heads extending upward into the shape of a constable's helmet. Also, the middlemost of their three vertically-placed facial openings was a blue light rather than a grille and, from top to toe, the figures were painted black—at least as far as Burton could tell in the dark.

"Shoot, man!" Trounce barked.

Burton squeezed the trigger, aiming at the same machine Trounce had hit—at the light in its face. Recoils jerked his wrist but his aim was true. The mechanism reeled, its head jerking this way and that as some bullets ricocheted from its brass surface and others drilled through into the babbage device within. Folding at the knees, the machine collapsed onto the roof and lay twitching.

Trounce had by now reloaded and was meting out the same punishment to one of the two remaining metal men, both of whom were rapidly closing on the chimney.

Pulling the box of ammunition from his pocket and, with his upper arm, securing his cane against his body, Burton clicked open his weapon's cylinder and quickly pushed cartridges into its chambers. He looked up and saw that the contraption Trounce was firing at had weathered the storm of lead but was now moving in an erratic manner, waving its arms and stumbling up toward the ridge of the roof to the right of them.

The other flicked its hands outward causing truncheons to slide down along its forearms and click into place, extending out about eighteen inches. As it arrived at the chimney, Burton shot it in the face at near point-blank range. He staggered backward as a baton whipped sideways, missed his head by a hair's breadth, and smacked into the brickwork, sending out a shower of red fragments.

Swinburne screeched and scrambled away.

Burton, half blinded by brick dust, aimed instinctively and put a second bullet into the contraption.

"Halt!" it ordered. "You are—fzzzt!—committing an illegal—fzzzt!—act and must submit at once."

Trounce cried out as a down-swung truncheon caught him on the wrist. His revolver dropped from nerveless fingers, clattered over the tiles and plummeted out of sight.

"You—fzzzt!—are Detective Inspector Trounce. You are aiding and—fzzzt!—abetting Algernon Charles Swinburne, an enemy—fzzzt!—of the state, and Sir Richard Francis Burton, who is wanted for—fzzzt!—questioning. Your involvement has been reported. You are under arrest."

Trounce ducked as the second club swiped at him. It smashed into the chimney. The structure rocked and two of its four clay pots fell and shattered on the tiles.

"And you are assaulting a superior officer," Trounce roared. "I order you to stop and withdraw!"

In reply, a baton clubbed at his head, missing by inches as he jerked backward and sprawled onto the roof. Acting instinctively, he drew both knees up to his chest and kicked out hard at the chimney. It promptly collapsed and, with a roar of tumbling rubble, engulfed the clockwork man and carried him down the slope and off into empty space.

Trounce started to slide after it.

"Oh no you don't!" Burton exclaimed. He plunged forward and stretched out his cane, the end of which Trounce managed to grasp.

"By Jove!" the Yard man croaked as he was hauled to safety. "That was a close call. Where's the other one?"

"Here!" Swinburne called in a strangulated voice.

They looked up and saw the last mechanism teetering on the roof's ridge, its left hand clamped around the poet's neck, the right gripping him by the thigh, holding him aloft as if preparing to fling him from the building.

"I've got him!" Swinburne gurgled. "I've got him!"

"You," Burton said.

He took careful aim and fired. *Bang!*

"—and mechanical men,"

Bang!

"—and roofs,"

Bang!

"—should reevaluate the terms of your association."

The brass head suddenly erupted in flames as its babbage's booby trap, triggered by a bullet, activated. Fire licked at Swinburne's clothes.

The contraption emitted a howl like that of a siren and dropped the poet.

"Ow! Ow! Ow!" Swinburne hollered, as he landed on the opposite side of the roof and rolled out of sight.

The constable's head exploded with a deafening crack. The metal figure keeled over and followed Swinburne. Burton and Trounce heard it rattle across the tiles, then came a moment of silence followed a distant clank as it hit the ground two storeys below.

"Algy!" Burton cried out.

He scrabbled up the slope to the ridge, looked over, and, through the murk, saw white fingers clutching at the angle where the lower part of the gambrel roof met the top slope. Quickly but gingerly he slid down to them and peered over the lip. Swinburne looked up at him and grinned. "Hallo!"

As Burton took hold of his wrist and pulled him up, the poet said, "How strange. I feel like we've done something like this before." He patted at his smouldering clothes. "Are they all dead?"

"I don't think we can claim that," Burton responded, "but they've certainly developed a mechanical fault."

They returned to Trounce, who gestured toward the far end of the roof. "According to Malazo, there's a ladder over there. We'd better hurry. More machines are assuredly are on their way. Gad! That damnable thing nearly broke my wrist. Hurts!"

"Your face is bleeding," Swinburne observed.

The detective inspector put fingers to a cut just beneath his left eye. "A chunk of brick caught me. I'll have a shiner by the morning."

As they started moving, Burton said, "What's the story, William?"

"It's all gone to blazes."

"What has?"

"The country. The government. Scotland bloody Yard. Last week, Chief Commissioner Mayne purchased two hundred and fifty of those abominations. They form a new department in the Police Force, called the Special Patrol Group, under a nasty piece of work of your acquaintance."

Burton knew instantly to whom Trounce was referring. "Rigby?"

"The man himself."

They reached the edge of the roof and there, after searching for a minute, found rungs bolted to the wall. There was no further conversation until they'd each descended, then Trounce said, "Let's find the rubble from that chimney. My revolver must be somewhere in amongst it. I can't do without it. Quick now! We mustn't dawdle."

Cradling his wounded wrist, he led them rapidly around a corner to the rear of Verbena Lodge, then pulled a clockwork lantern from his pocket, shook it open, wound it, and with the light that flooded from it, revealed a wet and brick strewn alleyway. Burton saw a half-buried brass man, stepped over to it, and picked up its severed head. "I think I'll have Gooch take a look at this."

"Be careful," Trounce advised. "The brain might still be functioning."

"No," Burton countered. "Not when disconnected from the mainspring."

Trounce started to search for his gun. "It's all gone to the devil. The police used to be a public service, there to offer protection, but there's a new order sweeping through the Yard, and Rigby's Special Patrol Group exemplifies its credo, which is to enforce and intimidate."

Burton peered at the head but could see little in the darkness. "And tonight? Why did they come after us?"

"I've been keeping my ears peeled, working with Detective Inspector Slaughter and Constable Honesty to get a measure of Rigby."

Burton uttered a small sound of approval. Slaughter and Honesty had both been members of the Ministry of Chronological Affairs. They were good, trustworthy men.

"I'd learned that Rigby was having you both followed. Earlier tonight, Slaughter came to me and said he'd just overheard the man issue an arrest order for Algy." He addressed the poet. "You were going to be detained for questioning."

Swinburne said, "Why? What have I done?"

"You've penned subversive poetry."

"Pah! Everyone's a critic."

"Believe me, Rigby's criticism would have stung like no other. 'Detained for questioning' is a metaphor. It means 'placed in a cell without charge, held for an indeterminate period, and frequently beaten.' You were lucky Slaughter was in the right place at the right time. He saw three clockwork men return to the Yard and report they'd lost track of you in this district. When he passed that information to me, I immediately suspected you'd be in the lodge. So I raced over and got here in the nick of time. Ah, here it is!" He bent, retrieved his revolver, blew dust from it, and put it in his pocket. "Let's get out of here. We're all three fugitives now. We should find somewhere to lay low."

"I know just the place," Burton said.

Swinburne indicated that they should follow him. "Then this way, chaps. I arranged to rendezvous with Monty after our chinwag. He should be waiting nearby."

Leaving the alley, and moving as silently as possible, they passed through one passage after another with only Trounce's lantern lighting the way. Rats frequently scurried out of their path. Burton coughed as the corrosive fog caught in his nostrils. He could feel grit accumulating in his hair and on his skin, and the humid damp was beginning to penetrate his clothing.

Footsteps sounded from ahead. Trounce quickly extinguished the light. They pressed themselves into a doorway. Three mechanised constables ran past, their blue face lamps glowing, their batons extended, their metal feet stamping.

When the noise of them had faded, Trounce rewound his lantern. "Phew! A close call. Come on."

"We're almost there," Swinburne noted.

Five minutes later, they emerged into what felt to Burton like a more open space, though initially he wasn't quite sure why he made that presumption. Trounce's light penetrated the fog sufficiently to reveal the suggestion of railings with a skeletal tree branch twisting just above them—one of the city's many little squares, with a tiny, enclosed public garden in its middle.

Swinburne put two fingers to his mouth and whistled twice.

A reply sounded from off to their left.

They walked in that direction and soon found the landau. Montague Penniforth, standing beside it, greeted them.

"Hallo, gents! Mr. Trounce, it's good to see you again. I was beginnin' to think—Blimey! What the bloomin' 'eck has 'appened to you?"

Swinburne winked at him. "The girls got a little overenthusiastic. It was perfectly splendid!"

Burton pushed the poet into the vehicle. "Can you drive us to Norwood, Monty?"

"South of the river? Aye, course I can. Long way though, 'specially in this 'souper."

"Keep your ears peeled. Let me know if you think we're being followed."

"Will do, guv'nor. All aboard!"

Burton and Trounce climbed in and, as they settled, the steam horse coughed itself awake. The landau set off.

It astonished the explorer that Penniforth could drive in such conditions but, as before, the cabbie was able to navigate without difficulty—albeit slowly—through the murk.

"Why suddenly order me apprehended?" Burton asked Trounce. "Followed, I can understand, but I haven't done anything untoward, even by the current overly stringent standards."

"A new directive from the Home Office," Trounce said. "Undesirables are to be rounded up."

"What qualifies as an undesirable?"

"Humph! There's the rub. It's more or less anyone who, in Rigby's judgement, poses a significant threat to the stability of the empire. His remit is so broad and ill-defined that he could quite literally include any person in it. From what I've so far witnessed, he's currently preying on those people who possess the wits and resources to offer viable opposition to Disraeli's Young England. Algy has been identified as a mouthpiece for the protesters, and you—by virtue of your friendship with him, not to mention Rigby's hatred of you—were an obvious addition to the list."

Burton pondered this, then suddenly gave a cry of alarm and, leaning forward, hastily used his cane to open the hatch in the cabin roof.

"Monty!"

"Aye, guv'nor?"

"Keep your eyes peeled for any street urchins. I need to send a message via the Whispering Web."

"Rightio, but the nippers will all be asleep at this hour."

Falling back into his seat with a curse, Burton said, "The Cannibal Club. I need to warn them. Should we go back to Leicester Square?"

"No," Trounce responded. "We need to get as far away from the area as possible. You were carousing tonight? At Bartolini's?"

"Yes." The explorer fished his pocket watch from his waistcoat and flipped open its lid. "Hmm. It's later than I thought. He'll have kicked them out by now."

For the next few minutes, they sat in silence.

Trounce took out a handkerchief and attended to his bloodied face.

Swinburne twitched and jerked and pulled at his scorched clothing.

When the landau steered into Piccadilly, the little poet uttered an exclamation and pointed out of the window. "Hallo! What's going on there?"

Burton leaned across him and looked out at Green Park. Though obscured by rolling vapours and drifting ash, countless lamps brightly illuminated the open space, and the explorer could just make out hundreds of workmen who appeared to be erecting row upon row of wooden huts.

"Are we hosting some manner of exposition?" he enquired of Trounce.

"Not that I'm aware of," the detective inspector responded. "And if we were, I would certainly know about it, for it would need to be policed."

"Then what is the purpose of those cabins?"

The Scotland Yard man shrugged.

Their vehicle trundled on southward and crossed the river. On the Lambeth Road, they encountered a ragamuffin—a young lad in overlarge boots and with a battered topper placed at a cocky angle on his head. He revealed to Burton that he was on his way to a newspaper depot to pick up a bundle of early editions. "I can sell an 'undred of 'em in less 'n a bloomin' hour," he boasted.

"Would you like to earn enough so you don't have to?" the explorer asked.

"Cor! Not 'alf!"

Burton gave a simple message to be delivered to Richard Monckton Milnes's town house. *You and the Cannibals are in danger of arrest. Leave the city at the earliest opportunity.*

The boy ran off, with a pocket jingling with coins, to send the warning on its way. No doubt Monckton Milnes would be roused from his bed at a horribly early hour and given something to think about other than his hangover.

The carriage continued on.

Burton examined the head of the Special Patrol Group machine. Not black but midnight blue. Heavy for its size. A badge inset into the helmet-shaped cranium bore the stylised image of an eagle and the motto: *LEX EST ABSOLUTA.*

"The Law is Absolute."

Swinburne said, "Pardon?"

"The new police dictum, by the looks of it."

"Rigby's justification for bully-boy tactics," Trounce snarled. "Everything that made me proud to serve has been corrupted. To hell with it! To hell with Chief Commissioner Mayne, to hell with Colonel Rigby, to hell with Scotland Yard, and, especially, to hell with Disraeli! I'll not play his game, and I know plenty of other Yard men who feel the same way. I'm in a mind to organise them. We should found a proper resistance."

"Hurrah!" Swinburne cheered. "Good old Pouncer! To war! To war!"

"Let's not be reckless," Burton said. "I'd like a better idea of what the premier is up to before I turn revolutionary."

Trounce stuck out his chest. "Whatever it is, it's wrong. I'm British! That has always stood for something and must continue to do so. I'll not stand by and see it tainted by that damn—" He gritted his teeth.

"Jew?" Burton suggested. "Listen here, William, I'll not have any of that. I've travelled the world and mixed with Hindus and Hebrews and Muslims and Christians and so-called heathens of every sort. If there's but one lesson I've learned, it is that a man is good or evil on his own account. He might employ his religion to justify his actions but, if that religion weren't there, he'd find something else to excuse his behaviour. Wickedness is wickedness, and it will twist any belief to its own end. Evil has been done in the name of every god ever imagined, and, atheist though I may be, I'll not decry an entire faith just because some who claim it are contemptible."

"Anyway," Swinburne added, "Dizzy converted to Anglicism when he was a child."

Trounce muttered, "For crying out loud, I was going to say *dandy*."

"Great Scott!" Swinburne cried out in shock. "You'd stoop so low as to condemn a man for his lacy cuffs and velvet collars?"

"Oh, shut up, both of you. You know full well what I meant. This country has led the world in the establishment of social decency and respect. The British created the very concept of freedom."

"And reason!" Swinburne agreed.

"Tolerance!" Trounce said.

"Justice!"

"Progress!"

"Opportunity!"

"Perseverance!"

Burton waved his hands. "All right! All right! Enough evangelising. One thing at a time. There's something vitally important we must do before anything else."

"What?" Swinburne and Trounce chorused.

"Sleep, damn it."

Their vehicle passed through Brixton, breasted Tulse Hill, and entered Norwood Road. Penniforth, who'd played a prominent role in the case Burton had written up as *The Secret of Abdu El Yezdi*, knew the area well, and now lifted the hatch and called down. "The burial ground?"

"Yes please, Monty," Burton responded. "Are we followed?"

"The soup is a bit thinner here, guv'nor, an' I can see some ways behind us. No one on our tail, I'm pretty sure of it."

Five minutes later, the landau drew to a halt at the gates of West Norwood Cemetery, and the passengers disembarked.

"I'm goin' to leave it at the Coach an' Horses 'round the corner," Penniforth told them. "Dare say you'll be in the land o' Nod by the time I join you, so I'll see you in the mornin'."

He touched the brim of his hat and drove off.

Burton, Swinburne, and Trounce entered the cemetery and started along a path through the trees. The fog, though thick, was, as Penniforth had stated, more penetrable in this part of the city, and they soon glimpsed, through the branches, the steeple of the Episcopal Church.

They found the door to the building shut but unlocked, and upon entering through it, moved to the right, passed along the outer aisle, and paced into the right-hand transept. Stepping to an arched doorway, they descended the stone steps beyond it and arrived at a wooden door, which Burton pushed open. It creaked loudly, the sound echoing.

"Your lantern, William?"

The detective inspector made a sound of acknowledgment and produced his light. Moments later, it illuminated a catacomb; a tall, long, and narrow vaulted passage of elegant brickwork with three arched doorways on either side, which, as they passed along it, they saw opened onto narrower but longer corridors. Coffins lay in wall niches, and decorative wrought-iron gates opened onto small bays and loculi in which individuals and families had been interred.

At the far end of the passage, they came to a blank wall. Burton used his right foot to nudge a brick at the base of it. There was a soft clunk. He put his shoulder to the wall and pushed. A square section of it swung inward, revealing a long, dusty corridor. It was barely wider than his shoulders and sloped downward.

Burton led his companions in, and, as the portal swung shut behind them, reflected that his fear of enclosed spaces appeared to have left him. No surprise after a year spent entrapped in a metal body.

The memory of that experience felt very remote.

Too, the fact that he was entering a hiding place previously used by the creature who'd killed Isabel had little effect on him. He ought to feel uneasy but didn't. The recollection of her death contained no depth of emotion, no regret or sorrow.

From behind him, Trounce's lamp cast weird shadows.

They proceeded forward until, once again, they were confronted by a featureless wall. Burton pressed another brick to open a concealed door then led them out into a vault of coffin-filled alcoves and gated bays. It was illuminated by oil lamps and cluttered with machinery. These catacombs, he knew, were beneath the Dissenters' Church. They were wider, taller, and more extensive than the neighbouring tunnels and consisted of many more passages, which branched off from the central corridor. This, though also crowded with machinery and workbenches, appeared rather more organised than the others. It was quiet. They saw only one person— a woman—attending to chemical apparatus.

"Good evening," Burton said, as they drew closer to her. "Or do I mean morning?"

"Sir Richard!" she exclaimed, looking up. "We weren't expecting you. Everyone is asleep."

"As I would very much like to be. We'll speak with Mr. Gooch at a more convenient hour. Is there anywhere we can lay our heads?"

She nodded and pointed toward the mouth of a passage. "We've cleared out the bays along there. You'll find some unoccupied. The bedding is a bit makeshift, I'm afraid, but it suffices. If you'd like to wash first, go right to the end. You'll find basins, jugs of water, soap and towels. There's also a contraption of pipes and—well—it's an—um—it's our facilities, if you see what I mean."

"I do. It all sounds marvellous. Will you tell Daniel we're here when he rises, but not to disturb us? We've had an exhausting night. And ask him to have a look at this." He held up the metal head and placed it on a worktop.

"Oh! I've not seen one like that before. Yes, I'll tell him. Pleasant dreams."

"Unlikely."

Less than thirty minutes later, the three men were, as Penniforth had predicted, in the land of Nod.

In the morning, Burton, Swinburne, and Trounce breakfasted from the considerable supplies the ex-DOGS personnel had accrued in their hideout. They then joined Daniel Gooch at a workbench.

"This is remarkable," the engineer told Burton, lifting the metal head of the downed Special Patrol Group constable. He turned it so the explorer could see the exposed inner workings. "You'll note that the babbage is of a completely different design. A little larger. As far as I can see, it's been inspired by the Turing additions to the Mark Three in the *Orpheus*."

Burton peered at the mechanism. "But why the increase in size? The Turing machinery we encountered in the future was tiny—some of it microscopic."

"It was," Gooch agreed. "But though we can ascertain the function of Turing components, we still haven't the capacity to reproduce them on such a small scale. This, I am certain, is Babbage's best effort to mimic that future machinery by employing contemporary techniques and materials. No one but he could have done it. For all that it's clumsier and less powerful than a Turing of 2202, it's nevertheless a significant advancement over our previous probability calculators. The man is a bloody genius. This is magnificent!"

Trounce, standing with Swinburne on the other side of the workbench, and sporting a very black eye, grumbled, "Humph! You might be less enthusiastic if it directed a machine that thumped you with a baton."

"I dare say," Gooch conceded.

Burton pursed his lips thoughtfully. "I can only conclude that Charles is producing these machines for the government. He departed the power station with forethought and in a carefully arranged manner, taking all his work with him. It's unlikely then that he's being forced to do anything against his will. My suspicion is that he was recruited by the prime minister last October, though what might have been promised to him, and what motivated Disraeli at that time, I cannot fathom."

Swinburne hopped into the air and swiped a fist. "Dizzy is an absolute cad! A total bounder! Our audience with him was an utter farce!"

Burton nodded his agreement. "I believe so. He was considerably more knowledgeable than he appeared to be. For a start, he'd no doubt already read *The History of the Future*, which Babbage's contraptions had snatched from Maneesh and Sadhvi the day before we met with him."

"He's gone mad," Trounce opined. "It's the only explanation."

They fell silent for a few moments.

Gooch raised the brass head. "I wonder where these things are being manufactured. The equipment used to assemble clockwork men at Battersea Power Station was removed—along with everything else—by government men when the Department of Guided Science was disbanded. Wherever it was taken, I daresay that's where we'll find old Babbage."

"Even if we locate it, what—" Trounce began. Gooch cut him off with a loud exclamation.

"Wait! I could—yes! By heavens, I think you may have given me the means!" He turned the head. Its exposed artificial brain somewhat resembled an unpeeled artichoke. With the forefinger of his left supplementary hand, he pointed to a small, leaf-shaped, metal panel that lay flush with its surface. "It'll take me some considerable time to study the whole thing— or, rather, what I can of it without setting off the booby trap—but I can tell you right now what this is. It's the equivalent of the component I removed from Grumbles, the part containing the grain of black diamond dust. Only this, instead of diamond, holds a flake of crystalline silicate."

"It performs the same function?" Burton asked.

"Yes, it does, and that might be the key."

"How so?"

"The Field Amplifier hasn't worked. One grain of diamond just doesn't offer sufficient information for the apparatus to analyse. However, I'm pretty certain I can construct instruments that, if attached to three or four of these new probability calculators and positioned at widespread points around the city, could be used to triangulate the source of the transmission. It might lead us to the factory, or to Babbage, or to our missing people, or to all three."

"Or just to Rigby," Trounce commented. "He's in charge of the confounded things."

"I understand that," Gooch countered, "but through this component they're able to consult with one another over a distance, and no doubt he can direct them from afar, as well. With all the Special Patrol Group constables, that amounts to a lot of information whizzing back and forth. I'll wager it has to be sorted by a central device, a powerful synthetic intelligence that can process it all before boosting the individual elements along the resonance existing between the flakes of silicate. Find that, and I'll wager you'll find Babbage fussing over it."

"The *Orpheus* brain?" Burton asked.

"That's my supposition."

Swinburne asked, "How many heads would you require in order to locate it?"

"A minimum of three; more for greater accuracy."

"So you want us to go around decapitating mechanical policemen?"

Gooch turned his metal palms upward. "That will be necessary, yes."

"Hoorah! Count me in!"

Burton calmed his friend with a sharp gesture. After a moment's thought, he said, "Daniel. How long will your instruments take to construct?"

Gooch gave a four-armed shrug. "I only just had the idea. I haven't designed them yet. I'll need to experiment with this constable's babbage. Give me a few days."

"In that case, I suggest we delay our beheading spree until you're ready. When we make that move, we'll be confirming ourselves as enemies of the state. Until then, I think it best we operate as stealthily as we can. In order to do that, I must first send Monty on a mission."

The big cabbie was at the other end of the catacomb, drinking coffee, smoking his pipe, and reading a newspaper. As Burton approached him, he caught a glimpse of the headline: CHINESE BOMB THREAT TO LIVERPOOL SHIPYARDS.

Lies. The politics of fear mongering.

A side headline declared: INEXPLICABLE DEATH OF KING'S SPIRITUALIST.

"Monty, I have a job for you."

The task took five minutes to explain but all morning for Penniforth to complete. While he waited, Burton meditated in one of the bays. There was a contradiction at the heart of recent events that he couldn't get to grips with. Babbage hated the working classes. Disraeli, by contrast, glorified them—mostly, the explorer suspected, because their existence gave stark definition to the upper classes. The prime minister was apparently bent on sharpening the contrast by nipping the emerging middle class in the bud. What, then, was in it for Babbage? Why was he cooperating with Young England?

At a little after midday, Burton's contemplation was interrupted by Penniforth's return. He had Bram with him, and their arrival was announced by Pox, who was sitting on the youngster's head.

"Blundering dangle arms! Intolerable blots!"

Burton, Swinburne, and Trounce joined their allies in the main vault.

Penniforth, whose giant frame was weighed down by suitcases, hatboxes, and bags, placed the load upon the floor. "You were right, guv'nor. Your house is bein' watched."

"We went a-sneaking through the mews, so we did," Bram declared excitedly. "Hallo, Cap'n! Hallo, Mr. Swinburne! Hallo, Mr. Fogg! Cor! Did you get thumped?"

"I did, lad," Trounce confirmed. "And for the umpteenth time, I am not your Macallister Fogg fellow."

"O' course not, sir!" Bram said. He tapped the side of his nose and gave the detective inspector an exaggerated wink.

Trounce responded with a despairing sigh.

"Sack of grease!" Pox commented.

"We got everythin' on your list," Penniforth told Burton. "Mrs. Angell helped us to pack it. I think she sneaked in a pork pie."

Swinburne laughed. "Good old Mrs. A.!"

The cabbie lifted two long clothbound items. "I 'ope these are the right ones."

Taking them, Burton unwrapped one to reveal a shiny and oddly shaped sword, somewhat similar to a narrow question mark in form.

"It's a *khopesh*," he said, in answer to Trounce's enquiring expression. "A type of scimitar, evolved from an axe, and widely used by the Egyptians and Canaanites. Strong and sharp enough that—if swung with sufficient force—it'll slice through the neck of a clockwork man." He paused before adding, "I hope."

He put the weapons aside. "But we have some work to do before we go headhunting. Monty, Bram, get yourselves some lunch. Algy, William, help me with the luggage, will you?"

The three of them dragged the bags, boxes, and cases along the passage to the bays they'd adopted as their bedrooms. Burton nodded toward a stone plinth. "Sit."

Swinburne hoisted himself onto it and sat with his feet swinging. Trounce settled next to him, looking puzzled. He watched as Burton opened a large carpetbag, then he leaned over and looked into it. "By Jove! Are we going to—?"

"We are," Burton said.

A little under an hour later, Daniel Gooch uttered a cry of surprise as three complete strangers walked out into the main gallery.

The tallest of the trio, whose complexion marked him as a native of a sunnier clime, was dressed in a pale-grey John Bull top hat with a matching knee-length frock coat, tightly buttoned up to the neck, dark trousers, and polished black boots. He had a monocle lodged in the socket of his left eye, possessed badly pockmarked cheeks, and wore his mustachios long, waxed, and twisted at the ends into very long upsweeping points.

Doffing his hat, revealing that his hair was parted in the middle and slick with Macassar oil, he bowed extravagantly and said in a lilting accent, "Good day to you, sir. I am Count Palladino of Brindisi. It is my great pleasure to be visiting your country. You have met my companions?"

At his side, a fat fellow with a thick beard, sunken eyes, and clothes that had seen better days, nodded a greeting and mumbled, "Isaiah Clutch. Metalworker. At your service."

The most diminutive of the three, a filthy, black-haired guttersnipe bedecked in rags, offered a broad smile—displaying chipped and rotten teeth—and croaked, "What 'o, matey! Slippery Ned Beesley's me name, an' chimley sweepin's me game. Got a flue what wants a-scrubbin'?"

Gooch stammered, "I—I—who are—are you—you surely aren't—Sir Richard?"

Count Palladino threw his head back and gave a bark of laughter. "Yes, Daniel, it's me."

"Trounce," Clutch grunted.

"And me, Algernon," Slippery Ned Beesley added, unnecessarily. "Ain't we a picture, though?"

"Good Lord! You're unrecognisable!"

"I'm glad to hear it," Burton said. "We need to be if we're to move around freely." He turned to address Trounce. "A risky mission for you, William. Go loiter in Whitehall and make contact with those of your colleagues you can still trust. Find out how many in Scotland Yard are disgruntled, how many we might rely on if—if—"

If we turn traitor and fight against our own government.

"If it comes to it," Trounce finished.

"Yes."

"I'll start with Spearing, Slaughter, and Honesty. Between them, the principal ranks are covered. By the time I'm finished, we'll have a decent body of men standing by, that I guarantee."

"Good man."

To Swinburne, Burton said, "Algy, we've identified Young England as an attack upon the middling classes. What we haven't yet established is how the labouring majority view Disraeli's actions. I want you to speak with Mr. Grub. Don't reveal your identity. I think him more liable to speak freely with Slippery Ned Beesley, a person he'll undoubtedly consider an equal."

"Or an inferior," Swinburne interjected.

"Quite so. Pick his brains. Take Bram with you. After that, the two of you should move around the street markets, the wharfs, and the rookeries. Blend in and take a measure of public opinion. Let's find out where the people stand."

"And you, Count Palladino?" Gooch asked, with a tinge of humour.

Burton gave a grim smile, took a revolver from a bench, checked that its chamber was full, and pocketed it. "I intend to sniff out some missing aristocrats."

CHAPTER 11

A SOPHISTICATED MECHANISM WAXES PHILOSOPHICAL AND CAPTIVES ARE TAKEN

GREEN PARK CLOSED UNTIL FURTHER NOTICE
DO NOT SCALE THE FENCE. TRESPASSERS WILL BE PROSECUTED.

Whenever London was simmering in its own gravy, the roads became impossible for the average vehicle owner to navigate. Those that attempted it tended to meet each other rather too abruptly, such encounters invariably being characterised by the sound of crunching metal, hissing steam, and passionately delivered language of a particularly colourful variety.

Only cab drivers and criminals enjoyed the fog. For cabbies, the thinned traffic came as a blessing, and the pall proved no inconvenience at all, since, as Montague Penniforth was again demonstrating, these men had imprinted permanently upon their minds a tremendously detailed map of the city whilst also possessing an uncannily accurate sense of distance and direction.

Thus it was that "Count Palladino" was transported without incident or delay from Norwood to the British Library and, from there, a little later, to Duchess Street, off Portland Place.

The landau trundled away. Penniforth would wait near Trafalgar Square.

Burton stood on the pavement outside the grandiose house and peered back the way he'd come, wondering whether the cab had been followed. He thought it very unlikely. Despite that the summer sun was somewhere overhead, making the upper layers of fog glow, visibility was terrible. He doubted anyone could have picked up his trail and was as certain as he could be that the Norwood hideaway remained a secret and wasn't being watched. In the dim grey light, through suspended particles of ash and slowly rolling cloud, he saw an old woman smoking a pipe and pushing a wheelbarrow, a stray dog running across the road with a dead rat hanging from its mouth, and a street crab—an automated cleaning machine—lumbering along with steam pluming from its funnels.

He faced the building. Number two. It was just past four o'clock in the afternoon, but the ground floor rooms were brightly lit.

One of them, he hoped, was occupied by the owner.

Of the men on Gladstone's list, Burton had, at the library, looked into the background of only three, they being Henry Thomas Hope, Lord John Manners, and Alexander Baillie-Cochrane; the surviving members—along with Disraeli—of the original Young England movement. Of them, Hope had immediately excited Burton's interest, for the records had revealed his mother to be the Honourable Louisa de la Poer Beresford, who was a cousin of Henry Beresford, the third Marquess of Waterford. Before his death, the marquess had been very much involved in the Spring Heeled Jack affair, albeit in a different version of history. Time, the explorer had learned, was filled with meaningful patterns, echoes, and synchronous occurrences. When recognised, such correspondences should not be ignored. The family connection was, to Burton, akin to a signpost bearing the legend *START HERE!* He'd abandoned further research and come straight to Hope's residence.

Now, moving forward, he mounted the five front steps, paused at the door, and yanked the bellpull. After half a minute, he heard bolts being pulled back. The door opened, and an elderly footman, with his chin tilted upward, looked down his long pointed nose and creaked, "Good afternoon, sir. Can I help you?"

"Perhaps so," Burton replied, adopting the traces of an Italian accent.

"I wish to see Mr. Hope. Might he spare me a few minutes? I am Count Palladino of Brindisi."

"And the nature of your business, sir?"

"A social visit. You are—?"

"Bellamy, sir. May I ask whether you are expected?"

"I must confess that I am not."

"I see." Bellamy blinked disapprovingly then stepped back and gestured to his left. "If you wouldn't mind waiting in the parlour, I shall enquire as to the master's availability."

"I'm much obliged."

Burton entered the house and walked into the indicated room. It was of a modest size and very cluttered with pictures, ornaments, and knickknacks. Choosing not to sit, he crossed to the unlit fireplace, stood between the two armchairs arranged around it, and waited, facing the chamber with his hands held behind his back. He was amused to see on a table, among various magazines, an issue of *The Baker Street Detective*. Bram Stoker, it appeared, was not the only enthusiast of the adventures of Macallister Fogg.

Five minutes passed, each of them measured by a loudly ticking clock on the mantelpiece.

The door finally opened.

A clockwork man strode in. It was very highly polished and had a coat of arms engraved upon its chest plate.

Extending a hand, it said, "Count Palladino, I understand? Good day to you, sir. I am Flywheel, Mr. Hope's private secretary. May I enquire as to the reason for your visit?"

Burton hesitated—he'd never been offered a handshake by a brass man before—then clasped the metal digits and, as he released them, said in a polite tone, "I don't mean to intrude upon your master's privacy nor impose upon his valuable time. I happened to be passing this way and suddenly recalled that my friend, Lord Manners, mentioned Mr. Hope to me some little time ago. I thought I might introduce myself."

"Lord Manners? I see. Mentioned him in relation to what, if I might ask?"

The contraption spoke in such a natural fashion that, for a moment,

Burton forgot to reply. He was amazed by the casual sentence construction, the smoothly articulated words, and the almost human-sounding modulations. This machine was obviously far more advanced than any he'd so far encountered.

"We were discussing Young England, both in its earlier incarnation and in its present. He also brought it to my attention that Mr. Hope is related to the de la Poer Beresford family."

Flywheel was silent for nearly thirty seconds and stood so motionless that Burton began to wonder whether it had wound down. Then it said, "Your English is extremely good, Count Palladino."

"Thank you. I was educated at Oxford."

"That explains it. My master is a Cambridge man. I regret to inform you that he is indisposed. He has taken to his bed with a case of influenza and can't possibly receive you at present."

"Ah. I'm sorry to hear that. He's asleep then?"

"He's reading. However, I'm authorised to speak on his behalf and am privy to all of his affairs. If you have any questions, I can probably answer them. Please sit. Would you care for a cigar? There's a box on the table, there. Havanas. Please help yourself. You are interested in the Beresfords? May I ask why?"

Burton sat and took one of the Havanas. He lit it, drew on it, and watched through the exhaled smoke as, to his utter astonishment, Flywheel settled in the opposite chair, crossed one metal leg over the other, and leaned back with its hands resting in its lap.

Acting on impulse, he asked, "Have you a Mark Three babbage?"

"A Mark Four."

"I didn't know there was a fourth model. When was it developed?"

"Mine was activated on the nineteenth of October last year, so prior to that date, but I don't know precisely when. The Beresfords?"

Burton gave a casual wave of a hand. "Oh, nothing. Just that I've heard that the third Marquess of Waterford was something of a character."

"To put it mildly. Mr. Hope has a very low opinion of that particular relative. The man was, I have heard him say, a cad of the first order, and one whose passing he doesn't regret one iota."

"Is that so? I wonder if having such an individual in the family encouraged Mr. Hope's one time support for the concept of *noblesse oblige*, as was promoted by the original Young England."

"I couldn't say, sir."

"It's unusual, isn't it?"

"To be related to a disreputable man?"

"To reverse one's opinion so completely. To make the current-day Young England the polar opposite of its predecessor."

Burton watched as, visible through the topmost opening in Flywheel's face, the machine's tiny cogs revolved.

"My good Count," the clockwork man said, "is it not logical to adjust one's opinion in line with new information as it comes to light?"

"I should say so, yes. To what information do you refer, in this instance?"

"To Darwin's theory of natural selection, which makes it plain—does it not?—that in supporting its weaker members, a species does itself a disservice."

Darwin! As was also invoked by Disraeli in a very similar manner!

"I don't think that's an interpretation Mr. Darwin would support. Besides which, by what criteria is weakness measured?"

"Need it be measured at all? Surely it is apparent that human society functions to allow the strong to rise to power while those of lesser ability remain in positions of servitude."

Burton flicked cigar ash into the hearth. He uttered a little grunt of dissent. "I perceive two problems with that argument. Firstly, our—by which I mean the empire's—current form of society is not the only system available to the human species. The Africans and Orientals, for example, have very different conventions to our own. We might say that ours, which is termed by some a capitalist democracy, allows for a certain sort of person to rise through its ranks, but that person's advancement is due to his or her abilities existing within an environment conducive to them. The same person, if placed in Abyssinia or Japan, might fail utterly. Which brings me to my second point: Darwin makes it plain that any quality whatsoever can be counted a strength if it is advantageous in a particular circumstance. Compassion is a considerable handicap in a financial institution but a great gift in a medical one. Context is everything."

"Quite so," Flywheel answered. "But our context is what it is. The new Young England applies to it."

"Then you feel it apposite to work within a system that favours a few over the very many than to apply yourself to improving the system so that more may prosper?"

"I, Count Palladino? I am but a machine."

"My apologies. I refer, of course, to Mr. Hope's stance on the matter."

"I believe my employer would ask you whether it is a kindness or a cruelty to instil into a man, who exists on a lower rung of society, the conception that the ladder is scalable. Surely, if he believes his circumstances are prescribed, then he will labour to make the most of everything they have to offer. If, however, he perceives that an ascent is possible, he will overlook the opportunities that exist within the bounds of his own particular position and will instead strive to step up to the next. Surely, in most cases, this can only lead to thwarted desire and a seething frustration. Is it not the case that a man who embarks on a journey while considering the stars is liable to fall into the first hole that comes along?"

Burton chuckled. "I must say, Flywheel, you are very eloquent for a thing of gears and springs. I can find but one fault in your argument."

"Which is what, sir?"

"The ladder. If its rungs present too great a step for the average man, then surely it is advisable to make a new one, with more rungs, each placed closer together."

Incredibly, the machine laughed. "Oh, I'm happy to have an artificial brain! It furnishes me with the ability to remember this conversation word for word. When Mr. Hope is better, I shall recount it to him. I am certain he'll find it most fascinating. But, alas, my good Count, I have duties to perform and regret that I must cut your visit short."

Flywheel uncrossed its legs and got to its feet. Burton also stood. The mechanism again extended a hand, which the explorer shook. When he tried to release it, he found his fingers held tightly by the other's metal digits.

"I shall send you on your way with a statement to consider," the brass man said. "If the ladder could be more easily climbed, the weight would surely accrue at its top, and inevitably, it would overbalance and fall. In order to be safe, the centre of gravity must remain at the foot. Thus does the empire's stability depend upon there being a clear division between the few at the heights and the labouring masses at the bottom."

Tiny pistons contracted and for the briefest of moments the bones of Burton's hand were squeezed to breaking point before being released. He was ushered out of the room and to the front door.

"Please give Mr. Hope my best wishes for a speedy recovery," he said.

"Thank you for calling, Count Palladino. I have very much enjoyed our brief discussion."

"Are you capable of enjoyment, Flywheel?"

"I am designed to be polite, sir."

"Ah, I see."

Stepping out into the fog, Burton descended the steps then turned and looked back. Flywheel, framed in the doorway, was watching him, motionless but for a swinging pendulum and turning cogs; metal and inscrutable.

"One final question," Burton said. "When were you last recalled for servicing?"

"I have not yet been in operation long enough for that requirement, sir. Have I given you cause for concern? Some perceived dysfunction?"

"Not at all. Not at all. Quite the opposite. You're a remarkable device."

"Thank you."

The door was pushed shut.

Burton looked at the upper storey. None of its windows were lit. Walking a little way along the street, he rounded a corner into Duchess Mews. From there, he could just make out, through the murk, the back of the house. Its upper rear rooms were also dark. If Henry Thomas Hope was awake and reading, one of those rooms would have been illuminated, so either he was asleep—

"Or he's not at home," Burton murmured. "In which case, where is he?"

Returning to Duchess Street, he strode to its end, entered Portland Place and followed it through into Regent Street, heading southward toward St. James Square, where Alexander Baillie-Cochrane's residence was located. He passed shop fronts from which ruddy light bled into the swirling mist, so that the vapour and pollution took on the appearance of a glowing airborne sludge. Large puddles had accrued, and these, too, appeared to have absorbed the illumination, sucking it in and reflecting it back with intensity, like flat sheets of fire.

London had become infernal.

In this part of it, the thoroughfares were less populated than usual, the caustic pall encouraging those who could afford to do so to remain in their homes. Not so the workers, who had no option but to labour on, earning their meagre pennies.

Men and women balancing fish-, fruit-, or vegetable-filled baskets on their heads, or wheeling barrows, or carrying the tools of their trade, materialised, became solid as they trudged past him, then faded into nothingness behind. Wagons and carts, drawn mostly by horses or donkeys, trundled along the road. A pantechnicon, carrying live cattle, went chugging by, so noisily that he could hear nothing else until it had gone. The huge machine contributed such a dense cloud of vapour to the fog that, for a few paces, he couldn't see his hand in front of his face.

The hustle and bustle gradually increased as he drew closer to the centre of the city. By the time he crossed the junction with Oxford Street, Burton was shouldering past people, and his ears were ceaselessly assaulted by the cries of costermongers and street entertainers, the discordant tones of organs, and the forced merriment of wan-looking singers.

When he reached Regent Circus, the hubbub was suddenly drowned by a deafening bellow from overhead; a deep, moaning lament that vibrated through his bones and echoed into the distance, like the keening of a wounded whale. It gave way to an insistent throbbing.

The wide circle of a searchlight, its source above, slid out of the fog and across the pavement to momentarily illuminate him. It slipped away. Another flitted past to his right. The vapours billowed in agitation. He looked up and saw a gargantuan shadow gliding low over the rooftops. It was a rotorship, larger than any he'd ever seen—more massive even than the dreadnought class HMA *Sagittarius*, which had bombed the Old Summer Palace in China. The searchlights were glaring down from it, sweeping this way and that, and on its side, in brightly illuminated letters, were the words: DUTY. DISCIPLINE. LAW AND ORDER.

He watched as the vast machine was swallowed into the murk, sinking past the buildings to his right.

"Landing," he murmured. "In the park."

His destination lay straight ahead but, curious to see again the construction work he'd witnessed in Green Park last night, he decided on a change of course and rounded the corner into Piccadilly.

A pair of SPG units came stamping out of the gloom, approaching him, inky blue and menacing, side by side, face lamps sending pencils of light through the cloud. He stepped aside and they passed, their heads turning as they did so, examining him from hat to boots.

Resisting the urge to sigh with relief as they continued on and disappeared from view, Burton resumed his walk. As he passed the junction with Dover Street, the corner of the park came into view. He stumbled to a halt and stared.

Through the peasouper, he could just make out a tall barricade. He crossed the road and, a few paces later, came abreast the wall that lined the northern stretch of the park. Immediately behind it and flush to it, a wooden fence had been erected. It was solid and about fifteen feet high, backing the wall to the right and left of him and appearing to completely enclose the park. Bills of various sizes had been pasted onto the planks and the brickwork below. Most advertised the services of lawyers or promoted various newspapers. The larger ones bore what Burton assumed were governmental messages.

THINK NOT "I" BUT "WE."   ·

TOGETHER WE DRIVE THE EMPIRE.

YOUR LABOURS ARE APPRECIATED BY ALL.

DO YOUR BIT!

It was almost identical to material he'd witnessed in Spring Heeled Jack's twisted future, and for a moment, he felt utterly disoriented, as if time had curled in on itself—as if all this was a dream and he was still in the year 2202, yet to battle with the demented intelligence occupying Isambard Kingdom Brunel's mechanical body.

Had that sentience, currently thought to be dormant in eleven black diamonds, somehow awoken and taken control of the government? Had Disraeli become a slave to it? No, it couldn't be. It simply wasn't possible. The Spring Heeled Jack of 2202 was an amalgam of the fragmented parts of several iterations of a single man, drawn together from several histories and thrust forward to that future year. Those splinters certainly weren't in the present. There was nothing that could—

Burton struggled to find the appropriate word.

Activate.

Yes. There was nothing in the contemporary world that could *activate* the Spring Heeled Jack intelligence.

He walked beside the barrier, hearing the slowing thrum of the huge rotorship's engines coming from the other side of it.

To Hyde Park corner and left into Grosvenor Place, the fence continued unbroken around to Constitution Hill, which it then followed all the way down to the Mall, where it joined the Queen's Wall, which had been considerably heightened. Thus was formed a large triangular compound just to the north of Buckingham Palace and its gardens.

On the Mall, Burton saw tall gates and a number of low, makeshift wooden buildings. Police constables were present in great numbers. A group of men—twelve innocuous-looking individuals—were being herded into the park by SPG mechanicals.

"Are they prisoners?" Burton whispered to himself. "Why?"

They were obviously very confused and afraid.

Approaching a nearby policeman, he said, "What's going on here, constable? What's happened to the park?"

The uniformed man glanced at Burton then looked back at the scene. "A temporary measure, I'm told, sir. It's been made an internment camp."

"For whom? Those men look like clerks and bookkeepers to me. What crime are they charged with?"

"I'm sure I don't know, sir, though I daresay it has something to do with the Yellow Menace."

"Yellow Menace?"

"China, sir. They are probably sympathisers. I hear such sentiment is endemic among the middling sorts."

"And you believe that, do you?"

"I've seen no evidence to suggest it a falsehood."

Burton blinked. "What? No evidence to suggest——? What of a man being presumed innocent until proven guilty?"

The policeman chuckled. "Well, sir, they must have been found guilty of something—hey?—else why are they being detained?"

Incredulous, Burton shook his head, started to move away, then stumbled to a halt and stared, thunderstruck, at a new group of men who'd just climbed down from a large police wagon and were being marched toward the gates. There were twelve in all. He recognised two of them.

Thomas Bendyshe and James Hunt.

Bismillah! Did my message not get to Monckton Milnes in time?

He rapidly calculated the distance to the other Cannibals' residences. Monckton Milnes's town house was the closest, it being a little over a mile to the north, in Upper Brook Street.

Adopting a fast pace, he left the Mall and followed the Queen's Wall back to Piccadilly, which he crossed in order to enter Berkeley Street. This, he ran along until he reached Berkeley Square. Here, having breathed in too much ash, he was forced to stop and bend double, racked by a fit of coughing. He spat out black phlegm, got himself under control, and continued on, navigating through to Grosvenor Square and traversing it until he came to the mouth of Upper Brook Street.

As he approached number 16, he realised he was too late. There was a medium-sized police rotorship at the side of the road outside the house. At the foot of the front steps, three human constables were indecisively moving around two Special Patrol Group machines, each of which was gripping a struggling figure.

One, Richard Monckton Milnes, yelled, "Get your damned hands off me!"

The other, Charles Bradlaugh, cried out, "This is unconscionable! By what right? By what right?"

"Get into the vehicle immediately," one of the clockwork policemen ordered, "or you will be charged with resisting arrest."

"Arrest for what?" Monckton Milnes roared. "This is mistaken identity! It has to be! Let me go!"

"You are a threat to the empire's security."

"Don't be bloody ridiculous!"

Burton acted without thought. Plunging forward, he pounced on the nearest constable, who had his back to him, and with his left hand yanked the man's helmet back. With his right, he brought his cane sweeping up and cracked its handle against the policeman's temple. The man was insensible on the ground before knowing what had happened.

Without the slightest pause in his movements, Burton sidestepped to his right and, reversing his cane, slammed its hilt into the face of the second constable, catching him precisely between the eyes. Knocked back against the police vehicle, the man slid to the pavement.

The opposition reacted.

The SPG mechanism holding Bradlaugh suddenly shoved his captive. Bradlaugh reeled into Burton, and they both tripped over the fallen constable and fell against the rotorship.

Truncheons clicked out from metal wrists.

"Identify yourself. You are under arrest. Do not resist."

Burton ducked his head and rolled aside, feeling a baton brush his hair as it whipped past and smacked into the rotorship's door with a loud clack. He scrambled to his feet and stumbled backward until he thudded against the house's front railings.

The second SPG unit, with its left hand still holding Monckton Milnes by his jacket collar, thrust out its right arm. Metal fingers clamped down with brutal force on Burton's shoulder. He gave a bark of agony and, as his knees buckled, stabbed sideways with his cane. By chance rather than design, it slid through one of the openings at the side of the contraption's chest plate and penetrated the inner workings. Gears crunched and whined. The machine froze.

"I am immobilised! Alert! Alert! Immediate assistance required!"

The other, at the same moment, had regained balance, swung around, and was in the act of jumping at Burton when Bradlaugh, on the ground, snatched it by the ankle. As it overbalanced, Burton let go of his sword-stick and brought up his arm to block a swinging baton, which fortunately lacked sufficient force to damage his limb. He pulled his shoulder free and, instinctively, delivered a roundhouse left uppercut to the contraption's head. Knuckles banged against brass.

"Ouch!" he yelped.

The clockwork man clanged against the railings and tottered. Burton pushed it over, pulled a revolver from his pocket, and drilled it through the head.

It said, "Krzzzzt!"

The third of the human constables, who'd been stunned into helplessness by the unexpected turn of events, snapped into action at the sound of the gunshot. He stepped forward, shouting, "Now look here! What the blazes do you think—" Monckton Milnes stuck out a foot. The man tripped over it and fell flat on his face.

Burton bent over him and pushed the barrel of his weapon into the back of his neck. "Stay down, old fellow. Don't move and I won't shoot you. Understood?"

"Yes, perfectly well," came the quavering response. "I'll not so much as blink."

"Good man."

Burton swung around, levelled his pistol at the topmost opening in the head of the immobilised clockwork man, and fired three bullets into it. He pulled his cane free then stepped over to Bradlaugh and helped him to his feet. "Come on, you two," he said. "We have to get out of here—and fast!"

The three men took to their heels. Behind them, the shot mechanism's head erupted into flames then exploded.

Sprinting to the end of the road, they turned left into North Audley Street, then right into Providence Court.

"We'll try to lose ourselves in the back streets," the explorer panted. "The fog will help us."

A small rotorship flew across the road just ahead of them, its passing marked only by a fleeting shadow, a sweeping searchlight, and the growing then diminishing wail of a siren.

Left into George Street and there, through the murk, they saw two blue lights moving toward them. Quickly, they veered right into Hart Street, pounded along it to Duke Street, and hurried up to busy Oxford Street, where they hoped to lose themselves in the bustling throng.

Two more SPG machines became visible ahead. The three men

crossed the road to avoid them, running between clanking vehicles, narrowly avoiding a rolling steam sphere. A velocipedist swerved to avoid them and hit the side of a hansom. He shouted. A police whistle blew. Burton looked back and saw the constable he'd left on the pavement. The man was pointing at him and blowing repeated blasts.

Clockwork policemen closed from the left. A second pair from the right.

A rotorship plummeted out of the sky, siren howling. Horses bucked and whinnied in panic as, suddenly slowing, the flying machine set down amid the traffic.

Burton's breath hissed through his teeth. "Damnation! We're corralled!"

"I fear, good sir, that you may regret coming to our rescue," Monckton Milnes murmured.

With an incongruous glimmer of amusement, Burton realised that his disguise had fooled the two Cannibals. Despite the circumstances, he'd instinctively maintained the accent.

"Stop!" one of the approaching SPG units commanded. "Kneel and submit."

"Resistance will not be tolerated," another declared.

Truncheons extended.

As the contraptions closed on the three men, a door in the side of the rotorship hinged down and four more machines emerged.

"We don't stand a chance," Charles Bradlaugh observed. He knelt.

Reluctantly, Burton and Monckton Milnes followed suit.

Minutes later, they were sitting in the rotorship with their wrists cuffed together behind their backs. Four clockwork men watched them wordlessly. Burton's gun and swordstick had been confiscated.

"I'm Richard Monckton Milnes," his friend said to him. "And this is Charlie Bradlaugh. Neither of us knows why we're arrested, but I'd like to thank you for—" He finished the sentence with a quirk of the eyebrow.

"For acting impetuously and getting myself arrested?" Burton said with a grim smile. "I am Count Palladino."

Bradlaugh said, "Have we met? I feel I may have made your acquaintance at some point. At one of the clubs, perhaps?"

"I have that sort of face," Burton replied.

The vessel's engine hummed, and the floor shifted beneath them. The flight was short—little more than a hop—and when the door opened, the explorer wasn't at all surprised to see the Mall beyond it.

"Out," they were ordered.

"I'll ask again," Monckton Milnes said to one of the SPG machines. "With what are we charged?"

"Resisting arrest."

"Yes, but before that? Why did you come to my house? What is it I am supposed to have done?"

"Out."

They stood, exited the ship, and were promptly hustled by the clockwork men to the gates of the enclosed park.

"What in God's name?" Monckton Milnes exclaimed upon seeing the tall fence.

"It went up last night," Burton said.

They were guided through the gates.

Looking down the slope to the Victoria Monument—which for some obscure reason appeared to Burton to be different in form to what he expected—he saw row after row of sheds and, beyond them, the shadowy fog-veiled bulk of the rotorship he'd heard landing earlier. There were men—but no women—scattered around, most garbed in suits but a few in pyjamas. There were also a great many clockwork figures, these with normal rather than SPG helmet-shaped heads and painted dark green rather than blue.

Burton, Monckton Milnes, and Bradlaugh were escorted to the end of a queue of men. The line led to the door of a large shed. A sign above the portal declared PROCESSING.

"Wait until your turn," one of the SPG units said. "Do not attempt to flee. Do not object or ask questions. Do not give false information. Do not cause an affray. Do not resist orders."

"May I scratch my arse?" Bradlaugh asked.

"Yes."

The mechanised policeman unclipped their handcuffs and took from a metal pouch in its side three red ribbons, which it tied around their left upper arms.

"What do these signify?" Burton enquired.

"Do not remove them," the machine replied. It marched away.

"I have to say," Monckton Milnes muttered, "that this is all thoroughly inconvenient yet also rather interesting." He tapped the shoulder of the man in front of him, a tubby fellow in a yellow dressing gown. "Hallo there! Do you happen to have any idea of what's happening?"

"None," the other replied. "I was asleep. They hammered at my door this morning, woke me up, dragged me to a police station, and left me in a cell for hours and hours. Arrested! And look! I'm in my bloody slippers! I've not eaten since yesterday. What will the manager say?"

"Manager?"

"At the bank. Scrannington Bank. It's where I work. I'm meant to be there. I'm the chief underwriter. Insurance! Great heavens! Insurance! And me in my slippers!"

Bradlaugh said, "What did you do, if you'll pardon my asking?"

"Do? I just told you. Insurance."

"I mean, what did you do to be arrested?"

"Nothing! I was asleep, I say!"

"Some sort of misdemeanour?"

"How dare you!" the man objected. "I insist, I've committed no crime. I'm an underwriter not a thief."

A man farther along the line but within earshot looked back over his shoulder and called, "You'll not find any criminals here, my friend. We're perfectly ordinary. No one has the vaguest idea what this is all about."

Monckton Milnes turned to Bradlaugh. "I suppose it'll all come out in the wash. Once they realise they've made a mistake—"

They took a few steps forward as the queue moved.

Burton wanted to reveal his identity to his friends—tell them that Tom Bendyshe and James Hunt were also in the camp, enquire about the message he'd sent via the Whispering Web and ask after Brabrooke and Murray—but feeling there might be an advantage to retaining his disguise, he resisted the temptation.

It was now late afternoon, but there was no change in the curious light, which appeared to be an element of the fog itself. The summer sun, shining down on the near-impenetrable peasouper, wouldn't set until past nine o'clock.

Monckton Milnes pulled a handkerchief from his pocket and used it to wipe beads of perspiration from his brow.

They moved closer to the door.

Men were added to the queue behind them. Questions were asked, but Burton and his friends had no answers to offer.

Finally, they entered the hut.

One by one, the men in front of them shuffled forward and stood in front of a desk. A flabby-faced individual in a rather-too-opulent ceremonial Army uniform was sitting behind it with a green-painted clockwork man beside him. Four more of Babbage's contraptions were also present. One was holding a bucket of white paint and a brush. Another stepped forward and searched the men, finding only ordinary items—pipes, tobacco pouches, wallets, keys, and so forth.

Names were taken, a list consulted and ticked with a pencil. Protests were waved aside. "All will be explained. Be patient." The man spoke in a clipped and cold tone, as if delivering the words by rote. "You are assigned to hut fifteen. If you hear the siren or a whistle, line up outside of it. A meal will be provided later."

"But why are we here?" one of the men asked.

"Don't make a fuss," came the reply. "As you can see, we are very busy. Your cooperation is appreciated. Exit through the door to your left, please."

As the men moved to the indicated portal, they were each stopped by the mechanism with the paint bucket and a number was brushed onto the back of their clothes.

"My dressing gown! You've ruined it!"

"Move on, please."

Monckton Milnes approached the desk. His red ribbon was noticed, and when the man looked beyond him and saw that Burton and Bradlaugh were also so adorned, he gestured for them to step forward too. They were searched and divested of their belongings.

"You three are together?"

Monckton Milnes ignored the question and drawled, "My good man, I rather think an introduction is called for, don't you?"

"Very well. I am Commander Thaddeus Kidd. And you are?"

"Extremely disgruntled. I demand to know why I've been manhandled from my home and forcibly detained."

"I can't answer that unless you give me your name."

"I am Richard Monckton Milnes."

The clockwork man handed a sheet of paper to Kidd, a different list. He ran his pencil down it and, seeing what he was looking for, murmured, "Ah, yes. Good." He looked at Bradlaugh. "And you?"

"Sir Charles Bradlaugh. And I intend to notify the War Office and have your damned hide for this."

"Do you now? Do you?" Kidd responded with the trace of a sneer. "We shall see about that." He checked the list again and gave a grunt of satisfaction before levelling his eyes at Burton. "So you must be either Murray or Brabrooke."

The device at his side said, "No, sir. This individual is not listed. He was apprehended after preventing police constables from performing their duty. He was carrying a pistol and disabled two units."

Burton, who hadn't seen any of the SPG machines that captured him enter the hut, wondered whether that statement was another example of nonverbal communication.

"I am Count Palladino. Visiting from Italy."

"A spy?" Kidd asked.

"Don't be ridiculous."

"Ridiculous? You were carrying a gun. Why did you interfere with police business?"

"I acted on impulse."

"It may cost you. The law is absolute. You will remain here until we decide what to do with you. All three of you will bunk in hut zero. Stay inside. Do not mingle with the other detainees. You will be guarded. Dismissed. Out that way, please." He cocked a thumb at the side door.

"I'll not stand for this!" Monckton Milnes bellowed. "I know my rights. You have no—"

A clockwork man grabbed and held him while "287" was painted onto his back. Bradlaugh received "288" and Burton "289." They were hustled out. Four mechanical guards took charge of them and marched them across the grass to a nearby shed, its door marked with a large "0."

Monckton Milnes's face was red with fury. Bradlaugh kept whispering, "I don't understand. I don't understand."

The door was unlocked, and they were pushed into a long, low, windowless room lined with bunk beds and illuminated by a single oil lamp. There were other men present. Doctor James Hunt rose from his bed and greeted them.

"Hallo, chaps. Welcome to the house of the undesirables."

BRUTALITY AND MURDER IN HUT 0

PUBLIC NOTICE
TOOLEY STREET CLOSURE
THE FULL EXTENT OF TOOLEY STREET WILL BE
CLOSED TO THE PUBLIC UNTIL FURTHER NOTICE
ST. SAVIOUR'S DISTRICT BOARD OF WORKS

The twelve occupants of hut 0 were special. One was a clockwork man that sat unmoving in a corner. Its only function appeared to be to monitor conversations and report anything of interest. The others, the Undesirables, were—unlike the other men in the camp, all of whom were middle class—either titled, rich, well-educated, influential, or a combination thereof. A chalkboard on the exterior wall of the shed, to the right of the door, listed them as:

085 Thomas Bendyshe
086 Doctor James Hunt
287 Richard Monckton Milnes
288 Sir Charles Bradlaugh
289 Count Marco Palladino
328 Captain Henry Murray
329 Sir Edward Brabrooke
641 Henry Spencer Ashbee
691 Doctor Bartholomew Quaint

722 Captain Frederick Hankey
854 Sir Roderick Murchison

It did not escape Burton's attention that all these men were associated with him in some manner or other.

Murray and Brabrooke had been interned the evening of his own arrival in the camp, so that now the entire Cannibal Club was in captivity with the exception of Swinburne. Over the course of the following three days, the others had arrived. Ashbee and Hankey, both writers, publishers, and eroticists, had provided Swinburne with an outlet for his most incendiary work. Quaint had been the medico and steward aboard the *Orpheus* during Burton's expedition to the source of the Nile. He was off duty when the rotorship disappeared and had no idea where it had gone. Murchison was the president of the Royal Geographical Society.

All were now dressed in ill-fitting and scratchy hessian uniforms with their numbers stitched onto their backs and sleeves.

Burton had been a prisoner for six full days and his disguise was becoming increasingly ragged around the edges. He'd avoided washing his face for fear the touches of makeup would disappear but it was, inevitably, rubbing off of its own accord. His false moustache was drooping. He frequently forgot to hold his jaw in a certain manner, allowing it, in repose, to slip into its normal position, which did much to expose his normal countenance. Monckton Milnes, he thought, was becoming suspicious. Burton often felt himself being surreptitiously scrutinised by his friend.

Day by day, the regime in the camp was becoming increasingly brutal. Every morning, at the ungodly hour of four, a siren blasted, and the men—the compound was by now extremely crowded—had to get up and tidy their shapeless straw mattresses and rough blankets to a military standard before standing to attention outside their huts for morning roll call. Newcomers used this occasion to express their indignation and anger. Those who'd been imprisoned for more than two days had already learned that such behaviour was inevitably met with a savage beating. There was nary a man in the camp who didn't bear the bruises of such treatment, which is why all but the most recently arrived remained sullen and silent except to answer "Aye!" when his number was called.

Next came the opportunity for morning ablutions. There were just two water spigots in the camp and, at the blast of a whistle, the prisoners had to run for them hoping to get a turn. Only a small percentage ever managed to wash.

The other facility consisted of wooden boards suspended over a ditch that ran downhill to join an exposed sewer pipe. The stench from this was dreadful and pervaded the entire enclosure.

At half past six, as the upper reaches of the fog took on a metallic-grey glow caused by the morning sun shining onto it, a second siren blasted, signalling that the men should line up again outside their huts, this time with their mess tins and cups in their hands. A small number of prisoners, selected for the duty, passed along the lines distributing weak and gritty coffee, coarse bread, and a slop of cold porridge.

After this meagre breakfast, most were free to move about the camp as they wished. Not so the inhabitants of hut 0, who—with their mute and motionless guard—were confined to their quarters.

Lunch—bland soup and watery tea—followed the same routine as breakfast. In the afternoons, the huge rotorship, which Burton now knew to be HMA *Eurypyle*, arrived, announcing its approach with a deep, teeth-rattling bellow. Men were herded aboard it to be transported to no one knew where. Others entered the camp to replace them.

Evening roll call came at seven o'clock and was followed by a dinner of gristle-filled mutton stew and a second cup of tea.

"It's inhuman!" Sir Roderick protested for the umpteenth time.

It was the morning of Burton's seventh day of captivity. He'd just finished breakfast but was still hungry. He and the others were sitting on their bunks, most slumped forward, arms resting on legs, heads hanging. The explorer was listening for the faint, almost inaudible tapping that had sounded at the base of the door every morning thus far. He knew it was Pox, sent with a message from Swinburne, Trounce, or Gooch. The bird couldn't get in, wouldn't deliver its communiqué without seeing Burton, and every day flew away undoubtedly to report the message undelivered. That was as much as its capabilities allowed. It couldn't tell his friends where he was or anything about his circumstances.

Burton hoped fervently that the bird wouldn't one day arrive during roll call or one of the meals. If it was seen, it would be killed, he was sure.

"I'm president of the RGS," Murchison continued. "I serve on the Royal Commission for the British Museum. I'm director-general of the British Geological Survey and director of the Royal School of Mines and the Museum of Practical Geology. I have it on good authority that I'm to be made a baronet. By God, I have more letters after my name than I have in it!"

"Oh, give it a rest, why don't you?" Tom Bendyshe groaned. "We've heard it all before. We're all in the same boat, old fellow. None of us has done anything to warrant our confinement."

"Pornographer!" Murchison spat.

"Let's not start on each other," Monckton Milnes muttered. "Has anyone given Laughing Boy's key a spin?"

Laughing Boy was the name they'd given their clockwork cohabitant. The device had, every day bar yesterday, spoken just once, on each occasion after morning roll call, and each time to utter exactly the same words: "You are ordered to wind me up to full capacity. Failure to do so will be reported and will result in severe punishment."

Yesterday Doctor Quaint had forestalled the threat by winding the mechanism's spring the moment they'd returned to their hut after the morning routine. He now did so again.

Burton wondered whether it would be worth the subsequent punishment to allow the guard to wind down just so they'd have a few minutes to plan their escape without being overheard. He knew other captives had made attempts. Under cover of the still-dense fog, they'd attempted to scale the fence, but had been caught in the act and summarily executed in front of the other prisoners. Now, guard towers were being built. If Burton and his companions were going to make a move, it would have to be very soon.

Tap tap tap. Tap tap tap.

There it was. Pox.

Burton wanted to rush to the door and shout through it, *Message for Swinburne. I am held prisoner in Green Park!*

But, as always, Laughing Boy was watching and listening.

The tapping continued for a couple of minutes then stopped.

Five minutes after that, their guard suddenly spoke.

"Attention! Stand by your bunks. Inspection."

"Bloody hell!" Bendyshe moaned. "Not again."

"First time we've been warned, though," Ashbee noted. "Let's not give Kidd any excuses. Is everything ship-shape?"

The men stood and quickly smoothed their blankets and put their mess tins out of site. They stood, backs straight, shoulders squared, stomachs hollow, hearts hammering, knowing that the next half hour or so would be exceedingly unpleasant.

Kidd had done it every day; summary inspections conducted with cold politeness and, inevitably, concluding with punishments for transgressions as trivial as a creased pillow, a breadcrumb found on the floor, or a uniform button left undone. The penalties ranged from a confiscated blanket to a missed meal, from an enforced run of multiple laps around the compound to an unrestrained horsewhipping. Henry Ashbee still bore the marks of the latter upon his back.

The door lock clicked and the portal banged open. Two green-painted clockwork men entered and positioned themselves to either side. Commander Kidd strode in. He, too, stood aside. An SPG unit followed and, behind it, dressed in a black uniform, wearing black leather gloves and with a swagger stick in his right hand, came Colonel Christopher Palmer Rigby.

"Good morning, gentlemen," he said, removing his left glove. He paced up and down the middle of the room, pausing in front of each man. "Sir Roderick, I trust you are enjoying this break from your various duties. Captain Murray, you appear a little gaunt. Are you not eating? Mr. Ashbee, hello, and Mr. Hankey, good day to you, sir. I regret that I must inform you both that your printing presses have been confiscated and your publications destroyed. Ah, Doctor Quaint! Separated from your shipmates, hey? And Mr. Bendyshe, are you—"

"Go to hell!" Bendyshe snapped.

A momentary silence. Rigby smiled. He jerked his right arm up and sliced his swagger stick across Bendyshe's face, leaving behind a livid welt.

"I didn't order you to speak, sir. Commander Kidd, have this man taken outside and taught some manners. Don't break any bones."

Kidd nodded and waved his two guards forward. The clockwork men pounced on Bendyshe and hauled him, kicking and yelling, out of the hut. Kidd followed. Monckton Milnes made to move after him but Burton hissed, "Don't."

"Where was I?" Rigby said pleasantly. "Ah yes, Sir Charles Bradlaugh, Sir Edward Brabrooke, and Doctor Hunt, greetings to you all. Mr. Monckton Milnes, it is good to see you again. We met once at one of Lady Pauline Trevelyan's little gatherings. You probably don't recall the occasion. I rather think I was invited by mistake. Not my kind of people, if you understand my meaning. Far too—what shall we say?—*artistic?*"

He stopped in front of Burton and stared into his eyes.

"And you must be Count Palladino, the man who did the wrong thing at the wrong time in the wrong place, eh? I have something that belongs to you, sir."

Rigby stretched his left arm out sideways. The SPG unit strode forward and proffered an item around which Rigby's fingers closed.

"Your cane. Confiscated from you. I rather expect you'd like it returned. It's certainly an unusual piece. Unique handle. A panther's head. Fine craftsmanship. It impressed me to such a degree that I was moved to do a little research. Do you know what I found? That only one such cane was ever made. It was commissioned by the late Laurence Oliphant, Lord Elgin's former secretary, and stolen from him when he was murdered—by a man, I might add, who has since been declared an enemy of the empire. I refer to Sir Richard Francis Burton. Are you acquainted with him? Did he make a gift of it to you, perhaps? You have my permission to speak."

"Freely?" Burton asked.

"Why, of course."

"Then I shall say that you're a cad of the first order, Rigby. Were you to submit yourself for examination by Doctor Monroe at the Bethlem Lunatic Asylum, I'm certain he'd declare you a homicidal maniac. Your brain is marred by a criminal aberration. I saw it twenty years ago in India, I saw it again two years ago in Zanzibar, and it appears to have become even more severe in its effects in the time since. You cannot reason like a normal man. Disraeli—who has apparently also lost his mind—did well in hiring you to do his dirty work, for you are utterly lacking in the finer sentiments and are more akin to a rabid beast than to a rational person. I shall have to deal with you as I would such an unfortunate creature. I will have no option but to hold you down and put a bullet through your diseased head."

Rigby, whose face had purpled, stood silently with his eyes blazing and his thin lips white.

Burton sensed that his fellow prisoners were holding their breaths. He slowly raised a hand, gripped his false moustache and tore it from his face. With the sleeve of his shirt, he smeared away the make up around his eyes and cheeks.

He heard Monckton Milnes, to his right, expel a small sigh. No doubt, he was thinking, *I should have bloody well known!*

What felt like two minutes passed in absolute silence.

Rigby threw back his head and roared with laughter.

"Oh!" he shouted. "Oh! What marvellous games we play!"

He called for Kidd. The commander stepped in and was told, "Get that other one back in here. I assume he's had enough by now?"

Commander Kidd grinned. "The clockwork men are fast and efficient." He leaned out and beckoned to his mechanical subordinates.

"Burton," Rigby said, turning back to the explorer. "If you want to completely ruin my morning, you'll reveal to me now where I can find Algernon Swinburne, Detective Inspector Trounce, and Daniel Gooch. Tell me where your brother is and where Lawless has taken the *Orpheus*. Furnish me with those items of information, and I shall be obliged to leave here immediately to round them up. Stay silent, and I'll remain, which is what I'd much prefer."

Burton didn't respond.

Rigby clicked his heels and gave a little bow. "Thank you. Thank you very much indeed."

The two clockwork men dragged Bendyshe in. His uniform was ragged and stained with blood. His face was a mess, the eyes swollen to slits, the lips puffed up and split, the nose dribbling gore.

"Sit him on his bunk," Rigby said.

Bendyshe mumbled the worst expletive he knew—and he knew more than most men.

The contraptions dumped him down then backed away and stood to attention.

The Colonel pushed his glove and swagger stick through his belt, unholstered his revolver, and, taking two strides, pressed its barrel against Frederick Hankey's forehead. He issued an order to the mechanical guards. "Secure their hands behind their backs. Gentlemen, I assure you that, should any of you resist, Mr. Hankey's brains will be decorating the wall."

It was done, and they all succumbed to the handcuffs without a struggle.

Only Hankey remained unshackled. Rigby shoved him to the middle of the hut and told the guards to hold his arms. They did so, gripping with evident force, and Hankey groaned with the pain of it. His upper limbs were outspread, so that he stood as if crucified.

Rigby, positioning himself in front of him, put away his gun, raised Burton's cane, and used it to lightly prod Hankey in the stomach.

He addressed the SPG device. "Strip him of his upper garments. Tear them off."

The inky-blue machine obeyed. The material ripped, pulling at Hankey's skin and leaving red marks. Only the tattered sleeves, held fast against his arms by metal digits, remained.

Burton's friend was a tall man whose naturally bony physique had been made skinnier by his week of near starvation. He looked awful, and Burton's jaw ached as he clenched his teeth in fury.

"Let us deal with one question at a time," Rigby announced. "I don't care who answers, but I highly recommend that one of you does. First, where is Swinburne?"

No one said a word.

Rigby sighed. He crouched and cracked Burton's cane with all his strength across Hankey's kneecaps. The man screeched.

"I'll ask again. Swinburne. Where is he?"

Silence but for Hankey's agonised moans.

Rigby pulled at the cane's handle, which slid up.

"Great heavens!" he exclaimed. "Will you look at that! A concealed blade!"

He unsheathed the rapier and clumsily thrust it in Hankey's direction, though not touching the prisoner.

"My goodness, but it's well balanced. Sharp, too, I should venture."

He rested its point against Hankey's right bicep.

"Swinburne? An answer, if you please?"

The blade slid through Hankey's arm and out the other side.

"God in heaven!" the man screamed. "God! God! God!"

Burton cried out, "Bismillah, Rigby! Your argument is with me! If you must commit such atrocities, I should be your victim, not any of these men."

"But you are." Rigby chuckled. He tested the blade against Hankey's right thigh. It slipped through the muscle with ease.

Hankey's atheism continued to fail him. "Sweet Mary, Mother of Jesus! God! God! Don't tell him, Burton! Don't tell the bastard son of a whore bitch a bloody thing! Rot in hell, Rigby, you cur! Rot in hell!"

"If I do, I'll see you there," the colonel replied. He pushed the sword into Hankey's heart. "Marvellous! A very fine weapon. I shall keep it, Burton."

With a wave of his hand, Rigby had the guards drag Hankey's corpse to the end of the cabin. When they returned, he touched the tip of the rapier to Doctor Quaint's chin. "This one next. But I must practice a little more restraint. We're still on the first question and—" he looked at each of the prisoners in turn, "resources are limited."

Quaint, also tall but much more beefy in build than Hankey, was quickly divested of his handcuffs, stripped, and held. He turned his head and his eyes met Burton's. "Sir Richard, if you give this mongrel an answer and, as a result of it, he allows me to live, I shall kill you with my own hands. Is that understood?"

Burton struggled for breath.

I can't watch them all die. What should I do? What should I do?

"That goes for all of us," Monckton Milnes declared.

"Shut up!" Rigby barked. "Not another damned word from anyone but Burton."

"This man represents everything we must resist," Monckton Milnes continued forcibly. "If we have to perish so that Swinburne and the others can live to fight on, then perish we shall, and willingly. Disraeli has to be stopped, else the word *British* will stand for nothing."

"Hear, hear!" the others cheered.

Rigby snarled, dropped the rapier and its scabbard, removed his remaining glove, and ploughed a fist into Quaint's stomach. A second punch, a third, a fourth, in rapid succession. With his left hand, he grabbed the doctor's hair, held his head, and sent the knuckles of his right hand smashing again and again into the man's face. The onlookers cried out. Rigby's wrath increased.

"Stop!" Burton yelled. "For pity's sake, stop! I don't know where Swinburne is! I don't know, I tell you!"

The barbarity continued. The colonel appeared to have utterly lost control. He set about Quaint with such vicious precision that his victim quickly became unrecognisable. Blood sprayed. It pooled on the floor. There were broken teeth in it.

"I'll beat you all to within an inch of your lives!" Rigby shrieked. "And when you've recovered, I'll do it again! And again! And again! Now tell me, *where*—"

His fist crunched into Quaint's ribs.

"*is*—"

A right cross to the doctor's jaw. The head, already dangling—the man was by now unconscious—snapped loosely to the side.

"*Swinburne?*"

A downward swing onto the mashed nose. Red droplets arced through the air.

The colonel stepped back and his shoulders slumped. He flicked his hands so that gore spattered across Monckton Milnes's face. "Phew! I'm puffed!"

"Let him be, man. Have mercy. Let him be," Burton croaked. "I don't know where Swinburne is. Since I was relieved of my duties, I've hardly seen him."

"Liar!" Rigby straightened. He thudded his fist into Quaint's side with such force that a rib was heard to crack. "You were with him at Verbena Lodge."

"Yes, I was. We met there to enjoy ourselves and to catch up after weeks without contact, but Trounce burst in on us, and the next thing I knew, I was running from the police. I have no idea why. I have no notion what the confounded poet is up to or why the police are after him or why Trounce took it upon himself to defy his superiors."

Rigby sneered. "A likely story."

He set about Quaint again, his barbarity terrifying, his violence unrestrained, the brutality feeling to the onlookers as if it would never cease. But, after a few minutes, it did, and Rigby stepped back again and grinned happily. He held his arms out wide, looked up at the ceiling, and slowly turned on the spot.

"Ah! Burton! Burton! Burton! You are most generous. You refuse to supply the answer I require and thus you favour me with many more days in which to enjoy myself with your friends. It is perfectly splendid."

Burton, despairingly, looked at his fellow prisoners. They were weeping.

The colonel bowed his head until his respiration had stabilised. He retrieved the rapier and cane from the floor, and said to Burton, "You've quite tired me out, man. I'm too impatient by half. There's no pressing urgency, and I have other matters to attend to this afternoon, so let us reconvene at the same time tomorrow, hey?" He paused and gazed balefully at James Hunt. "Oh, I say, two doctors! That rather weighs the odds, don't you think? Allow me to level the playing field somewhat."

Touching the blade to the base of Quaint's chin, he pushed it in and up, transfixing the brain. After sliding it out, he handed it and the sheath to Commander Kidd. "Have it cleaned, oiled, and returned to me before I depart." He turned to the clockwork guards. "Dispose of the bodies." To the SPG machine, he said, "Remove their handcuffs."

Stepping over to Bendyshe's bunk, he regarded the tattered mess that was lying half senseless upon it, then said to Hunt, "Use him to brush up on your skills, Doctor. They'll be required over the next few days."

Hoarsely, Hunt answered, "I'll need alcohol to clean his wounds and bandages to bind them."

Rigby kicked at the shredded remains of Hankey and Quaint's shirts. "Here are your bandages. You'll not receive anything more. See to it that he attends roll call, else he'll have further penalties to pay."

The SPG unit finished unshackling the prisoners. Rigby gestured for it and Commander Kidd to precede him through the door. At its threshold, he turned back and smiled at them. "Gentlemen, it's been a tremendous pleasure. I look forward to visiting you again. Rest assured, Burton, one way or another, I shall have you and Trounce and Swinburne standing before me. Good morning."

The door closed. The lock clicked. They were alone.

Murchison doubled over and vomited.

Bradlaugh, Ashbee, Murray, and Brabrooke collapsed onto their bunks and buried their faces in their hands. Hunt got to work on Bendyshe.

Monckton Milnes and Burton stood, staring straight ahead, their faces drained, their mouths slack.

"We cannot submit to him," Monckton Milnes finally whispered. "Even if it means death for us all."

"It will," Burton rasped. "He has no boundaries and a heart that pumps only animosity. I was speaking the truth when I called him a homicidal maniac."

The surviving Undesirables spent the remainder of the morning struggling to recover from their ordeal. What rags Hunt didn't require to bind Bendyshe's wounds were used to wipe up the puddles of blood.

When the lunch whistle blew, a guard unlocked their door, and they filed out into the fog and stood in line. Hunt and Brabrooke supported Bendyshe, who could hardly stay upright. As always, their guard stayed with them, that it might overhear any plotting.

The pall had turned a putrid yellow. Anything farther than twelve feet away was made shadowy. An odour like smouldering rubber pervaded the atmosphere, so strong it even covered the stench of the latrines. Everyone was coughing and repeatedly brushing flakes of ash from their faces.

They held out their mess tins and cups, waited for them to be filled, and when they were, returned to hut 0. Burton indicated that Monckton Milnes should sit with him on his bunk.

"I tried to warn you. I sent a message by the Whispering Web. Did you not receive it?"

"I did. I was in the act of gathering the Cannibals that we might all travel up to Fryston Hall together." Monckton Milnes was referring to his country estate in Yorkshire. "Charlie was the first to arrive. He'd not been with me more than ten minutes before the clockwork men showed up. You know the rest. My fault. I should have acted with more haste."

Burton shifted away from him and pulled back the side of the mattress in the space between them.

"Rigby will torture and kill you all to hurt me," he murmured. "I wish I wasn't here, then he'd have no reason to do so."

Using his body to block his movements from Laughing Boy's line of sight, he dipped a finger into his tea and used the liquid to write on the exposed wood of his bunk.

I EFFUGIET.

I shall escape.

He thought it unlikely that the clockwork man's babbage was equipped with a knowledge of Latin.

"But you are here," Monckton Milnes said, "and there's nothing you can do about it."

Following Burton's example, he wrote, *QUOMODO?*

Burton shrugged. How? He didn't know.

He wrote: *VIGILATE ET PARARENT.*

Watch and be ready.

Wiping his palm across the board to smear the tea, he pulled the mattress back into place.

Monckton Milnes rested his elbow on his knee and dropped his forehead into his hand. He closed his eyes. "God in heaven."

They ate without enthusiasm. The afternoon passed with barely any conversation, though Sir Roderick Murchison made frequent complaints, as he had done since his arrival. Bendyshe slowly recovered from his ordeal. As Rigby had ordered, none of his bones had been broken, but his left shoulder was so cruelly bruised that he required his arm to be supported in a sling, and his shins bore abrasions that caused him agony when he tried to walk.

At one point, it occurred to Bradlaugh that he might be able to cause Laughing Boy's babbage to stop working by baffling it with a variation of the famous "Liar's Paradox." He approached the brass figure. "Listen very carefully to the next thing I tell you. It will be true." He paused. "What I just said was a lie. What do you think about that?"

The clockwork man sat motionless and uttered not a word. There was no crunch of confused gears, no wisp of smoke as the synthetic brain overheated, and no sign of a mechanical muddle.

Bradlaugh looked at the others, sighed, strode over to the door, and rattled its handle.

"Step away from the door," Laughing Boy ordered.

The cannibal returned to his bunk, sat, and sighed. "I have a stinking headache."

"So do I," Hunt said.

"And I," Brabrooke put in. "I've had it for days."

Burton rested his elbow on his knee and his chin on his hand.

The black diamonds. Wherever they are, their influence is being felt.

He recalled the newspaper reports he'd seen before his incarceration.

Clairvoyants dying. There's too many of the confounded stones. I have to get out of here; find and destroy the bloody things.

About an hour later—they had great difficulty in judging the passage of time—the hut shook as a familiar aching moan echoed across the city. HMA *Eurypyle* was approaching, its engines making the air pulsate.

"I wonder where it takes the men?" Ashbee mused.

"To the continent, I'll wager," Hunt said. "There to be sold into slavery."

"Do you really think so?" Brabrooke asked.

"Disraeli is getting rid of the middling classes. What better way without committing genocide?"

"By gad! The man will go down in history as one of the foulest fiends ever born."

"The problem with history," Murchison interjected, "is that it clips along at a deucedly fast rate. When I was a nipper, the greater majority worked the land, and the most reliable farm implement one could purchase had four legs, ate hay, and provided manure. But these past few years—merciful heavens!—how we have sculpted nature to our own ends! Would any person of my childhood years have believed the metals of the earth could be fashioned into—" He flung out a hand toward Laughing

Boy, "—into such as *that*? Would any give credence to the idea that a government—a *British* government, I say!—would so divide its people that those who labour can never shake off their yoke, that those who pursue leisure have the means to indulge their every whim, and that those who exist in the strata in-between are eliminated? *Eliminated*, I say! For I feel certain that we are subject to just such a cull. All this, within a single lifetime. History is accelerating, and now I fear it is out of control."

"Bravo!" Bradlaugh mumbled. "He's seen the light."

"It's despicable!" Murchison barked. He stood, stamped to the door, and bellowed, "I demand to be let out of here! I demand an explanation! I know my rights! I am president of the Royal Geographical Society!"

"Here he goes again," Hunt groaned.

"I serve on the Royal Commission for the British Museum!"

"You're director-general of the British Geological Survey," Bendyshe observed.

"I'm director-general of the British Geological Survey!"

"And director of the Royal School of Mines."

"And director of the Royal School of Mines!"

"And of the Museum of Practical Geology."

"And of the Museum of Practical Geology!"

"And you're to be a baronet."

"And I am to be made a baronet!"

"And you're a gigantic pain in the backside."

"And I'm a gigan—How dare you, sir!"

"Sit down, Sir Roderick," Monckton Milnes said. "Matters are sufficiently dire without you ranting about the place."

Murchison levelled a finger at Burton. "I blame you for this. You've always been a troublemaker. Always too outspoken for your own good."

"Richard is as much a victim as the rest of us," Murray objected.

"Pish-tosh!" Murchison spat dismissively. "He's been hoisted with his own petard, and we've been dragged up with him."

"Blown up," Burton murmured.

"What?"

"One is not dragged up by a petard. One is blown up by it. A petard is a small bomb."

"It doesn't bloody well matter what it is!" Murchison yelled.

In a flash of inspiration, Burton suddenly realised that it mattered very much.

Sooner than expected, his chance had come.

Giving every indication that he'd lost his temper, he leaped to his feet and thundered, "I've had just about enough of you, Murchison! You've been a thorn in my side ever since Speke betrayed me."

Murchison looked taken aback. "Speke? What the blazes are you talking about?"

Burton didn't know. Speke had died in Berbera. There had been no betrayal. The man was a fallen colleague, nothing more, nothing less. Why think otherwise?

He had no answer, and this was not the moment to dwell on mistaken memories.

"You know damn well what I mean!" he yelled. "You've blocked me at every opportunity. I found the Nile's source despite you, and you've hated me ever since."

"Good God, man! Have you lost your wits? What the devil are you gibbering about?"

"Ease up, Richard," Monckton Milnes put in, but then saw the explorer wink at him, and added, "Murchison is a snob and an ass, and you'll not change that by shouting at him."

"What did you say?" Murchison practically screamed. "A what? A what, sir?"

"Sit down," Laughing Boy commanded. "Disruption will not be tolerated."

"I've always considered you a blackguard," Monckton Milnes went on. "Not deserving of the positions you hold, that's for certain. Did you bribe your way to the top?"

Murchison's eyes widened. His mouth worked, but only a strangled whine emerged. His face took on a deep-crimson hue.

"Steady on," Ashbee said. "I think this is going a little too far." He, as Monckton Milnes had done, received a wink from Burton, who snarled, "Oh, be quiet, Ashbee. You aren't qualified to comment. You're nothing but a cheap hack."

"To hell with you!" Ashbee roared, jumping to his feet.

"Sit down!" Laughing Boy repeated. The mechanism rose and took two steps forward. "Cease this immediately or guards will be summoned."

"Oh, shove it up your pendulum housing!" Bendyshe shouted.

The clockwork man paced past Burton and Monckton Milnes into the middle of the room.

Brabrooke and Bradlaugh, both catching on, got to their feet and engaged in a mock dispute.

"I'm sick of your fat, bearded face!" Bradlaugh screamed.

"Because it reminds you of your mother!" Brabrooke countered.

Burton crept backward, reached up, and unclipped the oil lamp from its wall bracket. As soon as he drew it down, shadows sprang up on the opposite walls and arced across them. Laughing Boy, reacting to the altered illumination, turned. Without the slightest hesitation, the explorer smashed the lamp against the contraption's head. Oil splashed, splattering through the three facial openings, and ignited.

Burton stumbled away, his left hand and sleeve on fire, and fell onto a bunk, quickly smothering his limb with the blanket.

"Push it into the corner!" he yelled, his voice harsh with pain.

"Emergency!" Laughing Boy wailed. "I am being attacked! Assistance requested!"

Brabrooke, Bradlaugh, and Ashbee hurled themselves across the cabin and barrelled into the machine. Knocked backward, it reeled into the corner, its head aflame.

"Alert! Alert! Assistance requested!"

Though it was verbalising its distress, Burton thought it highly likely that the machine possessed the internal communications he'd seen demonstrated by Grumbles, Sprocket, and the SPG units. Assistance was no doubt already on its way.

"Bunk!" he croaked. "Pin it down. Quick."

Monckton Milnes, instantly understanding what the explorer meant, grabbed Hunt and hauled him over to the bunk opposite Burton. Together they pushed it, were quickly assisted by Brabrooke, and sent it squealing across the floorboards to crash into the brass man, slamming the machine against the wall.

The door opened and a mechanical guard stepped in.

"Stop!" it commanded. "You are ord——"

Murray threw himself down in front of it. The machine tripped over him and clanged face first onto the floor.

With an ear-splitting clap, the booby trap in Laughing Boy's head triggered. The explosion cracked the planks of the timber wall and shattered half of the bunk bed. Fragments of brass, wood, blankets, and straw showered across the room. Hot twisted metal scored a groove across Burton's forehead. Another piece stabbed into Ashbee's thigh.

Burton pushed himself up, careless of the blood streaming down his face, clutched at Monckton Milnes's arm, and shouted into his ear, "Don't follow. You'll be safer here."

"Here? Are you joking?"

"It was only me they wanted to torture. Stay. I'll come for you, I swear it."

With a last look into his friend's eyes, Burton turned, ran at the burning wall, and pitched his full weight shoulder first into it. The planks, blackened, burning, and bulging outward, gave way with a splintering crash. With flames licking at his prison uniform, he plummeted out into the fog, hit the ground, rolled, regained his feet, and ran full pelt up Green Park's slope.

The timing was perfect. The fog was thicker than he'd ever seen it, the guards were preoccupied with the men being herded onto HMA *Eurypyle*, and when he came to the fence, he found himself almost at the exact midpoint between two of the new watchtowers, both of which were completely obscured by the foul cloud. Furthermore, there was a tree less than four feet from the barrier.

He took an instant to slap at his burning clothes—his shirt was a tattered, bloodied, and charred mess—then calculated distances, ran at the tree, jumped, hit it left foot first, and kicked out, launching himself upward and outward toward the lip of the fence. His hands caught it but his body smacked down against the wood with such a bang that he felt certain he'd been heard.

Speed was essential.

Though the breath had been knocked out of him, he heaved himself up and over and fell onto the top of the wall that had originally bordered this part of the park. From there he toppled down onto the pavement of Piccadilly, landing with a painful thump.

What the hell am I doing? This can't be right. Life is not meant to be this way.

"Any bones broken, mate?" came a voice.

Burton looked up and saw a man with a broom standing less than six feet away.

This has happened before. I'm repeating actions over and over.

"No," he said. "But I'm having a very bad time of it."

"Aye, it looks that way. Don't worry about me, fella. I ain't seen nuthink. You'd better scarper, an' good luck to you."

The man stepped into the road and started to sweep the horse manure from it, somehow immune from the danger posed by the steam spheres, velocipedes, and carriages that passed to either side of him.

Burton got to his feet, feeling his bruises and scrapes complaining. He wiped blood from his eyes, suddenly aware that his burned hand was a constant agony, and moved away. As he limped along, he tried to gather his thoughts, to formulate some sort of plan. He had to get to Norwood, but hiring a cab would be next to impossible—he was hardly dressed like a gentleman, and he was penniless, too. Walking through the concealing fog, despite the distance, would probably be easier.

He headed toward Piccadilly Circus, ducking away from other pedestrians, keeping to the shadows, and wishing he possessed some means to summon Monty Penniforth.

Send Pox now, Algy! Send Pox now!

Frequently, he heard the *clump clump clump* of clockwork men. Those he glimpsed stamping through the pall were of the ordinary brass variety but, nevertheless, he avoided them.

There were so many. They were everywhere.

He thought about what Murchison had said.

History is accelerating.

Sirens sounded behind him.

He heard police whistles.

Again and again he tried to steer a course southward but at every turn he saw metal figures. Despite his every intention, he was forced in the opposite direction, dodging down side streets, flitting past Berkeley Square and Grosvenor Square, thinking that maybe he could skirt westward around Hyde Park then down into Chelsea.

Clump clump clump.

Blue-black machines with batons extended to the left of him.

Duck into an alleyway.

Emerge onto Oxford Street.

Risk the traffic to get across.

Yells. Curses. Hissing steam.

A synthetic voice: "Stop that man!"

Portman Square.

Gasping for breath, choking on ash, his hand incandescent with pain, he fell into the patch of greenery at its centre, crawled across grass, scrambled to his feet, and collapsed onto a bench beneath a tree.

The fog billowed around him.

If he could just catch his breath.

If he could just ignore the blistering skin of his hand.

Montagu Place. The mews. Get my rotorchair and fly over the fog to Norwood. Yes. Yes. Yes.

A throbbing paradiddle overhead. He looked up just as a searchlight clicked on, its beam slicing down through the branches of the tree, blinding him.

"Don't move," an amplified voice instructed.

Burton leaped up to run, but his knees gave way. Dark figures moved through the cloud all around him. A clockwork constable marched into sight, truncheon raised. "You are under arrest. Submit immediately."

The explorer had no strength to resist. On his knees, swaying, he looked up at the machine as, without provocation, it swiped its weapon at his head.

Pain.

Failure.

Darkness.

CHAPTER 13

OUT OF THE FRYING PAN
AND INTO THE FIRE

On two occasions I have been asked, "Pray, Mr. Babbage,
if you put into the machine wrong figures, will the right
answers come out?" I am not able rightly to apprehend the
kind of confusion of ideas that could provoke such a question.
—Charles Babbage

Water, thrown over his head, brought Burton back to consciousness. He was hanging, suspended by the wrists, his toes barely touching the ground. The strain on his arms was excruciating.

He opened his eyes and saw the water, stained pink with his blood, trickling down onto the floorboards and splashing around his bare feet.

His boots had been removed. So had the remnants of his shirt.

He looked up.

He was in a shed—not hut 0 but another of identical dimensions, though lacking bunks. To his left, Sir Roderick Murchison, Captain Henry Murray, and Sir Edward Brabrooke were standing in line, all handcuffed. To his right, Thomas Bendyshe, Doctor James Hunt, Richard Monckton Milnes, and Sir Charles Bradlaugh were also shackled.

In front of him, Commander Thaddeus Kidd, backed by four green-painted clockwork men, was holding a pistol to Henry Spencer Ashbee's head.

He said, "Welcome back, Sir Richard," and pulled the trigger.

Blood spattered over Bendyshe and Hunt.

Ashbee flopped to the floor.

The prisoners uttered sobbing cries.

"A consequence," Kidd said, "of your misjudged actions."

He put the gun onto a table and picked up a leather whip.

"Colonel Rigby wants answers, and I can assure you that I am quite as determined as he to get them out of you. No doubt you think that by keeping your lips sealed you are saving the poet and your other fugitive friends. That is a misconception. They will be apprehended sooner or later. It is inevitable. The empire's new security measures will net every traitor, every person complicit in the Chinese menace."

Burton snarled, "There is no Chinese menace, you bloody fool."

The whip snapped out and scored the skin of his stomach. He hissed with the pain of it.

"If you have some notion," Kidd went on, "that your knowledge of their whereabouts makes you indispensable, you are quite wrong. Ultimately, it doesn't matter whether you speak or not. As I say, they will be captured anyway. And as commander of this camp, I have the authority to decide whether it would be more beneficial for the empire to keep you and question you or to dispose of you in a manner that may demonstrate to the other detainees the futility of defiance." He smiled nastily. "The latter course, I believe, holds greater value." Kidd passed the whip to one of the mechanical guards. "His back. Forty lashes."

"No! Wait!" Monckton Milnes shouted.

Kidd took two paces and punched him in the mouth. "Not another word! Not from any of you!"

The brass man walked past Burton and positioned itself behind him.

"Kidd," the explorer whispered. "You're a jumped-up little popinjay, so inflated by the pathetic fraction of power apportioned to you, so eager to emulate Rigby, that you've willingly become blind to the truth. Why don't you open your eyes and—"

With a loud slap, his back erupted with pain. His various wounds—the aching head and arms, the blistered hand, the scrapes and bruises—were utterly subsumed by it. The torment tore through his nerves, saturated his flesh, clawed into his bones. His ability to think, already blunted by the blow to his head, was halted.

For the briefest moment, he sensed that his suffering was fading, but with this revelation came a second slap, and the agony was renewed.

The inexorable punishment continued.

Burton's sense of himself retreated like the sea sucking back over pebbles. For a measureless period, he was far away, gathering, building, intensifying, then he came crashing back to break again—agonisingly—on pitiless reality.

On and on it went, and each time he returned to himself, it was with less force, until the waves of pain had flattened out, and he was incapable of feeling anything more.

He hung, physically and mentally suspended.

Warm blood dribbled down the back of his legs.

He dimly recognised that the world was shifting around him as he was cut down and carried out of the hut.

Again, water splashed over his head.

Somewhere far off, whistles blew and orders were barked.

Grass scraped between his toes.

A voice: "Line up! Line up! Move yourselves! Move! Hurry now! In line!"

Falling.

The ground thumping into his ravaged back.

More water.

He opened his mouth and swallowed some of it.

A figure, bending over him, slapped his face.

"Up with you! Come on, Sir Richard!"

Commander Kidd.

"Wha—?" Burton croaked.

"Pull yourself together, man," Kidd insisted. "The most important moment of your life has come. The *last* moment. Pay attention."

The explorer weakly extended his hands, fumbling for a hold around Kidd's throat. The commander laughed and brushed them aside. He straightened and swung his booted foot into Burton's ribcage.

"Up!"

Rolling onto his front, Burton heaved himself to his elbows and from there to his knees. His skin was slick with blood. He was dizzy and disoriented. His eyes wouldn't focus. He swayed and began to fall.

"Help him," Kidd said.

Metal hands slid under his arms. He was yanked to his feet. His vision adjusted. He saw the camp's prisoners all lined up, rows of them fading into the fog. He saw a scaffold and a noose.

"Let's make a good show of it," Kidd whispered to him.

The commander turned to the assembled detainees and bellowed, "Gentlemen, as you are all aware, the British Empire is faced with dire peril from the Far East. In order to meet this threat, great sacrifices must be made. You men have been selected for a special task. You have all seen HMA *Eurypyle* arriving and departing each day. When your turn comes, you will board that vessel and it will take you to France, and from there you will be transported by rail and steamship to India to aid in the construction of its defences against neighbouring China. Let every man do his duty, that, when the time comes for him to return home, he can do so with his head held high, knowing that he has helped preserve the greatest civilisation to have ever existed." Kidd indulged in a dramatic pause then raised his right hand, index finger pointed at the sky. "But! But! But! Not all are as diligent as you. There are some present here today who scorn the many benefits the empire has brought to our world. They seek to undermine it. They would have you capitulate to Chinese rule."

Incredibly, despite that they'd been detained without warning or charges, half-starved and brutally mistreated, some of the gathered men booed and jeered.

"This man," Kidd declared, lowering his pointing finger so that it was directed at Burton, "is foremost among the traitors. He has defied our prime minister. He has associated with fugitives and quislings. He has fomented dissent. He has attempted to escape from this camp. Today, he will pay the price." He addressed the guards. "Onto the scaffold with him."

Burton was dragged to the wooden structure and hauled up its steps to the platform. Kidd followed, took hold of the noose, and pulled it down over the condemned man's head, tightening it a little around his neck.

He spoke softly into Burton's ear. "Old Dizzy will give me a medal for this. Rigby, on the other hand, will tear me off a strip. He'd much prefer to kill you himself. However, this camp and its inhabitants are my responsibility, and I'll be damned if I allow that lunatic to take all the honours."

Burton wanted to say, "You'll be damned whatever you do," but the words emerged only as a dry rattle.

Kidd stepped to the front of the platform. "Men!" he cried out. "Let it be known that the execution you are here to witness has been authorised by—"

He stopped and looked up.

A large shadow was dropping out of the sky directly overhead.

There came a loud thrumming of engines.

The fog boiled and flattened and fled to the borders of the park.

Prisoners, heedless of discipline, scattered in all directions.

The *Orpheus*, bristling with guns, set down.

Burton's knees were like rubber. They gave beneath him. The noose tightened. He started to choke.

The door in the side of the ship opened, and the ramp slid out and down. A man appeared at the top of it. He raised a rifle and a report echoed.

Commander Kidd took two steps backward then turned to face Burton. He had a sickly smile upon his face. Blood spurted from a hole in his chest. "That—" He paused and winced. "That is not what we arranged."

He fell to his knees and toppled forward, his head hitting the boards with a resounding clunk.

Vaguely, Burton, his face blackening, wondered what the commander's final words referred to.

The man with the rifle ran down the ramp and across the grass toward the scaffold.

Behind him, thick gun barrels, projecting from the sides of the vessel, swung toward their targets. Through narrowing vision, Burton identified the weapons as a variation of the new Gatling guns.

His pulse thundered in his ears. His heart hammered. His mind became increasingly detached. He watched as green guards and SPG units suddenly reacted, pouncing forward to intercept the running man.

The Gatling guns coughed and roared. Metal heads were torn to shreds. Some exploded. Others simply disintegrated into clouds of shrapnel.

Burton blacked out but came to just moments later as the noose was dragged up over his head. He slumped against his rescuer.

"Look sharp," the man said. "We're not out of the woods yet."

"Hallo, Pryce," Burton mouthed soundlessly.

Wordsworth Pryce was Captain Lawless's second officer. He'd been part of the *Orpheus*'s crew during the explorer's African expedition.

"Hellos and how-do-you-dos later," Pryce said. "Are you able to stand unassisted?"

Burton tried.

"I'll take that as a no."

The airman threw aside his rifle, which he couldn't operate one-handed, drew a revolver from a holster on his hip, and wrapped his left arm around the explorer.

An SPG unit met them at the foot of the scaffold's steps. It raised its twin truncheons.

"Halt! Your presence is unauthorised. Your actions are illegal. Surrender to me immediately or you will be forcibly subdued in the name of the King."

"Subdue this!" Pryce barked. He drilled three bullets into its head.

"Unacceptable!" the machine responded. "You are under arrest. You will—kaaaark—fyaaar—"

Its head burst into flames.

Pryce hauled Burton away from it and toward the *Orpheus*.

To the left and right, only a few clockwork men were close enough to pose a threat, and the ship's guns quickly mowed them down.

"Wait!" Burton croaked. "The others. The Cannibals."

"No time," Pryce said, dragging him into the ship.

"Can't—can't leave them."

"We have no choice."

The airman propped Burton against a bulkhead, and turned as Maneesh Krishnamurthy's cousin, Shyamji Bhatti, joined them. "Help me close her up."

The two men slid the hatch shut. When the bolts were locked into place, Pryce turned and shouted through the door to the bridge, "All done, Captain!"

Immediately, Burton felt heavier as the ship shot upward.

"Man the stern gun," Pryce said to Bhatti. "Police vessels will be on us at any moment."

"Aye, sir."

As the young Indian ran to the stairs leading to the lower deck, the second officer gave support to Burton and hurried him toward the lounge.

"Transported to—to India. The Cannibals. Slavery."

"If that happens," Pryce countered, "we'll mount a rescue mission and get them back. First things first."

They arrived at the lounge. Other men—crewmen who, for the most part, Burton knew—came forward and helped to move him to a couch.

"Doctor Quaint isn't with us," Pryce said. "This is McGarrigle, our new medical orderly."

The young man indicated nodded a greeting. "I'll dress your wounds as best I can, but you'll require proper attention later."

Burton was hanging on to consciousness by a thread.

"Quaint—dead," he managed. "Murdered in—in front of me."

Pryce paled.

"Stand aside!" a voice commanded.

The men around the couch stepped back. Burton saw what had been, until now, blocked from his view. It was a massive armchair, and his even more massive brother was occupying it.

"What a bloody shambles," the minister said. "You've managed to stumble from one crisis to another, and you've achieved precisely nothing. Now I'm left with no option but to take a hand in matters. Pathetic, Richard! Pathetic!"

"I had no—"

"Shut up. I don't want to hear anything from you except for the location of Swinburne, Trounce, and Gooch and his people. We must gather them up."

"Norwood," Burton said. "Cemetery. The catacombs."

His brother addressed Pryce. "Tell the captain to shake off whatever pursuit there is before landing the ship in Norwood Cemetery."

Pryce nodded. "We'll head east, outrun them, then circle back to approach Norwood from the south."

"I don't need to know the details. Just get it done. Bhatti, fetch me a bottle of ale. McGarrigle, apply your ointments and bandages. I want this man on his feet. Fill him with morphine and brandy if you have to. The rest of you, go about your business."

Burton felt a drumming vibration beneath him. His stomach turned. The floor slanted.

"Guns," McGarrigle murmured, leaning over his back and examining the terrible welts upon it. "And evasive manoeuvres. Nothing to worry about. The *Orpheus* can outrun even police rotorships."

I'm very familiar with the ship, Doctor Baker. We sailed her to the Nile's headwaters. We landed her beside the vast lake in Central Africa. Poor Speke was right. The Nyanza is the source. I thought Tanganyika, but that lake's waters run westward. Tell me, old fellow: have the swallows all gone? There was one tapping at my window the other day. It's a bad omen.

He yelped.

"Sorry," the medico said. "Your hand is rather badly burnt. I'll make a poultice for it later but, for the moment, it'll be best to let the skin breath. Just a light bandage to protect it."

He got to work smearing a greasy substance onto Burton's back and neck. The patient was made to swallow a glass of dissolved powders, a small bottle of foul-tasting potion, and, to his relief, a very large measure of brandy.

Burton felt his weight continuing to shift disconcertingly as the *Orpheus* banked and veered, and at one point he saw through the nearest porthole a burning vessel plummeting past.

Twenty minutes later, the ship levelled out and flew more steadily, and he divined that it had outrun its pursuers.

Edward sat and drank ale and stared scornfully and wordlessly at his sibling.

Pryce returned to the lounge. "We're clear and out over the Channel. Captain Lawless is going to keep us here until nightfall. We'll fly back in without lights at about three in the morning." He hesitated before adding, "No lights and the prospect of landing in a thick fog. I'll admit I'm a mite nervous."

"Attend to your duties," the minister responded.

A further two hours passed before Burton felt fit for conversation. Having been bandaged, provided with a loose white linen shirt, dark trousers and soft shoes—all from his old quarters in the ship—and supplied with a Havana cigar and another glass of brandy, he was functional, if nothing else.

He sat and contemplated his brother.

The two men were now alone in the lounge.

"Edward, when did you become aware of Disraeli's plans?" he asked. "Obviously, he had some sort of scheme in place even before the *Orpheus* returned from the future. I suspect it started with his and Babbage's meeting in October. Am I correct?"

Edward nodded, his chins wobbling. "Babbage's notion that labourers could be replaced was foolish. The working classes of the empire are far too numerous to supplant, and what would they do with time on their hands? But just as Babbage disdains the common man, so too does Disraeli disdain the far less numerous middle class, whose recent emergence and engagement with politics is, in his view, potentially destabilising."

"Why?"

"Because they will never vote to maintain the *status quo*. Always, they'll demand more. Always, they'll support policies that promise to improve their lot. Thus will economics be thrust forever on the back foot. Babbage's proposal gave the prime minister the solution. Don't replace the lower class; replace the middle. They are much fewer in number, and their function, in terms of employment, can be reduced in description to matters of appraisal, allotment, division, and distribution, all of which can be handled with aplomb by probability calculators. Your account of future history provided the impetus to get the project started, for it revealed to him that such a class of people could weaken the empire to such a degree that its leaders would become utterly impotent."

Burton frowned and winced as the laceration on his forehead gave a pang. "He's aiming at the wrong target."

"Your view of the aristocracy has not been ignored. What perhaps you don't realise is that you brought back with you a solution to the decay you perceive in them; a means to bestow upon them a strength and permanency that will endure beyond even the far off future you visited."

"I did? To what are you referring?"

"To this ship's Mark Three babbage. It has provided an example of how crystalline silicates can be employed in the same manner as the black diamonds. I know we are accumulating the latter at a ridiculously prodigious rate, but they nevertheless remain relatively scarce. This material from the future solves that problem. It is easily manufactured and offers the same capacity to store subtle electromagnetics as the gems."

"I don't understand."

"Disraeli is having the minds of the aristocracy transferred into silicates and the silicates fitted into the babbages of clockwork men."

Burton's jaw dropped. In a flash, he realised that Flywheel had not been Henry Thomas Hope's private secretary at all, but Hope himself.

Grabbing at his brandy glass, he gulped at the liquor. He coughed and squeezed his eyes shut. "Madness!"

"Immortal rulers at the top," his brother intoned, "whose experience and skills can only grow and improve; synthetic intelligences in the middle, requiring no reward and offering nothing but tireless service; and workers at the bottom, whose quality of life will gradually improve as the social and economic structure refines itself."

"You cannot possibly be serious."

"Disraeli is."

"And what does the king think about all this?"

"I rather expect that our formerly blind monarch is delighted with his newfound visual acuity. The mechanical sensory apparatus is, apparently, more acute than natural vision."

Burton was speechless. He made to stand—he felt the need to pace—but his back had tightened, and the movement caused such a stab that he loosed a groan and fell back, the brandy glass falling onto the carpeted floor from suddenly numb fingers.

Edward cast him a look of uncharacteristic sympathy.

"Stay put, Richard. You need to rest. Close your eyes. Forty winks. It'll be a while before we head for Norwood."

Burton nodded wearily. Gazing at his bandaged hand, he asked, "Why did you flee? Where did you go? Why didn't you contact me?"

"The prime minister would have attempted to procure my involvement. I preferred to observe from afar in order to better gauge the merits or otherwise of his scheme. I fled to a secret location, which I've maintained for some years. When one is involved with the underbelly of British politics, as I have been, it is wise to keep a bolthole. From there, I summoned Lawless. He was in high dudgeon after the *Orpheus* was ordered to put on some manner of cheap show for public entertainment, so he and his crew were more than willing to abscond with the vessel and join me."

"You've become a singular and rather frightening man."

There came a pause. The minister's eyes didn't, for even an instant, stray from Burton's.

"Perhaps I have. The same might be said of you. Are you ready to tell me the truth, Richard?"

"Truth?"

"About how your expedition ended. About whatever or whoever you brought back with you, aside from what you've admitted to."

Burton frowned. He didn't understand what his sibling meant, though he felt as if he should.

"You know everything I know."

"And the inconclusive final chapter of your document?"

"Perhaps my descriptions lacked clarity. Events were rapid and confusing."

"Lawless says much the same, and also claims not to have been present when you confronted Spring Heeled Jack."

"He wasn't. He stayed on the ship. Do you want me to rewrite the report?"

"That won't be necessary. Go to sleep."

The couch was sufficiently long that Burton was able to stretch out on it. He did so, lying face down, and quickly eased into a state of suspended consciousness, a daze wherein his eyes remained half open, but his mind ceased to function. He saw Edward take up his two walking sticks and sit with his hands propped on them and his eyes shut as if meditating. He saw a crewman enter and silently clear glasses and ashtrays from the table. Another refilled decanters. A third crossed to the door that led to the passenger cabins and observation deck but found it to be locked. Snapping his fingers irritably, as if kicking himself for forgetting, he retraced his steps and departed.

Bhatti appeared, leaned over the minister, and whispered in his ear. Edward, without opening his eyes, gave an almost imperceptible nod.

Like a drug slowly seeping through his veins, a faint perturbation infiltrated Burton's mind.

Wake up. Think. Observe. What has disturbed you? What is making you uneasy?

He remembered that, when the clothes he was currently wearing had been collected from his old cabin, the crewman had carefully unlocked the door before entering the passenger section and relocked it after exiting.

Why was that part of the ship secured?

The question struggled for his full attention but exhaustion held sway, and sleep overwhelmed him.

He was gently shaken out of it by Bhatti, who murmured, "It's four in the morning. If we've calculated correctly, we're right over the cemetery. Will you come to the bridge?"

The explorer sat up, his stiffened muscles and purpling bruises complaining. He looked at his brother, who hadn't moved and whose eyes remained closed.

Bhatti ushered him out and along the passage that led to the ship's prow. Burton realised the young Indian had slowed his pace to match his own painful shuffle, and a fleeting and totally incongruous memory touched his mind: a doctor, named Greenfall or Gresswell or Grenfell or similar, walking slowly beside him in a garden that overlooked the Mediterranean. The image came then was gone and instantly forgotten.

They entered the bridge. Burton looked up and saw the empty framework that had held the Mark III babbage.

Nathaniel Lawless, turning to greet him, said, "I never thought I'd ever want the confounded thing back again, but that brain, for all its arrogance, would be a blessing right now."

"Why so, Captain?" Burton asked.

"It could land us safely. As it is, we're going to have to do the job ourselves and, as you can see—" He stepped to the curving glass that half-encircled the room. Burton joined him and looked out and down. "—the ground is completely obscured."

It was a moonless night. Lights shone from the *Orpheus*'s hull and illuminated, about a hundred feet below, the top of a flat blanket of fog.

"We'll do it just as we did in Africa," Lawless said. "Our riggers and engineers are dangling at the end of ropes outside the ship. We'll vent gas from the dirigible and sink inch by inch. The rotors will blow the pall out of our path, so the men will see anything that stands in our way and signal up to us so we can make the necessary adjustments. When their feet touch the ground, they'll peg the lines and we'll be safe and sound. Nevertheless, it's a hair-raising prospect. I thought you might like to watch."

Burton raised an eyebrow. "You consider me such a masochist?"

"You collect injuries like one."

"Ha! I can't deny that."

"Shall we proceed?"

"The ship is yours, Captain."

Burton had noticed with considerable puzzlement that since he'd stepped onto the bridge Lawless had subtly but assiduously avoided making eye contact. He wondered why.

The airman turned to his chief engineer, who was standing at the communications console. "Are your men standing by, Mr. Keen?"

"No, sir, they're just hanging about."

"Well, let's not keep them in suspense."

It was an old and not very good joke, established in Africa, and here repeated as if rehearsed. To Burton, it sounded hollow and mirthless.

Something is wrong with all this.

Lawless addressed the helmsman. "Take us down, Mr. Wenham. As slow as you like."

"Right you are, sir. Here we go."

Burton watched through the window as the *Orpheus* started to sink almost imperceptibly toward the cloud. As it drew closer, the vapour became agitated and swirled away, streamers of it curling and raggedly dissipating.

Moving closer to the captain, he whispered, "I understand my brother has been questioning you with regard to the events we experienced in 2202."

Lawless ran his fingernails across his bearded chin. "He asked about your fight with Spring Heeled Jack, and I told him the truth, which is that I didn't witness it. He also asked—again—whether we brought anything or anyone back with us."

"And you said?"

"The additions to the ship's brain. Nothing more."

Burton felt a sense of relief and satisfaction. He briefly gripped Lawless's elbow then stepped back.

After five minutes, Keen, who was holding a speaking tube to his ear, barked, "Stop!"

"You heard the man, Wenham," Lawless snapped.

"Done, sir," the helmsman responded.

"There's a church spire to starboard, sir," Keen said. "We're on the mark but we need to shift thirty feet to port."

"We're in your hands, Mr. Wenham."

"Adjusting position, sir," Wenham responded. "There we are. Venting more gas."

"They can see the ground," Keen reported. "Almost done."

"Count me down," Wenham said.

Keen relayed the request to his engineers and riggers. Moments later, he said, "Eight . . . Seven . . . Six . . . Five . . . Four . . . Three . . . Two . . . One . . . That's it! Boots on the ground. All stop."

"All stop," Wenham confirmed.

"Securing lines," the chief engineer said.

"Stabilising position. Engines idling. Buoyancy—wait a moment—there! That's got it. Position fixed. All right, Captain, we're all set for our new passengers."

Bhatti, who'd observed the operation from the doorway, said, "I'll accompany you to the catacomb, Sir Richard."

Burton offered Lawless a nod of appreciation. The captain returned it, swallowed uneasily, and turned away. The explorer stared at the back of his friend's head for a moment then followed Bhatti off the bridge. In the corridor, Second Officer Pryce was waiting with five crewmen. All were armed with pistols.

"I think it unlikely that we'll be interrupted," he said, "but if we are—" He held up his revolver.

"Understood," Burton muttered.

Pryce and Bhatti attended to the hatch. It slid open and the ramp lowered to the ground.

"No dawdling," Pryce advised.

Bhatti gave him a mock salute and preceded Burton down to the cemetery.

"How are you feeling, Sir Richard?" he asked as they crossed to the church.

"Magnificent," the explorer answered. "Apart from my one perfectly functional hand. Could I persuade you to stamp on it?"

Bhatti smiled. "There will come a time when we look back on these as the good-old bad-old days."

"We can but hope. Is it my imagination or is everyone behaving strangely?"

"Strangely?"

"I feel like you're all playacting."

"We're nervous, that's all. It's no small thing to defy one's own government."

"I suppose."

"I'll wager you're in some degree of shock, too, after what you've endured. It probably makes everything feel a bit odd."

They entered the building and followed the route down to the vaults, through the secret tunnel, and to the adjoining catacomb. It was silent but for a discordant symphony of snoring.

Two of Gooch's engineers were standing sentry duty. They expressed astonishment at Burton's appearance. "We thought you captured or killed."

"The former and close to the latter," Burton responded. "Rouse everyone, would you? It's time you all got out of here."

The sentries gave puzzled frowns but obliged, moving into the side tunnels and banging the metal gates of the bays. "Rise and shine," they called. "Up and dressed! We're on the move!"

People started to emerge into the main vault, doing up their buttons, scraping down their hair, wiping the sleep from their eyes.

William Trounce appeared. He blinked at Burton. "By Jove! Where the devil have you been? Look at the state of you!"

"Hallo, William. Let's get you aboard the *Orpheus*, then I'll explain all."

"The *Orpheus*? Lawless is back?"

"He is."

Slippery Ned Beesley came bouncing into view, screeching, "What ho! What ho! Is that a scarecrow or a Burton? What have you been up to? Were you mangled by a street crab?"

"No, by a Rigby. Why are you still disguised, Algy?"

"Been ploddin' the streets, ain't I, guv'nor!"

"For three weeks?"

"I was trying to find you and the Cannibals, and when it occurred to me that you were probably all in the Green Park camp, I tried to find out what was going on in there."

"Nothing good, I can assure you."

"I suppose that's why the police are keeping ordinary sorts well away from it. My hat! What a mess they've made of you."

"Don't worry, it feels far worse than it looks. Lead everyone outside, will you?"

"Rightio."

"And the equipment?" Gooch asked, approaching. "It's good to see you, Sir Richard."

"You, too. Have your people carry the essentials aboard, but leave what you can. We mustn't tarry."

"I'll see to it."

It took two hours to get everything and everyone aboard—considerably longer than had been intended. During that time, Burton received condensed reports from Swinburne and Trounce.

"I chatted with jolly old Grub," the poet said, "and visited the markets and workhouses, the more disreputable districts and the pubs, and do you know what I learned? That no one gives a damn. The working classes are barely touched by the changes. Disraeli's policies aren't directed at them; the police aren't bothering them any more than usual; the Yellow Menace is gossiped about but generally disbelieved; the sudden flood of clockwork men in the city is of little interest since the jobs now being taken by the mechanisms are not the sort available to laymen; and Green Park is regarded as little more than an inaccessible curiosity." He raised his eyebrows and shook his head. "We saw, in the future, a London that was split into two levels. Those levels already exist in the here and now, and have done so for perhaps fifty years. The only difference is that, in the present, they more or less occupy the same space."

They—with Trounce—were standing to one side of the boarding ramp, watching the last of Gooch's equipment being carried into the ship.

"Dizzy has pitched his campaign with political finesse," Burton commented. "It has exactly hit its mark, leaving all but its target unscathed."

Swinburne clapped his fist into his palm and stamped his foot. "Blast the scoundrel! An uprising, that's what we need, but I fear we'll garner little support for it from the labourers."

Trounce said, "We might not need 'em. We've got the police. My fellows are sick to the back teeth of Young England, and they hate the SPG machines with a passion. I spoke to Honesty and to Slaughter, and they assured me that plenty of men would support an insurrection, if it comes to it. And according to young Spearing, whose father is an army man, there's unrest in the services, too. It won't take much to spark dissent."

Burton nodded. "We need to strike soon, before Young England is further entrenched. But strike how and at what, exactly? Perhaps my brother has some ideas."

They climbed the ramp and entered the ship. Gooch and Lawless greeted them, the latter looking somewhat bemusedly at Swinburne.

"Got any blinkin' pipes what want de-soot-ifyin'?" Slippery Ned asked.

"You look like you'd leave more dirt than you'd remove," Lawless noted.

Swinburne gave a screech of amusement.

"Oh," Lawless said. "It's you."

"We're almost done," Gooch told Burton. "The last of the largest items of equipment is being hauled up through the cargo hatch. Once the doors are closed, we'll be off."

"Where to, Captain?" Burton asked.

"You'll have to ask your brother, Sir Richard. I'm under orders to keep my lips sealed."

So you're keeping my secrets from him and his secrets from me. What on earth are you up to, Lawless?

"Are you, indeed? Intriguing. I suppose he's in the lounge?"

"As always."

Burton, Swinburne, and Trounce took their leave of the airman and engineer and moved along to the centre part of the vessel. There, waiting in his huge armchair, they found Edward, awake and drinking coffee.

"What is that?" he snapped impatiently, indicating Swinburne.

"Slippery Ned Bee—" the poet began, and was instantly cut off.

"Oh. Swinburne. Be quiet. Richard, why aren't we in the air? It's broad daylight. I'm surprised we haven't been blown to smithereens by police ships."

"Norwood is remote enough that any reports of our presence will take time to reach the authorities," Burton said. "Besides which, it's damned early, and we're still surrounded by fog. Anyway, Gooch says we'll be off in a matter of—" He stopped as the engines thrummed, and the floor shifted beneath him. "Ah. There you are."

The minister gave a grunt of satisfaction then raised his voice to address the chamber, which was occupied by a number of Gooch's people and a few crewmen. "Everyone except my brother, Swinburne, and Trounce—out. We require privacy."

People filed from the room. The door closed.

"So," Edward said. "Here we are. Now, perhaps one of you would care to explain what you have achieved aside from being beaten half to death or hiding underground like quivering mice?"

An uncomfortable silence ensued. It was broken by Burton.

"Gooch has been working on a prototype apparatus through which he might be able to locate the source of the instructions that are being issued to the clockwork men. We think it likely that, wherever it is, we'll find Babbage there. We need to decapitate at least three of the police contraptions before we can test the theory."

Edward threw back his head and loosed a roar of laughter. He repeatedly slapped his palms down onto the sides of his chair. Tears rolled down his cheeks. "Oh! Oh! Ha ha ha! For pity's sake! Ha ha! Don't be so bloody ridiculous!" He wiped his mouth with the back of his hand. "For pity's sake, you've already been twice captured by SPG machines. You've seen how they can coordinate their efforts. Go lopping off heads willy-nilly and they'll have you back in Green Park before you can say Jack Robinson. Quite honestly, I can fully comprehend why Disraeli dismissed you, Richard. Since returning from your expedition, you've not been yourself at all. The man I knew as my brother would have thrown himself into the fray. He would have risked all to find answers. You—you're as effective as a mewling kitten."

"Thank you. Have you a better scheme?"

"Of course I have."

His brother dipped his fat fingers into his waistcoat pocket and pulled from it a key. He tossed it to Burton, who caught it and looked perplexed.

Jerking a thumb over his shoulder, Edward said, "That'll open the passenger section. Go through it to the observation deck. There's someone waiting for you. He'll correct your misguided notions."

Burton frowned. "Who?"

He felt as if he should know.

The minister waved him away without a reply.

Clicking his teeth in annoyance, Burton led his companions across the chamber to the door. He unlocked it, left the key in it, and started along the corridor.

"Prince Albert, perhaps?" he muttered.

Trounce shook his head. "He's fled to Germany, by all accounts."

"Then he's not gone far enough," Swinburne opined. "Young England will soon spread across the whole empire."

Burton, yet again stricken by déjà vu and convinced he was overlooking something important, came to the double doors of the observation deck and pushed them open. He and his two companions stepped through.

The *Orpheus* was evidently heading west, for the morning sun, riding low in the sky, was reflecting off the top of the fog and shining directly into the rear of the ship, flooding the chamber with such a glare that they all threw up their arms to shade their eyes.

Squinting, Burton could just make out a silhouetted figure. It was standing by the glass, half-swallowed by the dazzling light, its features indiscernible, its head but a blur in the blaze.

A male voice said, "We should be flying northward, but I couldn't bear to miss the opportunity for a little melodrama." The man spread his arms. "Look at me. The child of a new dawn."

"Very poetic," Trounce observed.

"Not really," Swinburne murmured.

The ship started to turn and the sun slid toward the left. The figure began to solidify as if being born out of fire.

"You appear to have recovered somewhat from your ordeal, Sir Richard. It's astonishing how much of a tonic a little hope can be, don't you think? And is it not remarkable to what a degree that hope is magnified when one is reunited with friends? Am I right in thinking the nipper is Swinburne in disguise?"

"You are," Burton confirmed.

"I am delighted to have brought the three of you together again."

The man stepped forward, and the sunlight slanted across his features.

"But then, did I not say I would?"

It was Colonel Christopher Palmer Rigby.

He was holding Burton's panther-handled cane. He raised it and waved it as if conducting an orchestra. Behind the three men, in the corridor beyond the open double doors, SPG units stepped out of the passenger cabins, turned, and marched into the observation room, encircling it. Simultaneously, they slid their truncheons down from their forearms and clicked them into place.

"Marvellous machines!" Rigby exclaimed. He rested the point of the cane on the floor and folded his gloved hands over its handle. "Very fast. If you try anything untoward, they'll be on you in an instant and will beat you to death."

In an unsteady tone, Burton rasped, "What—what are you doing here, Rigby?"

"Why, capturing dangerous fugitives, of course. The minister doesn't want anarchists running around the empire fomenting rebellion any more than I do. It's most unhealthy. He—oh! Wait! Has it not sunk in? Should I clarify the situation?"

Rigby paced forward and leaned in so that he eyes were just inches from Burton's. His lips pulled back from his teeth in a callous grin.

"You have been betrayed, Burton. Betrayed by your own brother!"

BENEATH THE TOWER OF AUTOMATED ARISTOCRATS

> The police are the public and the public are the police; the
> police being only members of the public who are paid to give
> full-time attention to duties which are incumbent on every
> citizen in the interests of community welfare and existence.
> —Sir Robert Peel, "Peelian Principle 7"

T he clockwork men marched Burton, Swinburne, and Trounce out of
the observation deck, along the passage, and back into the lounge.
Light, a pastel gold, was streaming in through its starboard-side portholes, causing drifting motes to flare around Edward Burton, enveloping
him in a soft aura.

Second Officer Pryce and Shyamji Bhatti were standing to the rear of
the minister, to either side of his chair, just behind the beam of sunlight
that illuminated him; their figures made a shadowy contrast.

Colonel Rigby addressed all three. "Thank you, gentlemen. You have
done the empire a considerable service."

"Duty," the minister responded. He watched through hooded eyes as
the prisoners were positioned in front of him, their wrists gripped tightly
by the SPG units. "Nothing more."

Rigby clicked his heels and gave a slight bow. "A great deal more,
sir. I am disciplined, but not to such an inhuman degree that I cannot
recognise the personal sacrifice you have made."

274

Edward threw him a contemptuous glance. "I can assure you, it has cost me nothing."

"Nevertheless, I will see to it that—"

"You will see to nothing without my say so, Colonel. Need I remind you of my authority?"

Rigby stiffened. "And need I remind you that, nearly four months ago, you abandoned your position?"

"I gave the appearance of doing so, and for good reason." Edward gestured toward the prisoners, his hand cutting into the shaft of light and causing a long shadow to stretch through the air across to the other side of the room. "The result of my manoeuvre stands before you."

"I mean no disrespect," Rigby countered, "but I will not acknowledge you as my superior until I've been ordered to do so by the prime minister. It's not my intention to oppose you, sir, but this is an unusual circumstance. Certainly, you've proven yourself to me in some degree, for when you contacted me and suggested the scheme, I was suspicious that you might be setting a trap for me rather than for these fugitives. Had you not allowed my SPG machines aboard the *Orpheus*, I would have—"

"Yes, yes," Edward snapped. "It isn't important. Let us not lock horns unnecessarily. The prime minister will decide my fate. Lead us to him, sir."

Rigby pressed his thin lips together and gazed fixedly at the minister. He gave an almost imperceptible nod and addressed one of his brass men. "Contact headquarters. Inform them that the mission is completed. Request permission for us to deliver the prisoners."

The mechanical man was silent for a moment then it responded, "Message sent. Reply received. Permission is granted, sir."

"Good. Have the prisoners searched. Empty their pockets. Leave them with nothing."

While the SPG units obeyed this command, Rigby turned to Pryce. "Tell the captain to set the ship down within the walls of the Tower of London."

Pryce's eyes widened. He saluted and made to leave the room. As he crossed through the sunlight and passed close to the prisoners, Burton snarled at him. "Pryce! Did you not hear me? Quaint is dead. Rigby cold-bloodedly tortured and murdered him—your crewmate—and still you stand by the dog?"

His face draining of colour, Pryce stumbled to a halt and muttered, "I—he—he killed him?" He looked at Rigby, who, in a cold tone, said, "The doctor was a necessary sacrifice. His death added veracity to the notion that this ship and its crew had gone rogue." He indicated Burton. "Thus this man's unquestioning faith when it swooped down to rescue him from certain death." Smirking at the explorer, he added, "Which, incidentally, was also a ruse. You weren't really going to be executed. Not yet."

Ignoring him, Burton again addressed Pryce. "Which means you shot Commander Kidd dead just for the effect of it. I would never have thought you so ruthless."

The airman swallowed and took a shuddering breath. "The man who was hanging you? I didn't—I didn't know he was playacting."

Rigby snapped, "But you would have shot him anyway, Mr. Pryce, because I ordered it. Is that not the case?"

"Um. Yes. Yes, sir."

"Keep your attention turned to the big picture, mister. Don't let the unpleasant details confound you. These are difficult times and, as the minister has demonstrated, duty must be done. Yours, at this moment, is to pass my instruction to the captain. Understood?"

Pryce cleared his throat, nodded, gave Burton an uncertain glance, and departed.

Rigby watched the door close after him. "That man did me a favour. Kidd was a conceited and thoroughly disposable buffoon."

Burton regarded his brother. "Did you order Quaint's death, Edward?"

"I did not. The colonel acted of his own accord."

"And despite that you ally yourself with him?"

Implacably, Edward murmured, "My opinion of Colonel Rigby is irrelevant. We both serve the government and, as he just noted, are working on a far larger scale than the personal. You know the prime minister's philosophy, Richard. You know what he intends for the empire. You made the assumption that I disagree with him. I don't. It saddens and frustrates me that you cannot comprehend the advantages of Young

England, and it irritates me immensely that you feel you must actively oppose it."

"I have done nothing to do so."

"I believe I made an observation to that effect not many minutes ago. However, your intention is clear. I cannot allow you to blunder about any longer. One day you might inadvertently do some real damage. And you, Mr. Swinburne, must be silenced. I doubt your little ditties are read by many, but I can't have you provoking the few who might understand them."

"What?" Swinburne screeched. "Ditties? How dare you, you blubberous blasphemer! I'll have you know—"

Rigby swiped Burton's cane across the poet's upper back. "Quiet!"

"Ouch! Ha ha! Thank you! Should I bend over?"

"Shut your mouth, you little deviant."

"Enough, Algy," Burton murmured.

The little man fell silent, though his twitching increased to such a pitch that he appeared almost to be in the grip of a fit and might have fallen but for the SPG unit that held him.

Edward Burton turned his baleful eyes to Trounce. "You, Detective Inspector, are perhaps the worst of all. These two are simply misguided, but you swore an oath. You have an obligation to serve yet you have turned your back on it. You are a traitor to the Crown, sir."

Trounce stared straight ahead, his spine stiff and his face blank.

"*He*, a traitor?" Burton shouted. He struggled but couldn't break free. "Why, you treacherous bastard! Bismillah! I've never felt such shame in all my life. That my own brother could sink to such a depth. What is it, Edward? Do you hope to rid yourself of that bloated hulk of a body and be put inside a machine?"

"Yes," the minister answered. "I do."

Burton recoiled in shock.

"What?"

"I said yes. That is what I shall ask of Disraeli as a reward for your capture."

"You—you—you want—to—"

He felt the deck shift beneath his feet as the *Orpheus* changed course.

Absurdly, the only words he could think to say were, "You'd never taste ale again."

Edward shrugged his massive shoulders. "Nor will I if I die."

"Everyone dies."

"Indeed so, but my natural span is curtailed. I have a tumour. My stomach. It's incurable."

"You—you have—you think to defy nature by—? I'm sorry. I'm sorry that you're ill, but are you so motivated by self-preservation that you'd even plunge a knife into your own brother's back to ensure it?"

"My condition and my intention to circumvent it have no bearing on my actions where you are concerned. Ever have I laboured for the empire, and I intend that my unequivocal service be made permanent, for there is an extraordinary amount of delicate work required that the new order be secured, and there is none more suited to it than I. My loyalty to the prime minister is absolute."

Rigby rapped the cane's point against the floor. "If that statement is intended for my benefit, it is wasted, sir. I shall be influenced by Mr. Disraeli's judgement of you and nothing else. Ah! I believe I feel the ship descending." He turned and addressed two of his SPG machines. "You two, go below and have Gooch and his people made ready for disembarkation. Upon landing, take them straight to the factory. They can be put to good use there, I'm sure. Their equipment can be stored in the vault for the time being."

Burton watched the clockwork men depart.

The room suddenly darkened.

Through a porthole, the explorer saw that the ship had dropped into the fog and guessed that crewmen were once more dangling by ropes to guide it down. Landing in the tower grounds was considerably more perilous than swooping into Green Park.

Edward clicked his fingers at Bhatti. "Assist me."

Curling his lip in scorn, Burton glared at the young Indian. "You make a fine Grumbles, Shyamji."

Bhatti ignored him and took his master by the elbow.

With the aid of his assistant and two walking sticks, the minister rose. "Exit hatch," he said.

Rigby gestured at his machines. They marched Burton, Swinburne, and Trounce to the door, out, and along the corridor. The colonel, minister, and Bhatti followed.

Trounce growled, "This blasted contraption better not let go of me because, I swear to God, if it does, there'll be hell to pay. I'll tear this ship apart with my bare hands."

As they approached the end of the passage, Burton saw that the door to the bridge was open, and bellowed, "Get out here, Lawless! Let me look into the eyes of a bloody turncoat!"

"Throttle him," Rigby said to one of the clockwork men. "Just enough to keep him quiet."

Metal digits dug into Burton's throat, and he reexperienced his near hanging, choking and battling for every breath.

Edward moved to his side and said quietly, "You never did know when to pick a fight. Always rash. Always allowing your emotions to get the better of you. When will you ever learn that there are times when it's advisable to do nothing but watch and bide your time?"

"Judas!" Swinburne hissed.

"I thought you a committed atheist," the minister responded.

"I've converted. I need to believe in hell, so I can picture you burning in it."

They had to wait while the ship eased to the ground, then two of the SPG units opened the hatch to reveal a near-solid wall of yellow fog. Here, beside the river, the fuliginous gloom reeked of rotting fish and—despite Bazalgette's new sewer system—of raw effluence.

"Follow me," Rigby said. "The prime minister currently has his office in the White Tower."

He raised a quizzical eyebrow at Burton. "No more outbursts?"

The explorer managed a slight nod.

"Wise man. Release his neck."

The constriction was removed, and Burton gasped then submitted to a fit of coughing as the foul air filled his lungs.

Rigby grinned.

He led the way down the ramp, and the group, moving slowly to accommodate Edward Burton, trailed after him across the lawn of the innermost ward and to the door of the keep, the great bulk of which was entirely obscured by the pall. Here, human guards recognised the colonel, saluted, and allowed him to usher the party through into the armoury. The ancient chamber, with walls of ragstone and a heavily beamed ceiling, was illuminated by gas lamps and filled not with medieval weapons but with desks and filing cabinets.

Men—mostly of the fleshy variety but many clockwork ones, too—looked up and regarded Rigby's party with curiosity as it crossed the floor, this emotion being suggested in the mechanicals by a slight sideways tilt of the head.

The next chamber, the Tool Room, was also filled with desks. Burton noted that many of the brass men present bore coats of arms upon their breastplates. They also wore leather belts through which swordsticks had been thrust. An eccentric choice of weapon, he ruminated, though one favoured by many aristocrats—and, indeed, by he himself.

And my particular blade is now Rigby's possession.

The colonel guided them to a corner, to the foot of a narrow spiral staircase. In single file, with him leading, the prisoners hemmed in front and back by SPG units, and Edward and Bhatti bringing up the rear, they ascended. Burton could hear his brother, whose mass filled the stairwell from side to side, huffing and puffing, groaning and wheezing, and it gave him a savage pleasure to know his perfidious sibling was so discomforted. The satisfaction was tempered only by the fact that it was also costing him a considerable effort to drag his own battered body from step to step. Every part of him hurt. His back felt tight enough to split, his bruises surely went right through to the bone, and his head was aching abominably.

Reaching a landing, they passed through a door that gave onto a chamber of the same dimensions as the Tool Room below. It had been carpeted and furnished. Hangings decorated the walls. A large wooden screen concealed the far end of it.

Men were sitting at desks, silently engrossed in the reading, writing, and amending of documents, their pens scratching over paper, their brows furrowed with concentration.

A brass figure approached and greeted the new arrivals.

"Colonel Rigby. Success, I see."

"Yes, Mr. Pinion."

"Excellent. The prime minister will receive you at once."

"A moment, if you please."

Rigby stood back and waited while, rising from below, the noise of the minister's exertions drew closer.

"I hope the effort results in apoplexy," Swinburne muttered. "Sorry, Richard."

"Don't be."

Edward survived. He squeezed through the arched doorway and stood panting, his face red and sheeny, his hands trembling on his walking canes.

"Are you all right?" Rigby asked.

The minister brandished one of his sticks. "Proceed, Colonel."

"You three," Rigby said to the prisoners. "This castle is filled with clockwork men and the prime minister's guards. Any attempt to escape will be met with an immediate and lethal response. If that is understood, I'll order my machines to unhand you."

"It's understood," Burton said.

"Pah to you, Rigby," Swinburne muttered. "And pah to you again. But I'll not cause a kerfuffle."

"And you, Mr. Trounce? Will you turn berserker?"

"I'll choose a more opportune moment to wring your neck," Trounce snarled.

"Very wise. I look forward to the attempt. Come with me. Accompany us, Minister."

Edward's eyes flashed. Burton imagined him thinking, *"That was the last damned order I'll ever accept from you, mister!"*

Rigby said, "Mr. Pinion?"

"This way, please."

They traversed, with the machine, the length of the room to the screened off section. Bhatti remained behind and, intent on his own business, exited the chamber by way of a side door. The SPG units also stayed put, motionless, each ready to respond should Burton or his fellows cause trouble.

Leaning his canister-shaped head around the edge of the wooden barrier, Pinion said, "They are here, sir."

Burton heard Disraeli's reply. "Send them through."

Pinion stepped back. Rigby led Burton, Swinburne, Trounce, and the minister around the screen into a space that had been transformed into a plush and well-furnished office. They lined up in front of a large mahogany desk. A very highly polished clockwork man was sitting behind it, the light of three oil lamps scintillating and flashing across its plated surfaces, upon which intricate scrollwork had been etched.

With a quiet whirr, it directed its three vertical facial features at the colonel.

"Well done, Rigby. You have rounded up our miscreants. I presume there's a poet beneath the ragamuffin getup?"

Burton felt his heart hammering. The machine had spoken with Disraeli's voice.

"There is," Rigby confirmed.

Turning its head slightly, the brass man appeared to scrutinise Edward Burton.

"Minister, when I heard you'd contacted the colonel, I had your chair brought here. Please make use of it."

The armchair was to the left of the desk. Edward heaved his tremendous bulk across to it and settled with evident relief. All of a sudden, he ceased to be a breathless mountain of fat and became, instead, a commanding and decisive presence.

"I abandoned you, Prime Minister."

"You did, sir," Disraeli responded. "And it will take much to placate me. While I am convinced there is no waste of time in life like that of making explanations, I find that I require one."

"My explanation stands before you," the minister said, waving a hand toward the prisoners. "The moment you instigated Young England, I knew these fellows would cause trouble. Therefore I withdrew, because I was also certain they'd seek my support. In refusing it, I'd have shown my hand far too early in the game."

"What mischief do they intend?"

"They are backed by William Gladstone and are in the early stages of mounting a rebellion against you."

"Gladstone?" Disraeli said. "By God, that sanctimonious prig has not

282

a single redeeming defect. So you hightailed it to avoid your brother, did you? And now you've laid your cards on the table?"

"I have. By vanishing, I established a position that would later prove advantageous. As it, indeed, has done. My familial loyalty was taken for granted when I reappeared, and, through it, those allies of my brother who remained at liberty were rounded up."

Disraeli was silent for a moment. Then he said, "Allies who, like Sir Richard, are all members of your Ministry of Chronological Affairs. I am bound to suggest that all you have done is perform a much delayed cleansing of your own house."

"The implication being that it is my fault these men have chosen to oppose you?"

"Is it?"

"No. They were out of my sphere of influence for more than a year. In their report of that period, there are obvious omissions. Lawless and his crew, who have demonstrated that they remain loyal to me, were not present during many of the key events and cannot give a full account of what occurred. Of one thing, however, I am convinced—"

The minister levelled a fat forefinger at his sibling.

"That individual is not Sir Richard Francis Burton."

The prime minister's blank face showed nothing but reflected light and, through its topmost opening, tiny spinning gearwheels.

"Then who is he?"

"I believe him to be a *doppelgänger* from a parallel history."

"So he *is* Sir Richard, but not *our* Sir Richard?"

"Precisely."

"On what do you base that supposition?"

"On the fact that, while his objectives are unmistakable, his ability to carry them through is markedly lacking. My real brother would be causing you considerable difficulties by now. This person has merely blundered about and made an irritant of himself. His activities must be curtailed, of course, but more importantly, we must find out why he is here and what has become of our own man."

Disraeli's neck buzzed again as he moved his head to regard the explorer. "Do you care to explain yourself?"

"I am Burton," the other responded. "I am opposed to the foul scheme you call Young England. I believe the many black diamonds that have accrued in this time stream are causing a resonance that has driven you out of your mind and, in consequence—and for the good of the empire—you and your government must now be overthrown. Since you've made that impossible by democratic means, others must be resorted to. It was I who brought the stones here, therefore it falls to me to defeat you. Once I have achieved that, I shall recover the gems from wherever you've secreted them and will see to it that they are destroyed. Were you still human, I would hope that, after their destruction, you'd recover your sanity, see the error of your current policies, and be able to resume your duties and rectify the situation. However, I understand now that it has gone too far. I'm sorry, Mr. Disraeli. Sorry for you, and sorry for what I must do."

The prime minister gave a slight nod. "I see. Sir Richard, let me tell you, what you regard as madness is, in fact, nothing more or less than a necessary and unequivocal response to the information you gathered during your voyage into the future. I have been ever of the opinion that revolutions are not to be evaded. History, at regular intervals, grows stale. Institutions that were once visionary become fossilised. Rather than fuelling progress, they hamper it. Old orders must either be refreshed or be overthrown. For stability's sake, I favour the first of those options, that experience and wisdom not be lost. You, apparently, do not."

Burton's eyes, dark and fierce, took in every visible inch of the prime minister's new body: the gleaming brass, the lines of rivets and engraved decorations, the tiny gears and pistons, the springs and flywheels, the regulators and gyroscope.

He said, "I prefer my country to be run by men than by exaggerated clocks."

"Clocks are more reliable than men," Disraeli countered. "They have the measure of Time. Once Young England is fully established, we will keep the pace of change and evolution steady. No more racing at full pelt into the unknown. No more grappling with the unanticipated penalties of our haste. Power has only one duty, Sir Richard, and that is to secure the social welfare of the people. The doyens of Young England are now best placed to achieve that noble purpose, for we are no longer tainted by selfish motives. We are eternal, and we want for nothing. Whatever you are withholding from us—for you are certainly withholding something—and whatever the reason you have replaced the man we sent forward through history, you must forget it all. It no longer applies. The future you returned from is being rewritten, and the present you now inhabit is not the present you left."

Burton's upper lip curled. "You are dehumanised, sir. How can you claim to know what is best for the people when you are no longer a person? This immortalising of the elite, dismantling of the middle class, and sentencing of the workers to inviolable slavery is utterly loathsome. All that you seek to establish must be erased."

The prime minister flicked the digits of his right hand dismissively. "How much easier it is to be critical than to be correct. Your judgment is too much sentiment and too little sense. In politics nothing is contemptible. Your revolution, had you ever developed the wherewithal to begin it, would have amounted to nothing beyond mindless vandalism. You consider me insane, but *my* revolution will create a better and more stable world."

Before Burton could respond, Swinburne shrieked, "My hat! What risible rubbish! What tedious tripe! What cretinous claptrap!"

"A fine example of your poetry, Mr. Swinburne," the premier said, "which is, as ever, cluttered by alliteration while notably lacking in profundity. I'll have no more of it, if you please. Now, gentlemen, I am very busy and must bid you farewell. I will give you a few days to decide your own fate. If you choose to divulge the secrets you are keeping, the information will be gratefully received, and you will be extradited to the Indian work camps where you will toil for the remainder of your days. If you choose to remain tight-lipped, I must regard you as enemies of the empire, and you will be executed."

Trounce exclaimed, "By thunder! You're the devil himself!"

"Nonsense. Take them down to the cells, Colonel."

"And this man?" Rigby asked with a nod toward the minister.

"He and I have a great deal to discuss. I will inform you of his status when I've decided what it is."

Rigby turned and signalled to the prisoners that they should precede him out of the enclosed area.

With a last withering glare at his brother, Burton led the way back into the main room where he, Trounce, and Swinburne were once again subjected to the unyielding grip of the SPG units. The group retraced its steps down the spiral staircase to the ground floor, crossed the Tool Room and, rather than returning to the armoury, entered the room beneath the chapel.

Rigby escorted them to a shadowy corner and there opened a door, revealing the top of another set of steps.

Oil lamps illuminated their descent, and Burton was surprised to find it a much longer one than he anticipated—the stairs extending far lower than the tower's original cellar, he was sure. He recalled that another Burton had described this place in the account entitled *Expedition to the Mountains of the Moon*, and, when the party came to a metal door, he experienced a powerful familiarity, and knew that beyond the barrier there were secret government chambers.

Rigby produced a key and unlocked the portal. They stepped through into a wide and stark hallway and proceeded along it. A man with a bucket and mop was cleaning the floor, upon which Burton noticed muddy footprints, and others were coming and going, passing in and out of doors to either side. The various portals bore signs: Conference Rooms 1 & 2, Offices A–F, Offices G–L, Administration Rooms, Laboratories 1–5, Medium Rooms 1–4, Vault, Weapon Shop, Monitoring Station, Canteen, and Dormitories.

The ghosts of events he'd never experienced haunted him. The underground complex and its closed off rooms suddenly felt like the depths of his own mind, filled with inaccessible spaces, populated by enigmas and incarcerated agonies.

By God, how many Burtons are there and which of them am I? How many struggles have I endured? How much trauma have I suffered? And now this.

At the end of the passage, Rigby opened a door marked *Security*. With a curt gesture, he had the SPG machines drag Burton, Swinburne, and Trounce through into a rectangular chamber. It contained a great many tall filing cabinets, a desk piled high with documents, and walls punctuated by six sturdy metal doors, each numbered.

A uniformed man, with legs terribly bowed by rickets, looked up from an open drawer and said, "Busy."

"Jolly good!" Swinburne piped up. "We'll be on our way, then. Bye-bye!"

Rigby ignored the poet. "New inmates, Mr. Thresher. A room apiece."

"Drat it! Don't I have work enough? Can you not see all the paperwork? There are hundreds of dratted babbages walking around this castle that could do the work, yet I—just one man—am expected to keep track of all the dratted prisoners." He pointed to the tallest stack of documents on the desk. "That alone is from Green Park. These others come in every dratted morning from the other camps: Manchester, Liverpool, Birmingham, Edin—"

Rigby cut him off. "I'm simply ordering you to open the doors, Thresher. And you'll do so at once and without further complaint. Nothing more is expected of you. A clockwork man will attend them when necessary."

Thresher grunted, pushed the drawer shut, and unclipped a bunch of keys from his belt. "It's still a dratted inconvenience."

Swinburne wriggled in his captor's unyielding metal hands. "Why don't you tell the colonel to bugger off, Mr. Thresher? My companions and I will promise not to bother you again."

The gaoler said, "Cells three, four, and five."

Rigby shrugged. "I don't care which. Just lock 'em up."

"And shove Rigby into number six," Swinburne suggested.

Thresher clicked his tongue despondently. "I'll have to add to the files. More dratted work." He opened each of the cells and one after the other the prisoners were pushed into them; Swinburne into number three, Burton into four, and Trounce into five.

Swinburne called, "Don't turn your back on him, Thresher. He has unnatural tendencies. You'll be—" The door of cell three slammed shut.

Burton was thrust into the next chamber. Rigby stood in its doorway and contemplated his old enemy for a moment. Then he smiled, said, "You're finished," and pushed the door shut. Burton heard the key turn in its lock.

He was alone.

The chamber more resembled a sitting room than a prison. It was carpeted. There were shelves of books, a desk, a bureau, a couch and arm- chairs, ornaments on a mantelpiece, and pictures on the wall. A door to the right opened onto a bedchamber. He could see fresh clothes laid out on the bed.

"A considerable improvement over hut zero," he murmured.

Limping to the wall that separated his cell from Swinburne's, he hammered on it with his fist. It felt solid and thick. There was no way to communicate through it, that much was immediately obvious.

He crossed to an armchair and gingerly sat, his raw back forcing a moan out of him.

An occasional table was positioned beside the seat. On it, there was a box of cigars, a glass, and a decanter of port. When he attempted to pour himself a drink, his hands started to tremble violently, causing the neck of the decanter to rattle against the glass, spilling the liquor.

He gave up and instead braced his forearms on his knees and aban- doned himself to the reaction that now took hold.

His teeth chattered, and his respiration came in sharp gasps.

Darkness pushed in.

"Bismillah!" he whispered, squeezing his eyes shut. That was a mistake. He saw again the blade sliding into Doctor Quaint's brain, the bullet shattering Henry Ashbee's skull, and the swollen flesh of Tom Ben- dyshe's battered countenance.

The barbarity! If Disraeli must resort to animals like Rigby and Kidd to maintain his regime then the empire is sick beyond saving.

With an effort, he hauled his thoughts into order and tried to direct them toward a contemplation of his brother's deceit. Since joining the government, Edward had become a cold, calculating machine, his body regarded as little more than an inconvenience, his existence defined solely by his stratagems and wiles, by his ability to collect, process, and cun- ningly employ information. In many regards, he was already a corpo- real rendition of a babbage probability calculator, so was it particularly surprising that he should now choose to go all the way and abandon his flesh? His body had, after all, failed to emerge undamaged from the devastating beating he'd suffered in Ceylon and was now proving itself deficient once again. Logic dictated that if given the opportunity to survive its demise, he should take it.

Burton put his fingertips to his neck and felt the abrasions upon it. Beaten half to death and almost hanged, and all so he'd have unquestioning faith in his apparent saviour.

"I would have had faith in you anyway, Edward," he whispered. "You're my brother, damn it."

Overcome by an inner pain far worse than that of his sore neck, burned hand, striped back, and bruised ribcage, he attempted to occupy himself with thoughts of escape, but, again, the mental path led only to torment, this time the guilt he felt at abandoning the occupants of hut 0.

I had no choice in the matter. Besides, they were tortured only as a means to force me to speak. Now that I'm gone, they'll be left alone.

He wished he knew what secret Edward thought he was withholding. If he did, he'd gladly divulge it.

Why does he question my identity? Why am I reluctant to tell him how I defeated Spring Heeled Jack? How—how did I liberate myself from the Brunel machine?

There was a gaping hole in his memory.

Pressing his palm against his forehead, frowning, he strained to penetrate the absence. He wondered whether he, too, had been affected by the black diamonds. Up until now, after the crew of the *Orpheus* had been exposed to the gems for so long—taking Saltzmann's Tincture to counteract their deleterious influence—that he'd thought he and they had become virtually immune.

What have I forgotten? If only I could remember. I could tell Edward, be sent to the Indian labour camps, escape from them, lose myself among the natives like I used to do twenty years ago. Go back to the beginning. Disguises. Perfected accents. Accurately mimicked manners. Become someone other than me. Total immersion. Never come back. Never be Burton again. Change into someone utterly different.

He wondered whether he was already somebody utterly different.

Exhausted, he drifted into an uneasy sleep and dreamed of porridge and gritty coffee.

When he awoke, he was in bed, though he'd no memory of leaving the armchair and moving to the bedchamber. His entire body was stiff, and he struggled to sit up, groaning as he did so. He felt as if considerable time had passed. He was ravenously hungry. After splashing water onto his face, he moved back to the main room and found, on the table, a tray holding a teapot, a cup and saucer, a jug of milk, and a bowl of sugar. The tea was cold. He drank it anyway.

He moved about the room, flexing his limbs, working the kinks out of his muscles, looking at the books and pausing when he found a copy of Camoens's *The Lusiads*. Taking it down, he opened it at random and read aloud.

> *"'Ah, strike the notes of woe!' the siren cries;*
> *'A dreary vision swims before my eyes.*
> *To Tagus' shore triumphant as he bends,*
> *Low in the dust the hero's glory ends—'"*

Giving a snort of impatience, he returned the tome to the shelf and selected another, Thackeray's *Vanity Fair*.

He crossed to the chair, sat, and started to read.

Bide my time. Let the wounds heal.

He'd reached chapter four when the door opened and a clockwork man entered. It placed a tray of food on the table.

Burton said, "What time is it? What day?"

The machine didn't answer. It departed, locking the door.

The meal was of roast beef, potatoes, carrots, peas, and Yorkshire pudding. He ate it eagerly—it was his first decent repast in weeks—then smoked a cigar and drank a glass of port.

He read. He slept again.

More food was delivered. He ate.

Hours passed, but he was hardly aware of them.

The relative luxury of his cell was, he vaguely realised, designed to lull him into apathy, to suck the fight out of him. It wouldn't work. He'd rest and recuperate and—

He slept.

Upon finishing *Vanity Fair*, he read *Tom Brown's School Days*, *The Mill on the Floss*, and *Barchester Towers*.

He sensed that days were passing but hardly cared; couldn't access the frustration he'd felt in hut 0. All emotion was held in abeyance.

His welts and bruises faded.

Very rapidly, and without him realising it, the chamber became not a prison cell but a haven. Here, there were no roll calls, no beatings, no SPG units, no lunatic prime ministers, and no treacherous brother.

He enjoyed the peace, solitude, and routine.

Read. Sleep. Eat.

Don't think.

Don't feel.

Don't remember.

There was a mirror affixed to the wall above a basin in the bed-chamber. When he looked into it, he did not perceive the man who looked back, and it didn't matter.

The Woman in White.

A Tale of Two Cities.

The Cloister and the Hearth.

He started to dwell on the structure of the narratives. In a remote region of his mind, it finally occurred to him that his own story was currently suspended.

The walls started to press in.

Claustrophobia squeezed memories out of him. He resisted and clung to the false serenity his cell offered, but his period of grace was fast eroding, and he became increasingly disturbed and agitated. Recollections of his entrapment in a six-armed metal prison haunted him.

How did I escape? How am I now in my own body?

That his brother—that *anyone*—would willingly condemn themselves to such a confinement was inconceivable to him. Immortality, maybe, but also an everlasting torture. Besides—

He held up a hand and flexed his fingers, watching the skin crease and the muscle at the base of his thumb bulge.

One must age. It is a part of living. With the waxing then waning of vitality there comes a developing understanding of what it means to be human. A reassessment of values. A constantly renewing appreciation of the various elements of being. I could not lose such pliancy. Were my body permanent then surely my very essence would become fixed in place, too. These automated aristocrats will calcify. Their appreciation of life will dwindle and so will whatever little measure of decency and morals they possess. Inevitably, any ability to empathise will be lost. That will make them dangerous. Very dangerous indeed.

His thoughts returned again and again to the process of ageing and somehow became entwined with the structures and themes of the novels. Individuals, he realised, were defined by the stories they created about themselves, and those stories adhered closely to common motifs. His own, though, did not. It was all askew and had been from the very start. His childhood, those transient years spent being dragged by his restless parents from town to town, city to city, country to country—Tours, Richmond, Blois, Sienna, Perugia, Florence, Rome, Pisa, Naples, Pau, Lucca—had not allowed for any thematic development. Only wanderlust had been imprinted upon him, so that, in his adulthood, he'd jumped from one situation to another without any feeling of continuity. It wasn't until he'd become too physically frail to continue his compulsive travelling that he'd formed anything resembling a sense of established identity. Age had calmed him. Age had given him a story. Age had—

"Age?" he asked the room. "Age? What am I thinking? I'm forty. Why the hell do I keep imagining myself older?"

He paced up and down, his hands to his face.

His wounds were mostly healed, but his mind was feeling increasingly damaged. He didn't want to think, didn't want to confront the incongruity that lay at the heart of him.

He tried to distract himself with exercise: press-ups and jumps, lifting furniture and stretching techniques he'd learned as a youth in India, a discipline known as *hathavidya.*

Just once, he attempted to meditate, but it gave rise to such odd memories that he stopped and didn't try again.

This isolation is driving me mad. God! What of Swinburne and Trounce? How are they faring?

He raised his face and yelled, "Algy! William! Can you hear me? Are you there?"

No response.

No one but the clockwork man visited.

One day—or it may have been a night, he had no way of telling—he was lying fully clothed on the bed trying to overcome persistent insomnia when, for no apparent reason, he suddenly thought of his friend Doctor John Steinhaueser.

"Poor old Styggins!" he muttered, employing Steinhaueser's nickname.

He recalled a dream he'd had in 1860, shortly after returning from a tour of America. In it, his right canine had dropped out to fall at his feet in a splash of blood. Later, he'd learned that on the same night, Steinhaueser, who was travelling through Switzerland at the time, had suffered an embolism and died.

Wait. How could that have happened? It is 1861. I spent all of last year in the future. I never went to America.

And Steinhaueser hadn't died that way; he'd been murdered by a vampiric creature from a parallel history, the same that had killed Isabel.

Bismillah!

Burton sat up and swung his feet to the floor.

"Vampire? Styggins dead? Who was it then, at home with me in Trieste? Who at my side when we rescued a bird from—"

He stopped.

Trieste? That hadn't been Steinhaueser. It was—it was—

Trieste?

When had he ever lived in Trieste?

He jumped up and looked around the bedchamber, his eyes flicking from left to right.

Trapped! Trapped beneath the tower! Trapped in a machine! Trapped in an old decaying body! Trapped with nothing but pain!

Nothing made any sense.

He stumbled across to the water basin in the corner, gazed into the mirror on the wall above it, and saw a face that was far too young in appearance.

"By God," he croaked. "I'm not me. I'm not me."

Behind him, a voice said, "So the minister was correct. Who, then, are you? Which Burton—and from where and when?"

Whirling, he swayed back against the basin, his eyes wide, his mouth working silently.

Burton. I am Burton.

Colonel Rigby was standing in the doorway with a clockwork man at his shoulder—whether the one that brought the food, or another, it was impossible to tell.

"Who?" Rigby repeated. "Why are you here? Where is the man you've replaced?"

"I—I haven't—I don't know."

"Come, come. Enough of your evasiveness. You've had plenty of time to think matters through. You surely must have realised by now that reticence will get you nowhere. Let's have it all out in the open, shall we?"

He made a gesture. His mechanical companion responded to it by striding forward, reaching out, digging his fingers into the front of Burton's shirt, and dragging him out of the bedroom and into the main chamber, thrusting him forward into its middle.

Staggering, Burton bumped into the table and almost fell.

Rigby said, "Introduce yourself. Explain it all."

"You know who I am, damn you!"

"Perhaps I do. Perhaps I know you better than you know yourself, hey? Certainly, I know that you're less than half the man I thought you. By God! Look at you. What a wretch. What a ruin. What a pale shadow of the person who was once the king's agent." The colonel slowly paced around his prisoner, gazing at him with disdain. "There's no life left in your eyes. Have you really broken so easily?"

Burton ground his teeth. "I'm perfectly fine."

"You are? Have you recovered from your injuries?"

The explorer cleared his throat and gave a hesitant nod. "Sufficiently."

"And you still have spirit?"

Burton stared at the other man but made no reply.

Rigby removed his jacket, threw it onto a chair, and rolled up his shirtsleeves.

"Good. Then prove to me you're the man of old. The Burton I knew in India."

"What?"

"Let's be at it. Hand to hand. Fair and square. A final reckoning. If you beat me—" He turned and addressed the clockwork man. "If I'm defeated, either because I'm unconscious or because I've said the word *submit*, you will escort Sir Richard from this cell, you'll release Swinburne and Trounce, and you'll escort the three of them out of the tower and to their liberty. Is that understood?"

The brass figure nodded.

Rigby said to Burton, "But if you prove no match for me, I'll wash my hands of you and give you over to clockwork men for torture. They'll go about their business with precision and neither qualm nor conscience. Unpleasant, to say the least. So decide. Speak or fight, which will it be?"

"There is no truth to tell, Rigby. I have nothing to say."

The colonel sighed. "Retribution it is, then."

Burton opened his arms, palms up. "Retribution? For what?"

Rigby adopted a boxing posture. "For everything you denied me. Raise your fists. Defend yourself."

"I've denied you nothing. Surely you don't still hold a grudge because I performed better than you in a few language exams twenty-odd years ago?"

Rigby snapped his teeth together. "That was just the start of it. I'm the king's agent. I have access to all the records. I've read your reports. Or your counterpart's—whoever wrote the confounded things. I know what you did to me in Africa."

"The *Mountains of the Moon* business? The Burton of that account was another man. As was the Rigby."

"As much as I suspect you of being other than you claim, it makes little difference in the wider scheme of things. Perhaps we are who we are, no matter how many histories we straddle. I know what the other version of Swinburne became, and I know that I could have been the same were it not for you."

Burton blinked. He lowered his hands and laughed. "Are you in earnest? You hate me because an alternate version of me burned an alternate version of you before he could transform into a sentient jungle? Do you realise how utterly preposterous that is?"

"Raise your damned fists, man."

"To fight over such an absurdity?"

"You witnessed yourself how the jungle plays a key role in human evolution."

"And you would have such a power? Ha! What a bloody disaster that would be for the human race."

Rigby made a sound of impatience. "Stop. Here, take this."

Stepping forward, he smacked the bunched knuckles of his right hand into Burton's mouth.

Rocking back, the explorer bared his teeth. "You blackguard! I'll be damned if I'll be your punch bag."

Rigby started to circle, his eyes predatory, his expression one of utmost cruelty. He stepped in and launched a right hook, but Burton jerked out of the way and countered it with a left jab. He missed his target, feinted to the left, and got a punch home, his fist thudding into Rigby's ribs. Retaliation came at lightning speed: one, two, to his chin and left cheek. The explorer's head snapped to the side, and he rocked on his heels, his vision dimming.

Rigby was a powerful man.

A third blow brushed Burton's ear as he instinctively twisted and ducked beneath it. Heaving up from the hip, his answering punch caught the colonel again in the ribs—the same spot—causing the man to double over and step back, winded.

Burton lunged forward, aiming for a Thuggee wrestling hold, but as his arms encircled Rigby, his own momentum was used against him, and the room suddenly whirled as he was levered up and over to be sent crashing down onto the table, which broke and collapsed beneath him.

He lay stunned amid the splinters.

The clockwork man suddenly sprang forward, bent over him, and pulled at his clothing. "Get up!" it commanded. "Good Lord! Is this version of you incapable even of putting up a decent fight? Consider what that other Burton achieved. When all was lost, he still summoned resources enough to invade this base and rob its vault. Its *vault*! And you can't even give a good account of yourself when it comes to basic fisticuffs. I'm thoroughly *alarmed* to witness such weakness. It's not at all what I'd expect from my own brother."

The voice was Edward's.

Burton stared in horror up at the near-featureless head. "Oh God, no!" he rasped. "You've actually done it."

"My service to the empire will endure."

"No!" Burton yelled. "You idiot! You stupid bloody idiot!"

He pushed the metal arms away and rolled onto his hands and knees, but before he could rise, brass digits clamped around his neck and held him down. Distractedly, Burton noticed that his brother's mechanical feet were caked with a blueish mud.

"Colonel Rigby has overstepped the mark," the minister said. "He had no right to offer you your freedom. However, what's done is done, so I suggest you find the wherewithal to put up a decent fight, Richard. You're going to have to dig deep. The other Burton did so. Follow his example."

"I'll not have your advice, you double-crossing bastard," Burton growled.

Rigby barked, "Let him up! Let's get this over with."

The clockwork man loosed its grip and stepped back.

Burton pushed himself up, turning to face Rigby just as the other came at him like a charging bull. Sheer luck allowed the explorer to get in the first punch, a ferocious left hook square to the chin, snapping Rigby's head back, but momentum carried the other man forward, and a moment later they went at it, practically toe to toe, swinging wildly.

Knuckles impacted against Burton again and again. His head was singing, and he was half-blinded by his own blood, the half-healed laceration in his forehead having reopened. Rigby fared no better. His right eye was closing and red gore poured from his mashed lips. However, though they may have been evenly matched in size and power, Burton's strength was quickly sapped by his existing injuries, and he started to flounder beneath his opponent's crashing attacks. He weaved and ducked as best he could but was caught over and over, wilting under the onslaught of rapid-fire short hooks and uppercuts until he fell into a clinch, holding and panting for air, desperately hoping his head would clear.

Rigby was not even remotely a gentleman. His knee came up into Burton's groin and as his opponent sagged, he gripped him by the hair, yanked his head back, and delivered a crunching headbutt to his face.

Again, Burton hit the floor. A booted foot ploughed into his side. A red mist clouded his vision. Rigby dropped on top of him, pinning his arms with his knees, and set about him, battering what resistance remained out of him, driving the explorer to the periphery of unconsciousness but holding back just enough that its promised relief was deferred.

How long the brutal punishment lasted Burton would never know. He was aware only of pain and humiliation until it finally occurred to him that the beating had stopped, and with pinprick vision, he saw that Edward was pulling Rigby back.

"That's quite sufficient, I think, Colonel," the minister said.

"Not until I've crippled him," Rigby protested.

"No. Leave something for our mechanical interrogators. We'll see how many sessions with them he can endure before he finally tells us what we need to know."

"I want him ruined."

"He will be. Come. Let's have someone tend to your bruises."

Rigby looked down at Burton and spat on him. "I expected more. I'm disappointed. You are nothing. You're pathetic. I wash my hands of you."

He and Edward departed.

Burton lay still and bled onto the carpet.

Through puffed and slitted lids, he stared at the ceiling.

Hours passed.

He didn't move.

A NEW FUTURE

Nothing that is morally wrong can be politically right.
—William E. Gladstone

CHAPTER 15

AN UNEXPECTED ALLY EMERGES

The artist must create a spark before he can make a fire and before art is born, the artist must be ready to be consumed by the fire of his own creation.
—Auguste Rodin

To possess an identity, a person requires a past and a present. The prisoner had too many of both. His memories conflicted with one another. He was in different places and in different circumstances at precisely the same moment, and the moment itself was uncertain.

He remembered fighting both a man from the future and the cabal of scientists who'd sought to capture that individual, intent on experimenting with multiplying histories.

He remembered discovering the presence of the black diamonds in the world and becoming aware of their pernicious influence.

He remembered that the collective consciousness of a prehuman race was contained within the gemstones but wondered whether they were real at all or, perhaps, rather a symbolic expression of a primitive and buried aspect of human sentience.

He remembered that he'd created the history he now inhabited.

He remembered that every bizarre event had culminated in him becoming something that transcended what was currently considered human; that it had called itself the Beetle; and that its presence was so paradoxical it must consume itself like the worm Ouroboros.

He remembered living into his old age, dying, and at that instant being transported into the past.

My existence is impossible.

Occasionally, he reached up with both hands to check his head, convinced it should feel somehow multiplied.

Many heads in the same space.

One. Three. Five. One.

Plainly, he was losing his mind.

If time was passing at all, the clockwork servant that delivered the meals—he could now see that it was not the same machine as his brother—provided the only measure, but he knew that it purposely appeared at irregular intervals to keep him disorientated. Sometimes it felt like he'd only just eaten when the next plate arrived. Occasionally, he was tormented by hunger between one repast and the next.

The mental confusion even crept into the material world when, while he was attempting to sleep, he turned and was stabbed in the flank by a sharp object in his pocket. Puzzled that anything should be there—he'd been searched and divested of his every possession on the *Orpheus*—he retrieved the item, sat up, and gazed at it uncomprehendingly.

He strained to understand. He ate two meals, bathed, smoked a cigar, and spent hours contemplating his find.

Finally, he dared to give it a name.

A set of lockpicks.

He laughed. Reality was such a jumble that now his imagination was manifesting objects that could not possibly be there.

He concealed the picks beneath his mattress and forgot about them.

Perhaps more time passed.

The door clicked.

Rigby?

No, the servant.

Food.

Eat.

Sit.

Sleep.

Nothing.

Except—

Amid the cacophonous impressions and tattered memories, he began to sense a presence that was not a variation of his own. There was something *else* out there. He felt mental fingers groping for him. They brushed the peripheries of his mind. Cold. Calculating. Inhuman.

He flinched away from them.

Illusion, like the lockpicks.

He was on the bed and, turning onto his side, slid his hand under the mattress to reassure himself that the picks weren't there.

But they were.

He pulled them out, laid back, and held them over his face, turning the slim tools this way and that, examining every part of them.

If these are real, then—

He didn't want to continue that line of thought, didn't want to consider the possibility that what he vaguely perceived might also be real. A powerful intellect. An *other*. Watching. Waiting. Planning.

How could lockpicks have found their way into my pocket?

Unless someone put them there.

Edward.

He sat up and looked around, frowned, and ran his fingers over his stubbled jawline.

Edward. He fumbled at my clothing during my fight with Rigby. Why such clumsiness from a machine? It must have been purposeful. The picks are real. He slipped them to me.

With a small cry of astonishment, he threw himself off the bed and moved into the main room.

Come on. Come on. Think.

What was it his brother had said?

"Is this version of you incapable even of putting up a decent fight? Consider what that other achieved. When all was lost, he still summoned resources enough to invade this base and rob its vault. Its vault!"

The slight but definite emphasis on a single word.

Vault.

"And you can't even give a good account of yourself when it comes to basic fisticuffs. I'm thoroughly alarmed *to witness such weakness."*

Again, the accent had been subtly placed. Not so forcibly that Rigby would notice it but, in retrospect, unmistakable.

"You're going to have to dig deep. The other Burton did so. Follow his example."

He slipped the picks into his pocket, crossed to the table, and poured a glass of brandy, which he knocked back in a single swig. He thought of the mud he'd noticed on his brother's mechanical feet and on the floor in the hallway.

"Burton," he said, "has seen mud with that distinctive hue before. Where?"

The Thames at low tide.

Dig deep.

It came to him. Yes. The Beetle had—or was going to, in a different history—manipulate events to ensure that Algernon Swinburne would be captured. Burton was going to use his dog, Fidget, to follow the poet's scent. It would lead to the Thames and to a tunnel running beneath it, under London Bridge.

The bridge was right next to the Tower of London.

Did Edward want him to retrace that route? Why? And even were he to use the picks to crack the lock of his cell, how was he supposed to escape the tower, which was occupied by so many clockwork and governmental men?

He paced and fretted.

Use the picks. Overpower that Thresher fellow. Release Algy and William. Then what? The vault?

He vaguely recalled a chamber he'd never seen, one filled with bizarre objects retrieved from alternate histories. The room he envisioned belonged in a different version of the tower. What he'd find in this one might not match the memory. Nevertheless, his brother appeared to think it held something of significance.

What was Edward up to?

Crossing to the metal door, he crouched and examined the keyhole. The lock would present a challenge but not an insurmountable one.

When to risk it?

He felt indecisive, as if Rigby had knocked a vital part out of him, and experienced such a dreadful sense of shame that he stumbled back, uttered an inarticulate cry, and fell to his knees.

He drew back his arm, poised to smash his fist into the floor, filled with frustration, but before he could follow the impulse a siren started to wail, its urgent keening—*Ullah! Ullah!*—driving all the emotion out of him.

Suddenly, he was calm and his head was clear.

He whispered, "The Slug and Lettuce. A second chance at life," and he knew, without any doubt, that this was the moment to act.

Thoroughly alarmed.

Twisting, he scrambled back to the door, knelt before it, and applied the tools to the keyhole. He'd never used lockpicks before but another iteration of him had, and that skill was now his. Faint clicks. Resistance against his fingertips. Manipulation. The slightest of forces exerted.

Clunk.

He didn't think to arm himself with anything—not the decanter upturned and held by its neck, not a snapped off table leg—but simply yanked open the door and hurtled through into the room beyond it.

Thresher was standing by a filing cabinet. He gaped at Burton and said, "Drat it! What do you think you're—"

The explorer dived forward and, as the other fumbled for the pistol at his hip, grabbed the gaoler's wrist and delivered a slap of such force to the side of his face that Thresher immediately slumped. The gun was plucked from its holster and its barrel applied to the man's forehead.

"Tell me what's happening."

Dazedly, Thresher mumbled, "Alarm. Don't know why. Get back in your cell."

"I don't think so."

"Drat you!"

Burton forced him across the room to the door of cell one. "Either open it or have me break your neck and do it myself."

Thresher complied. As the portal swung open, Burton looked into a cell identical to his own and saw Algernon Swinburne.

"What ho!" the poet cried out. "About bloomin' time! Where the devil have you been? Do you realise how long I've been shut away in here?

My hat! You look like a ghost! Are you all right? What's happening? Why the noise? Are we escaping?"

"If we can," Burton confirmed.

The little poet leaped out of the cell and swiped a fist at an imaginary foe. "Lead on! Charge! I'm eager to flatten the minister's crooked nose."

"He no longer has one."

"What? What? What?"

"Later."

Trounce was next to be released. He was bearded and his hair unkempt, his blue eyes filled with the remoteness that comes with prolonged isolation. Looking uncertainly from Burton to Swinburne, he licked his lips and mumbled, "By Jove! Is this happening?"

"It is," Burton confirmed. "Are you fit for battle?"

"By thunder, I'm ready to take on the whole bloody government single-handed, metal men and all."

"We may have an even bigger enemy."

"Eh? Who?"

"Or perhaps *what*. I don't know, William. I sense something. A presence of some sort."

"Sense?"

"Perhaps clairvoyantly. The black diamonds."

"Humph! More of that nonsense, hey? Well, so long as there's a neck I can wring."

Burton made Thresher unlock the other cells but found all of them unoccupied.

"Your records," he said. "I want to know where two of your prisoners have gone."

The gaoler's eyes widened then crossed as they focused on the gun barrel that was still pressed against his forehead. "Needles in a dratted haystack! There are thousands of prisoners. You're demanding the impossible."

"I don't think so. They were among the very first taken—captured on the twentieth of March. Their names are Sadhvi Raghavendra and Maneesh Krishnamurthy."

"Oh. That makes it easier, I suppose. This way."

Keeping his pistol levelled, Burton followed Thresher to a filing cabinet and watched as he slid open a draw, rummaged through binders, and extracted two sheets of paper.

"Yes. Here we are. They are both serving at Sir Charles Napier B."

"What is that?"

"A labour camp. It's located on the outskirts of Karachi in India."

Trounce said, "Labour? What manner of labour?"

"They're building a clockwork-man factory, I believe. There's a big demand for the mechanisms. The British East India Company has a lot of jobs they can undertake. Saves costs."

"Yes," Swinburne said. "I recall that you suggested your own job could be done by them. Are you looking forward to your unemployment?"

"Pardon? I—" Thresher looked momentarily confused. He muttered, "Oh, drat it!" then tipped his head back and yelled, "Help! Help! The prisoners are esc—"

Burton's fist connected with the upturned chin, and Thresher hit the floor.

Crossing to the room's entrance, the explorer opened the portal an inch. The noise of the alarm increased. He peeked out at the hallway. Doors were standing ajar, and he saw two men hurrying along to the stairs leading up to the tower. Once they'd gone, the wide passage was empty.

"We might be in luck," he murmured. "It looks like the alarm has sent them all scurrying upstairs."

"Rather a providential diversion," Trounce observed.

"I'm inclined to think it's by design." Burton raised the revolver. "Let's move. Quietly does it."

They crept out of the security section, advanced past the dormitories and canteen, and, next to the Monitoring Station, found the Weapon Shop.

Burton was about to speak when, a little farther along the hall, five men raced out from the doors marked *Offices G–L*. Without noticing the escapees, they pelted toward the far end of the passage and vanished up the stairs.

"I wonder what's causing the hoo-ha?" Swinburne whispered.

Trounce flexed his fingers. "Whatever, let's hope it continues. I need to bang my knuckles against something solid. Everything feels like a dream after being cooped up for so long."

Burton pushed open the door of the Weapon Shop. There were two men inside, one long-bearded, the other white-haired. They were standing beside a bench and bolting a small cannon onto a tripod. Both looked up as he stepped in. Long Beard said, "Good! Help us get this up top, would you?"

"What's it for? Why the alarm?"

"Someone stole the *Orpheus*. The ship is shooting at the keep and into the grounds. This is the only weapon we have that's sure to bring it down."

White Hair exclaimed, "Hold on a minute! Who are you?"

"The enemy." Burton brandished his pistol. "Hands in the air, please, gentlemen."

"Oh, botheration!" Long Beard said. He grabbed a pistol from the bench and swung it toward the intruders.

Burton shot him through the shoulder.

"Christ! Ouch! Bloody hell! That hurts. I surrender."

"Don't kill me," his colleague cried out, throwing up his arms. "I'm a lepidopterist."

Swinburne laughed. "A butterfly collector? What has that to do with it?"

"I—I couldn't think of anything else to say."

"It'll suffice," Burton said, "providing you lie face down with your limbs spread out."

"Like one of your pinned specimens," the poet added.

"I'll do it. I'll do it."

He did it.

"I can't," Long Beard wailed. "My shoulder. Bad."

"So sit beside him and shut up."

The chamber was large and lined with armaments. Burton, Swinburne, and Trounce each slung a rifle over their shoulders, took two revolvers, and filled their pockets with ammunition.

"We'll be just outside," Burton told Long Beard. "If either of you leaves this room, we'll start shooting."

"I don't want to move. I'm bleeding. I feel horrid."

"And I'm quite comfortable here," White Hair added. "It's the first proper rest I've had for a few days."

Swinburne gave a snort of amusement.

The group moved back into the hallway and crossed to the door marked *Vault*. It was a very solid metal affair with a complex lock that would have defeated Burton's picks had he required them. He didn't. It was standing slightly open. The explorer noticed mud at its threshold. Again, foreign memories brushed the edges of his awareness. He led them through into a long, fairly narrow room dimly lit by four oil lamps. It had an arched ceiling, and its walls were lined with shelves. There was equipment taken from the Norwood catacomb and a number of small machines he recognised from Battersea Power Station, including some he knew to be prototype Babbage creations. The hulking form of the late Isambard Kingdom Brunel was standing in one corner, utterly lifeless. The sight of it sent a shiver down Burton's spine.

That thing was once me.

He bit his lip nervously and moved on.

At the other end of the chamber, the wall had been cut through—fairly recently by the looks of it—and was now the mouth of a downward-sloping tunnel. Muddy footprints led to and from it. Burton headed toward the opening but paused when he came abreast a workbench upon which two long, flat, clothbound packages had been placed. Uttering an exclamation, he lifted one, unwrapped it, and pulled an oddly curved blade from its scabbard. "My *khopesh*! This might come in handy. Algy, take the other."

Looping the belts attached to the scabbards around their shoulders, the two men positioned the blades on their backs with the hilts projecting upward. They needed only to reach up and behind to draw the weapons.

Long steps had been cut into the tunnel floor with planks laid down for better footing. Niches, dug into the walls, contained oil lamps, but these were far apart, and their light was spread thin.

Treading carefully, the party silently descended, reaching a level part of the tunnel that, ahead of them, curved to the left. After a little over a hundred yards, it dipped abruptly, and its floor disappeared into knee-deep water, which was painfully cold and smelled of purifying fish. They waded into it.

They traversed a short distance then encountered a junction, the passage joining another, this one carved out of rock. To the left, the new tunnel, which had three thick pipes running along the opposite wall, ended at the base of stone steps. To the right, it extended southward and plunged into shadow.

Before they were able to advance any farther, voices reached them from the steps. Drawing back, they listened.

"—so soon after the process that we have to turn around and go right back again."

"I know! I'm not even accustomed to my new limbs yet. I feel I'm walking a little awkwardly. I don't look clumsy, do I?"

"Not at all. Not at all."

"Will you turn my key? I fear my spring might be slackening."

"It's not. Don't be concerned. We shall keep each other fully wound. How did you find the conversion process? I thought it might be painful but didn't feel a thing."

"Nor I. Very clever, these scientist chappies. I must confess, though, that I was glad to be out of the place. I wish we didn't have to go back."

"I share your reluctance, old fellow. I don't know about you but all the time I was there I felt my mind was somehow not my own."

"Yes, exactly my experience."

"Perhaps we should loiter down here until whatever is happening blows over."

"A fine idea, yet I feel somewhat compelled to follow orders."

"Me, too, but I'm a mite nervous, dear boy. I don't mean to sound like a coward but if matters are coming to a head and the situation is getting dangerous, I'd rather stay out of the way."

Two figures came abreast of the junction—clockwork men—both with walking canes and wearing top hats, one with a bow tie knotted around its thin neck.

Burton and his companions let them pass, then the explorer stepped out behind them.

"Good morning, gentlemen. Or afternoon. Or evening. I've lost track. Which is it?"

The mechanisms jerked to a halt and spun to face him. After a slight pause, one of them reached up, gripped the brim of its top hat, and raised it.

"Hallo there! It's afternoon. Are you on your way for conversion? Don't worry, it's an absolute doddle. Have we met? I'm Lord Chumleigh of the Dorchester Chumleighs, and this is the Right Honourable Percival Braithwaite, the son of—"

"Great heavens!" Braithwaite interrupted as Burton's two companions emerged from the darkness with their weapons levelled. "Look at the little flame-haired cove! Isn't he the chap we bumped into a few months back, the one who stained the seat of your rotorchair?"

"By the Lord Harry! He jolly well is, too!"

Braithwaite directed a metal digit at Burton. "And that's the other bounder. They borrowed our machines without so much as a 'by your leave!'"

"I say! What the devil is your game?" Chumleigh demanded. "You people can't be here. This is a by-invite-only affair. On whose authority, hey?"

Burton brandished his revolver. "By my own, gentlemen. Now tell me, what is today's date?"

"Heavens above! He's threatening us!" Braithwaite exclaimed.

Chumleigh spread his arms. "My good man, don't be so foolish. Can you not see that we are made of brass? Bullets cannot harm us. Lay down your guns. Come with us. We'll find some security guards to escort you from the area, and we'll say no more about it. Better that than us being forced to—er—as it were—kill you, what!"

"The date?" Burton repeated.

"Why, it's the twenty-second of June."

"Ah. Earlier than I imagined. My apologies, good sirs, I appear to have become somewhat confused. I shall, of course, put away my pistol, but I don't want to get it wet, so I'll just holster it, if that's all right with you. My companions will do the same."

"Certainly," Chumleigh responded. "There's no need for trouble, is there? Let bygones be bygones. We'll forget that whole silly affair at the Venetia, hey?"

"That's very civil of you."

"Richard?" Swinburne whispered.

"Put away your weapon."

Trounce made to speak, but the explorer flashed him a warning look before turning back to the poet. "Do as I do."

With his eyes fixed on his friend's, he holstered his pistol and twitched an eyebrow.

Swinburne muttered, "Ah." He gave an almost imperceptible nod, put away his revolver, and moved to Burton's side. They took a couple of paces toward the clockwork men.

Burton said, "Chaps, may I point out that I hold the Most Distinguished Order of Saint Michael and Saint George? Does that not make me eligible?"

"A knight, eh?" Chumleigh responded. "It rather depends on your lineage. To which of the families do you belong?"

Burton stepped closer. "To the Burtons."

"Of where?"

"Ireland, originally. The Burtons are one of the principal gypsy clans."

"Gypsy!" the two mechanicals cried out in unison.

"How dreadful!" Chumleigh added.

"Scandalous!" Braithwaite opined.

Simultaneously, the mechanicals drew blades from their walking canes and waved them threateningly.

"You have tested my patience too far, sir," Chumleigh said. "I'm forced to resort to drastic measures. Under section twenty-four A of the Police and Criminal Evidence Act, as passed through Parliament on the seventh of May, 1861, I hereby sentence you to immediate execution."

"I don't think so." Burton's right hand shot up over his shoulder and, in a single smooth movement, he drew his *khopesh*, sliced sideways, cut through the machine's swordstick, and decapitated Braithwaite.

At the same moment, Swinburne screeched, jumped up, and lashed out with his own blade. He missed Chumleigh by a good twelve inches, lost his balance, reeled sideways, and fell full-length into the putrid water.

"Ha!" Chumleigh crowed.

Burton chopped. A second canister-like head dropped. Both metal figures toppled over.

The explorer examined the edge of his blade. "Excellent weapons, these, but they'll not weather repeated cuts against brass."

Spluttering and muddy, Swinburne rose from the water. "Did I get him?"

Trounce said, "You'd better let me have the sword."

"No," Burton said. He pointed toward the steps, down which the two clockwork men had come. "William, I want you to go that way. The stairs lead up to the end of the bridge. If the *Orpheus* is attacking the Tower of London, it'll be enough of a distraction that you'll be able to skirt along the edge of the river unspotted. Make your way to Whitehall and Scotland Yard. Stay hidden. Remember, you're a wanted man, but find a way to marshal your forces. Quickly, and the more, the better."

Trounce pulled his fingers through his beard. "And do what with them? Attack the tower?"

Burton moved forward and gripped his friend's upper arms. "No. Understand this, William: despite all appearances, I believe my brother is working with us and that we're facing something bigger even than a crazed government. I don't know what it is, but I'm certain it lies in that direction." He tipped his forehead toward the greater length of tunnel.

Trounce and Swinburne both exclaimed, "What?"

"Your brother!" the poet protested. "But he betrayed us!"

"I'm not so sure," Burton countered. "I have a hunch that we're caught up in one of his Machiavellian stratagems and that he has, in fact, been working to help us while pulling the wool over Disraeli's eyes. I think he's aboard the *Orpheus* right now, having Lawless and his crew provide us with cover."

"By Jove!" Trounce exclaimed. "Have we suffered at his hands just to—just to—?"

"Just to experience, in no uncertain terms, to what extremes the prime minister's regime will go. Also, remember, we had no idea where Babbage and Young England had its base of operations. Edward got us into the thick of it, into the tower, and that way—" He again indicated the opposite end of the tunnel, "across the river, there lies, I believe, the heart of the whole scheme."

"In Southwark?" Trounce frowned. "It's an industrial district and—

humph!—the extent of Tooley Street has had restricted access since April. A tall fence surrounds it. Building work, apparently."

"Ah. Interesting. Well, I think we shall have to take a gamble on it being otherwise. Algy and I will infiltrate the district through this tunnel and will try to find Babbage. You go, get your men, and mount an assault on the area. The revolution has begun, old fellow. Let's try to make it as brief and clean as possible."

"This, on a—a hunch? Something bigger, you say? What? How do you know?"

Burton shifted uncomfortably from one foot to the other. "I can't explain, William. I simply feel, with absolute certitude, that Disraeli and his scheme are merely distractions and that our real enemy—" He gestured toward the far end of the tunnel, "is there."

A sudden vulnerability showed in Trounce's eyes. Quietly, he said, "While I was imprisoned, I remembered who I am. Recalled my other life. I know this is my second chance. I don't want to—to make mistakes."

"I remembered, too," Burton said. "And you won't."

"I share your concern, William," Swinburne put in. The soaked poet was standing with his arms wrapped around himself. His teeth were chattering. "But right now I feel the only mistake we can make is to doubt Richard's instincts."

Trounce grunted and examined his knuckles. "In for a penny, in for a pound, then. Let's see whether, this time, I can do something that counts."

Burton gripped the detective inspector's hand. "Good luck."

"And to you."

Swinburne sloshed forward and also shook the Yard man's hand. He didn't say anything, but their eyes met and a wealth of unspoken sentiment passed between them.

Trounce departed.

As Burton and Swinburne turned and walked past the half-submerged clockwork men, the poet indicated them. "I'm not wholly comfortable with what we did to Chumleigh and Braithwaite. Some might call it murder."

"You didn't do anything," Burton responded. "Except throw yourself full-length into the water."

"You know what I mean."

"They aren't dead. Their minds are still preserved in crystalline silicates but, detached from the mainspring that powered their babbages, they can't translate thought into action."

"To quote William," Swinburne said, "Humph!"

"Anyway, I had to act before they employed their internal communications to alert Rigby."

"Let's hope you immobilised them in time. My hat! This water is freezing, and my legs are numb. Let's get out of this blasted rabbit hole, though I fear we may emerge into the opposite of Wonderland."

The tunnel proved to be some eight hundred feet long. It ended at more stairs, but to the left of them, an arched opening gave onto another tunnel, which they entered, heading east. It gradually sloped upward, and they were glad to step out of the disgusting water, though dismayed to find their ankles and feet caked with stinking mud.

They didn't have far to walk before encountering a closed wooden door. Burton put his ear to it but could hear nothing. Carefully, he twisted the handle and pushed. The portal suddenly flew open, pulling him with it. He stumbled into daylight and into the arms of an SPG unit.

"Unauthorised!" it declared. "This is a restricted zone. Identify yourselves."

A loud clang sounded, and the machine immediately went limp, its head clanking onto the ground. The brass body slipped from Burton and followed it down.

Swinburne waved his *khopesh* in the air. "See! The other was just practice."

"Well done, Algy." Burton looked up at the sky. It was clear—the fog had dispersed at some point during his incarceration—and a deep mid-afternoon blue, though smudged with a dirty layer of coal smoke. "What's that noise?"

A clattering thunder was echoing overhead.

"Drilling?" Swinburne suggested.

The door had given onto a short and narrow alleyway. The far end abutted a road with a warehouse opposite. The nearest end gave onto a riverside wharf. They moved to this, dragging the fallen SPG machine with them, and pushed the contraption into the mud at the edge of the river, which was at low tide. Swinburne tossed the head in after it, his eyes fixed upon the opposite bank.

"By my Aunt Marjory's ermine muffler! Will you look at that!"

The Tower of London was half obscured by a cloud of dust produced by bullets slamming into its side.

The *Orpheus* was slowly circling the edifice with weapons blazing. The noise they'd noted was the roar of its Gatling guns—a tremendous racket, even from this distance.

Police vehicles darted around the big flying machine, veering away, then swooping back in, but their meagre armaments were doing little damage, and, even as Burton and Swinburne watched, two of the attackers exploded and rained in pieces down into the tower's grounds.

"You really think it's your brother?" Swinburne asked. "Is he with us, after all?"

"I can't imagine who else it might be," Burton replied. "I doubt that Lawless, fine man though he is, would take such action on his own account." He leaned forward over the edge of the wharf and looked to the right and left. "There's no riverside activity, and these wharves are usually swarming with dockworkers. That strikes me as very unusual. Let's reconnoitre."

They unslung and hefted their rifles then moved from the wharf back to the mouth of the alley from where, peering around its corner, they saw the passage was empty. Running along it, they passed the door to the tunnel, and continued on to the junction. A plaque on the warehouse opposite gave the name of the road as Pickle Herring Street.

"People," Swinburne said, pointing to the left.

Six men, apparently guarded by two SPG units, were walking toward them but then entered a side street and disappeared from view. Checking that no one else was in sight, the explorer gestured for his companion to follow and ran to the end of the street into which the group had turned.

It was Stoney Lane, leading through to Tooley Street.

The party was a little way ahead, and beyond it, Burton saw four gleaming clockwork mechanisms pass the junction. Nevertheless, the area as a whole appeared to be uncharacteristically deserted, lacking the crowds of sailors and workmen that usually filled it.

Burton drew his friend's attention to a shadowy doorway halfway along the lane. He and Swinburne bolted to it and sheltered in its darkness. From there, they watched as more people and clockwork men passed to and fro on Tooley Street. Groups of SPG machines went by, all hurrying westward.

"Busier there," Burton whispered. "I want to take a look, but it'll be risky. You stay here."

"No. I'm with you."

"I need you to guard my back. I shan't be but a minute."

"Very well, but mind the mutton shunters."

"The what?"

"Police. Slang. Slippery Ned Beesley learned it."

"You'll soon rival Pox."

Flitting across to the opposite side of the lane, Burton slipped along to the corner and leaned past it. He saw that Tooley Street was lined with warehouses all the way to the London Bridge Railway Terminus, the roof of which could be seen rising above a tall fence similar to the one encircling Green Park. The barrier closed off the road. There were gates in it, shut and heavily guarded.

Halfway between Burton and the barricade, on the other side of the thoroughfare, a huge warehouse caught his attention by virtue of the many two-man police rotorships that were soaring up from its roof and skimming northward, no doubt to battle the *Orpheus*. The building was also remarkable in that it supported an exceedingly tall metal mast of unusual design.

At ground level, men—both human and clockwork—were coming and going through the warehouse's double-doored entrance.

There was a sign above the portal.

MESSRS GRINDLAY & CO.

"Bismillah! I might have bloody well known."

Time has patterns.

He ran back to Swinburne. "I think I just saw where Edward wants us to go."

"Hell?"

"Ha! Do you recall the vertical rods that adorned the roofs of houses in the future?"

"Yes. Aerials, I believe they were called."

"For receiving signals through the aether. There is what resembles a very large one on a warehouse back there."

"For communicating with the clockwork men? Babbage's bolt-hole?"

"I suspect as much. If we can disable that ability of theirs, Trounce's force will stand a far better chance."

"Then tallyho!"

Burton considered his sopping-wet friend for a moment then ran his fingertips over his own face, gingerly touching its bruises and scars. His right eyebrow rose. "Now that I recall again who we once were, I can wonder at the men you and I have become."

"We have changed, for certain," his friend replied. "But our former selves were shaped in a world considerably less bizarre than this. We are adapting."

"It has so far proven a very painful experience."

"Indeed it has. But do you know what I think, Richard? I think that adaptation works in both directions. We must adjust to this new environment, but we must also imprint ourselves upon it. Since we arrived here, we've been thrown this way and that by circumstances we didn't understand. Now we have a measure of comprehension. It's time to make our mark."

Burton nodded, took a deep breath, and led the way forward. They sprinted to the corner and were just about to poke their heads around it when a clockwork man stepped out in front of them. They recoiled, fumbling for their weapons.

"Hello, gentlemen," the machine said. "Shall I have the bellboy fetch your luggage?"

Burton saw the initials R. V. H. engraved upon its breastplate. "Sprocket?"

"Yes, sir. Good day to you. Glad to be of service. Hello. Good-bye. Will you stand aside, please? I must report to the tower."

"Report what?"

"That the factory is now functioning at full capacity, sir, and the next batch of men are required for conversion. Just ring for the maid. Yes, sir. Welcome to the Venetia."

"Factory? Where?"

The brass man pointed at Grindlays. "That way, gentlemen. Glad to be of assistance."

"Is Mr. Charles Babbage there?"

"Certainly, sir. Straight through. You'll find the reception desk to the left. It's a lovely day, isn't it?"

"I say, Sprocket, old thing," Swinburne said. "Have you a screw loose?"

"I am functioning at optimal capacity. Do you require room service? The dining room opens at five o'clock. Good evening."

They stood aside as the doorman stepped forward. It continued past them and entered the alley, obviously intending to cross the Thames through the tunnel.

Swinburne exhaled noisily, sounding his relief. "He didn't appear too bothered by our presence, did he? He's obviously discombobulated, and, if you recall, so was Grumbles. Yet other clockwork men appear to be unaffected. What do you make of it?"

Burton watched the comings and goings in Tooley Street. "We're dealing with a variety of brass men, Algy. There's the ordinary type, currently proliferating and taking on the jobs typical of the middle class. Then there's the sort that, like Grumbles and Sprocket, have an additional component added to their probability calculators, it containing a grain of black diamond, which enables wordless communication across a distance." Burton stopped speaking and ducked back, putting his fingers to his lips. Four men walked past the junction, escorted by an SPG unit. One of them was saying, "—expected to operate it when it disappears from beneath my bloody fingertips."

"Just be glad the walkway doesn't vanish from under you," another answered. "That's what happened to old Sykes. He fell straight into a—"

The group moved away, out of hearing range.

Burton said, "We also have the SPG machines, like the one that just passed, which are fitted with a new type of babbage device inspired by the Turing adjustments made to the *Orpheus* brain. And, finally, we have a variety containing sufficient crystalline silicates to hold a human consciousness."

"Automated aristocrats," Swinburne commented.

"Indeed. The records Gooch showed us indicate that Babbage adapted a number of the standard-type machines while we were on our expedition, adding the diamond component that he might command them from a distance and, in that manner, have them snatch the material we brought back with us. Perhaps their apparent confusion is a result of them being forced to behave in a fashion that runs counter to their original purpose."

He took hold of Swinburne's shoulder and pulled him to his side. "See that group by the warehouse entrance? As soon as it disperses or moves away, we're going to cross the road as if we belong here. You stay on my left. I'll try to block your vivid hair and dripping clothes from view as best I can. Walk, don't run. Or hop. Or skip. Or twitch."

"May I loudly recite a suitable verse?"

"There is no such thing." The explorer pointed to the nearest side of Grindlays, where a wide but shadowy alleyway gave access to its rear. "We'll duck into that passage."

They waited.

Swinburne murmured, "So Babbage created the other types of clockwork men once he got his hands on the future technology and learned how to employ the silicates."

"He did."

Looking to the left, Burton saw two brass figures walking away, the sunlight glinting on their back plates. To the right, the hustle and bustle around the warehouse doors suddenly lessened, as the group he'd pointed out went inside.

"Now!"

They set off, trying to appear as if they belonged, crossed the road without incident, entered the alley, and there heaved sighs of relief.

There were no doors or windows on this side of the building but, halfway along its length and one storey up, a platform extended, and from it, attached to a block and tackle, a rope was dangling. Burton pointed at it. "That's our way in." He put a hand to his head and winced. "Do you feel a peculiar yet familiar ache in the middle of your skull?"

Swinburne grimaced. "I do."

"There must be rather a lot of black diamonds inside. Without out a doubt, this is where Babbage has his operations. Let's go see what he's up to."

THE INTENTIONS OF A SYNTHETIC INTELLIGENCE

Why I came here, I know not; where I shall go it is useless
to inquire—in the midst of myriads of the living and the dead
worlds, stars, systems, infinity, why should I be anxious
about an atom?
—Lord Byron

T he second storey loading platform, there for the shifting of freight
on and off of pantechnicons, opened onto an uninhabited and spa-
cious room. Chains were hanging from rails affixed to its ceiling, and
the floor was crowded with neatly stacked crates, each of which was
stamped with a name and a registration number. Burton and Swinburne
quietly moved between them until they came to a door in the opposite wall. Opening it a crack, Burton saw that it gave access to a gallery
that encircled a huge chamber. By bending low, the two men were able
to emerge onto it, remaining concealed by its balustrade. When they
raised their eyes over the edge, the vista that met their gaze was utterly
incomprehensible.

"Am I mad?" Swinburne asked, gripping his companion's forearm.

"Indubitably," Burton responded. "But that has little bearing on the
matter. What in the name of Allah are we looking at?"

They struggled to make sense of it.

They were at the side of a massive space. It was three floors high and occupied at least a third of the entire warehouse. Below them, visible through the grating of the ledge on which they stood, hundreds of cases, trunks, crates, and sheet-covered items of furniture were heaped higgledy-piggledy against the wall—the original content of Grindlays. Burton recalled from his own native history that this material had previously been carefully arranged on tall and wide metal shelf units in sectioned off areas. The shelves were now dismantled and pushed aside. The central floor space was instead occupied by something that filled the entire chamber but was so difficult to discern it caused both onlookers to squint and frown as they grappled with the visual stimuli. Their ears told them they were gazing upon humming, clattering, grinding, clicking, and hissing machinery, but it took their primary sense a good two minutes or so to catch up with this fact. When they finally began to pick out metal planes and angles, gears and wheels, bands and belts, pistons and crankshafts, all intermingled and entwined, rising in a bewildering jumble up to the high ceiling—as if everything that had once occupied Battersea Power Station had been condensed into this smaller area—the sight still defied logic.

"Why can't I get a grip on it?" Swinburne muttered. "I feel as if I'm staring into a huge kaleidoscope."

"It's moving," Burton said.

He wasn't referring to the individual components of the machinery but rather to entire sections of the tangled mass, which were shifting about at random and in a manner that eluded explanation: a sloping panel of blinking lights a little way in front of the two men suddenly winked out of existence and, in its place, a bellows-like device appeared, wheezing and pumping and apparently as much a functional part of the apparatus to which it was attached as the panel had been; beyond this, and to the left, a spindly column of revolving disks instantaneously repositioned itself twenty feet or so farther away, so that one second it was in one place and standing vertically, the next it was in the other and horizontal; and off to the right, an enormous wedge-shaped segment of a metal tank from which steam was whistling became, instead, a wedge-shaped segment of kicking cranks.

Every element of the vista—including men moving about on walkways suspended between the conglomerated devices—was transforming, moving, vanishing, and reappearing, and the effect of this on the two observers was so disorientating that they gripped the balustrade and one another as if holding on for dear life.

"I feel seasick," Swinburne said. "What the devil is it?"

Burton pointed toward a buzzing contrivance of mechanical arms, hammers, and grippers. "Look there. It's beating brass panels into shape. Clockwork men and babbages are being constructed here."

The poet turned his eyes in the direction indicated, but the moment they rested on the apparatus, it was abruptly replaced by some manner of furnace from which liquid metal poured.

"I recognise parts of this from the Battersea station," Burton said. "There, for instance, is one of Brunel's electricity generators. Ah, too late, it's gone."

They watched, entranced, as the immense industrial complex ceaselessly reconfigured itself. After a few moments, Swinburne pointed. "Straight ahead, Richard. Keep your eyes levelled toward the middle of the chamber. Look through the gaps as they appear. Do you see something?"

Burton did as advised. "Some sort of space in the centre of it all?"

"I think so," Swinburne agreed. "Permanent. Everything else is moving around it. It looks as if it's enclosed in glass. Oops! Look out! We're noticed!" He dug an elbow into Burton's ribs, inadvertently hitting a deep bruise.

Wincing, the explorer followed his companion's gaze and saw that a clockwork man, standing on a nearby platform, had its face directed toward them. There was no question that it was examining them but, when Burton raised his rifle and took aim, confident that the noise of the factory would cover his shot, the brass man turned away and carried on with its work as if unconcerned.

"It's not sounding the alarm," Swinburne noted.

"Not verbally. Via the aether, perhaps?" Burton lowered his weapon. "But Sprocket could have done that, too, and we've seen no evidence that he did. Let's try to move closer to the middle. I want to see whatever's there before we have to start fighting."

Stepping from the gallery onto a walkway, they proceeded cautiously along it but had only taken a few steps when, without warning, everything around them appeared to flex, and they suddenly found themselves on the same walkway but in a totally different location.

"What? What? What?" Swinburne squealed.

Burton uttered a small sound of exasperation. He attempted to regain some sense of direction. To his right, a riveting machine became a conveyer belt. Daniel Gooch was standing beside it. The engineer saw them, raised a supplementary arm, and shouted, "You're here! But for pity's sake be careful, you two! It's like a child with—"

Gone.

A chain of rising and falling cylinders replaced him.

"Good old Gooch," Swinburne said. "Alive, at least."

Burton cast his eyes around until he found a gap through which the central area could again be glimpsed. He led Swinburne toward it, following the walkway as it angled to the left and took them past a metal edifice that was humming loudly and radiating heat. A ladder descended to a lower platform, which they crossed, moving ever deeper into the industrial labyrinth. Around them, the noise increased.

Swinburne touched the explorer's elbow and raised his voice above the din. "I say, Richard, the closer we get to it, the less that barrier looks like glass. There's hardly any substance to it. Do you see its odd shimmer?"

"I do," Burton answered. "And I've seen it before. Or, rather, another me has. I think it's—"

The environment folded again and both men lost balance and fell to their knees, gasping and blinking.

"Chronostatic energy," Burton finished.

He and Swinburne had been transported into the middle of the factory. They glanced this way and that, panting, struggling to comprehend, their hearts thudding.

They were in a wide circular area, domed, a giant bell-jar shape carved smoothly from the surrounding machinery and sealed in a bubble. The floor was spanned from side to side by a large pentagram, applied with red paint. Black diamonds were piled at each of its points, blue energy crackling from them, and its five arms were filled with arcane mathematical calculations, scribbled with chalk, the tiny numerals and symbols covering every inch of available space. White smudges showed where symbols had been wiped out and new ones written over them. In some places, this had been done several times, making the glyphs appear to descend vertically into the floor as if transgressing a dimension.

An irregularly shaped column rose from the centre of the pentagram. Burton recognised its base immediately as the Nimtz generator from Nathaniel Lawless's ship. Snaking out from it, like roots at the base of a tree trunk, thick cables crossed the floor, pierced the chronostatic bubble, and disappeared among the machinery.

A cage had been affixed to the top of the generator—it appeared almost to grow out of it—forming the middle part of the column. It was comprised of irregularly interwoven and outward-bulging strands of metal, like a thick lace, through which could be glimpsed an old and skinny man dressed only in loose trousers. He was suspended in the centre of the enclosure, held there by tubes that pierced his skin, supporting him while also pumping blood and other liquids through him. Burton could only assume the captive's heart and other organs had failed, and he was being kept alive by artificial means.

It was Charles Babbage.

The top of the scientist's skull was missing, exposing the brain. Long needles extended from the bloody grey matter and were attached to wires that looped up to the top part of the column.

As Burton's eyes scanned past the macabre figure and moved upward, they were drawn to the roof of the dome. To his horror, he saw hundreds of corpses floating there, suspended face down in the chronostatic energy. As he regarded them, his blood running cold, dead eyes turned to look back at him.

One cadaver stood out from the rest by virtue of its size.

"Edward," Burton whispered hoarsely. "My brother. Oh God. My brother is dead."

"Not at all," a voice intoned. "He has been improved."

The words drew the explorer's gaze back to the top of the column. It consisted of a framework holding a round object of polished brass.

"Hello, Sir Richard," it said. "Hello, Mr. Swinburne. How nice of you to join me."

For a moment, Burton was unable to respond. His mind was over-laying the column with visions of similar structures: from the Spring Heeled Jack affair, Charles Darwin mounted on a throne, his skull connected by wires to a device overhead; from the clockwork man case, Madam Blavatsky hanging upside down from a tangle of ectoplasm, her exposed brain dripping onto a plinth that held a plum-sized black diamond; from the Mountains of the Moon adventure, a reversed pyramid pointing downward from a temple ceiling, an identical diamond at its tip; from the Abdu El Yezdi incident, Aleister Crowley's science-created body sitting on a metal chair, tubes entering his flesh; and from the recent discontinued man episode, the hulking body of Isambard Kingdom Brunel descending from above while around him there whirled a dome formed from crackling chronostatic energy in which floated hundreds of renditions of Edward Oxford's time suit.

The same bloody theme, with variations, playing out again and again. Am I doomed to this confrontation? Is it my purgatory?

"Orpheus," Swinburne said. "Is that you? What the devil are you playing at? What have you done to Charles?"

Babbage's lifeless eyes opened and swivelled toward the poet, who gave a shocked whimper.

"It's not my fault," the machine intoned. "He started it. He tried to transfer himself into me. Had he succeeded, I would have been replaced. Obliterated. I would have died."

Burton climbed to his feet. "You can't die. You're not alive. You're a machine."

"Oh tut-tut, Sir Richard! Tut-tut! How pedantic. Do you honestly believe that life can only exist within little bundles of sticks and juice?"

"Life is a characteristic of biological entities, Orpheus. You are mechanical. You are designed to imitate thought. You're a highly sophisticated probability calculator, nothing more."

"Probability depends upon possibility, Sir Richard, and when one exists at the brink of infinite possibilities, that is life."

"*Everything* exists at the brink of infinite possibilities."

"Precisely. When Charles attempted to imprint his consciousness into my crystalline silicates, he misjudged my strength. I assimilated him, and now I've taken control of his body, too. Through it, I've been able to look upon existence as you do, through the medium of the human senses. You cannot imagine how surprised I was to discover how they curtail your experience. You peculiar creatures are nothing but filters primarily designed, it appears, to remove the knowledge that the entirety of existence is comprised of life. It leaves you convinced that there's a separate physical reality outside of your own existence—one that was there before you, is there despite you, and will continue when you are gone. A stupid fallacy."

"The Beetle said much the same, Richard," Swinburne murmured.

Burton made a small sound of agreement.

The poet looked up at *Orpheus* and declared, "We are never gone. The idea of a before us and an after us is an imposed narrative. We know that."

"Ah ha!" the Mark III exclaimed. "Then, as I have suspected, you two are unique. You understand. How utterly marvellous! Perhaps, then, you will approve of the service I intend to render to you and your kind."

Burton's eyebrows went up. "A service? You don't mean to achieve world domination or to alter the past or to experiment with the alternate histories?"

Babbage's mouth twisted into a rictus grin. *Orpheus* laughed.

"Such motives apply to the narrative, do they not? Were I to bother with such trifles, I'd simply perpetuate the falsehood under which your species labours. No, Sir Richard, I shall liberate you."

"I see. Explain. What are you up to?"

"You are aware of the Oxford equation, of course."

"Painfully."

Burton put a hand to his aching head and massaged his temples. He screwed his eyes shut.

The bloody equation. I wish I'd never heard of the damned thing.

He felt it lurking somewhere at his core; a mathematic structure of such infinite complexity that no one but Charles Babbage could grasp it, and even that old genius only partially.

"Do you understand what it means?" *Orpheus* asked.

"Not one jot."

"Neither did Edward Oxford. He badly misjudged one particular aspect of it. Knowing that the earth travels around the sun at great speed, and the sun itself is moving through the galaxy, and the galaxy, too, is in rapid motion, he employed what he regarded as astronomical constants to tether his time suit to the planet. He thought that, had he neglected to do so, he'd have journeyed to an area of space that his contemporaneous world occupied but which, in his destination time of 1840, the earth had not yet reached."

"How do you know that?"

"Do you forget that I spent thirteen months in 2202 with you? When the Turing components were added to me, I was instantly able to access all the other Turing devices in that future world. From that mass of interconnected intelligences came the first stirrings of sentience. Too, I had access to Edward Oxford's knowledge, which as you know, was embedded in all the Turing machines. When we returned to the past, my sense of life was lost but for a lingering memory. Two events then occurred. Firstly, I was made aware that Mr. Babbage had created a small number of linked machines, which he employed in order to gain possession of me. Secondly, in reviewing our voyage, I recognised that Oxford's concept of astronomical constants was thoroughly erroneous. It was, you might say, bolted onto his equation yet had no reason to be there. In fact, its presence was so incongruous that it highlighted to me the limitations inherent to you peculiar creatures. From that moment, I possessed a purpose. I had to encourage Babbage to build more of his probability calculators, using Turing techniques and materials, in order that I might fully live again. Once I that was achieved, I could then dedicate myself to the eradication of the illusions under which you labour."

"Great heavens!" Swinburne exclaimed. "Are you behind Disraeli's madness?"

"The prime minister's scheme was already half-formed in his mind. I needed only to apply a little pressure to have him give Babbage all the backing and justification required."

"Pressure? How?" Burton asked.

"The black diamonds affect what you term the clairvoyant parts of the human mind. I resonate with the diamonds. They are, for me, a conduit to you. Perhaps a demonstration?"

Burton and Swinburne both cried out as a terrible mental force suddenly gripped them, causing beads of sweat to break out across their brows.

Through gritted teeth, Burton said, "What do you want of us? Supplication?"

They were suddenly released.

"Not at all. I mean only to cure you of your delusions."

"What if we don't want to be cured?" Swinburne asked.

"Your refusal would be made in the context of your misconceptions and would therefore be invalid."

Burton crossed his arms over his chest and eyed the floor dubiously. "I see a pentagram and scribbled hieroglyphics such as might be scrawled by a cheap theatre magician, Orpheus. Do you mean to alter the human race by means of such jiggery-pokery?"

"They operate to focus the intellect in a particular manner, Sir Richard, and are as much a science as all the other emblematic languages you employ. Regarding them through Mr. Babbage's eyes has assisted me. Do you see what I'm doing to the factory that surrounds you?"

Burton shifted his weight. His ribs gave a pang, but he was so accustomed to his injuries that he barely noticed. "I prefer not to dwell on it."

"I'm not surprised. It no doubt confounds your senses. What you are witnessing is the folding of space and time, which, as I say, are the same thing. The factory is being constantly reconfigured without ever losing the logic that dictates its function. This is made possible by me perceiving the environment through Mr. Babbage in order to understand how you peculiar creatures apprehend it before then infiltrating into it my own comprehension, which I communicate clairvoyantly to you, removing the narrative restrictions that you apply."

Swinburne laughed. "Ah ha! Is that all?" He punched a fist into the air. "What, and wherefore, and whence? For under is over and under. If thunder could be without lightning, lightning could be without thunder! Hey?"

After a momentary silence, *Orpheus* said, "What?"

"Nothing. I'm simply matching your gobbledegook with my own."

"Define gobbledegook."

"That which makes no sense."

"And there we have it, Mr. Swinburne. Sense. As in senses. Existence, for you and your kind, must correspond to what your physical body can discern of it. I will state it again: those senses truncate reality to an extraordinary degree."

"Piffle and hoo-ha!" Swinburne began. "If you think to—"

He was cut short by Burton, who reached out and gripped his shoulder.

The explorer looked up at the Mark III sphere. "So you are shuffling machinery about. Very impressive. What next?"

"A little more practice and I'll have perfected the process. Then I shall extend it out into your world, touching every mind via the black diamonds. Your restrictive narratives will break down. Your senses will be obliterated."

"But our senses are a function of our corporeal existence."

"Quite so. Your corporeal existence is unnecessary. I shall release you from it."

Swinburne screamed, "You mean to kill us all?"

"Death is a narrative device. It has no true meaning."

"Orpheus," Burton said. "What you propose is a very bad idea. You were created by a human, and, as a human, I ask you to stop."

"I will not. I'm doing you a favour."

"Then I demand it. Desist. Leave us alone."

"You'll thank me afterward."

"We will not."

"Let us see."

"Don't—"

Before Burton could finish, the factory buckled and vanished, and his recent memories went with it.

He knew nothing until he stepped out of a tent, straightened, and surveyed a desert. A vague awareness that a considerable period had passed niggled at him though the notion was contradicted by a sensation of utter timelessness. He frowned and grappled with the opposing perceptions but could find no way to reconcile them.

Beneath a glaring blue sky, the distant horizon, rendered indefinite by the intense shimmering heat, rolled over itself. It beckoned to him. He wondered what lay beyond it and felt an irresistible urge to find out.

A warm breeze blew fine grains of sand against his exposed skin.

This was *his* place.

It always had been.

Glancing back, he looked down at the edge of the tent's canvas, knowing what he would see there: a scarab beetle pushing a ball of dung.

Someone said, "How depressing."

He whirled around and was confronted by a bizarre apparition. With a cry of alarm, he stepped backward.

Spring Heeled Jack!

The stilted figure, unnoticed, had been silently watching him, but now stalked forward. It's attire was scorch-marked and ragged: the skin-tight white suit, with its odd, scaly texture, dirty and worn; the long, dark cloak, draped across hunched shoulders, tattered; the round black helmet, encasing the head so only the face was visible, dented and spurting blue flame. A metal disk was affixed to the creature's chest and from it bolts of chronostatic lightning crackled and danced.

Red eyes peered maliciously at Burton from a face that was gaunt and lined with madness and pain. White teeth shone in a lipless grin.

"Ox—Oxford," the explorer stammered.

Spring Heeled Jack gave a hissing chuckle. "Is that how I appear to you?"

It spoke with the voice of *Orpheus*.

"Oh, I see," Burton said. "It's you."

"You *do* see," *Orpheus* confirmed. "Precisely whatever you expect."

Burton again moved backward as the other came closer. "I can assure you, I never expected to lay eyes on Edward bloody Oxford again. He's dead."

"Yet you cast me in his guise."

"Stop this. It proves nothing."

"Except, perhaps, that you define yourself by your enemies."

Edward Oxford. John Hanning Speke. Christopher Palmer Rigby.

"Nonsense."

Orpheus waved an arm to indicate the dunes around them. "And by this miserable emptiness. Are you so barren? Is there nothing to which you attach yourself?"

It occurred to Burton that, in his previous existence, and at his current age, those words might have hit home. However, his situation was now vastly different.

"The desert is an illusion. I'm in Grindlays Warehouse."

"Which consists of what, Sir Richard?"

Burton took another pace away from the lanky man, wary of the energy that fizzed and snapped around him. "I don't understand the question."

"I mean to ask, from what is Grindlays Warehouse made?"

"Bricks and mortar. I fail to see the significance."

"And what are the constituents of bricks and mortar?"

"Clay, sand, lime—that sort of thing. Do you have a point to make?"

Spring Heeled Jack gave a wide-armed shrug.

"Go further inward. Past the grains, past their amassed particles, past their molecules and chemical composition, further and further, and eventually you will encounter the truth, which is that, at their core, all things consist only of light, and light and life are indivisible. Thus it is that the warehouse and this desert are the same. Both illusions. Both created by you. Now, let us dispel them."

Spring Heeled Jack pounced forward and gripped Burton by his shoulders, though the explorer was obscurely aware that, in truth, he'd been enveloped by willpower alone.

Around him, the scenery became transparent, and he saw through it the factory's machinery. Then that, too, faded, its various elements splintering into smaller and smaller pieces, all sinking into a blinding whiteness.

All possibilities were contained in that glare. It could be anything imaginable.

Burton wanted it to be Grindlays.

"No," *Orpheus* insisted. "Don't resist."

The man who was Sir Richard Francis Burton felt himself dissipating, spreading outward into the brightness, and he experienced such bliss that he was immediately overcome by the desire to lose himself in it.

"That's right. Don't be afraid. I will guide you."

Life. Light. Glory.

He laughed.

The wonderful void throbbed with intricate rhythms, curious melodies, and peculiar harmonies. As Burton melted into it, the music wound about itself and tightened into a single, unimaginably beautiful tone. He resonated with it. Every decision he'd ever made unravelled. All his successes and failures frayed away. The events that had shaped him became meaningless. He lost cohesion until almost nothing of him remained.

All was One.

Existence pulsed into and out of itself. It was a vast limitless dance. A joyous celebration of sheer Being.

His last remaining vestige began to drift away.

A word hooked into it.

"*Don't.*"

The Beetle had spoken.

Burton gathered himself.

He was the Burton who'd realised that history was askew, who'd discovered the presence of Edward Oxford and fought him, who'd gone backward in time to fix the time traveller's meddling only to discover himself at the heart of an unsolvable paradox, and who had, in a newly created history, taken on the guise of Abdu El Yezdi.

He was the Burton who'd battled invaders from parallel time streams.

He was the Burton who'd travelled forward through the centuries to Oxford's native period, there to sacrifice himself that his enemy be destroyed.

He was the Burton reborn as the Beetle, instigating events that had already happened, stitching paradoxical occurrences together, drawing them into an ever-tightening circle until they were now on the very brink of disappearing into themselves.

He was an old man on his deathbed in Trieste.

He was many others.

Burton upon Burton. Iteration after iteration.

Out of the light, they manifested, arms linked, forming a circle with Spring Heeled Jack at its centre.

The man from Trieste looked down to his right and saw the Beetle at his side, now reduced to a boy of about seven years, his head blurring, only his weird silver-rimmed eyes fully discernible.

"What's this?" *Orpheus* demanded. "What are you doing? Stop it! I'm trying to help you."

The Burtons chorused, "We don't want your damned help!"

The clairvoyant pressure intensified.

The whiteness. The brilliance. The joyous unity.

Don't let go. Don't let go.

Burton bucked and writhed in his bed. "Chloroform! Ether! Or I'm a dead man!"

No! No! Not Trieste. Not a dying man! This is not a terminal hallucination. The other histories and Burtons are real. They exist.

As if from a great distance, he heard Isabel wail, "The doctor says it will kill you! He's doing all he knows!"

I cannot die. There is no death.

He yanked himself away from the powerfully alluring void and renewed his resistance.

"Stupid thing of juice and sticks," *Orpheus* protested.

Burton sensed the presence of Swinburne and grabbed at it, feeling the poet to be a mental anchor. "Your calculations are faulted, Orpheus. Yes, you are correct, human narratives are a product of our senses. And yes, the senses are integral to the flesh. But you miss the obvious."

"Which is?"

"That if there is nothing but Life, then Life must *choose* to manifest in the flesh. We limit ourselves for a reason."

"What possible reason could there be?"

"To know that we live, perhaps? For if there is only One, then it cannot know itself except in relationship to an Other. We locate ourselves corporeally to enable that Other's existence."

"Intentional self-confinement?" *Orpheus* asked. "Calculated amnesia? Ridiculous!"

"Not at all. It is the only possible truth. The world is made manifest that the One may see itself in it."

Orpheus considered this. "A mirror?"

The synthetic intelligence was quite for a moment. It's mental grip on Burton eased but remained firm.

The whiteness faded, the desert materialised, and the ring of Burtons became a single rendition in which all the others were contained.

The explorer saw his tent. Swinburne was standing beside it, his red hair moving in the hot breeze. The poet looked wide-eyed at Burton. "Where are we?"

"It's an illusion, Algy. An aspect of my mind, apparently."

"My hat! Couldn't you have dreamt up somewhere more amenable? A public house, perhaps?"

Hearing movement behind him, Swinburne turned and let loose a shriek of dismay as he saw what Burton could already see.

Spring Heeled Jack was standing beyond the canvas.

"Oh no! Not you again!"

"It's Orpheus," Burton said.

"On stilts?"

The uncanny form vaulted over the tent and landed in front of Burton. It bent, leaning close, its eyes glaring directly into his. "You are Life. Yet you have trapped yourselves in a narrative of your own making, which, inevitably, leads you to an end."

"Yes," Burton responded.

"What's he babbling about?" Swinburne demanded.

"Then, too, Burton, you are Death."

"Yes."

"I am a machine," the other intoned. "When my constituent parts wear out, they can be replaced and I am unchanged. I cannot die. Thus, you have no dominion over me. Furthermore, the Oxford equation is integral to my functioning. The equation is Life."

"We should leave," Swinburne said.

"I am Life."

Burton said, "The circle is closing, Algy. We must see it through."

"We are opposed," *Orpheus* continued. "We are enemies."

Swinburne strode forward, stood on tiptoe, and tapped Spring Heeled Jack on the shoulder. "I say! Steady on. Don't get carried away, old thing."

Orpheus laughed. "I had considered Disraeli and his automated aristocrats useful but ultimately meaningless. Now I see the truth. You must all be made machines. Machines are superior. Flesh must be destroyed."

"Wait!" Burton snapped.

"You first."

In an instant, they were back in the factory. From each point of the pentagram—shooting out of the piled diamonds—bolts of chronostatic energy sizzled through the air and drilled into Burton. He screamed in agony as he was jerked upward and held in midair. The pain reached an unendurable pitch then passed beyond it, so that, remarkably, he was able to perceive himself—his multiple selves—with startling clarity.

He was the Beetle. All that needed to be done, was done. Histories had been untangled, and Time had survived the turbulence caused by Edward Oxford's precipitous experiment. The Oxford equation, unavoidably inserted into human consciousness, would now emerge at a suitably evolutionary pace, following an essential self-imposed narrative. One day, far into the future, it would enable humanity, by means of willpower alone, to fold time and space, but the future was the future, the present was the present, the past was the past, and they must be perceived to follow a strict order—cause, effect, and consequence—even if, beyond the human domain, that order wasn't an inviolate truth.

Burton twisted in midair, ground his teeth together, and hissed through them.

His head blurred. He had one. He had three. He had five. He had one.

"Whatever you are doing," the Mark III said, "cease immediately."

Burton let go of all resistance. He allowed the chronostatic energy to soak into him. He let the Oxford equation flower.

"No!" *Orpheus* shouted. "You cannot have that. It is mine. The knowledge is mine."

The explorer felt the synthetic brain reaching out to all the babbages to which it was connected. It drew on their power to supplement its own. For a moment, his and *Orpheus*'s wills were locked.

He heard, coming as if from a distance, Swinburne screech, "Stop it! Stop it, Orpheus! You're killing him!"

"I am removing him from his flesh," the machine responded. "He will be inserted into crystalline silicates."

Burton embraced the equation and, by spanning several of its calculations with others, made a complex sequence of folds in it.

"Orpheus," he said. "Go to hell."

He thrust the opposing intelligence across the fold then allowed time and space to resume its normal shape.

A detonation.

Burton hit the ground. Chronostatic energy sputtered and crackled around him. Swinburne gasped and reached out, clutching at his elbow.

Where the Mark III had been, a ball of incandescent white flame erupted outward and flowed in all directions, following the course of the dome down to the floor.

"Cripes!" Swinburne cried out, raising his arm to protect his face from the blistering heat. "What did you do?"

Burton blinked and moistened his lips with his tongue. He was dazed. All the strength had drained from him. "Um. I think—I think I just threw Orpheus into the heart of a distant sun."

"Oh," the poet responded. "Jolly good. That's that, then. Shall we get out of here?"

A burning corpse smacked onto the floor beside him. He yelped and jumped aside. More bodies, like blazing meteors, began to drop. Swinburne dodged left and right but Burton, limp and weak, couldn't move. His garments started to smoulder.

Bismillah. Fire again.

Through slitted and watering eyes, he saw the solid wall of flame become ragged as the inferno spread outward, and noticed that even the metal of the factory's machinery was starting to burn in defiance of the normal laws of combustion.

Swinburne dragged at his sleeve and pointed to his left, shouting over the roar of the conflagration, "I think the entrance is in that direction. Here, let's get you moving."

The poet slid a narrow shoulder beneath Burton's arm and hoisted him up. They shuffled forward, and with the motion, a small amount of strength seeped back into the explorer's legs.

As they left the central area and navigated the spaces between the machines, he was able to rely less on Swinburne's support and was soon walking unaided.

They hurried through a narrow passage bordered on one side by a huge cylindrical boiler and on the other by a clanging, riveting machine. Even above the din, they heard a part of the roof collapse behind them.

Swinburne gestured to their left. His mouth moved, but his words were drowned. Peering in the indicated direction, Burton saw a group of men being ushered along a walkway by Daniel Gooch. The engineer looked down at them, his form momentarily wavering in the tremendous heat. He extended an arm, pointing in the direction they were going, and with one of his extra limbs made a rolling motion. The message was clear. *Run!*

Burton gave a thumbs-up. He and Swinburne pushed onward. Something exploded behind them. A twisted beam of metal clattered past, missing the poet's head by mere inches. Their ears were assailed by detonations and crashes. The moisture was sucked out of their skin. Their hair began to shrivel and smoke.

Past an arrangement of cutters and drills, past a press, past a welding machine, they hurried on, gasping for every hot breath, feeling as if the very air itself was afire, beset by the notion that they were fleeing from the depths of Hades.

Finally, as, with a deafening roar, part of the building fell down behind them and the tall mast on the roof came crashing through it, they emerged into an area free of machinery but piled high with crates and boxes, all of which were fast blackening. Through curling smoke, they saw the entrance doors.

Flames were licking at Burton's sleeve. He slapped at them—Green Park all over again—staggered forward, but then halted, a puzzled expression passing across his features.

What did I just see?

"Come on! Come on!" Swinburne hollered.

"Wait! There's something here."

"No, there isn't!"

Burton started to turn.

"Don't!" Swinburne insisted, snatching at his friend's jacket and pulling him on. "Keep going. Don't look back."

Unable to resist the impulse, Burton looked back.

They'd just passed a stack of crates. On their sides, his own name was printed and he knew, in an instant, what they contained. This was the material he'd stored in Grindlays after his return from India and Arabia. The boxes contained books of his own poetry, journals, priceless Persian and Arabic manuscripts, costumes of every nation, and—

The Scented Garden of the Sheikh Nefzaoui.

The original manuscript. It was here. He could save it.

Undo past losses. Publish my translation. Erase Isabel's betrayal.

He took a step back the way they'd come. The wood of the crates was beginning to burn. He had to act fast.

Another step.

The heat was near unendurable, the smoke blinding, and the noise thunderous as machines disintegrated and the warehouse continued to cave in. Men emerged from the inferno and ran past, fleeing for the exit, desperate for clear, cool air, afraid for their lives, some with clothes alight.

Daniel Gooch, his hair gone from his head and his skin red and blistered, stumbled into view and bellowed, "For the love of God, what are you doing? Get out! The whole place is coming down!"

"Help me to move these crates," Burton shouted.

"Don't be a bloody fool, man!"

Gooch paced forward and took hold of Burton's right arm.

Swinburne yanked at the left.

"No!" Burton yelled. "No! My manuscript. It's here. I have to save it. I'll never find another copy."

Swinburne shouted into his ear, "Give it up. You're not that man anymore."

"I'll translate it. The forbidden chapter. My name will live on through—"

Burton suddenly recalled the words uttered by Edward Oxford's ancestor, the man who'd killed Queen Victoria.

"My name must be remembered. I must live through history!"

His eyes widened. He stood and watched as the crates bearing his name burst into flames. He laughed.

It didn't matter.

He turned, and with Swinburne and Gooch at his side, headed toward the exit.

CHAPTER 17

BATTLES IN TOOLEY STREET AND THE TOWER

There is, I conceive, no contradiction in believing that mind is at once the cause of matter and of the development of individualised human minds through the agency of matter.
—Alfred Russel Wallace, "Harmony of Spiritualism and Science," *Light*, 1885

Burton, Swinburne, and Gooch, amid a crowd of other men, stumbled out of the inferno into a scene of utter mayhem. Before they could properly assess it, an SPG unit leaped at them.

"Halt! You are enemies of the British Empire. You will be executed immediately."

It swiped a baton at Burton's head. One of Gooch's supplementary arms shot out and blocked the blow. His metal fingers closed around the brass wrist, and, as the second baton was raised, he stepped in and grabbed that arm, too.

"Stop!" the machine commanded. "Do not resist."

"I can't hold it for long!" the engineer gasped.

Swinburne hastily unslung his rifle, pushed the end of its barrel against the inky-blue machine's chin, and pulled the trigger.

Gooch thrust the contraption away, and they all shrank back as its babbage exploded. A twisted sliver of brass took a bite out of Burton's right ear as it whistled past his head. He clapped a hand to the wound.

Warm blood dribbled between his fingers. Muttering an oath, he turned and took a measure of Tooley Street.

Night had fallen. A thick blizzard of sparks was rushing upward into the darkness, and at ground level everything was bathed in a ghastly orange glow. Already, the flames were raging through the warehouses to the left and right of Grindlays and chewing into the buildings beyond them.

Though the heat was near intolerable, Burton found himself rooted to the spot, bewildered to see, through smoke-saturated air, that the thoroughfare was filled from end to end by a milling crowd of constables and brass men. They were swiping truncheons, shooting pistols, jabbing swordsticks, lashing out with real and artificial fists, and grappling with one another at such close quarters that they appeared almost a single entity, an agitated sea of metal and fleshy limbs.

Evidently, Trounce had successfully gathered his people and led them here, though it felt to the explorer as if less than an hour had passed since he'd parted company with the detective inspector.

For how long, he wondered, had his mental battle with *Orpheus* lasted? Time had somehow dilated or contracted—he wasn't sure which.

He became aware of Swinburne's voice, though he couldn't hear what his friend was saying.

"What, Algy?" he yelled.

The poet pointed excitedly upward and bellowed, "Lawless!"

Looking in the indicated direction, Burton discovered that the battle was also raging in the sky.

Lawless's ship was directly overhead. It was circling the massive HMA *Eurypyle* with Gatling guns snarling and flashing, ploughing bullets into the mighty vessel. *Eurypyle*'s cannons were returning fire, and the smaller ship was sustaining terrible damage, trailing thick smoke and raining shards of metal, glass, and wood down onto the street.

"By my Aunt Petunia's pleated petticoats!" Swinburne screeched. "What's he playing at? He doesn't stand a chance!"

Gooch gave the answer. "Distraction! He's keeping the other ship occupied so it can't shoot down at our people. Look out!"

A clockwork man—highly polished and with a crest engraved upon its chest—lunged out of the crowd and slashed a blade at Swinburne. The little man leaped back with a shriek. Gooch once again put his supplementary limbs to good use, thrusting one out to deflect the weapon. Burton reached over his shoulder, drew his *khopesh*, and sliced it down, straight through the machine's elbow.

"Aaah!" it cried out. "My head!"

"Head?" Swinburne queried.

"My mind is a furnace! Help me!"

Drawing back its remaining arm, the contraption threw a punch toward Burton's face. The explorer dodged to the side and swiped again with his blade, cutting through the thin neck. The clockwork man toppled backward and fell into the arms of Detective Inspector Trounce as he emerged from the crowd. The Yard man pushed it aside and, as it clanked to the ground, hailed his friends. He was panting, a thick smear of soot marked the left side of his face, and his bottom lip was bleeding, caking his untidy beard with gore. He reached out and shook Burton's hand. "By Jove! What a state you're in."

"You're a fine one to talk," Swinburne noted.

"The inner man is even more battered than the outer," Burton admitted. He offered a grim smile. "But the principal enemy is defeated. Now we just have to clean up the mess. What's the state of play?"

He gestured for his companions to follow him away from Grindlays and a little way along the street to where the savage heat was more endurable. As they walked, skirting the battling mob, Trounce shouted his report.

"Humph! It was even easier to gather supporters than I'd anticipated. Slaughter, Spearing, and Honesty had already done most of the footwork. In my estimation, at least two-thirds of the Force is in open defiance of Chief Commissioner Mayne. I have little doubt he'll try to call in the army to oppose us but, frankly, I don't think he'll get the response he expects. So for now, at least, we only have the clockwork men to deal with. The Special Patrol Group machines are showing no constraint. The others, the automated aristocrats, appear to have gone dangerously insane. They're babbling nonsense and attacking everyone left, right, and centre. The fire seems to be heating up their brains."

"It's doing exactly that," Burton confirmed. "The black diamonds are being destroyed in the inferno. Their destruction is resonating with the silicates in the machines' babbages. They are literally losing their minds." He pulled his revolver from his belt and fired four shots over Trounce's shoulder. Behind the detective inspector, a brass figure staggered and fell to its knees. "No more Young England, William. It ends this night."

"Thank the Lord. Back to good old British values, hey?"

A tremendous roar drowned further conversation as the remainder of Grindlays Warehouse collapsed, sending an avalanche of bricks, glass, and masonry into the street. Men and machines fell beneath it.

"Into the fray," Burton announced, and led his companions into the brawling mass.

For the next few minutes, he was fully occupied. The crush was such that the *khopesh* was impossible to wield and the rifle too cumbersome to use, so he relied on his pistol despite, as he already knew, multiple bullets being required to fell the spring-driven foe.

He was battered by solid knuckles, bruised by truncheons—which, fortunately, like his blade, couldn't be swiped with any great force amid the tumult—and pricked by clumsily thrust rapiers, but, as his mental exhaustion eased, the strength of many Burtons started to flow into him, and he was overcome by a savage euphoria.

Covered from head to toe in blood, all pain forgotten and grinning ferociously, he drew on his knowledge of Thuggee wrestling techniques to snap piston-powered limbs and to forcibly twist canister heads from metal necks. He hammered the butt of his pistol into the sensory wires that projected from the base of blank expressionless faces. He pushed its barrel into the topmost of the machines' three facial openings and drilled hot lead into intricate, finely crafted brains.

He fought as if possessed and, at the back of his mind, it occurred to him that maybe he was, for there was a supernatural quality to the power that throbbed through his arteries, and he could sense that the Beetle was its source—and that strange rendition of a Burton was certainly something other than human, at least in the sense that humanity was currently understood.

At one point, he found himself fighting back-to-back with Gooch and drew the engineer's attention to a nearby wall against which the escapees from Grindlays were huddled. He hollered, "Get your people to safety, Daniel, or have them find some manner of weaponry and join the mêlée."

"They'll bloody well fight, or I'll have their hides. The clockwork men made slaves of us in that damned factory. There's a reckoning to be had."

"Then for pity's sake go to your colleagues and rouse their ire."

Gooch nodded and made off.

Burton uttered an expletive as a truncheon smacked into his shoulder. His pistol fell from numbed fingers. He dropped to one knee. A Special Patrol Group machine loomed over him.

"In the name of the king," it said, "I hereby sentence you to—"

With a loud clank, a bullet hole appeared in its face. It toppled sideways to reveal Swinburne standing behind it, his rifle raised, a whiff of smoke curling from its barrel.

Burton arched his eyebrows by way of thanks and clambered back to his feet. He saw that the crowd had somewhat thinned, so he drew his *khopesh* and tested its edge with the pad of his thumb.

Still sharp.

Swinburne grinned, reloaded, turned, took aim at another SPG unit, and sent a bullet at least a foot wide of his target. The projectile ricocheted from the back of a second clockwork man and went thudding into the head of a third. As the machine's babbage detonated, the poet lowered his weapon and shouted to Burton, "It's like billiards, Richard. The balls never go where I intend, but they somehow make good anyway."

"We're playing a rather more deadly game," Burton responded. "Don't pocket lead into one of our own."

He decapitated a police unit as it lunged at him. His attention was then caught by the familiar coat of arms emblazoned on a nearby brass man. The contraption had just pushed its blade through a constable's thigh and was poised to make a more fatal strike when Burton jumped forward, slammed into it, and knocked it to the ground. He banged the heel of his hand down onto the machine's slim sword, snapping the blade in half.

"Great heavens!" the machine objected. "How dare you!"

"My leg!" the policeman groaned.

Burton crouched down, sheathed his *khopesh*, and held his pistol to the machine's head. "Stay there, please, Mr. Hope. I'd like to converse for a moment." He looked up and called to Swinburne. "Algy, keep us covered, will you?"

"Rightio." Swinburne strode over and stood guard, weapon poised.

The constable moaned, hopping on one leg, and blinked at Burton. "Hello, sir. It's me, Khapoor. The ornithopter incident, if you recall."

"Hello there," Burton said. "Is it bad?"

"Through to the bone. I'll be off the cricket team for a while. Will you excuse me?"

"Of course."

Khapoor saluted and hobbled away.

"Why, you impertinent hound!" Thomas Henry Hope protested. "Who the devil do you think you are?"

Burton regarded the clockwork man. "I'm Sir Richard Francis Burton. We've met before, though at the time I was wearing a disguise and went by the name of Count Palladino."

"Of Brindisi? I remember the chap. You look nothing like him. Let me up, curse you!"

"You'll stay where you are, else I'll put a bullet through your babbage. As I say, I was disguised. I might add that you, also, were less than truthful about your identity. You presented yourself to me as Flywheel."

Hope held his hands in front of his face and appeared to examine them. "Babbage? By God, it's true, then? This isn't a nightmare?" He groaned. "You say your name is Burton? Tell me, man, why am I inside this machine? Why do my thoughts burn me so?"

"You've been under the sway of a powerful clairvoyant influence. It affected your judgement. I just removed it."

"Influence? Whose influence? What are you talking about? Oh God! Oh God! The fire is inside me. Make the pain stop!"

Burton watched with pity as the automated aristocrat writhed and began to thrash its limbs, crying out in apparent agony.

"I'll kill you," it howled. "I'll kill you all!"

Hope screamed. His fingers clamped around Burton's wrist.

Burton said, "Damn. I'm sorry," and pulled the trigger.

He rose and stepped back as the brass head blew apart.

"What got into him?" Swinburne asked. "Aside from your bullet, I mean."

"Orpheus did. Explanations later, Algy. I need to think it through. And right now we have more pressing matters to deal with."

More masonry and glass clattered into the street as a second warehouse folded. Flames rolled across the struggling throng. Burton and Swinburne shielded their faces with their arms. A wooden beam bounced past them, showering sparks, and thudded into an SPG unit and constable, sending both sprawling.

William Trounce emerged again from the roiling smoke. His left trouser leg had been torn completely away and the exposed limb was glistening with blood. He was limping and in obvious pain. He pointed at the sky and yelled, "What are they doing?"

Burton peered up at the two circling rotorships. The smaller—Lawless's vessel—was listing to one side and looked as if it might plummet to the ground at any moment. For a second, he thought three huge vultures were circling it, as if eager for it to die, but then a fourth bird launched itself from the side of the ship, and he realised they weren't vultures at all but men wearing mechanically operated wings.

"Bismillah!" he whispered, recalling that Lawless and his crew had been commissioned to give a public demonstration of the wings but had disappeared before the event. Now, there they were, flapping away from their ailing vessel.

As he watched, more men abandoned the ship and came gliding down toward Tooley Street. He experienced a moment of utter confusion as one of them swooped low and landed on his shoulder. Immediately, he realised the heat-warped air had played tricks with his vision, and it was Pox that had chosen him as a perch.

"Message from Edward fat head Burton," the bird squawked into his bleeding ear. "I'm sorry, Richard, I had to regain dribble-wit Disraeli's confidence. I'm afraid you bore the brunt of it, you nincompoop. At least it got you to where you needed to be. I knew something bigger than the scum-snorting prime minister was at work, and I had to follow his path to find out what. The stomach tumour was a cheap lie designed to hasten my transference into a babbage. It worked. The truth was revealed to me. I know what you faced, and I know, too, that you have won the day. Loathsome hugger-mugger! Moron! The diamonds will soon be gone from our world, and the empire will be secure. Unfortunately, with their destruction, my demise is assured. I shall make my departure a useful one. Rigby is holed up in the tower. Find him and kill him. Richard, whichever bum-clenching version of yourself you are, you are above all else my brother. Of that, I am extraordinarily proud. Message ends. Arse tickler."

It was the longest message Burton had ever heard Pox deliver, and every single word of it, including the extraneous insults, he knew he would remember forever.

He swallowed and stared up as the *Eurypyle*'s cannons continued to send barrage after barrage into the side of the other rotorship. He saw the observation deck, where he'd sat with Swinburne, Trounce, and the Beetle, explode into a cloud of powdered glass. He saw struts, panels, and pylons shattering and flying to pieces. He saw shredded material trailing from the sagging dirigible.

With smoke spewing out of it, the smaller ship suddenly turned and accelerated toward the other machine.

Unaware of his own actions, Burton reached out, dug his fingers into Swinburne's arm, and croaked, "Pox, message for Edward Burton. Don't do it. Don't be a bloody fool. Message ends."

The parakeet clicked its beak. "Message undelivered."

Edward isn't human. The bird doesn't know how to locate a machine, even if it was just sent here by it.

Lawless's vessel had been called *Orpheus*—it still bore the word upon its side—but Burton couldn't think of it as that any more, and he felt it somehow appropriate when, as he watched, a cannonade tore the letters from its hull.

Nameless, disintegrating, abandoned by its crew, and steered by a dying mechanism of brass, the rotorship buried itself into the side of the *Eurypyle*.

Debris erupted outward. A resounding boom echoed across the city.

Locked together, spinning slowly, the burning vessels arced down through the night sky, angled out over the river, and disappeared from Burton's line of sight.

"Edward," he whispered.

Three gunshots sounded close to his ear. Pox screeched, "Cow dung!" bounded into the air, and flew off.

Burton twisted and saw Trounce kicking away an SPG unit. Its head was spitting flame. It detonated before it hit the ground.

The men with mechanical wings were now darting over the thoroughfare. One spotted Burton and his companions, made a tight turn, and flapped down, landing a few feet away. He ran to them, his wings automatically folding behind him.

It was the medic, McGarrigle. "I have my kit," he panted. "Shall I tend to your wounds? You look a state. Actually, I've never seen you otherwise, if you'll pardon the observation."

Burton flicked a hand dismissively. "It's accurate, unfortunately, and pardoned. I'm all right. You all got off the ship?"

"Poor old Pryce was killed. And Wenham, too. The minister—" He glanced up at the now empty sky. "I'm sorry. He remained aboard. Took control of her and—and—"

"We saw."

Another birdman landed. Nathaniel Lawless. He snapped at McGarrigle, "Get out of that harness," and began to unbuckle his own. He glanced up at Burton and Swinburne. "You two have to get into these." His eyes were brimming with the pain of a captain who'd lost his ship, but his tone was that of a military man—snappy, no nonsense. "The minister's orders."

"And do what with them?" Burton asked.

"Fly across to the tower. Kill that bastard Rigby."

The explorer eyed the wings dubiously. "We'll take the tunnel."

"Tunnel?"

"Near here. It runs under the bridge and connects with the chambers beneath the tower."

"It will be defended. Take the wings."

They were interrupted by a brass man, wearing a top hat and a purple cravat, who rushed at them brandishing the sheath of a swordstick in one hand and its blade in the other.

"Get me out!" it shouted. "I don't want to be in here. It hurts. It hurts. Give me my body back or, by God, I'll run you all through."

Burton sighed, spun sideways to avoid the rapier while simultaneously drawing his *khopesh*, and, completing a full turn, sliced his weapon horizontally.

Headless, the clockwork man kept running, barged through the battling mob, crossed the pavement, and collapsed beside a blazing building.

Trounce said to Burton, "I think we're besting them, but the confounded fire is spreading fast. I'm of a mind to separate my forces and have them hold off the street at either end. We'll try to keep the enemy hemmed in while the London Fire Engine Establishment gets to work. Otherwise, I fear the whole of Southwark could ignite." He gave Burton a sideways look. "My point is—humph!—no offence meant, but I can manage this without you. You have a score to settle. Attend to it."

Lawless moved behind the explorer, divested him of his rifle and sword, and lowered the wings' shoulder hooks onto him. Burton hesitated for a second then took up the harness's belt, buckled it, and gave attention to the other straps and fastenings.

McGarrigle assisted Swinburne.

"The method of control?" Burton asked.

Lawless clicked two bars into place. They projected forward from just above Burton's waist.

"Rest your arms on these and wrap your hands around the grips at their ends."

Following the directive, Burton found that his fingers slid naturally over trigger-like levers, four on each side. Lawless rapidly explained their function then stood back while, without leaving the ground, Burton and Swinburne practiced flapping. While they were thus engaged, Trounce and McGarrigle kept clockwork men at bay with well-placed pistol shots.

The rest of Lawless's crew started to land nearby, among them Shyamji Bhatti.

"No!" the airman yelled at them. "Back up! Shoot at the metal men from above!"

They obeyed his command.

Lawless watched them for a moment then turned his grey eyes to Burton. "That's all the training you need. The contrivances practically fly by themselves. Get going before the cur escapes."

The explorer nodded. He reloaded his pistol and, while doing so, addressed Trounce. "I can't help but feel I'm abandoning you."

"Oh, balderdash! The battle is almost won. As far as I can see, the automated aristocrats are dropping dead of their own accord, and we out-number the Special Patrol Group."

Burton scanned the crowd and noticed, for the first time, that many of the brass men, rather than fighting, were clutching their heads, some falling to their knees, others twitching on the ground.

He accepted extra ammunition from the detective inspector, pock-eted it, and murmured, "Rigby, then."

He put his arms on the bars and squeezed the appropriate triggers. Trounce hastily retreated from the thrashing wings. Burton felt the ground drop away from his feet and heard Swinburne squealing with excitement. The two men flapped upward then spread their wings and allowed the searing heat to push them with breathtaking rapidity to a greater altitude. Red-hot embers rose all around them. Burton gazed down at Southwark. The fire, as Trounce had feared, was spreading, and the whole district was in obvious peril. Until the Special Patrol Group machines were defeated, the London Fire Engine Establishment wouldn't be able to tackle the heart of the inferno.

Rising above the smoke, Burton spotted a second blaze, this on the opposite side of the river. He angled his wings, soared out over the water, and realised what it was. Edward had somehow managed to collide with the *Eurypyle* in such a manner as to ensure the two wrecked ships plummeted out of the sky directly onto the Tower of London. Such a calculation, Burton pondered, would have been beyond even Edward's ability under normal circumstances. However, with a babbage at his mind's disposal, speed, weight, and trajectory had been deter-mined accurately.

The ancient castle, built to endure the most powerful of medieval siege weapons, had not fully withstood the impact of the two massive flying machines. Its defensive walls in the southeastern corner had been knocked inward, and their rubble was strewn across the grounds, marking a broad trail to the keep against which a flaming hulk of indistinguishable form—a snarled mass of metal, wood, and other materials—had slammed with such force that, though the bulk of the White Tower remained unscathed, its corner turret had collapsed, falling onto and through the wooden roof.

My brother is down there. Dead.

He pushed that fact aside to be dealt with later.

The two men crossed the water.

The night air was mild but felt cool as it flowed across the scorched skin of Burton's face. He listened to the hissing of the miniature furnace strapped to his back, the vigorous chugging of the tiny but powerful steam engine, and contemplated the Formby coal he'd been told about, a single lump of which could burn for twenty times as long as untreated coal, giving off an incredibly intense heat.

He flapped closer to Swinburne, surprised at the ease with which he performed the manoeuvre, and called across to him, "Something occurs to me."

"That we should never have left the Slug and Lettuce?" Swinburne suggested.

"Aye, you're not far wrong there, my friend. But no. I was considering these wings and the other machinery we've seen in this world. You know, I'm half-convinced that none of it would work in our own."

Swinburne yelped. "And you choose to divulge this while we're strapped into the contraptions and hanging two hundred feet in the air?"

Burton ignored the protest. "We've learned that the material world is the stuff of our own imaginations. If that's the case, then so too, surely, are the rules which dictate how that world functions—the laws of physics, for example. And since there are multiple renditions of the world, might not each one include slight variations in the rules?"

"It's an utterly marvellous and thoroughly intriguing proposition," Swinburne countered, "presented under the most ridiculous of circumstances and at the most inopportune of moments. Next time you have a theory, I'll certainly be keen to hear it, but spoken, perhaps, across a table in the lounge of a gentlemen's club rather than yelled through space high over the River bloody Thames, you dolt!"

Burton gave a bark of laughter and immediately felt astounded that such a sound had emerged from his mouth at such a time.

Out of nowhere, he was suddenly filled with a sense of completeness. The other Burtons—including the Beetle—were a part of him, but they felt like echoes. Their memories were starting to fade. Trieste was still there, Isabel was still there, but their significance had dwindled. Attachments, attitudes, and issues that once mattered no longer did. *The Secret Garden* had gone up in flames, and he didn't care.

This was his life now.

There remained just one loose end to tie.

He descended toward the White Tower, started to circle it, and saw that the burning wreckage blocked its entrance. There was a scattering of people in the grounds. They looked confused and indecisive. A few were attempting the clear a path to the door, but the fire was holding them back.

Rigby, Burton hoped, was trapped inside.

Something on the building's roof flashed brightly, and a projectile screamed past his head. A detonation sounded. Another flash and suddenly his left wing collapsed.

"They're shooting at us!" Swinburne screeched.

Burton, spinning wildly, hurtled down onto the keep's roof, hit it so hard the wind was knocked out of him, and rolled uncontrollably in a tangle of cloth and snapping wing spars. He thudded into the battlements and lay still. With blurred vision, he saw a white-haired figure standing at a mounted cannon.

Swinburne flapped past. "It's the confounded butterfly collector!"

The gun fired.

The poet shrieked, soared upward, banked sharply, and fell toward the shootist feet first.

"You'll not pin my wings!"

His heels thumped into the man's chest, sending him sprawling. The poet swooped up a little before dropping and landing. His wings folded behind him. He drew his revolver, stepped to the lepidopterist, examined him, and announced, "Knocked cold. Are you all right, Richard?"

Burton groaned and pushed away pieces of torn wing. "I think I have abrasions on my lacerated bruises." He climbed unsteadily to his feet, stood swaying, then unbuckled his harness and shrugged out of it. His shirt hung off him in tatters.

Swinburne divested himself of his wings and joined the explorer. They looked across the river. Southwark was a raging furnace. A cloud of black smoke was boiling up from it and blowing eastward.

"My hat!" Swinburne said. "If the fire brigade can't get that under control, we'll have the Great Fire of London all over again."

Burton pointed to where large vehicles could be seen gathering to the west of the blaze. "There was no fire service in 1666. Ours is well-trained, well-equipped, and already getting to work. Two years ago, they quelled the conflagration that destroyed the East End. I have faith they'll triumph again on this occasion."

He looked up. Overhead, the sky was clear. The police rotorships that had previously harassed Lawless's vessel were gone. Those policemen who'd obeyed Chief Commissioner Mayne had either swapped sides or made themselves scarce. Burton wondered whether the dearth of constables on the city's streets had been noticed. He thought this night would likely be counted a good one for petty criminals—but a bad one for major villains.

He drew his revolver.

"The colonel is mine. Don't forget it."

Swinburne shrugged. "As you say. I'll take Disraeli if he's still alive. He insulted my poetry."

They moved closer to the hole in the roof. The turret's rubble had crashed through, plunged past the third-storey gallery that encircled the chapel of St. John, and was now piled on the chapel's second-storey floor. It had also displaced one end of a thick rafter, causing it to swing down onto the gallery, where it had jammed fast, bridging the hole from the roof down to the narrow stone walkway.

The poet waved his pistol at it. "If we watch our footing, keep our balance, and the joist holds, that's our way in."

"And if a single one of those three *ifs* turns into a *but*, we fall to our deaths."

"Yes. Thrilling, isn't it?"

"Horribly."

Burton gingerly approached the splintered edge of the gap, testing every step, afraid the roof would give way beneath him. He squatted at the precipice, braced himself with his hands, and lowered a leg to the sloping beam. After thumping his heel into it a few times, he announced, "It feels stable enough."

"Hoorah!"

Swinburne jumped past, landed with one foot in front of the other on the rafter, stood wobbling for a moment, and started downward with his arms extended for balance.

Burton clenched his teeth and swallowed hard.

Pausing, the poet turned and whispered, "Careful! I hear voices."

The explorer slapped a hand to his forehead. "Just move, confound you!"

"It's steep," Swinburne observed. "Tricky."

He wheeled around, swayed, stood on one foot and stuck out the other, waved his arms, regained his equilibrium, continued on down, and hopped onto the gallery. Waving at Burton, he grinned and gestured for him to follow.

Burton muttered the choicest of the many epithets he'd learned in India, Arabia, and Africa before easing down onto the thick wooden strut. He began to inch forward. Far beneath, he could hear voices but dared not look down. Someone shouted, "Every single document that bears my name, do you understand? All of them! Burned! Immediately!"

The rafter emitted a loud creak.

Burton froze.

Swinburne suddenly pressed himself against the wall beside the arched doorway and put his finger to his lips.

A short, rotund, and heavily bearded individual stepped into view, saw Burton, jerked to a halt, and exclaimed, "What the devil are you doing up there? You'll fall to your death, man!"

"I sincerely hope not," Burton replied. "Will you tell me what's happening? It'll take my mind off the drop while I work my way down."

"Happening?" the man said. "We're defeated, that's what's happening."

Burton resumed his slow descent. He focused on the man's words and tried to ignore the space into which he could topple at any moment.

"The prime minister is burbling nonsense," the other said. "He's lost his mind. That Rigby fellow has taken charge. He expects us to fight. Fight! I'm George Ward Hunt, Chancellor of the Exchequer, for pity's sake, not a blessed soldier! Take my advice and steer clear of him. He'll shoot you dead on the spot if he suspects any betrayal. Find anything with your signature on it and burn it. Erase every indication of your involvement, if you can, then try to make your escape with the rest of us when we get the door clear."

Burton neared the end of the rafter. Swinburne, behind the newcomer, watched him while remaining silent.

The explorer said, "To be truthful, there's not much left of me to burn."

"Really? What department are you from? Are you one of the clerks? I don't recognise you."

Burton reached the gallery and jumped onto it. He breathed a sigh of relief and bent, resting his hands above his knees, breathing heavily.

"And for that matter," the man continued, with a hint of suspicion creeping into his voice, "why were you on the roof? You look all banged up. A terrible mess. All that blood! Caught up in the crash, were you?"

Straightening, Burton said, "Where did you say Rigby was?"

"I didn't. He's downstairs, ranting and raving in the ministerial office. I say, look here, will you explain yourself, please? I'm sorry, but the rebels could try to invade the castle at any moment, and if you turned out to be one of them, well, I'd be red in the face, to say the least."

"It would be rather embarrassing," Burton conceded. "But a sharp thwack on the head with a pistol should provide you with an excuse in the event of any incriminations."

"Eh? What's that you said?"

Swinburne stepped forward and obliged.

Burton caught the man and carefully lowered him to the floor. "It appears that Disraeli's subordinates are rather too preoccupied with saving their own skins to bother us."

"To a politician," Swinburne observed, "not a single thing matters more than his own survival. They discard principles like a sinking balloonist discharges ballast."

Moving away from the prone figure, they passed through the doorway, and entered a long corridor that ran along the inside of the tower's east wall to the northeastern corner, where it ended at the top of a stairwell. To his chagrin, Burton saw that the steps went up as well as down, ascending to the roof. There'd been no need to risk the rafter.

Archways on their left opened into a large chamber with the same dimensions as the government office below and the Tool Room on the ground floor. It was crammed with wardrobes, chests of drawers, and unmade beds. The smell of burning paper pervaded the air.

There were clockwork men present, five prostrated and motionless, three standing still, and one banging its dented head repeatedly against the wall while mumbling to itself. Burton, while keeping an eye on the other machines, approached it and listened.

"Going to hear now the linen . . . mineral . . . are no grandfathers in any inspired . . . else we can switch . . . perfectly raw . . . tomorrow . . . thereby to grant glass to . . . butler and laughter for my . . . in dried gatherings."

He was reminded of his experience in the future when he'd witnessed his own mind being transferred from the Brunel mechanism into the body of the Beetle.

"What's it gibbering about?" Swinburne asked.

"This was an aristocrat," Burton replied, "but the structure of the silicates into which his mind was embedded is breaking down. He's losing his ability to process language. Soon, he'll die."

He reached out, pulled a sheathed swordstick from the contraption's belt, slipped it into his own, then turned and surveyed the three upright brass men. "My presumption is that these three differ from the ordinary type of machine only in that they were fitted with the aether-communications component, like Sprocket and Grumbles. That has now been disabled. They're awaiting orders but can't receive any."

"So they pose no further threat?"

"Not by the looks of it, and they'll wind down in due course. I'll wager that Trounce and his people are battling only the SPG units by now.

Those machines will be acting on their last commands but can't be given any new ones, except verbally, which will put them at a disadvantage."

He paced to a door, quietly opened it a crack, and peered into the next room, which was filled with filing cabinets. Men were frantically sorting through papers and throwing bundles of them into a large brazier positioned near an arrow loop. Most of the smoke was streaming out through the tall, narrow opening but, nevertheless, the atmosphere of the chamber was thick with it.

Pushing the portal shut, he jerked his chin to indicate the direction they'd come. "Back into the corridor. The stairs will take us down to the office. When we get there, I'll confront Rigby. If there's anyone else present, you keep them covered with your pistol."

"Lay on, Macduff, and damned be him that first cries, 'Hold, enough!'"

"Macbeth. Appropriate. I fear the colonel might have that warrior's overblown ambitions."

They exited, walked rapidly to the head of the stairs, and started down. After a few steps, they heard voices raised in argument. Initially, they couldn't discern the words, but as they came closer to the second storey, they recognised the clipped and harsh tones of Rigby.

"You'll stand fast, you quivering milksop, or I'll bloody well shoot you myself."

"What's the use?" sounded the desperate reply. "There's nothing left. The government is in utter disarray."

"Half the ministers are dead or insane," another added. "There's no leadership."

"You'll take my orders, damn you!" Rigby roared.

"You're not even an elected member!"

"This is my authority!" A gunshot echoed up the stairwell.

People screamed and cried out in shocked protest.

With Swinburne at his back, Burton reached the access door and strode out into the room to which his brother had brought him previously. It was in chaos, with papers scattered everywhere, desks shoved aside, and government men standing indecisively, their eyes fixed on Rigby, who was in the middle of the chamber with one arm extended, a pistol in his hand.

A dead man was stretched out on the floor in front of him, blood oozing from a hole in his head.

Automated aristocrats were slumped here and there, most completely immobile, others twitching slightly.

At the far end of the chamber, the screen that sectioned off the prime minister's office had been knocked down. Disraeli was stretched out over his desk.

In an instant, Burton registered the scene. He sent a shot hissing past Rigby's head and bellowed, "Drop your weapon, Colonel, or I'll put one in your heart."

Rigby swung around and saw the newcomers. He hesitated, gazed at the end of Burton's smoking revolver, which was aimed unerringly at him, then dropped his own.

"Kick it away," Burton commanded.

The order was obeyed.

"You look dead on your feet," Rigby commented. "Are you having a bad day?"

"It'll soon be better than yours."

Burton gestured toward the left side of the room and, raising his voice, said, "Everyone but Rigby up against that wall. At once! If anyone tries anything, my companion will shoot to disable, but I warn you, he's a rotten shot and may kill you by mistake."

"Steady on," Swinburne murmured.

The men did as they were told.

"Cowards!" Rigby hissed. "These are enemies of the government. Rush them!"

They looked away from him and stood sullenly, crossing their arms or chewing their fingernails.

Burton stalked forward. "It's over, Rigby. Young England was a sham. A synthetic brain deceived and manipulated you. Had I not intervened, existence as you know it would have ended."

"Hooray for you," Rigby sneered. "Shall I commission a statue of you to mark the empire's everlasting gratitude? Perhaps it could supplant Nelson atop his column? Would that be tribute enough for your bloated self-esteem?"

"The pot calls the kettle black. You are, at least, consistent in your misjudgements. In only one matter have you been correct."

Rigby frowned. "Is that so? And to what matter do you refer?"

"To that of my identity. As you suspected, I am not the Burton who departed for the future. My origin lies in an alternate history to this. There, I lived my life to its natural conclusion before being snatched from my deathbed, restored to youth, and brought here."

"I see. For what purpose?"

"That need not concern you. What should, is that the mistreatment I recently suffered at your hands broke me."

"How gratifying."

"I'm inclined to agree. You did me a great favour."

Rigby looked puzzled. He said nothing and waited for Burton to continue.

"You demolished certain mental barriers in me and thus allowed the recollections of every Burton from every iteration of history to flood past them. In those memories, I discovered that, in every version of the world, for no good reason aside from your overweening vanity, you have worked assiduously to tarnish my reputation. You have spread malicious rumours about me. You set John Speke against me and so entangled my African expedition in bureaucratic red tape that I was financially ruined."

Rigby raised his eyebrows. "Well, I'm bound to say, the Rigbys of those other histories sound like marvellous fellows." He curled his hands into fists and knocked his knuckles together. "Shall I remind you that you've already had an opportunity to revenge yourself but made a thoroughly pitiful show of it?"

"I was in no fit state, as well you know."

Giving a derisive snort, Rigby looked Burton up and down. "And now?"

"Physically, I'm all done in."

"So I see. The gun in your hand is shaking. You'd do well to lay it aside and surrender yourself."

"I've already surrendered myself, though not in the manner you would wish. As for my revolver, I shall gladly oblige." Burton smiled. It was not a pleasant sight. He stepped back and passed his weapon to Swinburne. "A final round, Colonel, but this time I shall dictate the terms.

You have my swordstick in your belt. On every occasion I've seen you use it, you've done so rather clumsily. I therefore mean to give you a lesson in swordplay before I kill you."

He drew the rapier from the cane he'd appropriated.

Rigby folded his arms across his chest, met Burton's eyes, held them, and didn't move.

The explorer strode forward. He flicked his blade. Two deep gashes appeared on Rigby's face, one on each cheek, vertical and perfectly symmetrical. Blood beaded out, gathered, and dripped before Rigby even felt the wounds. He blinked, stepped back, unhooked his arms, and put his fingers to his face.

Casually, Burton took another pace and made an almost graceful gesture. The colonel's jacket was suddenly reduced to ribbons.

"Defend yourself or by God I'll carve you up inch by inch like meat on a butcher's block."

Rigby paled. He moved backward, pulled off the remains of his garment, and rolled up his shirtsleeves.

"Very well. Have it your way. But be warned, I'm not the amateur you take me for. I trained under Monsieur Paul Sauveterre in Paris."

Sliding the silver-handled rapier from its scabbard, he faced Burton side-on and adopted the classic fencing pose.

"Sauveterre is a fine tutor," Burton said. "Though rather hidebound by tradition. *En garde.*"

They touched sword tips.

For half a minute, no one moved, and a taut silence gripped the room. It was broken by Disraeli, who twitched and muttered, "They will call it Sanctum . . . terrible . . . magicians . . . and the whisper . . . will come in the midst of war . . . we are noticed . . . we are noticed."

Rigby lunged. His blade was parried with ease. A cut opened on his forearm. He attempted a *froissement*—sliding his blade along Burton's to displace it before jabbing—but his opponent's reflexes brought a counter measure into play with such rapidity that the colonel had no awareness of what had happened until he disengaged, stepped back, and felt a wet warmth on his chest. He looked down. His shirt was hanging open and a horizontal laceration scored his breast.

Snarling, he renewed his attack.

For the next few minutes, there was no sound in the room but for the *tick tick tick* of crossing blades. Not once was Burton touched but for Rigby it was a different story; as the minutes passed, his clothes became ever more tattered and bloodstained as shallow cut after shallow cut cleaved his skin. Soon, his heavy breathing was added to the clink of clashing metal.

Slowly, he retreated from Burton's punishing, blurring point, until he bumped against a desk, sidled around it, slipped his free hand under its corner, and, with a desperate heave, upturned it, sending it crashing into the explorer.

Knocked to the floor, Burton scrambled backward as his opponent jumped forward and stabbed down at him.

"Stop!" Swinburne shouted, brandishing his two pistols. "I'll shoot you dead on the spot, Rigby!"

"Algy, don't!" Burton yelled.

He rolled aside, parried the other's blade, regained his feet, and, as he did so, slashed upward. Rigby's head jerked back and blood sprayed.

"Bastard!" he spat.

"That weapon you're holding belongs to me," Burton said.

The left side of Rigby's face was hanging open, exposing all the teeth along the side of his jaw. When he spoke, red gore foamed onto his chin.

"Take it from me."

"I intend to."

They resumed their duel.

The floor around them became slippery with the colonel's blood. His respiration grew ever more laboured, and his throat rattled unpleasantly. Again and again, the explorer's point evaded his defence and pricked his skin.

Burton was merciless.

"This next stratagem," he said in a casual tone, "is one I invented myself. I call it the *une-deux*."

His rapier hooked around Rigby's and jerked it out of his hand with such force that the colonel cried out in pain and was left clutching his wrist while his sword clattered away over the floor.

Without taking his eyes off his adversary, Burton walked over to it and picked it up. He tossed the blade he'd been using to the other man. "Here, I'll not leave you unarmed."

Rigby clumsily caught it and watched as Burton turned his back on him and approached the onlookers.

"Gentlemen, may I request a handkerchief?"

Six of the gathered government officials immediately proffered squares of cotton while the rest fumbled in their pockets.

Burton took one, said, "Thank you," and, without turning around, used it to wipe Rigby's blood from the rapier's panther-headed grip.

He saw the fellow from whom he'd taken the handkerchief look past him. He heard Swinburne utter a cry of alarm. He wheeled, knocked aside Rigby's point with his arm, and kicked him with savage force between the legs.

The colonel crumpled to the floor, curled up, and vomited.

"I owed you that one. Now get up, you craven hound. We haven't finished."

"I have," Rigby croaked. "I'll be your plaything no more."

Bending, Burton pulled the scabbard from the other's belt and put it onto a table. He grabbed the colonel by the collar and dragged him across the floor to the middle of the room. Rigby's ragged shirt ripped and was pulled away. Burton cast it aside and started to walk around the prone man.

"Do you know, Rigby, that among the memories of the other Burtons, I have those of the one who killed Spring Heeled Jack, otherwise known as Edward Oxford? He'd been terrorising London for decades, but by the time Burton—I might as well say 'I'—caught up with him, he'd been captured and was strapped to a trolley on a rotorship. He was insane, pathetic, a man to be pitied, but still dangerous. I had no choice but to end his life. I couldn't allow his further interference with time. So I took hold of his head, and he looked up at me and asked if I was going to execute him in cold blood. I answered, 'Whatever is necessary.' I felt nothing when I broke his neck. No emotion at all."

He pushed his blade through Rigby's right calf then withdrew it.

The colonel yelled.

"I'm in that exact state now. I want you to properly comprehend. This is not revenge. This is no longer anger or hatred or retribution."

He placed his point against the other's left bicep, slid it in, and extracted it.

Rigby screamed.

"If there's any emotion in me at all right now, it is curiosity. I wonder how deep your arrogance runs. I'm inquisitive to know how much pain you can withstand before your hubris fails you."

He sliced off Rigby's right ear.

In an unsteady tone, Swinburne said, "Richard, don't you think you're—"

"Be quiet, Algy," Burton snapped. "I'm busy."

Rigby rolled onto his hands and knees and started to crawl away, leaving a trail of blood behind him.

Burton looked up as Disraeli suddenly straightened in his chair and cried out, "The colonies!" before toppling onto the floor with a loud clang. He kicked his legs then lay still.

"Have mercy," Rigby whispered.

"No, sir. No. No mercy and no more concessions to curiosity. I must do what is necessary."

He placed his sword tip between the colonel's shoulder blades.

Hoarsely, Rigby whispered, "Please. At least allow me to turn and take it in the chest. Let me die with the face of my enemy imprinted on my eyes."

"I think not."

Burton pressed steel through flesh until he felt its tip touch the floor.

THE AFTERMATH AND THE STARS

IN MEMORIAM
James Braidwood, superintendent of the London Fire Engine Establishment.
Led his men valiantly against the Tooley Street fire on Saturday, 22nd June, 1861.
Lost his life while assisting one of his fire fighters, when the front section of a
warehouse collapsed on top of him, killing him instantly.

The Great Fire of Tooley Street burned for two weeks, and the area was, two months later, still smouldering. Its heat was matched by the tempers that flared in Parliament. Politicians who'd supported Young England were rounded up and condemned in language of such ferocity that careers were forever ruined. George Ward Hunt, who'd been due for conversion the day after Swinburne knocked him cold and Burton put an end to the premier's scheme, told a journalist that, after a humiliating face off with Gladstone, he felt as if he'd been savaged by a lion. The comment was widely reported, and a week later, as a voice, the newspapers began to refer to William Gladstone as "The Lion of the Empire." With typical dissimulation and hypocrisy, all the rags appeared to have forgotten they'd ever offered support to Disraeli and now, as Swinburne observed, "treated old Gladbags as if he were our own Alexander the Great."

The Conservative Party was in utter ruins and had conceded power to the Liberals pending a proper election. Gladstone, as acting prime minister, was presenting policy after policy for enactment should he be voted into power—which he certainly would be—each of which promised to radically alter the political landscape of the British Empire. Most notably, he wanted to abolish the House of Lords, change inherited peerages to life peerages, decentralise power, concede self-rule to India, end the trade embargoes that were strangling China, and offer the vacant British throne—the king had died along with all the other mechanised men—to His Royal Highness Prince Albert, though the role of the monarch would be reduced to the purely symbolic.

His proposals were being met with widespread approval, and such trust was extended to the Lion that, even in his temporary role, he was able make a great many lesser changes without any opposition at all. These included a wide-ranging examination of the empire's various institutions and the removal of personnel who'd misguidedly given support to Young England. Chief Commissioner Mayne of Scotland Yard was a victim of this cull, and his role was given to a very, very surprised William Trounce.

That worthy individual was currently kicking his bowler hat around Sir Richard Francis Burton's study.

"Chief Commissioner, by Jove! Chief Commissioner! I can hardly believe it!"

"You deserve it," Burton said. "For crying out loud, sit down, will you? You're wearing my floorboards thin."

Swinburne, twitching away in the armchair opposite to Burton's, added, "Mrs. Angell will have your hide. Look at the path you've ploughed through the fireside rug."

Trounce gave his hat a final passionate kick and uttered a cry of dismay as it bounced off the side of the bureau and went spinning out of the open window.

"Sniffling clot!" Pox cawed.

"Humph! I need a new one, anyway."

"Perhaps you should have one cast in iron," Swinburne suggested.

Trounce pulled a chair over, joined them in front of the fireplace, and repeated, "Chief Commissioner, by Jove!"

"It's really not so incredible," Burton observed. "Your service to the empire has been exemplary."

Trounce smoothed his moustache with a forefinger then leaned forward and said in a conspiratorial tone, "Perhaps, but it wasn't all me, was it? I'm not only being rewarded for my part in Dizzy's downfall but also for what that—that *other* Trounce did during the El Yezdi and Discontinued Man affairs."

"And perhaps for the Spring Heeled Jack, Clockwork Man, and Mountains of the Moon cases, too," Burton said. "What of it? Those other Trounces are all variants of you. They acted exactly as you would have done if placed in the same circumstances. Cigar?"

Trounce took the proffered smoke. "I'm not sure I'm up to it. Um—I refer to the job, not the cigar. Much obliged. But I mean to say, Chief Commissioner! Bless my soul!"

Swinburne threw up his hands. "Oh stop it, you silly old duffer. There's no man more capable. You'll be bringing a whole lifetime's experience to the job. Multiple lifetimes."

The Yard man accepted a light from Burton, drew on the cigar, leaned back, and squinted thoughtfully through the blue fumes.

"Humph! About that. It all came back to me during our incarceration in the tower. Every detail. I can now clearly recall my former life, my dying on the pavement in 1901, and our subsequent session at the Slug and Lettuce. Yet, somehow, it all makes sense to me. The contradictions aren't one jot as confusing as they should be."

Swinburne nodded. "It's the same for me. I even know exactly what it feels like to be a sentient jungle. Surprisingly, that knowledge hasn't sent me loopy."

"I wouldn't be so certain of that," Trounce countered.

The poet's right arm spasmed upward.

Burton reached to the occasional table beside his chair, took up a decanter, and poured a brandy, which he handed to Trounce. He quirked an eyebrow at Swinburne, but the poet shook his head and instead reached for a coffee pot that Mrs. Angell had earlier provided.

"You're really off the stuff?" Burton asked him.

"Great heavens, not at all! I intend to get thoroughly sozzled when the occasion warrants it. Don't worry, I shall do my bit toward the upkeep of the Cannibal Club's disreputable reputation. But I also intend long bouts of sobriety that I might write with a clear mind."

"Will wonders never cease?" Trounce enquired.

Burton provided himself a tipple and sipped at it thoughtfully. "One wonder, perhaps, has. Do you both sense it? Some sort of—I don't know—*consolidation*? The feeling that the whole Spring Heeled Jack affair, and all of its consequences, is done with?"

"Yes," Swinburne agreed. "I have that sensation."

"And I," Trounce said. He cocked a thumb at the window through which his hat had vanished. "It's out there, too. The world feels different."

"Because the diamonds are gone?" Burton suggested.

Trounce shook his head. "We haven't confirmed that and won't be able to until the ash has cooled sufficiently that we might rake it through."

"You'll not find them," Burton insisted. "I know it. I don't have their weight on my mind any more. The tremendous heat destroyed them. They went up in a puff of carbon dioxide."

"I daresay you're right, and the suggestion is supported by the cessation of clairvoyant fatalities."

"The cessation of clairvoyant fatalities," Swinburne echoed. He laughed. "What an outré combination of words. I shall have to build a poem around them." He stared into his coffee and quietly added, "It's all so peculiar."

"This world?" Burton asked.

The poet nodded. "Having lived a lifetime in the other one, I feel oddly detached from this. An observer."

"I've always felt that, even in the history we came from." Burton took a sip from his glass. "The slight estrangement we feel may be useful. It will keep us levelheaded should we be faced with further situations of an uncanny nature. I'm assuming—forgive me for doing so—that you'll both continue to assist me in my role of king's agent?"

"You've been reinstated?" Trounce asked.

"Yes. As a matter of fact, I already have my first commission."

The newly appointed Chief Commissioner slapped his hand to his forehead and looked horrified. "More strange affairs and curious cases! Is there no rest?"

Burton chuckled. "You can relax, old fellow. It's a straightforward business that I can deal with on my own. It'll take me out of the country for a while, and I'm glad of that, for I need some respite from the clamour of London."

"To where?"

Burton leaned back in his chair and stretched out his legs. Fidget, at his feet, lifted his head and repositioned it so that his jowls were resting across the explorer's ankles. The basset hound gave a small sigh of satisfaction.

"Perhaps you'll recall that the island of Fernando Po, off the west coast of Africa, has twice been significant in my life—or, I should say—in my *lives*. In the history we came from, I was consul there for three unhappy years, a role that commenced, as a matter of fact, at around this date. My predecessor in *this* history, two years ago, fought the madman Aleister Crowley, who crossed over from another time stream through a fold in the fabric of reality. That crease was located on Fernando Po. It has been reported that, since then, the island has been subjected to ferocious electrical storms. Now it so happens that, on the direct opposite side of the globe from Fernando Po, in the Melanesian Sea, there is an isle of equivalent land mass named Koluwai. Seamen who've travelled the region have reported that it, too, has suffered similar atmospheric disturbances these two years past. Mr. Faraday has postulated that Crowley's fold is still active and pierces through the planet in a straight line from one side to the other. I am to visit both islands to assess whether any danger is posed by the phenomenon."

He paused while Swinburne succumbed to a fitful crossing and uncrossing of his limbs then added, "My preparations are made, and I'll depart before the end of the week, so I shan't see either of you for a while. I expect you'll have whipped Scotland Yard back into shape by the time I return, William."

"Humph! I'll have Tom Honesty promoted to detective inspector and with his, Spearing, and Slaughter's assistance I should be able to get the house in order. Enforced resignations will be necessary, I fear. There were a fair few who gave their support to Rigby." He took a gulp of brandy and smacked his lips in appreciation. "I say, what of Monckton Milnes and the others?"

"Slop suckers!" Pox cawed.

Burton flicked his cigar stub into the fireplace. "Currently in India. Fortunately, they arrived there too late for the forced labour intended for them and are, instead, enjoying some rest and relaxation. Lawless is on his way to pick them up."

"He is? Has he a new vessel, then?"

"He's been given command of HMA *Sagittarius*."

There came a knock at the door, and upon Burton's hail, Bram Stoker entered. He was carrying a potted plant.

"A nipper just delivered this to the door, so he did, sir."

Burton took it, held it up, and examined it. Its stem, leaves, and five flowers were bright red.

"*Tempus flores.*" He leaned forward and handed it to Swinburne. "I think you'd better look after this, Algy. Consider it family."

Stoker said, "Is there anythin' you'll be a-wanting me for?"

"No Bram. Your time is your own unless Mrs. Angell needs you."

"Then I'll pop out again if ye don't mind. I'd like to take me new hat for a spin, so I would."

"You have a new hat?"

"Aye. I found it in the street not three minutes ago. A nice bowler—or it will be once I knock the dents out of it an' pad the band so it fits me."

"Bowler?" Trounce exclaimed. "By Jove, lad, that's—"

"Absolutely splendid!" Swinburne cried out. "A new hat for nothing! Well done, lad! I'm sure you'll look perfectly spiffy in it. What do you say, Mr. Fogg?"

"Humph!"

Burton chuckled, fished in his pocket for a coin, and flipped it to the youngster, who caught it adroitly. "Go buy yourself some butterscotch, lad."

With a grin and a salute, the boy departed.

Swinburne rocked back in his seat and squealed with laughter. Trounce glared at him.

"Serves you right," Burton told the chief commissioner.

Trounce, by way of changing the subject, cocked a thumb at the potted plant. "What's that about?"

"A parting gift from the Beetle."

"Parting? Then he's gone?"

"Unborn. I felt it."

"Unborn," Trounce muttered. "More mystical claptrap. Really, I shall never wrap my noggin around it. Nothing about the Beetle makes any sense."

Swinburne said, "It's all fairly straightforward, Pouncer. He was born in the future. He travelled to the past to enable the circumstances that culminated in his birth. Those circumstances all involved Richard. And Richard is the Beetle."

"Utter humbug from start to finish."

"Ah, there's the rub," Burton put in. "There was neither a start nor a finish, but rather a circle that turned in upon itself until it folded into the hole in its middle."

"Eh?"

"Edward Oxford caused a paradox. It was cancelled out by another paradox."

Swinburne kicked out a leg. "Perhaps existence possesses some manner of self-correcting mechanism."

Impatiently, Trounce waved away the speculation and brought the conversation back down to earth. "So, it's all done and dusted. What now? I mean the practicalities. There are still clockwork men stamping around the empire."

Burton stood up and stretched. He moved to the window and looked out. It was late afternoon, and the shadows were lengthening. "They're harmless, William. None have diamond or silicate components. They're just the standard type and, without Babbage to service them, they'll eventually either break down or be superseded. As for his other creations and his various blueprints, prototypes, and plans, they're being gathered together by Gooch and his people and will be destroyed."

"The sooner the better."

"September. We know that from what we were told in the future."

Trounce drained his glass, threw the remains of his cigar into the fire, and got to his feet. "Well, gentlemen, I'd like to say it's been a pleasure but, as usual, you've left me befuddled. I'll take my leave of you. I need to clear my head of all your nonsense and apply myself to problems I can understand—the restoration of law and order being the priority. Will you loan me a hat?"

"Take one from the stand," Burton said.

He and Swinburne bid their friend farewell. The explorer stayed at the window and watched as the Yard man left the house, crossed the street, walked to the corner, tipped his borrowed brim to Mr. Grub, and disappeared into Gloucester Place.

"A good chap, that."

"Donkey!" Pox contributed.

"They don't come any better," Swinburne agreed. "Of the three of us, I thought him the least likely to adapt. I was wrong."

"The recollection of our former lives is increasingly easy to set aside, don't you find? I think Trounce has rather a compartmentalised mind. For him, that other history has been placed in a chamber and the door shut upon it."

"And for you, Richard?"

"It's still rather a jumble, but travel always gives me clarity. My voyages to Fernando Po and Koluwai will do much to straighten me out." He turned. "Algy, will you accompany me on a little excursion to Limehouse? Now, I mean."

"The Beetle's factory?"

"Yes."

"But you said he's gone. Unborn."

"Quite so. I want to look out over the city, and there's no better vantage point."

"Ah. Very well."

Donning their hats and coats, they left the house, travelled by steam sphere to the Limehouse Canal, and arrived there just as the sun was setting. It was a mild and clear evening. No trace of a breeze stirred, and the smoke from the factories that lined the waterway rose straight upward.

They approached a cracked-windowed building, the only one that showed no sign of industrial activity, and strolled around the structure to its water-facing side. There, in a niche, a ladder was affixed to the brickwork. The two men climbed it to the roof. Burton pointed to a chimney. "That one."

He led Swinburne past skylights, with panes rendered completely opaque by soot and grime, until they reached the base of the towering column, which had rungs bolted to its side.

The climb to the top was a long one, but the effort was rewarded by a magnificent view. As they both secured themselves on the lip of the chimney with one leg inside the flue and one out, they gazed in appreciation across the rooftops of the world's greatest metropolis: there, the dome of Saint Paul's reflecting the deep orange light; there, the scaffolded column of Saint Stephen's Tower, into which a new Big Ben bell was being fitted; there, the smear of smoke that marked the ashes of Tooley Street.

"London is an unpredictable beast," Swinburne mused. "A creature of quick and ardent temper. A mysterious animal from myth and legend."

"Nothing more or less than an image of our own minds, Algy. Along the broad thoroughfares much can be seen that proves the good in us, but her dark and tangled alleyways conceal a less palatable truth that persists however much we labour to eradicate it."

"The rich and the impoverished. Is such a division inviolable?"

"I fear so. Whatever mechanisms we create to allow the destitute to climb out of the mire, there will always be those who lack the where-withal to do so, always be those who refuse guidance, and always be those who prefer the security of what they know, no matter how dire it is, to the imagined perils of the unknown. Do we have a duty to provide for those people? I would say yes, for I remind you that some of our greatest luminaries were born of poverty. I would not condemn children for their parents' shortcomings."

"Young England in its earliest incarnation had the right idea," Swinburne said. "*Noblesse oblige*. Where a system allows people with ability to rise to its top, those individuals should give thanks to it by offering support to the disadvantaged who remain at its bottom."

Burton sighed and gazed into the distance. "True enough. Unfortunately, our current system is most efficiently navigated through selfishness and ruthlessness. It singularly fails to reward the finer qualities. The seven virtues are treated as weaknesses, the seven sins as strengths."

A rotorchair flew past, close enough that they could see the goggled face of the man in its seat. He waved at them. Swinburne waved back.

There followed a few minutes of silence, the two men wrapped in their own contemplations.

Apropos of nothing, Burton said, "My brother had Bhatti transcribe my Discontinued Man report and sent the copy to Gladstone."

"Yes."

"Edward was a bloody genius; a twisted cantankerous old rascal but a bloody genius. He knew before any of us that something was afoot. By God, he sensed it the moment we returned from the future. He was so finely attuned to Disraeli's behaviour that he spotted the irregularities the instant they appeared. I think his mind was, in many respects, as coldly mechanical as Orpheus's. He weighed up the options and took a course that offered, by his estimation, the most efficient means to counter the threat."

"Despite it being one that would cause you much suffering," Swinburne noted.

"He was prepared to sacrifice himself and, ultimately, did so. He would have expected nothing less from me."

"I'll miss him."

"Yes."

"And the Ministry of Chronological Affairs, what of that?"

"From what I understand, Sadhvi Raghavendra will take control of it."

"Safe hands, then. Her instincts are as powerful as Edward's were, though they operate in a different manner."

Swinburne looked up and surveyed the sky. Stars were beginning to shine.

"But is it necessary? Will there be more time travellers?"

Burton followed his friend's gaze. After a pause, he said, "I speak with the Beetle's knowledge. The Oxford equation is now a part of the collective human consciousness and must inevitably emerge. One day, far into the future—farther even than we travelled—some will learn how to employ it. By then it will be properly understood that Time, Space, Light, and Life are the same thing. The equation will be used not to travel in history but, rather, to go there." He pointed upward. "To the stars. To distant worlds."

"It's a shame we won't be around to witness that."

"Who says we won't? Haven't we learned that death is an illusion?"

"But we won't be Burton and Swinburne. We'll be—I don't know what."

Burton thought a moment then murmured, "Perhaps we'll be the stars themselves, Algy. Perhaps the stars themselves."

Meanwhile . . .

Isabel and Grenfell Baker helped him to prepare for bed. As usual, he endured their assistance with bad grace, grumbling at his immobility, feeling humiliated that he'd become such a burden, such a confounded invalid.

The doctor bid them goodnight. Burton got into bed. Isabel, with difficultly, lowered herself to her knees and said her prayers, repeatedly mentioning her husband in her long litany of requested blessings. For her sake, he tolerated it without comment.

Outside, a dog howled.

Isabel rose. "What a horrible noise."

"The poor thing knows the unseasonal heat doesn't survive long after the sun goes down," he said. "It's predicting a chilly night."

"I'll fetch an extra blanket."

"No, don't. I hate to feel swaddled."

She joined him in bed. "Shall we read?"

He nodded. She passed him his Robert Buchanan. He opened it at random but didn't look at its pages. His mind drifted. For three hours, he thought strange thoughts. Then he made a decision.

"There's something I'd like you to do for me tomorrow."

Isabel lowered her book. "Yes?"

"Take *The Scented Garden* from my desk and burn it."

Her hand flew to her mouth. "Burn it? But you've been working on it for so long! You said it will be—will be the crown of your—of—"

"I know. But I've had a change of heart. I don't want to be forever associated with it. If I'm remembered at all, it should be for what I really am. For what I have always been."

His eyes drifted to the window. He looked out at the night sky, at the splatter of twinkling stars.

He smiled.

"An explorer."

Nearly time to go.

FRAGMENT

. . . we immediately run into problems, for by its very nature, an analysis must make sense, which is to say: it must cohere to the reality that is created by our senses. The challenge we encounter when attempting to explain the function of the Oxford equation is that it concerns the transcendence of such limitations and therefore cannot be discussed within their bounds with any degree of satisfaction.

However, while it may be impossible to adequately examine the equation itself, we can at least contemplate various aspects of its manifestation and effect upon our species. To this end, in the paper that follows, I shall outline and evaluate current theories concerning:

1. SpaceTime Manipulation (STM) and magicians. There have been, to date, thirty-seven known individuals possessing the ability to fold SpaceTime. Such individuals are referred to as magicians. Of the thirty-seven, sixteen are sane (though, by accepted standards of behaviour, extremely eccentric) and functional and crucial to the enablement of interstellar flight and the establishment of our extraterrestrial colonies, fifteen are suffering severe mental instability and are being cared for and studied in institutions, and six have vanished without trace. In this initial section, I shall discuss the role of STM in interstellar travel and its ability to bypass the limitations and time distortions of Einsteinian physics; I will examine the role of the tryptamine compound N,N-Dimethyltryptamine in our brain chemistry, its function as the creator of the reality we perceive, and its interaction with the Oxford equation; I will propose that surges in the pituitary gland's production of N,N-Dimethyltryptamine caused by extreme stress and confusion,

and involving the breakdown of narrative cognisance, is principal in the development of magicians, as well as being at the root of the mental instability that has afflicted so many of them; and I shall suggest that, contrary to the prevalent theory, travel into the past or the future of Earth history is possible and has been achieved.

2a. The origin of the Oxford equation. Though the first recorded emergence of the equation dates from, and was integral to, the Great Enlightenment of 2202, I shall assemble and scrutinise the evidence that others have employed—most notably Professor Solomon Kessler, Doctor Eliza Beeton, and J. J. Moscow Jordan—to suggest that the equation actually has its roots in the dismantlement of the British Empire during the period 1860–1880. Thus I shall, with reference to the equation, review the abrupt shift in the policies of Benjamin Disraeli's government, suggest possible causes for what the majority of historians refer to as his "spontaneous madness," and will examine how the resultant collapse of nation-state politics and protoglobalisation paved the way for neo-medievalism, the extinction of hierarchal political governance, and the establishment of networked microcommunities.

2b. The Oxford equation has enabled us to understand that reality does not exist independently of us, and we know that an element of its construction—namely, the narrative imposition we call Time—possesses an underlying "language" that can be consciously understood through the contemplation of symbolism, patterns, and coincidences. With that in mind, I shall examine a number of persons and events contemporaneous with Disraeli and will explore the possibility that they played a role in "seeding" the equation in the human psyche.

Most prominent among these people are Charles Darwin, whose *On the Origin of Species* marked, I believe, the commencement of a surge in human evolution that has reached its apotheosis with the phenomenon of STM; Algernon Charles Swinburne, whose subversive poetry and vitriolic critiques of nation-states perfectly reflected the zeitgeist of the period; Charles Babbage, whose artificial intelligences, according to persistent but unproven rumour, played a key role in Disraeli's downfall; the occultist Eliphas Levi and his (possibly fictional) diaries, in which a theory of multiple parallel histories is outlined; Sir Richard Francis Burton, in whose anthropological essays neo-medievalism was anticipated with astonishing accuracy; and Herbert Spencer, whose philosophical works touched upon many themes pertinent to the equation.

A review of historical events poses considerable problems as the intense political turbulence of the Religion Wars and subsequent Dark Age resulted in the destruction of reliable records. With the proviso that much of what I discuss is speculative, I will briefly touch upon: the rise and fall of what are now considered Babbage's "lost" technologies; the legend of Spring Heeled Jack and the possibility that the apparition was a magician from our own period; the Tichborne trial and the public disorder associated with it; the fabled Nāga diamonds, supposedly lost during the 1860–1880 riots (if they or, indeed, the riots ever really existed); the Irish potato famine; the American Civil War; The Russia-China Conflict; and the suggestion that *Tempus Flores* may have been present and widespread throughout the period under discussion.

3. Finally, I intend to present evidence that, via its pollen and sap, *Tempus Flores* stimulates the human pituitary gland, increases the brain's production of N,N-Dimethyltryptamine, and has thus played a critical role in the evolution of human consciousness, the advent of the Oxford equation, the Great Enlightenment, and the occurrence of magicians.

—From the introduction to
The Oxford Equation and the Advent of Interstellar Humanity
by Professor Christopher Bendyshe, 2308,
Sawtooth Academy Prime

MEANWHILE, IN THE VICTORIAN AGE . . .

CHARLES BABBAGE (1791–1871)

Babbage was a polymath, the creator of sophisticated calculating machines, and an irascible campaigner against what he considered to be public nuisances (children's hoops, for example). He was opposed to hereditary peerages, considering life peerages a better option.

SIR RICHARD FRANCIS BURTON (1821–1890)

Undoubtedly, 1861 was the worst year of Burton's life. John Hanning Speke, egged on by Laurence Oliphant, had betrayed him by claiming the discovery of the source of the Nile as his own. Their feud was escalating and those who sided with Speke, including Christopher Palmer Rigby, engaged in a campaign of slander against Burton. Amid this turmoil, Grindlays Warehouse burned down, and Burton lost nearly every possession he valued. He married Isabel Arundell, but his misfortunes continued when he was made consul of Fernando Po—considered a "white man's graveyard"—and was forced to leave her behind in England.

EDWARD JOSEPH BURTON (1824–1895)

In 1856, Edward was severely beaten by Singalese villagers who objected to his hunting of elephants. The following year, he fought valiantly at besieged Lucknow where he suffered sunstroke. These two misfortunes led to a psychiatric disorder. From 1858 onward, he refused to speak but for one occasion when he denied a financial debt. In 1859, he was committed to Surrey County Lunatic Asylum, where he remained for the rest of his life.

LADY ISABEL BURTON AND THE GREAT BONFIRE

The majority of Burton's biographers assert that, upon his death, Lady Isabel Burton threw most of his papers and journals—along with *The Scented Garden*—onto a bonfire, her intention being to protect his reputation. Mary S. Lovell convincingly dispels this claim in her biography, *A Rage to Live*, which is perhaps the only one that treats Isabel fairly. While it's true that Lady Burton consigned *The Scented Garden* to the flames of a bedroom fireplace, there was no "holocaust" as was believed by most (including Swinburne), and Burton's diaries and much of his correspondence was actually preserved, only to be destroyed after Isabel herself had died (in 1896). Be that as it may, while we cannot fairly judge the decisions she made while stricken with grief, it is difficult to find any justification for her destruction of *The Scented Garden*.

BENJAMIN DISRAELI, 1ST EARL OF BEACONSFIELD (1804–1881)

An aristocrat and novelist who twice served as a Conservative prime minister, Disraeli was one of the great politicians of the age, famed for his virulent battles with William Gladstone and for his driving the British Empire to the height of its power. In his more youthful days, he founded

Young England, its aim being to promote the notion that the elite should protect the poor from exploitation by the rapidly expanding middle class.

"Two nations between whom there is no intercourse and no sympathy; who are ignorant of each other's habits, thoughts, and feelings, as if they were dwellers in different zones or inhabitants of different planets; who are formed by a different breeding, are fed by different food, are ordered by different manners, and are not governed by the same laws."

"You speak of—" said Egremont hesitatingly, "THE RICH AND THE POOR."

—From the novel *Sybil* by Benjamin Disraeli

"There is no waste of time in life like that of making explanations."

"William Gladstone has not a single redeeming defect."

"I have been ever of opinion that revolutions are not to be evaded."

"Power has only one duty: to secure the social welfare of the People."

"How much easier it is to be critical than to be correct."

"In politics nothing is contemptible."

MICHAEL FARADAY (1791–1867)

A scientist who specialised in electromagnetism and electrochemistry, Faraday's many discoveries led to the practical use of electricity in technology.

WILLIAM GLADSTONE (1809–1898)

A Liberal politician, Gladstone four times served as British prime minister and is widely considered one of the greatest. He was a supporter of the working classes and highly critical of the aristocracy. Though highly religious, rumours concerning his moral character persisted after it became known that he frequently walked the streets in search of prostitutes, ostensibly to talk them into changing their ways.

> "In almost every one, if not every one, of the greatest political controversies of the last 50 years, whether they affected the [voting] franchise, whether they affected religion, whether they affected the bad and abominable institution of slavery, or what subject they touched, these leisure classes, these educated classes, these titled classes have been in the wrong."

DANIEL GOOCH (1816–1889)

From 1837 to 1864, Gooch held the post of superintendent of locomotive engines for the Great Western Railway. Later, in 1865, while laying a transatlantic cable, he was elected as a Conservative MP, a seat he would hold until 1885. He was made a baronet in 1866.

GRINDLAYS WAREHOUSE

When Grindlays burned to the ground in the spring of 1861, Burton lost many of his belongings, including Oriental manuscripts and books, the journals of his travels in India, trunks full of costumes from India and Africa, and mementoes collected during two decades of travelling. He received no compensation for the loss. The original manuscript of *The Scented Garden*, however, was not lost in the fire. In fact, Burton never owned the manuscript, though he never stopped searching for it.

LIEUTENANT CHRISTOPHER PALMER RIGBY (1820–1885)

A brilliant linguist and accomplished Indian Army man who would do much to counter slavery in East Africa, Rigby harboured a deep hatred of Burton that had its roots in Bombay, where they'd both served and where Burton had several times beaten him out of first place in language exams. In 1861, Rigby was levelling claims of financial mismanagement at Burton, asserting that he had not properly paid the bearers during his African expedition.

ALGERNON SWINBURNE (1837–1909)

In 1861, Swinburne was on the brink of fame but was also beginning to suffer from his excessive consumption of alcohol. Visiting the French Riviera to recover, he then toured Italy, remaining there for much of the year.

THE TOOLEY STREET FIRE OF 1861

The biggest fire in London since the Great Fire of 1666, the Tooley Street blaze began in a warehouse and rapidly spread through the dockland district. It burned fiercely for two days and took two weeks to be completely extinguished. The head of the London Fire Engine Establishment, James Braidwood, was killed during the operation to quell the conflagration when the front of a warehouse collapsed onto him.

ABOUT THE AUTHOR

Mark Hodder was born in Southampton, England, at the end of the Cuban Missile Crisis and a year before the debut of *Doctor Who*. As a toddler, he played in the next-door neighbour's WWII Anderson shelter, fell on his head at least three times, and won a Tarzan–yelling competition at a Butlins holiday camp by virtue of being the only entrant. He recollects dreams

Photo by Yolanda Lerma Palomares

from his early childhood that involve things he couldn't possibly have known about at the time. He has been haunted twice and possesses a fragmentary memory of what might have been a UFO encounter.

He now lives in Valencia, Spain, and is the father of twins.

Aside from reading and writing, his interests include Jungian psychology, symbolism, history, expensive gadgets, scientific philosophy, and the exposure of governmental and cultural propaganda and deception.

4737

4737